PRAISE FOR KIM LOCK'S
THE OTHER SIDE OF BEAUTIFUL

'Mercy Blain is a character you find yourself cheering on. Kim Lock mixes the transformative journey of Alice Hart with the quirkiness of Eleanor Oliphant in this story about embracing life, even when it threatens to overwhelm you.'
—Tricia Stringer, bestselling Australian author

'Mercy Blain is an unforgettable character who will capture your heart from the first pages and hold it through until the end. Her madcap journey towards forgiveness— of herself and others—is moving and funny and all other good things that will make you want to keep reading and make you sad when your time with Mercy comes to an end.'
—Sophie Green, bestselling author of *The Shelly Bay Ladies Swimming Circle*

'Tender, funny and quietly profound, *The Other Side of Beautiful* is a breath of fresh air.' —*The Sunday Times*

'A colourful, engaging story of escape and road-trip adventure ... also compellingly cinematic and features an endearing narrator-heroine with plenty of meaty real-world troubles.' —*Sydney Morning Herald*

'An engaging story about second chances and a life changing road trip ... a heart-warming story.' —*Canberra Weekly*

'Exquisite, tender and wry, this break-out novel about facing anxiety and embracing life firmly establishes Kim Lock as an extraordinary new talent and an author to keep an eye on. —*Better Reading*

'A treat from beginning to end. Mercy's travails as she negotiates her uncertainty and fear are both funny and moving … A real and heartfelt story.' —*Herald-Sun*

'*The Other Side of Beautiful* is an exquisite blend of heartache and hope. Life affirming and bittersweet, this novel is like a breath of fresh air.' —*Theresa Smith Writes*

'Redolent, compassionate, heartfelt and accepting, *The Other Side of Beautiful* by Kim Lock is fully deserving of a five-star rating.' —*Mrs B's Book Reviews*

Photo: Louise Agnew

Kim Lock is an internationally published author of five novels, including the reader-acclaimed *The Other Side of Beautiful*. Her essays and opinion pieces have been published widely and her fiction appears in translation. She lives in regional South Australia with her family.

Also by Kim Lock

The Other Side of Beautiful
The Three of Us
Like I Can Love (published in the UK as *The Good Mother*)
Peace, Love and Khaki Socks

THE
FANCIES

KIM LOCK

First Published 2023
First Australian Paperback Edition 2023
ISBN 9781867251620

THE FANCIES
© 2023 by Kim Lock
Australian Copyright 2023
New Zealand Copyright 2023

Published by
HQ Fiction
An imprint of Harlequin Enterprises (Australia) Pty Limited (ABN 47 001 180 918),
a subsidiary of HarperCollins Publishers Australia Pty Limited (ABN 36 009 913 517)
Level 13, 201 Elizabeth St
SYDNEY NSW 2000
AUSTRALIA

A catalogue record for this book is available from the National Library of Australia
www.librariesaustralia.nla.gov.au

Printed and bound in Australia by McPherson's Printing Group

FSC
www.fsc.org

MIX
Paper | Supporting
responsible forestry
FSC® C001695

For Ben
This one has boats

ABIGAIL

Well, damn. Here she was.

Never, she'd said. *Never* coming back of her own free will. Yet as she sat in the taxi crawling up the darkened esplanade, no one was holding a gun to her head.

The taxi inched along and Abigail knew it wouldn't make the driveway. Wind peeled up from the sea, as if to urge the cab further, but it drew to a halt well short of its mark. Surely the driver mocked her, the way he crept so slowly even though the meter continued to count up in the way dollars only did when you had to pay them. The taxi sat there idling, headlights pushing out cones of light and she felt an impotent fury.

'That's fifty,' said the driver.

It was almost ten pm. She had forgotten how utterly dark night time could be: stars winked, surf flashed at the edge of the headlights' beam and then—nothing. No light anywhere. With effort she craned forward, looking up the hill, but her view was blocked by what she knew was a row of old pines.

'Can't you just—' Abigail gestured towards the driveway, maybe two hundred metres further.

'You got more?'

'No.'

The driver shrugged. 'You said go as far as fifty.'

She sat back. Stuffy hot air blew from the vents in the dash. Salt spray, or drops of rain, or flakes of some crusty coastal crap blew through the headlights. It would be cold out. This enraged her too. Inside the taxi was too hot; outside was too cold. When was the last time she had felt comfortable? Just pleasantly, mildly content?

Abigail considered the man's stomach, the way it lolled towards the steering wheel. She probably couldn't find his dick under there anyway, so she handed him the fifty—she hadn't earned it, but it was the only money she had, and when he took it she experienced a sense of finality so complete she almost laughed—and she got out of the car.

The taxi drove away and Abigail stood on the side of the road. She could hear the suck and froth of the ocean but couldn't see it. She could hear the wind in the pines but couldn't see them, either. But she could feel the familiar cold stinging her cheeks and hands, and she could taste the brine in the air, and smell the rotting mounds of kelp piled along the shore. Same stinking shit, different pile. The smell made her fifteen all over again and in spite of herself she felt nostalgic and homesick. Or maybe what she felt was the relief of a homesickness she didn't know she'd had. Tears pricked her eyes but it was just the wind.

The plastic bag of underwear hanging from her fingers twisted as she walked, first one way then the other, digging the straps in and out of her knuckles. Strands of hair tore around her face, whipping into her mouth. Her cardigan was a loose spring-time thing without any buttons; she'd last worn it in November in Adelaide and now, five months later, late autumn and five hundred kilometres closer to the South Pole, she was freezing her tits off so she hunched her shoulders, trying to pull the cardigan tighter. Her dress fluttered about her bare knees. Gravel crunched beneath her boots. She walked briskly to warm herself and it worked, or at least provided a distraction, as soon enough she was puffing.

Hunger announced itself in her stomach. The last meal she'd eaten was the two Big Macs she'd wolfed down at the bus station, a good seven—eight?—hours ago now. On the bus, someone bought hot chips at a stop halfway and her mouth watered at the memory of how good those chips had smelled, filling the bus with their hot greasy scent.

Headlights lit across the scrubby bush lining the road. An awkward glance over her shoulder and she saw the car. It was in the distance, but coming faster than it should have been along the main street, and something in noticing the car's speed caused an urgency in her that she didn't know how to resolve. No instruction had been given, no command barked with which she must comply, and she was paralysed over how to respond to this simple occurrence: a car, in the middle distance, coming at a clip.

'Shit.'

Should she wave and keep walking? Step onto the road and flag down a lift? Ignore it entirely? *Because it's not just about knowing* what *to do, is it?* Abigail thought. *It's about knowing the* right *thing to do.* The acceptable, respectable, *good* thing. And it was these things—*acceptable, right, good*—that needed to remain her focus. In the same way that someone whose clothes are on fire needs to focus on not being on fire.

So what would a *good* person do?

Casting about, she hurried off the road and scrambled into the bushes. Sticks scraped her cheeks, the plastic bag snagged and her left foot was suddenly bare and treading in mushy leaf litter. She swore again, dabbing blindly about with her naked toes, but then the car's headlights lit up the bush and she folded to an awkward crouch, hiding her face.

A ute roared past, bass beat thumping from the stereo, before it slowed and turned into her parents' driveway.

She said, 'That'd be fucking right.' Because if, instead of fleeing, she had stuck out her thumb she might now be at her destination, not crouched in a bush in the dark.

Wind shook the leaves around her, raining fat drops, and it occurred to her that she also needed to pee. Something crawled behind her knee and when she tried to flick it away, it bit her. A needle of pain radiated up the inside of her thigh.

'Motherfucker,' she yelped.

Silent cries of rage built in her throat as she fought her way from the bush. She emerged panting, one foot bare, and slapped her hands all over her body, up and down her legs, over her head and arms.

Lots of girls cried in prison. Almost all of them. But Abigail had not. It could be said that she hadn't wanted to give them the satisfaction but that would be a lie, because no one was satisfied in that place. That whole vile business was miserable and soulless—no one was getting any joy seeing people reduced to snivelling like a toddler. They'd have to *care* in order to do that—even if what they cared about was making people bawl. And no one there cared.

So would it be this, then? This? Standing on the side of the Port Kingo esplanade at night, wearing only one boot, some pissed-off insect munching its way up to her fanny? The feeling of homesickness that wasn't homesickness. The way the wind was *whooing* through those pines exactly as she remembered, as it probably had for a hundred years. The salty stink that was somehow god-awful rotted and also bracing, brand new. Abigail felt the whole lot of it well up inside, inflating and stretching and going transparent-thin.

Then it deflated.

So, no. It would not.

Several minutes spent rooting in the undergrowth did not produce her missing boot and her toes had gone numb anyway, so she limped back to the road without it. One-booted, she stumped along the bitumen and began the long steep walk up her parents' driveway.

And, there it was: the house of her child-self, two storeys of local stone, windows hailing yellow against the night sky. The house had been her grandfather's, now her father's, and could have been one of her brothers', eventually, if any of them still cared about primogeniture or whatever.

Her grandfather liked to say he built this house with his bare hands, which meant he kept a couple of brickie mates in beer and crays for a few months while they built it and in his good graces for the rest. The site, flattened into the hillside, was selected for what could be viewed from the house: town; the harbour; the violent Southern Ocean. But its position was a kind of parlour trick. You could see out, but not in. As a teenager Abigail would see the girls coming—Em and Sal, or Jo and, of course, Honnie—and sneak down the drive to ambush them from the pines. They'd fall about laughing. It never grew old. Once, a year or so ago, she thought she'd seen Em come into the restaurant but it wasn't her. Beyond profile pictures, she hadn't seen them in decades.

Ranged about the house was a crowd of dual-cab utes, gleaming beneath the house lights. *Nose in and suckling*, Abigail thought. The cheesewood bushes—still there—on the edge of the lawn gave off their cloying scent, stewing with the salt and seaweed and catching her in the feels again.

At the front door was a sleek new security screen, one of those expensive, invisible steel mesh things. Overhead the light was out and she stood in the dark, trying to catch her breath. Her bare right foot was numb. From around the back of the house came the sound of laughter and men's voices.

She knocked.

Nothing happened.

After a while she knocked again, harder, rattling the screen. The chorus of voices from around the back continued and through old habit she found herself searching for the potted cactus that used to hide the spare key. But the cactus wasn't there, of course. Her mother had thrown out the cactus and hidden the spare key even before Abigail left. She recalled the sound of the pot dropping into the wheelie bin—*thud*—and the way her mother had turned to her and said, 'I really liked that pot.'

Taking a few steps back, she peered into the upstairs windows. No movement. Returning to the screen, she gave it one last rattle and was steeling herself to creep around the side when the overhead light came on. The front door opened and Nell Fancy stood behind the screen.

Abigail felt Nell's eyes take her in, raking from the top of her head, down the length of her body to her feet. Slinging the plastic bag behind her legs, Abigail popped one hip, lifted her chin, shook the hair from her eyes.

'Hi, Mum.'

Her mother slammed the door shut.

THEM

The barbecue began not as an intentional barbecue but as a few sausages on a grille. And the grille was not so much a grille as it was a forty-four gallon drum sheared in half with a rack fixed over a pile of smoking stringybark chunks that didn't fit in Young Dick's slow combustion in the lounge.

It began when Col Morton showed up, not long after the sun went down. Col, a fisherman in his late thirties—young for a skipper—had come to the back door because he was that kind of man and assumed he had that kind of relationship with Young Dick Fancy. (He did, but Young Dick wasn't the kind of man to make other men feel necessarily assured about that.)

Col stood at the back door, squinting pensively, and said, 'You hear?'

'Of course I did,' said Young Dick.

'Whatcha reckon? We got a problem or what?'

Young Dick took a long moment to consider the moths butting against the porch light. Col was holding his breath because this was where it all hinged, the moment that decided whether what had happened earlier that day would fizzle away to nothing, like so many other incidents, or if it would become Something. And little made the locals of Port Kingerton happier than when something did indeed become Something.

Finally, Young Dick stepped back and said, 'You better come in, I reckon.'

A text message from Col to Spike, Young Dick's deckie—*at Young Dicks bring a few cold ones*—resulted in three more arrivals, because Spike happened to be dropping an outboard motor at Ricky Leake's old man's when the text from Col came in. So Spike came with Ricky Leake and his old man, then more messages were sent and more cold ones brought and the grille was fired up and here we are. Six men standing around, each nursing a beer except Young Dick with his can of lemonade.

'The dog found it,' Col Morton was saying. 'Otherwise the old lady wouldn't have seen it.'

'I heard some kid found it,' said Ricky Leake. 'One of them Lofts.'

'Anybody named Loft couldn't find their own arse if it was on fire,' pointed out Spike, who was only saying that because Trisha Loft wasn't here. Six people was about five too many for Trisha.

'Yeah, except ole Lofty has about forty-five kids, so he can obviously find his wife's—'

'Hey, Rick,' Nell Fancy broke in from her deck chair nearby. 'Get us some more sausages.' She jerked her chin in the direction of the kitchen. Ricky Leake's face turned sheepish and he slunk away.

Up to this point Young Dick had said little. Sipping his lemonade, staring into the glowing coals, he'd listened to the blokes' speculations and mulled it over in his head. He'd have to tell them. It was hardly a state secret. Dettwyler, the senior constable down at the cop shop, had already told him the bone was human, so there was no doubt about that. No doubt, either, that everyone would know soon enough anyway. Harder to say, however, was how long the thighbone had been in the water; even harder to say was whose thigh it had once been.

Young Dick glanced at his phone and frowned. A message from Twitch had come in saying he couldn't make it; one of his grandkids had a fever and Twitch had to make the run into the bigger town for paracetamol. It didn't feel right to Young Dick, telling the blokes without Twitch here. But it couldn't wait. By morning this story would have taken on a life of its own, bloating and mutating, scattering poisonous spores, and then it would be too late. Best to get to it before it starts breeding. Better still, chop it off at the roots.

'It could be an animal though, couldn't it?' said Little Jase Turner, Col Morton's deckie, who'd only just arrived. 'Cow? Or kangaroo?'

'It's not a cow or roo.' Col shook his head. 'It's too big, mate.'

'Some roos get pretty big.'

'Well, cows aren't small, are they?'

'Depends. What kind of cow?'

Col shot Young Dick a look, but the older man was still staring into the flames, the expression on his face inscrutable.

Ricky Leake had returned from the kitchen and was slapping sausages onto the rack. Fat hissed onto the coals.

'How would a cow bone end up on the beach, anyway?' someone asked.

'It's not a cow bone.' Col was getting indignant.

'Are we sure it's just one bone? I heard down the pub it was half a skeleton.'

'It was just one bone,' said Col through gritted teeth.

Young Dick lifted his lemonade as if to take a sip, then hesitated. He lowered the can slightly, brows furrowed, and looked at the group of blokes. Col saw him looking and was relieved, because finally Young Dick would get things back on track, all this nonsense about cows and kangaroos could end, and they could get on with sorting out if this was going to be a problem or not. But Young Dick's gaze continued past the men and came to rest on his wife.

'Nell? You hear something?'

Nell looked up. 'Huh?'

'I thought I heard knocking.'

Straightening in her chair, Nell glanced back at the house. 'Your dad's watching *Doc Martin*, so I doubt he'll have moved.'

Young Dick set down his can. 'I'll check.'

'No, I'll go,' said Nell, getting to her feet. 'I'm tired of this lot anyway.' She put a hand on her husband's forearm, felt the ropes of muscle and sinew there, taut from years of hauling craypots. Under her breath she told him, 'It could be nothing.'

He sighed. 'I don't think so.'

'You could leave it alone. You don't have to fix this.'

A long look passed between them, the men's voices fading away. Recently Nell had seen a meme that caught her attention: a picture of Spider-Man, bodily holding back a bus filled with angry people while a child sat in the roadway in front of the bus, headphones on, looking down at a screen, oblivious to his own saving. Nell thought of this image now as she saw in her husband's eyes the thankless, held-back weight of a generation.

They both glanced away as the sound came again. This time Nell heard it too: someone was knocking on the front door.

Port Kingerton, at the southernmost tip of South Australia, was a town where if something was happening—an upgrade to the T-junction kerbing; a new assistant for Mrs Dinwiddle at the post office; wifi—the Fancys knew about it. But the things the Fancys knew about were not just nice things like public works and postal assistants. They knew about the not-nice things, too. The things many locals *didn't* know about.

Or at least, didn't *really* know about.

Some folk might have claimed to know, but the truth was they didn't. Because that's the way the Fancys preferred it: in Port Kingerton, knowledge was disseminated on an 'as needs' basis and many people, much to their own chagrin, simply didn't need. For instance, the time Lewis Roosevelt's new thirty-three-foot Powercat disappeared from the breakwater and was found adrift two kilometres offshore, diesel tanks filled with salt water, or the time some gel-haired pretty boy from the city had fiddled with a woman he shouldn't have and required persuading that if he wanted to keep them,

Queensland would be a safer place for his testicles. These were the things about which only the Fancys knew the truth. The *real* truth. And only the Fancys chose who else would know.

So when Abigail arrived at the barbecue and no one knew she was coming, not even her mother, well, that was momentous. Because everyone knew that twenty-three years ago, sixteen-year-old Abigail had hung out the passenger-side window of Zac Murphy's Corolla, both middle fingers held high, swearing she'd never come back.

And she hadn't. Until now.

OLD DICK

They hid the ladder from me again today, the bastards.

You'd think an old bloke could get some peace in his dying bloody days, but apparently around here that's too much to ask.

All I wanted was to look at the stars. Like white surf on a black sea, spread out and glittering like that. Watching them stars would be a good place for an old bloke to go and get on with the business of dying. Retrieving my corpse from the roof would be inconvenient. The way my toast was burnt this morning? Trying to get my body down would serve them right. Ha ha, imagine that! It'd be like trying to wrestle a shop mannequin down the ladder, all stiff-legged.

But, no. The ladder was nowhere to be seen and unless I fancied myself capable of shunting up the drain pipe— which I don't, not with these hips grinding like a pair of rusted wingnuts—there was no getting up on the roof for me. Instead I just sat on my arse at the window like a useless prick, looking at those cheesewood bushes when I'd much rather be watching to make sure no bastard's stolen my mooring in the breakwater.

It's daytime, Richard, the woman told me. *Why are you looking for stars in the daytime?*

How else would I find the bloomin' pots? I told her. A man's not a sextant. Seventy-eight pots to pull and them seals have been a bloody nuisance lately, getting in to tear the bait out. Crays not crawling, especially if there's no bait. What bloody use is there in pulling up empty pots? Who pays for empty pots? Nobody, that's who.

Then she told me I'm not out at sea, and she was craning her neck at the window again—what in god's name was she looking at? All morning she was there, blocking a man's view of the boats. And she was huffy because she wanted the binoculars but I don't know where the binoculars are. Maybe they're with the ladder.

Just squint, I told the woman. Back in my day we didn't have binoculars, we just squinted. A man doesn't have time to look for binoculars when there's craypots to pull and he's got the business of dying to attend to.

Here's your toast, she told me and turned back to the window.

It wasn't toast. It was a slice of charcoal. But Luce would have my guts if she ever heard me being impolite to a lady so I ate the toast and said nothing. Didn't stop her from blocking the damn window all morning though.

Now *Doc Martin* is on the telly and I like him, the cranky Pom who acts like his patients are dimwits. I've met a lot of dimwits in my time and frankly he's much nicer to them than I ever could be. He's such a funny bastard. I don't know if I could be funny around dimwits. Seems to me like the best thing to do is serve them to the crays.

Dad, come on, says the young fella. *No need to talk like that.*

Where'd you come from?

Just downstairs. You all right?

Get away, you're blocking my view of the telly.

And go answer the door, I say. Someone was knocking.

ABIGAIL

The last time Abigail broke into her parents' house she was sixteen and the size of a curtain rod. Now she was thirty-nine and a pallet of curtain rods heavier, but before she could stop to reminisce, muscle memory kicked in and she found herself creeping along the side of the house like it was 1999.

The shade was drawn on the downstairs bedroom window, a square of light escaping from the edges. From inside she could hear the muted sounds of a TV. It used to be the twins' room, and although her mother could never be said to be sentimental, it had taken a good year or so after the boys moved into their own place before Nell had removed their stuff: bunk bed, posters of Porsches and Pamela Anderson, half-empty cans of Lynx spray, dented cricket bats and scruffy tennis balls. Growing up, Abigail always thought her older brothers' room vaguely dank, smelly and grim—the same descriptions she'd have given them. When she'd heard Hamish and Dylan had also finally left town she discovered a caved-in feeling inside her. She hadn't liked it. She'd never admit it.

Standing outside the twins' old bedroom window now, Abigail ran her fingers along the frame until she found the dented edge of the fly screen. Still there, of course—the new screen on the front door was just for show. Her family name was its own security.

It was still breaking and entering if it was your parents' house. Which was why she hesitated, at least for a beat.

The screen lifted out easily. She set it against the wall. The catch on the window popped when she rattled it—just like it had when she was sixteen, just like her brothers had shown her—and she slid the window open and heaved herself onto the bricks. One leg through, pushing the shade aside and light flooding her eyes, then the other, and for the first time in twenty-three years she was standing in her brothers' old bedroom.

An elderly man in a wheelchair was glaring at her, brandishing a bread plate over his head. Flannel pyjamas, wisps of white hair, skinny as a whip. On the TV screen, images of a quaint seaside village.

'Who the bloody hell are you, and what the hell's wrong with your eye?'

'Hey, Grandpa,' she said.

The plate inched higher, threateningly. 'I said—'

Abigail closed the window, straightening the shade. The door into the hall was open and she hobbled over, darting a glance up and down, before retreating back into the room.

Putting one finger over her lips, she turned to her grandfather and hissed, 'Ssh.'

'Don't shush me, you little trollop.'

Although her grandfather gave it everything he had, the bread plate sailed harmlessly into the carpet. She tried to bend down to retrieve the plate but settled for shoving it under the bed with her bare foot. The carpet was gorgeously soft, cleaning the grit from between her toes. What a goddamn luxury.

Her grandfather backed away from the television and was searching for a new weapon. A tube of lotion thudded to the floor before she took the handles of his chair and wheeled him out of reach of anything else he could throw.

'Hey,' she said, crouching awkwardly in front of him, 'it's me, Abigail.'

He glared at her. 'Who?'

'Your granddaughter.'

'I don't have a granddaughter. Are you soft in the head?'

A wave of exhaustion hit. Her back hurt, her bare foot throbbed as the feeling returned and the inside of her thigh was on fire. She was so hungry it felt as though her stomach was carving teeth into her spine. All she wanted to do was lie down on this luxuriously soft carpet and sleep for weeks.

She dropped the plastic bag, slumping onto the bed. Her grandfather eyed her warily. When had she last seen him? Since she'd been away he had become older, frail; she knew his mind and memory had begun to betray him. But the memories she had of Old Dick Fancy were of a spritely, late middle-aged man, a fourth-generation fisherman and farmer. Grey haired and running to paunch but knocking about in his ute, re-straining fences, castrating calves. *Now look at him*, she thought. *As licked by time as we all are.*

'You the young fella's missus?'

'The young fella is Richard,' she said. 'Your son. I'm his daughter.'

He went very still. Then his eyes softened.

'Ah,' he said. Wheeling closer, he reached a hand towards her face. 'What've you got there, kiddo?'

His fingertips grazed her bruised cheekbone. In spite of his frailty his hand was steady, the touch on her cheek tender, assured. Without thinking, she found herself tilting her head, leaning into his touch. His palm was warm and he gave her a smile and it was the first time someone had touched her with care in forever. She took a deep, shuddering breath.

He narrowed his eyes. 'Was it a bloke? You tell me who. I'll knock his block off.'

She straightened, retreating from his hand. 'No, Grandpa. It wasn't.'

'Get too close to the back end of a horse?'

'It's nothing.'

'Doesn't look like nothing. Looks like someone clocked you.'

A burst of laughter came into the room. Someone cheered. The scent of grilling sausages wafted in and her mouth flooded with water. 'What's the party for?'

'Useless pricks,' he said. 'Seventy pots to pull and they're out there slacking off. The young fella's too soft on them. A good hardening up, that's what they all need. Back in my day we didn't slack off until the cray season was finished. And even then we had too much work to do. Do they think the steers are gonna drench themselves? Or firewood cut itself? I tell you, these days, no one knows what hard work is if it bit them on the …'

It was late April; cray season was over for the year, but there was no interrupting her grandfather now, ranting about the price of fence posts and timber in general, imported all the way from Sweden when forests of the stuff grew just up the flaming road.

He stopped mid-sentence and squinted at her.

'What happened to your eye?'

'Just a little bump, Grandpa.'

He drew back, affronted. 'Who the hell you calling grandpa?'

She went to pat his knee but he scooted out of reach. She'd lost him.

She stood up, because great Christ was she hungry, and she needed to find some motherfucking Stingose.

THEM

Nell had unlocked the downstairs bedroom window, of course.

Sentimental she might not be, but Nell was a mother of three children and that meant some part inside always pulled to want her kids with her, even when she didn't. So, after she found Abigail on the doorstep, bedraggled, one-booted and looking risky as a loaded gun, Nell had shut the door, walked calmly to Old Dick's room, popped the window latch and returned outside to the back deck, acting as though nothing had happened.

Because Nell knew that Abigail would find her. Nothing stopped Abigail from getting what she wanted. When Abigail was a child, she'd once hidden the pregnant stable cat in the bottom shelf of her wardrobe for almost three weeks, diligently bringing the cat food and water, removing the dirtied litter before any smell could escape, because Abigail knew that as soon as the kittens were born they'd be euthanised. (The Fancys always said one cat in the stable was good for keeping down rats and mice; more than one was just feral.) When Old Dick eventually discovered and dispatched the kittens, Abigail staged a two-day hunger strike. It only ended because Nell made a peach crumble.

Nell knew that if Abigail had finally deigned to show her face in Port Kingerton after all these years, she must want something very much indeed.

Out the back, conversation eased as a second batch of sausages was eaten. Young Dick had broken the unfortunate truth about the bone's provenance—'it's a leg bone, coppers said' and pointed to his thigh in case anyone needed visual aid—and the men were as outwardly nonchalant yet inwardly thrilled as any group of white men from a small town would be upon hearing such news. Human remains. Right there on the beach. Big day.

Nell returned to her chair, betraying nothing except to bite off a sliver of fingernail. She deliberately didn't look at her husband. Young Dick was engaged in an earnest-looking conversation with Col Morton. Nell gazed beyond the backyard, towards the stables and the night-dark paddocks beyond, and waited.

It only took Abigail a few minutes.

Having swapped her single red cowboy boot for Nell's Ugg boots, Abigail strode onto the back deck. Squared shoulders, flared nostrils, pushed-out breasts, but other than a few eyeballs sliding in her direction, the odd eyebrow lifting, the men were momentarily too consumed by gossip about a human femur to properly register her arrival.

Until she hugged her father. When Young Dick saw Abigail appear on the deck, all five-foot-nothing of her mustered and blazing, he dropped his can of lemonade. He took three large strides—*bam, bam, bam*—across the deck, making the boards shudder and everyone lower their beers in surprise, and folded Abigail in his arms.

Nell took that moment to slip away. She was off the deck and into the backyard, heading for the stables, before anyone noticed.

'Give a man a heart attack, kid,' Young Dick mumbled down at the top of Abigail's head. 'What are you doing here?'

'I wanted a sausage,' Abigail said into his shirt.

He blinked rapidly, cleared away a sudden gruffness in his throat and released her. 'You're out then?'

'It would seem that way.' Abigail jutted her chin and that's when her father noticed the black eye: a plum-coloured bruise deep in the corner of her left eye socket, a dark crescent across the top of her cheekbone.

It wouldn't be a good idea to bring it up.

'Dettwyler would know you're here, yeah?' he said. Then he frowned. 'I only just saw him today. He didn't say anything.'

'The copper here in Kingo? He wouldn't know. They only alert the locals in, you know, the area.' Abigail gestured north, the direction of Adelaide, a six-hour bus ride away.

Young Dick felt a frisson of alarm. 'You didn't tell them you were coming down here?'

'I didn't have to. No parole, remember? I'm free.'

But, oh, her face when she said it! Young Dick saw the steel in her expression and it hit him like a crowbar to the guts. She said she was *free* but she wasn't, he knew that. They all knew that. Freedom was the biggest lie told to ex-prisoners. The first time she got out the guards actually said to her, *See you next time.* It was only made crueller when it turned out to be true. Because if prison succeeded in anything at all, it was in making it easier to go back.

'So,' Young Dick said, 'you want a snag?'

'Sure.'

'Jase,' he barked. 'Get the tongs.'

And Little Jase Turner was out of his chair, plucking a sausage from the grille and handing it, cradled in a piece of bread, to Abigail.

Young Dick said, 'You want sauce?' and Little Jase jumped for the bottle, but Abigail shoved the sausage into her mouth as if she hadn't eaten in a month. Little Jase hovered hopefully nearby with a bottle of tomato sauce, but after a few minutes it became evident that Abigail was ignoring him completely, or perhaps couldn't be bothered noticing him in the first place, so he slunk away.

'Did you see your mother?' Young Dick asked, glancing around. 'She was here a minute ago.'

'She was as thrilled to see me as you'd imagine.'

'She was surprised.'

Abigail shrugged.

'She'll be glad you're here, you know,' he said.

'Funny way of showing it.'

They had moved so they were standing side by side, not looking at each other as they spoke. Instead their gaze was across the deck, past the men, into the darkened yard and paddocks. Young Dick could see the stable lights were on. *That's where Nell's gone*, he thought.

'How'd you get here?'

Abigail took a bite of her sausage. 'Bus,' she said around her mouthful.

'You walk here all the way from the station?'

'God, no.' She finished chewing and swallowed. 'Cab. Their fifty bucks got me to about two hundred metres down the esplanade.'

He felt another low stab of alarm. 'Whose fifty?'

'Oh, Jesus.'

'Well—'

'I didn't steal it. That's my head start into a new and respectable life, courtesy of the Commonwealth, remember? Fifty whole bucks.'

He wanted to know where she got the money for the bus ticket but he knew better than to ask that, too.

One of the older men chose to sidle up to Young Dick at that moment. With a respectful nod to Abigail, the man leaned in and murmured that he was real sorry but he was going to have to take off, but he wanted to know if there was *anything needing to be done about … you know?* So Young Dick and the other man made for the shadows at the far edge of the deck.

They all knew who Abigail was. A couple of the younger men—Col Morton, Ricky Leake—were closer to Abigail's age and had therefore only known her as a gangly, wild and slightly terrifying teenage girl. To see this grown woman, about whom they had in the intervening years gleaned only the occasional snippet from Young Dick, was a bit like coming face to face with a comic book hero: it didn't seem real.

Once Young Dick had been taken away from the barbecue by the unexpected arrival of his daughter, no one had known whether or not to continue talking about the problem of the thighbone found on the beach, so conversation turned awkward. A bunch of blokes with beers generally abhor silence, so no one wanted *not* to talk, but no one could think of anything to say because all they really wanted to talk about was the bone. They couldn't even turn to Nell for assistance because she seemed to have disappeared.

So when Abigail strode towards them, the men found themselves shuffling sideways, automatically making a place for her in the circle. She stood eating her sausage, lifting her chin and meeting each of their eyes in turn, catching Col Morton until his cheeks turned pink and he became tremendously interested in how the last three sausages were faring on the grille. Feet scuffed; throats were cleared. Silence descended whether they liked it or not, and it was torturous. Abigail finished her sausage and helped herself to another. Little Jase Turner held out the tongs but Abigail whipped the sausage off the grille with her fingers, and this minor spectacle provided something for the men to focus on. It was a temporary interruption, they consoled themselves, and they could get back to discussing the bone any minute now.

Any minute now.

But Abigail kept eating her sausage and no one seemed able to look away. She gripped it and stuffed it into her mouth in a way that turned Col Morton's cheeks a deeper shade of crimson. Abigail was wearing a sort of dark blue, floaty, many-layered dress and as a breeze cut across the deck, the dress undulated about her bare knees, lifting goose-bumps on her shins. The skin on her legs was mottled blue and white, disappearing into Nell's Ugg boots. Before they realised what was happening, Abigail had finished the second sausage and started on a third. The tongs opened and closed impotently in Little Jase's hand. For this third one, Abigail hadn't even bothered with bread; she ate the sausage right as it was, a stick of meat in her hand. When her front teeth closed over the sausage, cracking the casing and smearing grease onto her lips, each man experienced a sensation like physical pain. Or yearning.

By the time Abigail started on her fourth sausage, the men had sweat trickling down their spines. Col Morton's vision had blurred and Little Jase was gripping the tongs as if they could save his life.

Was it the tender bare knees, the floaty fluttering dress? Was it the suggestive devouring of four sausages? Or was it just the fact of her, Abigail Fancy, barely taller than any man's nipples yet larger than their memories and imaginations—a stacked, lush, blonde-haired powerhouse, appearing the same day as a human thighbone washed ashore?

Whatever it was, no one could say. But at that moment, there on Young Dick Fancy's deck, as a tomorrow promised a tantalising uncertainty, more than one man tumbled help-lessly in love.

OLD DICK

As far as I can tell I'm eighty years old. Eighty-two, maybe eighty-five. You'd have to check with Luce.

I've got one new hip and one shit hip, courtesy of osteo-arthritis. The doc wants to replace the shit one like he did the other, but no thanks. The first one hurt like buggery and I couldn't even wipe my own backside afterwards, so one is enough. A man can limp. Back in my day we didn't have fancy things like artificial hips, we just limped. Billy Loft only had one eye—the other one got poked out with a gaff—but he didn't go having some fancy replacement eye-ball fitted in his head, he just winked.

I've also had gout, tinea and, if it's hot, eczema. I'm miss-ing the last two fingers on my left hand after they got caught in a rope tying two boats together. When I was a little tacker I had mumps, measles, chicken pox, whooping cough and whatever it was that, before I went to bed, made Ma pin a flannel soaked in vinegar and metho around my neck. I've had three broken arms, a busted nose, two cracked ribs and I'm pretty sure a dose of crabs after getting a bit too fresh with that young red-headed sheila who came to town once looking for an uncle. Or was she running away from an uncle? Either way, she didn't stay long and it's just as well as I had to stick some nasty gunk on places I'd rather not mention, if it's all the same.

Sorry, Luce.

Point is, I've had a lot of things happen to me, health wise. So I don't know why that short hefty woman with the black eye has come back in here, interrupting my show again, and asking me about bug spray.

Stingose, she says. *I can't find any in the bathroom. Mum's out at the stables ignoring me, and this bite itches like a bitch.*

I don't know what you're talking about, I say, and it makes me nervous because does she know about that young red-headed sheila and her uncle? Just thinking about it is making me itchy. I consider taking a quick peek in my trousers but I'm a gentleman so I don't.

You remember me now?

She puts her hands on her hips. She goes to the window, checks behind the curtain, jiggles the window lock. She belches and I'm rattled.

Sorry, she says, but she doesn't sound it. *Four snags.*

What in the blazes is she on about? Now she's laughing her head off, really cackling, and I'm worried there might be something wrong with her, because she's holding a plastic bag. Holding up the bag and laughing like a maniac. Doubled over and howling.

Twelve hours, she's saying. *Twelve hours I've been carrying this sack of undies and I've finally left it on my grandfather's bedroom floor.*

Oh shit, she says. *I think I'm gonna wet myself.*

ABIGAIL

After the barbecue—after the men left, her grandfather was asleep and the house was quiet—Abigail sat at the kitchen table and waited for Nell. She had not dragged herself and her sorry sack of undies five hundred kilometres, had not spent six hours famished on an overheated bus, only to be ghosted by her own mother. So Nell could have her temper tantrum, but she could have it to Abigail's face.

Abigail's first stint inside was nothing. Two weeks; her wrist slapped by a magistrate whose temper she'd worn thin. *I don't know what else to do with you*, the judge said, throwing his actual hands in the air. That was two years ago. Abigail hadn't come home after that; she hadn't needed to. But now—shouldn't her mother be *glad* she was here? Couldn't Nell understand that facing this town again meant she'd reached a certain level of desperation?

For Christ's sake, wasn't it obvious she needed them?

She splayed her hands on the tabletop. There was the mark she'd made with a butter knife, trying to trap Dylan's hand. There was the knot in the wood missing its centre, making a divot the size of a cornflake. The tap was dripping into the empty sink, very slowly: *Plink. Plink. Plink.* The fridge hummed a while then clicked off and the house fell into the kind of silence that was less an absence of sound and more a skin-crawling noise of its own.

She stood, chair shrieking across the floorboards.

'Hello?' she said in the hallway. The lounge she found empty, so too the dining room, office and downstairs bathroom. As she went she clicked lights off, methodically and purposefully plunging the house into blackness.

The house was the same but it was also different. On the hallway side table the press-dial phone was gone, replaced with a blinking modem. In place of the paisley hall runner was a chic woven beachside mat. Fewer photos, more art: this house she'd grown up in had the same old body, the same old bones, but its dressings were foreign, belonging to someone else. Abigail was at home but she was also intruding.

At the front door she reached out and snapped the lock. She went back down the hall, through the kitchen to the back door, pressing her forehead to the glass panels like she had done as a child. Beyond the dark backyard she could see the glow of the stable lights. She could go out. She could try and talk to her mother.

Instead she locked that door, too.

Returning to the stairs, she hauled herself up one step at a time. All she could hear as she ascended was her own laboured breathing, the familiar squeak of the fourth then seventh steps. On the ninth she trod close to the banister, avoiding the most strident squeak, before she reached the landing and stopped to catch her breath. She used to take those stairs two at a time.

Her parents' bedroom was empty. In the ensuite, she startled at her own reflection, gingerly poking the bruise around her eye. She muttered under her breath, fluffed her hair, bared her teeth.

'I'm going to use your toothbrush,' she called out, taking one from the holder. 'Stop me if you want.' When no answer came, she shrugged. 'Suit yourself.' She squeezed a wad of paste over the bristles.

What had once been her room was now a tidy spare. Gone were the *TV Hits* posters, the desk painted with glitter nail varnish, the CD player that used to blast 'Coco Jambo' until her mother confiscated the power cord. Now: plain double bed; narrow Ikea bookcase; neat grey curtains.

At least the bed was made up. When she sat on the edge it felt as if she sank for an eternity, the softness just kept on giving, and once again she had that unnerving feeling of homesickness she hadn't known was there. With great care, she reclined until gravity took over and she tipped, and was lying on her back.

Abigail gave a short laugh. On the ceiling, the lightshade she'd made when she was very young as a craft project with her grandmother Lucy was still there, hanging over the bulb. Strips of lace and ribbon tacked around a wire frame. Her room had reeked of craft glue for days.

Undressing to her knickers, she crawled into impossibly soft sheets. Only when she was under the covers did she remember the lights would not be turned out by someone else, so she got up again, turned off the light and went back to bed.

She tried not to think of her.

Abigail was born in the hospital car park. The story went that Nell had been busy that morning in July, trying to negotiate the sale of a particularly showy gelding over the phone, while Hamish and Dylan had chicken pox. It also happened to be one of the coldest, wettest July days on record. As Nell liked to tell it, the tight-arsed man in Sydney trying to talk her down four grand for the pony that would go on to sweep up supreme championships all over the east coast had nothing on the twin three-year-olds mutinous with itchy spots and the frigid rain belting in sideways, threatening to tear off the stable roof. Neither, apparently, did the imminent arrival of Abigail. When she could ignore it no longer, her mother said, she reluctantly got in the car and Young Dick drove to the hospital but it turned out she needn't have bothered. Shooting efficiently onto the passenger seat, Abigail arrived before anyone could get their hands on her.

Which was, her family liked to say, Abigail's first middle finger to the world.

THEM

Word of Abigail's return spread fast.

After the barbecue at Young Dick's, Col Morton, starry-eyed, headed straight downhill to the pub and told the publican, Larry Dinwiddle. Larry told his wife Beverly, the postmistress, who then told Sheila Rocket, who was the first through the post office doors the next morning. Shelia went straight next door to Bram's Deli and told Penny Bram, who immediately phoned her daughter Jessica, who'd gone right through school with Abigail and choked on her morning coffee before texting her entire contact list. The news fizzed along the esplanade, blazed through the shops and into the back streets, flaring out over the swamps, scrub and dairy farms. Men paused mid-paddock to check their phones, women jigged babies on hips while their thumbs flew across screens. Young Dick

Fancy's daughter back, the same day a leg bone washed up on the beach, for crap's sake.

If considered from above, Port Kingerton is a tiny curve of town jammed into the pointed southern tip of South Australia, like sand shoved into the toe of a shoe. The esplanade—the town's main street—runs east–west along the coast. On one side of the main street is a strip of shops and along the other side is the sea: breakwater; beach; jetty. Mostly, travellers arrive in town from the north, where a bigger town (and the bus station) sits an hour away, or Adelaide five hours (six by bus). It's possible to come into Port Kingerton from the east—Melbourne way—but the only ones who do that are generally lost.

So travellers come from the north and find themselves at a T-junction whereby they turn right onto the esplanade. The strip of beachfront shops goes like this: the first fish-and-chip shop; the post office; Bram's Deli; a hardware-cum-surf store; a gift shop selling wind chimes, crystals, incense, oil burners, slipper socks and, behind a black curtain with an 'adults only' sign hanging above, a thought-provoking selection of dildos and plugs. Then there is a vacant block, the second fish-and-chip shop and the church. Beyond that, land begins to rise up over the cliffs and wind-whipped houses huddle side by side. After a kilometre or so there's the stand of Norfolk Island pines and the Fancys' steep, curving driveway. And then? The lighthouse, the cemetery and finally scrub and more scrub.

So it didn't take long before the entire town knew about Abigail's return. In fact, before Abigail had even woken up in her childhood bedroom, everyone knew.

Literally.

Everyone.

What they didn't know, however, was *why* Abigail was back. Not that this hindered anyone in hypothesising. Nor would they admit their hypothesising was exactly that: a guess. Everyone who heard Young Dick Fancy's daughter was back and passed it along either took someone else's conclusion and modified it—put their own personal flavour on it, like ice-cream toppings—or made up a conclusion of their own. Because who would turn down a chance to create the ultimate narrative? That would be like turning down the chance to have your story included in the Bible. You just wouldn't.

With Abigail Fancy's arrival came the chance to make history. And as history proves, the stories that stick need not be factual, nor even especially believable—they just have to be credible enough. Which is to say, scarcely credible at all.

OLD DICK

I have made no secret of the fact that I am dying. Death, you could say, is in the offing. But the young fella keeps talking to me like there's something I need to do tomorrow, or something or other is happening next week, or he's even mentioned plans for next Christmas and to be honest it's starting to piss a dying man off.

How many times do I have to tell him? I'm not gonna be here tomorrow, let alone next bloody Christmas.

I'm carking it, I say. Dropping off the perch. Taking a dirt nap. Shuffling off this mortal coil. Dying, I tell him. Are you thick in the head?

In my time I've seen a few dead men. I can't say it's particularly pleasant to see a man without breath in his body. It tends to be a bit spooky, if that doesn't make me sound like too much of a ding-dong to admit. One minute there's a person, this whole animated fellow, moving about and mouthing off and having opinions, and the next moment—where'd he go? The thing that makes him a *life*—where does that go? Death comes and now he's just a body: an object that takes up a bit of space but is *empty*, like a piece of furniture. Just as heavy, too.

It might not be pleasant to see, but I've never understood why people are so afraid of death. Not like the clap—now there's something to make a man run screaming. All right, it's unnerving to witness death when it happens—one minute alive, the next minute furniture—but it happens to every single one of us. Not a man on the planet can weasel his way out of sleeping with the fishes. Same way I never much understood the blokes who drop like swatted flies when the missus has her time and pops a kid out—what, they reckon they didn't come head first and bawling from the same place? If you ask me, there's a lot of hypocrites in this town. A lot of people could do with reminding where we all came from, where we all end up. Too many men don't think with anything but their knobs and they forget—women are the beginning of us and oftentimes the end, too.

Sorry, Luce.

Maybe I need to remind the young fella. I know what I'm talking about when I talk about a man dying.

ABIGAIL

The next morning, Abigail decided to go back for her boot.

Supple cherry-red leather, Cuban heel, swirls of white embroidery. The boots had cost her the equivalent of working straight through Christmas and they made her calves look spectacular. She was not about to leave one in the bush on the side of the Port Kingo esplanade for some coastal insect to eat or shit or nest and spawn within.

First, she would need warmer clothes. When she'd opened the front door a gust of glacial wind straight from Antarctica flattened her dress and spring-time cardigan against her skin, chilling her to the bone, and she'd sworn heartily and retreated inside.

She could have gone to Nell's closet. Last night, no one had stormed in and kicked her out. She'd remained in her bed unmolested, uninterrupted, and she had taken that as forgiveness—or, at the very least, licence. It may have been two decades since she'd set foot in Port Kingerton but it wasn't that long since she'd seen her mother. There'd been Christmases, long weekends, birthdays. Only a year ago, Nell had come to the city because she'd decided a specialist naturopath could help with her sudden dairy intolerance (he hadn't, but the intolerance resolved itself when Nell decided she liked cheese too much and would simply tolerate it anyway) and they'd spent an afternoon in the Botanic Gardens, eating Reubens on the lawn and watching the old Adelaide Hospital being torn down. So she knew the unlocked window, the made-up spare bed? That was all Nell. She could help herself to a pair of her mum's jeans and a jumper. She could.

But would a *good* person continue to enable her mother's silence? Was it *respectable* or *right* to maintain a mother–daughter freeze-out? No. If she was going to take her mother's pants she would have to speak to her mother first. Or at least try.

Abigail headed out the back door. Hesitating, she took her mother's parka from the hook. She'd get permission for that while she was at it.

Cold wind cut against her bare legs and she attempted to wrap the parka tighter. Hair whipped into her eyes. Again she noticed that briny-fresh marine scent doing weird things to her emotions. The back lawn had been recently mowed and clods of grass clippings stuck to her mother's slippers, making her mince awkwardly, trying to keep them clean.

She approached the stables. New rails topped the fence, the oily smell of creosote mixed with the earthy waft of horse. Beyond the stables, the grazing paddocks rose uphill to a stand of pines, grey-black in the distance.

When she was a kid, Abigail had a clubhouse in those pines. Gnarled roots made the walls, thick mats of pine needles the floor. It was a clubhouse of one, but that just meant no other shitbag could get in the way. Holed up in her clubhouse, she would fill a notepad with evidence of potential crimes: *Mr Loft's tractor abandoned on Half Mile Road—suspicious?* (It wasn't; the tractor had just chucked a fan belt.) *Post office closed before school finished today—Mrs Dinwiddle kidnapped (or dead)?* (Neither. Just a bad pork pie and no one to fill in.) *Brian Wimple selling pot?* (Yes. But the Wimples were fifth-generation locals; Wimple Street was named after Brian's great-great-great-grandfather. Permission was implicit.)

Gripping the fence rail and looking at the pines, it occurred to her that she couldn't remember a time in her life that wasn't coloured by suspicion or wrongdoing. It didn't matter what kind: made-up, whispered about or real—villainy followed her like a stench.

And just as she was dwelling on this, on villainy and stench, she was assaulted. Or rather she was *assailed*, from all angles and through all senses: a terrific honking went into her ears; clammy webbed flesh slapped the bare skin on her hands; a demonic wheeze raked primal fear up her spine and electrified her skull. The sun darkened. She tasted dust. She smelled feathers.

Abigail was no stranger to noise. She was no stranger to fear. But she *was* off balance, and more tired than she'd been in her life, and the amount of patience she had left in her entire being was about the size of a bee's dick.

A goose. She was being attacked by a goose. A savage, hissing, darting—'Piece of shite!' she yelped—goose.

Somehow she was running, in what direction she did not know. Although it couldn't exactly be called running, the gait she was doing now—more a kind of constipated side-stroke, a sea lion humping up the sand.

After a minute or a half-hour, Abigail found herself around the side of the house, alone. Breathing heavily, heart hammering. Mighty pissed. Edging along the wall, she peered towards the back lawn and there it was on the grass, shaking itself out and tucking away its wings. Sleek white feathers, golden beak. Innocent and straight out of a nursery rhyme. The goose rolled one beady eye towards her and she jerked back, flattening herself against the wall. Fists clenched, she swiped her wrist beneath her nose and it came away bloodied. She looked again at the goose in surprise.

'Bitch.'

The goose waggled its tail and loosed a squirt of turd.

That's when she heard laughter. Gales of it, drifting across the back lawn. Her mother was standing outside the stables, head thrown back and laughing into the sky. Score one to her mother. Payback for the door locking last night, or, more likely, for the effrontery of having arrived herself on the doorstep.

She waited until her mother caught her eye. Then she gave her the finger, before heading back inside to find Nell's nicest pair of jeans.

Her mother's jeans did not zip up, but they would protect her from the cold. So, warm in Nell's parka, Ugg boots and jeans, Abigail set off to retrieve her boot.

The ocean was a restless grey and from the top of the drive she could see the breakers far out to sea, the southerly hurling spindrift into the air. Rough deep water, surging with power. She was struck by a sense of being very small, pitifully human.

By the time she reached the end of the drive she was sweating. The stand of old pines threw shade. The unzipped jeans had slipped down, crotch sagging around her thighs and rubbing the insect bite into a raging itch. After her encounter with the goose her bruised eye socket had returned to throbbing.

Last night the taxi had dropped her off in the dark and now, in the daylight, Abigail could see all the way down the hill into town. A memory came to her of Hamish's face, grinning. *Don't tell Mum*, he said, handing her the skateboard. *No, don't stand up, you'll fall.* The feel of awkwardly centring her butt on the board, feet tucked, knees wobbling. Hands gripping the thin ply. The panicked elation of gathering speed, Dylan alongside her, whooping, because there were two skateboards for two boys, but three of them. A few days later, she had carried her roller skates down the drive, sat under the pines to lace them, then tottered into the middle of the road. Rumble-roar of tiny wheels on bitumen, the whistle of wind in her ears. She made it almost all the way into town before she fell, tearing the flesh off her palms and knees (she still had a small, puckered scar on her left knee). Limping home, gravel studding her skin and blood soaking into her socks; Nell had not spoken to her until the next morning, when she'd said, coolly, *Just because the boys do it doesn't mean you should, too.*

Thickets of low bushes lined the road, waving in the wind. Somewhere in there was her boot. Abigail tried not to picture the red leather muddied and scuffed, the inside bristling with antennae. As she walked along the edge of the road, peering into the vegetation, she heard the sound of an engine. She willed it not to slow, to pay her no attention and pass by.

It didn't. The ute pulled up behind her, engine idling.

'Hey, stranger.'

When she turned, the sun was in her eyes. A man was leaning out the window but his face was in shadow.

'Heard you were back in town.'

She tried to recognise the voice. 'Did you now?'

'What've you been up to?'

Was she supposed to answer that? They all knew she'd been in prison again. It wouldn't be Kingo if they didn't.

She sauntered towards the ute: dark-tinted windows; chrome roll bar; checker-plate running boards. At least there was mud up the sides, she thought. *Not just a show pony.*

Then she got close enough to see his face. *Oh, Jesus.*

'Ab Fab Fancy,' he said.

'Adrian Turner,' she said.

The first time she kissed Adrian Turner—a few years older than her, a supplicant of her brothers—Adrian had initiated the kiss, catching the corner of her mouth at a party, and for his trouble she'd kneed him lightly in the groin. The second time was all her. Whirling on him at a bonfire on the beach, she'd pushed him off balance and he'd stumbled, but the sand was soft and Adrian had been grateful.

'Wow.' Adrian gave a low whistle. 'How'd you manage that black eye?'

Abigail folded her arms and studied him. He had turned into a bean pole of a man, scruffy blond beard and oil-stained knuckles, but she could see the boy there in his kind blue eyes. 'You got old,' she pointed out.

'Easy,' he said, laughing nervously. 'You looked in the mirror yourself lately?' Then a look of mild horror crossed his face. She could almost see him wishing he could suck the words back inside.

A long moment passed. She did not help him.

'My little brother saw you last night,' he blurted. 'At your mum and dad's. I couldn't make it, I was working. Otherwise I would've been there.'

'No doubt,' she said.

'What're you looking for?' He nodded towards the bushes.

'Lost my boot last night.'

'Oh, yeah? Have a big one, did ya?'

'Medium. Size seven.'

He laughed, a bit too hard.

'You been in trouble, or what?' he asked, again indicating her bruised face.

She didn't answer. The ute idled. Gulls cawed. She watched Adrian try not to stare at her, watched him grow increasingly uncomfortable, looking everywhere except directly at her.

Once upon a time, Abigail had kissed the few boys of Port Kingerton and they had acted grateful and goofy, as if she'd gifted them something precious. Because the truth was she *had* given them something precious: her attention. Maybe it was Hamish's and Dylan's favour the boys craved, but her brothers had been a tough duo to crack, preferring the company of each other to anyone else. Not that it stopped every Kingo boy from trying. And if they couldn't crack Hamish and Dylan, in Abigail—willing, welcoming, harmless, sweet, stupid girl—they could have the next best Fancy.

Until they couldn't. Until Abigail's attention was worth nought, her currency flat-lined.

Abigail thought that now, even fresh out of prison, they were not worthy of her attention. Not a single damn one of them.

Slapping the ute's door pillar in farewell, she turned back to the bushes.

But the engine continued idling behind her.

'Did you hear?' Adrian called.

Abigail frowned into the shrubbery, hoping to spot a glimpse of red leather. 'Hear what?' she said distractedly.

'About what they found on the beach?'

Slowly, she turned back to Adrian. 'What did you say?'

'They found something on the beach yesterday,' Adrian said, sitting in his idling ute, hopeful face staring out at her. 'Did you … know? Oh. You … I guess you didn't hear. Uh, well, I'd better get going …'

Suddenly the ocean was too loud. The seaweed rot too strong. Time reeled backwards: Abigail was thirty-nine and out of prison for the second time; she was twenty-five and stinking of beer and smoke at three am; she was fifteen, rocks and red paint flying, the entire town pointing at her, faces alight with outrage.

Before she knew what was happening, she had stalked back to the ute. Grabbed hold of the window frame, lunged in at Adrian Turner, whose head shrank back on his neck like a startled turtle. He kept trying to retreat but there was nowhere else for him to go. He was trapped, pinned against the seat as she somehow leaned her upper body into the cab and thrust her face into his.

'You ever mention this shit again,' she said, 'I'll tear your fucking balls off.'

Three minutes later Abigail found her boot. Other than a bit of dirt and seagrass stuck to the toe, it was perfect. Stepping out of the Ugg, she slid her foot into her boot. Then, wearing one slipper and one red boot, Abigail headed back up the drive, whistling.

She left her mother's slipper in the bushes.

THEM

Adrian Turner, forty-three years old, diesel mechanic and amicably co-parenting father of two, drove down the hill into town with his hands shaking and a raging boner pressing into his jeans.

Parking out the front of the hardware-cum-surf store, Adrian had to wait a full five minutes, during which time he pretended to look at his phone, before he could emerge from the ute. When he did he was still a little shaky, so he lit a cigarette and stood on the kerb. This was an invitation, of course, for anyone passing by to stop and have a yarn.

First up was Sheila Rocket, having recently come out of the post office. Sheila was seventy-one, and because it was April, which to the locals meant it was not cold, she was wearing a floral dress.

'Did you hear the prodigal daughter has returned?'

Adrian sucked on his smoke. 'I did,' he said, without exhaling, so his voice came out strangled. Against his better judgement, Adrian was replaying the feel of Abigail's breasts pressed against his hand on the ute's window frame. So unexpected. So heavy. He felt movement in his jeans again and sucked harder on his cigarette.

'Returned to the family bosom,' said Sheila, a comment which made Adrian, against his own will, take note of Sheila's, presently only about two feet from his nose. It seemed his mind had not quite made it down the hill with him and was still up there, on the side of the esplanade by the Fancys' driveway, with Abigail launching herself at him like a wildcat, trapping him with her warm, slightly tea-scented breath and heaving breasts.

Oh no, thought Adrian, as his jeans tightened.

Sheila Rocket went on. Distressingly for Adrian, Sheila also stepped closer. Came right up under his chin. Trying not to move, Adrian flared his nostrils. Smoke seeped out.

'Were you there?' demanded Sheila. 'At the Fancys' barbecue last night?'

Adrian replied that he got caught at work.

'I'm trying to find someone who was actually *there*. So far everything I've heard is secondhand, and you know how I don't like to tell tales.'

'Jase was there.' Adrian turned his head to the side, lifted his smoke and sucked like a drowning man on a snorkel.

Sheila looked delighted. 'I've been meaning to pop by your mum's and get that recipe for her lemon slice. You know, the one she made for the Scouts' fete. Does she have it handy?'

'The Scouts' fete from twenty years ago?'

'Well, time flies.'

'I don't know,' Adrian said truthfully. 'You'd have to ask.'

Which was exactly what Sheila Rocket wanted to hear, as they both knew the recipe was of little interest to Sheila: Adrian's brother, Little Jase Turner, who had been at the Fancys' last night, still lived at home.

But Sheila wasn't quite done. Casting her eyes left and right, she leaned even closer to Adrian, lowered her voice and said, 'A certain Miss Bram isn't going to be happy.'

Adrian shrugged helplessly. He couldn't care less for girlish politics at regular times, let alone when he was being unexpectedly bailed up by bosoms.

Fortunately the conversation ended up working for them both. Sheila got what she wanted—an attendee of the barbecue—and so did Adrian. Memories of his mum's lemon slice caused a considerable easing, pants wise.

Next, Adrian went into the hardware-cum-surf store, a narrow, dim space crammed with rope, screws, expensive power tools and cheap surfboards. Behind the counter hung the obligatory faded and curling Chiko Roll poster, the model in her tiny denim shorts condemned to straddle a motorbike and hold a deep fried log of batter since 1987, despite the fact that the store had never sold Chiko Rolls, nor any food at all.

Col Morton and two other blokes (dairy farmers from out of town) were leaning against the counter.

'Definitely,' Col was saying loudly, 'one hundred per cent *not* a kangaroo bone.'

'Who said, though?'

'Coppers.'

A snort. 'What would they know?'

'Forensics and shit? Oh hey, Adrian. You hear?'

'Yeah, mate,' Adrian replied, because whether Col was referring to the bone or Abigail's return, Adrian had heard enough.

'Pretty nuts, eh?'

The word 'nuts' took Adrian right back to Abigail's threat to rip his balls off and he shuddered.

'Young Dick reckons it's nothing, though,' Col said. 'So I don't reckon there'll be any ... you know.'

'Trouble?' offered one of the dairy farmers.

'Won't there be, though?' countered the other. 'If it's a human bone, they're not going to ignore it. They'll want to know, like—what human did it come from?'

There was a pause as the men absorbed the truth of this.

David Wimple, the store's owner (after his father and before that his grandfather) looked troubled, and said, 'I hope not. I've gotten used to town being ... polite.'

The dairy farmers nodded. They had gotten used to that, too—one of them was about to head to the deli for a hazelnut latte, for Christ's sake. Their grandfathers would laugh from their graves.

But Col Morton, having only moments ago had the glory of being the person who could deliver the words right out of Young Dick's mouth—*the bone is a human femur but it's no business of ours*—now stiffened in irritation. Col's irritation didn't come from the potential threat of a police investigation, however. It came from the suggestion that Young Dick Fancy could be both right and possibly wrong.

This aggravating sense of conflicting beliefs was further compounded when Adrian Turner, recovered and newly emboldened, voiced aloud the thing they had all been thinking, but so far no one had actually had the chutzpah to say: 'Takes you back, though, doesn't it?'

The distance was stared into wistfully as minds cast back twenty-four years, to the time when something else suspicious and shocking was found by the beach. Something that turned the town upside down. Something much worse than a thighbone.

Col Morton sometimes walked with a limp. The reason Col sometimes walked with a limp was the main reason he felt comfortable going to the Fancys' back door.

After leaving the hardware store, Col limped into Bram's Deli. Penny Bram was behind the counter and observed that today was a day when Col was wearing his limp like a trophy. She muttered, 'Give me strength,' under her breath but called cheerfully to Col, 'How was the barbecue?'

'Well,' said Col, limping to a halt. 'You wouldn't believe who turned up.'

'I've already heard,' said Penny, setting her elbows onto the counter, feeling the radiant heat of the pie warmer against her backside. 'And Nell didn't even know she was coming, eh? Her own daughter, turning up unannounced. After all these years.'

'Didn't look like she did.'

'How is she?'

'Hmm,' said Col, not wanting to admit that he had not spoken a word to Abigail and did not have a clue about her wellbeing. 'She's a bit rough, as to be expected. Got a shiner of a black eye.'

'How long was it this time—six months?'

'Five,' Col said knowledgeably.

There came the sound of plastic flapping as Penny's daughter, Jessica, thrust through the hanging strips at the rear of the store.

'Not long enough, if you ask me,' Jessica said.

Penny looked at Jessica in surprise. 'Aren't you supposed to be opening the gift shop today?'

'In a minute.' Then to Col, Jessica said, 'If it's a toasted ham and cheese you're after, we're all out.'

Col considered the mother–daughter pair side by side: the Brams.

Well, what was left of them. Penny Bram's mother split when she was a small child and her father died twenty-four years ago. For a long time it had been just the two of them: Penny and Jessica. Everyone knew Jessica's father had never been on the scene, a blow-in who had lasted long enough to knock up Penny and run off with the good set of silverware she had inherited from her late grandmother.

Now, Col looked at Penny and Jessica, a thirty-year before-and-after of curly hair, wind-ruddied cheeks, poker faces, and he could have spared a thought for what the events of yesterday might mean to them—the discovery of human remains, the return of a nemesis. But Col was not overly inclined to sparing thoughts for others. Unless they were a Fancy.

'Darn,' Col said. 'I was.'

Penny side-eyed her daughter. There were four ham-and-cheese toasties in the pie warmer. Penny watched as Col headed over to the fruit and veg stand, exaggerating his limp. 'Foot playing up today?' she asked, trying to keep the disdain from her voice.

'A little,' Col said valiantly, inspecting a tomato. 'Must be gonna rain.' He set the tomato down and picked up another, identical to the first. 'I can always tell if there's rain on the way. It plays up where the bones were broken.'

'The rest of us just check Weatherzone,' said Jessica, then winced as her mother's elbow dug into her ribs.

'You got any of that good ham?' Col asked.

Penny bent towards the cabinet but Jessica spoke up again. 'Fresh out,' she said. 'Used the last of it for sandwiches. Only got the other type, the not-good ham.'

Penny's side-eye changed to a glare.

'I guess I'll take some of that,' Col said, picking up a loaf of white bread and setting it on the counter with a tomato.

'So why's Abigail back?' Jessica asked. Her mother shot her another wary glance, before reaching across her to set the tomato on the scale.

Col managed his best evasive expression. 'I can't really say. You know I can't.'

'*Do* I know that?' said Jessica.

Penny rung up the total. All she wanted now was to get Col Morton out of the store so she could find out what on earth had gotten into Jess.

And then Jessica said, 'It's a bit too much of a coincidence, her coming back right when the bone washes up.'

'That's twelve twenty-five,' Penny announced brightly. 'You'd better get to the gift shop,' she said to Jessica. 'You don't want to be late.'

'It *is* a coincidence,' said Col. 'A prison sentence ends when it ends; she couldn't choose that.'

'Pfft,' said Jessica. 'As if the Fancys don't have sway with a judge. They've got fingers everywhere.'

'Happy to make it twelve,' Penny shouted.

'Maybe you should hold your tongue,' Col said to Jessica, lightly, as if he was still making enquiries about ham.

Now Penny could see it in Jessica, a pilot light that had been clicking away for years. And with the arrival of Abigail Fancy suddenly: *whoosh*. A flame.

'Sorry,' Penny said to Col, because although she thought he was a bit of an idiot she wasn't completely unaware of who she was talking to. 'I think Jess is tired. The baby kept her awake last night—right, Jess? You'll go home later and have a nap, won't you? After you've *gone and opened the bloody gift shop*?'

'Probably a good idea,' Col agreed.

'I'm not afraid of her,' Jessica said.

'Oh, look, Jess, I'm sure there's no need for that,' Col said, magnanimously. He shifted his weight with a grimace.

'You should take some fish oil,' Jessica said, 'for that foot.'

Col looked down. 'Why?'

'Helps with inflammation.'

'Can a bullet wound stay inflamed for ten years?'

'Only if you're a dickhead. That's twelve twenty-five.'

Col pointed to the tomato. 'Weigh that again without Jessica's finger. Then you can keep the change.' He put a tenner on the counter.

Forty minutes after the post office opened, Nell Fancy stepped inside.

Lucky it was Wednesday, because had the bone washed up and Abigail returned on a weekend it would have been harder for the three women gathered at the post office counter to purchase the office supplies they all suddenly needed.

Nell walked in to see Sheila Rocket (back again; she'd forgotten she also needed bubble wrap) and two fishermen's wives (both inconsequential) tucked together, with Mrs Dinwiddle behind the counter.

When Nell entered the other women went silent.

Nell headed straight for them. 'Morning, ladies.'

'Hi, Nell.'

'Morning.'

'Good, thanks.'

Nell turned to the postmistress. 'Bev—have the parcels come in today?'

Mrs Dinwiddle hesitated. The parcels had come in. But the postmistress was presently feeling like a teenage girl whose heart-throb has just crossed her path: tongue-tied, yet dying to draw the encounter out as long as possible. 'I'm not sure,' she said.

Nell tapped a foot.

'Wait here, Nell. I'll go see.' The postmistress disappeared.

Sheila Rocket and the two inconsequential women shifted. Someone cleared her throat. Someone opened her mouth as if to speak, then shut it again.

Nell said nothing. The smell of molasses and horse lifted from her jeans, but that's how Nell always smelled so no one minded. It was far better than fish, which was how everyone else always smelled.

It was a minute before Mrs Dinwiddle returned, empty handed. 'Doesn't look like the courier's been yet,' she lied.

Nell waggled her phone. 'I've got a notification there's a parcel to collect.'

'Oh? Could be a glitch in the system. Let me check again—sometimes the young girl puts them in the wrong place. Wait here.' And the postmistress went out back again, wondering how she could keep Nell Fancy in the store for longer without having to keep leaving the room, which was counterproductive.

'I hear you've got a visitor,' said Sheila Rocket, who couldn't take it any longer.

'Yes,' said Nell, making sure to smile. 'It's wonderful. I'm so glad to have her back. She looks amazing.'

Sheila Rocket and the two fishermen's wives didn't know what to make of that. Based on what they'd heard, the last thing they had been expecting from Nell was a display of maternal pride. It made them question if what they'd heard was actually true. At such a notion, they chafed.

Mrs Dinwiddle returned, a box in her arms. 'Found it.'

'Great.' Nell came forward to take the box.

In a sudden desperate brainwave, Mrs Dinwiddle took a step back from the counter. 'I'll just need to see some ID.'

There was a long, tense pause.

Nell said, 'You'll need what, Bev?'

'Some ID, Nell. It's a rule they're enforcing now.' The postmistress pointed to a few leaflets sticky-taped to the counter: *Support Our Farmers The Life Of The Land; NO FRACKING – SIGN OUR PETITION; Pre-paid SIMs available.*

'I don't see anything about ID.'

'Oh, well. I need to make a new sign. So anyway, how is Abigail? Is she just visiting or returned for good? How do you feel—you and Dick?'

Another stiff pause ensued. Sheila Rocket and the two other women dared not move, only their eyes flicked back and forth. Mrs Dinwiddle's forehead grew damp. A tractor growled past out on the street. Seagulls squawked.

Finally Nell said, 'Keep it.'

And Nell turned and walked out of the post office.

No one knew what to make of that, either.

OLD DICK

I did not steal those sheep.

What would I want with six sheep? (Or was it eight?) Look, it doesn't matter—I didn't steal them, such a puny flock as it was. A man doesn't have the time or inclination to nick a few wethers when he's got craypots to pull and heifers to drench, and the damn bull's got pink eye again, the useless lump of nutsack.

And no, I don't know who did steal the sheep either, so quit harping.

It's okay, Dad, the young fella is saying. *That's not why the cops were here yesterday.*

All right, I probably do know who stole them. But it's been dealt with, so that's the end of it.

I know, Dad. Don't worry about it.

They've been fussing, the young fella and the woman, fussing all morning and blocking my view of the boats.

Coming and going, faces all tense, talking in low tones so I have to ask them to speak up because I can't hear them when they're whispering. And then they tell me *Don't worry about it?*

Ha! I'll show them. Try getting my corpse out from inside the hay baler. That'd make their day difficult.

The young fella's asking the woman if she's got any ID, which is a fair enough question, but the woman looks royally pissed about it.

Can you believe that? the woman says. *She actually asked me for ID.*

For some reason the young fella finds that incredibly funny. The woman does not.

Come on, the fella says. *It's not Beverly Dinwiddle you're mad at.*

The woman hands me a sandwich in a bowl. I don't recall asking for a sandwich in a bowl, but I take it because I'm polite and Luce would have my guts otherwise.

She should have called, the woman says. *I would have picked her up.*

You know Abigail.

The bus! She took the stinking bus, all that way.

It's only a few hours.

Six.

Compared to five months inside?

Why didn't she tell me? She looks awful.

You know what doesn't stink? A boat. Well, unless the deckie doesn't hose all the guts off properly, then it can get a bit ripe. Back in my day though, deckies knew what hard work was, and who the captain was, and boats sparkled like they should. Nowadays kids don't know what proper work looks like. Slumping around with their video games and their insolence. Bring back the rod in school, I say.

You know what we used to do when people didn't listen?

Not now, Dad.

Feed 'em to the crays.

I'll never get to relax, will I?

I wait for the woman's answer to that, but they just go on staring at each other. Excellent. Now they're distracted I can make a hasty getaway. I've got important business with the hay baler.

ABIGAIL

Huffing, Abigail made her way back up the drive. The elation of retrieving her boot turned out to be momentary as now the boot was rubbing against her toes. Any relish she'd felt in leaving her mother's slipper on the side of the road was also gone, as if the steep driveway was a moral high road: the further up she got, the more petty and rueful she felt.

She made it to the top of the drive, cursed, then turned and headed back down. She retrieved the slipper and climbed back up. By the time she reached the house again she was blowing like a racehorse. Propping her hands on her thighs, she tried not to throw up, but her conscience felt less stricken. A tiny sense of relief in a wrong made right.

As she straightened up, a goose waddled around the side of the house.

'You've got to be kidding,' Abigail said.

The goose appeared to double in size. It lowered its head and stretched its neck, sending out from somewhere deep inside its body a long guttural hiss.

Her eyes went to the front door, then back to the goose.

They both took off.

Abigail reached the door just before the goose reached Abigail. 'You want a date with an axe?' she yelled, when safely on the other side of the screen. Unperturbed, the goose resettled its feathers and toddled off.

Muttering about paté, Abigail went into the lounge room. Her grandfather was seated by the window, peering through the glass. In the distance she could see the breakwater, a line of colossal boulders curved around a little harbour while the Southern Ocean raged against it. Breakers smashed against the rocks, shooting foam into the air. Inside the shelter of the breakwater a scatter of cray boats floated, calm on their anchors.

Old Dick was unmoving, intent.

'What're you looking at?' she asked.

He didn't answer.

'Grandpa?'

'Ssh. You hear that?'

Abigail came alongside him, looked out the window. Ocean, pine trees, desultory beach. Not a person in sight. 'Hear what?'

'Sirens. I reckon them coppers are back.'

A prickle crept up her spine. 'The cops were here?'

'All bloody morning, yesterday. Parked across the road like they own the joint, stopping a man from strolling down the beach if he wanted. And maybe I would've wanted a stroll down the beach?'

'Oh, yeah?' she said. 'When's the last time you strolled down the beach?'

Her grandfather finally looked at her. 'You teasing?'

'Sorry,' she said.

'S'alright, love. I'll take you for a walk later. I've just got to watch a while, make sure no bastard steals my mooring.'

'Why were the cops here?'

He frowned. 'Some palms probably need greasing.'

'Is that so?'

'Listen,' he said, wheeling closer. 'There's something you should know.'

Abigail bent to his eyeline. 'What's that?'

'North of the lighthouse. Twelve degrees, eighty yards. Don't ever dig there.'

'Got it,' she said.

'Now, if the coppers need oiling, there's stacks of hundreds in the—'

'Enough, Dad!'

The shout came from the kitchen.

She looked at her grandfather in surprise. 'What's that about?'

The old man shrugged. 'Stuffed if I know.' He went back to gazing out the window.

Squeezing her grandfather's shoulder, she left him and entered the kitchen, where she found her father bent over the sink, replacing a washer on the tap. Tools and tap innards scattered about the benchtop, a film of water dripped down the cabinet.

'You need help with that?'

Her father held the wrench towards her. 'Be my guest.'

'That was rhetorical.' Making her way to the table, she pulled out a chair and sat down with relief.

Abigail watched her father, elbows pitched out, knees jammed against the cabinet. In the years she had been away his hair had turned silver and sparse, but he was the same size and shape, as tall and wiry as her mother was short and athletic. Watching him work, seeing a man undaunted by four metre swell now bested by a dripping tap, she felt a surge of affection and security. But immediately following that comfort was a feeling of terror: the idea that it could be taken away. It had been a year since she'd smoked but a craving for a cigarette hit her so hard she put a finger to her mouth and ripped off a nail.

'You shouldn't yell at Grandpa,' she said.

Young Dick set down the wrench. 'I know. But it gets to me.'

'He's just talking.'

'I know,' he repeated, and she saw him struggling to formulate a reply. 'But when he talks about the past ... His memories get jumbled. He doesn't always have a handle on when things come up and out anymore. Some things are best kept ... private.'

She gestured about the kitchen. 'There's no one here.'

'He doesn't know that. Whether we're alone or in a room full of people, he'll talk.'

'Talking's not a crime.'

'No,' her father said. 'But what he talks about could be.'

Abigail's heart kicked. The craving continued to buzz along her nerves. 'At least Grandpa talks to you,' she said. 'Mum's still ignoring me.'

She could see him considering a way to deny it, his face lifting as if he were going to chummily cajole her that *Surely not, she's just busy*, but he seemed to change his mind. 'She just needs a little time, is all. Give her a chance.' He pointed to his tool bag. 'Pass me the Teflon tape.'

Pushing herself to her feet, Abigail went to the bag and plucked out a roll of plumber's tape. She put her index finger through the hole in the centre of it.

'How many chances does a person have?' She spun the roll and it wedged down over her knuckle. 'Because I've run out.'

Setting down the wrench, her father clicked his tongue and came forward. The tape wouldn't come off her finger. After a moment's tugging and fussing, during which her knuckle grew even fatter, she was about to suggest he fetch the butter when he unwrapped a length of tape right from her finger and snipped it off.

'What are you going to do?'

She braced herself. 'Know anyone who's hiring?'

'Here?' He held onto her finger as a slow grin spread across his face. 'Sure I do. But hire you? No.'

'Bullshit.'

'Not a chance, Abs.'

'Are you kidding?'

'No. I'm telling you.' He let go of her hand. 'Sorry, kiddo.' He returned to the tap, offering over his shoulder, 'It's nearly lunch time. You must be hungry. Help yourself to something to eat.'

The roll of Teflon tape was still stuck on her finger, but Abigail went to the fridge. While her back was turned she heard her father say, 'So, do you have anything at all?'

'These boots,' she replied.

'Anything else?'

'The dress and cardigan.'

'Oh.'

'I didn't get bail, remember?' Fumbling open a jar of gherkins, she sniffed, recoiled and put the jar back.

'Right,' said her father. 'You made that additional, uh, threat.'

'"To his person",' she quoted, peeling a foil lid from a tray and inspecting the contents. Cannelloni. *Hell yes.* She took the tray in delight.

'So I guess you didn't have much time to sort things out.'

'No.' She opened the cutlery drawer and picked out a fork. 'Remanded in custody, then straight into His Majesty's finest. One hundred and fifty-two days. Three thousand six hundred and forty-eight hours, give or take a few for the strip searches and bureaucratic dicking around.'

At 'strip searches' her father looked as though someone had kicked him in the shin. 'So it's all gone?' he said. 'You've got nothing?'

'Not a cent,' she confirmed. 'I didn't even have my phone on me when I was arrested. This stupid dress has no pockets. Without time to cancel anything it doesn't take long for a few direct debits to clean it all out. Rent, electricity, phone … *poof.* Gone.' She offered a wry smile. 'Not that there was much there to begin with—' she lifted a foot, waggled her red boot '—too much Afterpay debt. And now all my boots are gone, too. This is all I have left, literally the clothes on my back. Landlord took the rest, the cocktrumpet.'

It had, perhaps, been the worst of the salt in her already smarting wound, the loss of her boots. None of Abigail's

clothes were expensive—her salary from the restaurant
hardly allowed for it—but she was a junkie for good boots.
The higher the better. She thought now of her black suede
thigh-highs and wanted to weep. And although her landlord had seized all her possessions when her eviction had
been made formal while she was inside, Afterpay didn't give
a shit. She was responsible for the debt and its eye-watering
interest until it was paid off, even though all the boots were
god knows where—landfill, eBay, her landlord's basement
for his dark web dress-ups. It did not matter. Debt trumps
humanity.

Her father was quiet for a while. Abigail stood at the bench
forking up cold spinach and ricotta cannelloni and thought
it was possibly the best thing she'd ever eaten. 'Grandpa said
the cops were here yesterday.' Swallowing, she added carefully, 'Is that true?'

Young Dick was quiet so long she thought he wasn't going
to reply. When he spoke, his voice was measured. 'Yes. For
most of the day. But they're gone now.'

'Why?'

If Abigail knew one thing about her father it was this:
he could not lie. His life was structured around keeping
information safe and the weight of that—a generation of
guardedness—meant he had to be able to remember everything he said and the easiest things to remember are facts.
And that meant never telling an outright lie. Even when the
truth could never possibly come to light.

Which was why she watched her father wrestle internally
with her question—*why were the cops here?*—and knew he
was trying to figure out what he could say that was true.

And this, his clear grappling with the truth, meant that the facts were uncomfortable.

'Maybe you should sit down,' he said.

'No thanks.'

'I said sit down.'

'And I said no thanks.'

'All right.' The wrench hit the sink with a clang. 'The cops were here because yesterday morning Mrs Potts found a bone on the beach. A human thighbone.'

Ludicrously, Abigail heard herself say, 'A fresh one?'

'Don't know. It's been in the water. Seals gave it a hard time.'

Putting down the fork, she pressed two fingers to her lips, holding the cannelloni inside. She swallowed several times, but it didn't work. Hurrying to the sink, she bent over and closed her eyes as spinach and ricotta came back up. At least it lubricated the Teflon tape, which popped off her knuckle. Her father didn't want the tape returned to his tool bag. He took it from her gingerly and dropped it in the bin.

THEM

There were several people in Port Kingerton who considered themselves to be Young Dick Fancy's right-hand man, even though Young Dick had stated adamantly over the years he had neither need nor desire for one.

There was Col Morton, young and strong, skipper of his own boat already and the kind of man who came to the back door. And of course, there was that time he'd taken a bullet in his foot for Young Dick.

There was Tim 'Twitch' Witchens, in his sixties like Young Dick, also a fisherman, but the kind of man who always texted first (Twitch had five kids and eighteen grand-kids spread all over the state; his phone was welded to his hand whether he liked it or not).

Trisha Loft, one of many Loft grandkids and a stealthy, introverted type, had also proved herself loyal to Young Dick on several occasions, most of which remained known only by way of urban legend, but one verifiable instance was the time Young Dick found himself tipped from his boat a kilometre offshore, clinging to a craypot buoy, and Trisha had plucked him from the water with only the strength of her upper body.

A shortlist of others were possible: Adrian Turner; another Loft; David Wimple from the hardware store in a pinch.

The point is, Young Dick had a lot of support from the men and women of the community. A lot of muscle, too, should persuasion be necessary.

So why had Young Dick told his daughter no one would give her work?

The kitchen tap was still leaking, but Young Dick packed away his tools and headed outside. He crossed the back-yard, pushed through the gate and walked into the stables. His footsteps echoed on the stone floor, shafts of dusty light fell across the sawdust. All but two stalls were empty; most of the horses were turned out on the autumn grass. In the third stall, a nose poked over the door, briefly assessed Young Dick then disappeared, uninterested.

'Nell?'

'In here.'

Young Dick went into the feed room. Grain bins, molasses-stained buckets and scoops lined the walls, and a stack of lucerne hay in the corner gave off a grassy scent. Sitting on that stack was his wife. She was dressed in old jeans, fleece vest over a black T-shirt, scuffed riding boots. Hair pulled away from her face. She was reading a book.

Young Dick climbed onto the bale alongside Nell. Even sitting down she was much shorter than him. Tucking his chin to his shoulder, he looked down at the top of his wife's head. The grey peeking at the roots of her hair sent a rush of tenderness through him. Picking a piece of straw from her crown he said, 'How can you read in this light?'

'I don't need light. It's not all that interesting.'

'Then why are you reading it?'

Nell closed the book and considered the cover as if it might offer a reason for the use of her time. 'Truthfully,' she said, 'it's something to look at that doesn't need anything from me.' She set the book aside. 'What's Abigail doing?'

'Helping herself to the leftover cannelloni.' He didn't add that it had taken her two goes at it. After Abigail had washed the vomit from the sink, then gone upstairs to wash herself, she had come back for seconds. Nothing, it would seem, was going to stand between Abigail and those tubes of baked ricotta.

Nell nodded in satisfaction. 'Good.'

'She thinks you're ignoring her.'

'I am ignoring her.'

Young Dick knew better than to ask why. 'How long for?'

'The same length of time anyone of my generation ignores someone. Until I can figure out my thoughts and feelings enough to stop blaming the other person for them.'

'I believe they call that *projection*, my love.'

'Call it whatever you like. She's made such a mess.'

'You know Abigail.'

'But that's the thing,' Nell said, suddenly wild. 'Clearly I *don't*. Showing up here, looking like she is—it's the last thing I expected. Nothing's ever *easy* with her. Why does she have to make everything so hard?'

From the stalls came a thud, followed by a lazy snort. Nell leaned over to tug her phone from her pocket.

'I told the boys,' she said, thumbing the screen. 'Hamish wrote, "good news hope she stays and gets her shit together" and Dylan hasn't written back.' She shoved her phone away. 'So I guess it's not only my generation.'

Young Dick considered offering an excuse for Dylan's non-response—he was busy; phone service was sporadic in Far North Queensland; maybe he was working nights and asleep—but decided against it. 'What did you tell them?'

'That she was back, and that I can't face her, so don't ask me any questions because I don't know.'

'Well, there you go. If you're pissy, Dylan will side with Abigail—he always has. You know that.'

Nell didn't respond. She picked up the novel, turned it over a few times in her hands, set it back down.

'She wants a job,' Young Dick said. A little sheepishly, he added, 'I told her she wouldn't be able to find anything.'

'Why would you say that?'

'Because I don't want her in town.'

Nell bristled. 'You want her to leave?'

'No,' he hastened to say. 'I'm glad she came back. I don't know what she's going to do, but if she's here, I can finally keep an eye on her.' He tipped back his head to consider the roof. 'Like I should have done twenty-odd years ago.'

'You can't keep her confined to the house,' Nell said. 'Whether she's here or in town, people will talk. People will think and say and do whatever they want. Are you trying to protect her from that?'

'Yeah.'

Nell laughed softly. 'She doesn't need protecting.'

'I know that.'

'Well?'

Young Dick plucked a stem of lucerne and began breaking it into small pieces. 'The timing is unfortunate.'

'Actually the timing is perfect, if you take a look at her.'

He shuddered, brushing the hay from his hands. 'That black eye, Christ.'

Nell stared into the middle distance. 'Whoever it was,' she said mildly, 'I'll kill them.'

'Now you sound like Dad.'

Nell lifted her face to look him directly in the eye and Young Dick saw flint there, the same steely conviction he saw in Abigail.

'She can't go back again, Richard. She can't. *Look* at her.'

'I know.'

'Well?'

'Shit,' Young Dick said, glancing at his watch. 'I'm late. Twitch's got the tractor at the ramp, he'll be waiting. There's rough weather on the way.'

From the stall came another thump, another snort, the sound of a hay bag being thrashed against the wall.

Nell put a hand on her husband's arm. 'The boat can wait.'

'The weather won't. If I don't get it into dry dock and get that anti-foul on—'

'What are you going to do?'

He gave a heavy sigh, taking up Nell's hand and squeezing it. 'What was it you said last night? That it wasn't my problem to fix?'

Nell narrowed her eyes. 'That was about three seconds before she knocked on the door.'

'Ah.' He kissed her knuckles. 'So *she's* my problem, is what you're saying.'

They both went quiet as from inside the stall came a shrill, indignant whinny. A moment later a fainter answering cry came from the paddocks.

Young Dick inclined his head in the direction of the stall. 'How much longer has she got?'

'Not long,' Nell replied. 'It seems everyone is running out of time.'

OLD DICK

My father once shot a man over a pair of horse clippers.

In the leg, I should add—not somewhere fatal like the chest or neck or balls. The way my father told the story, the man he shot used to work for my father but hadn't for a few years, then one day the man came waltzing into my father's kitchen while Dad was innocently eating his supper and demanded my father give him the horse clippers.

'Where are those horse clippers?' the man said, in an offensive manner.

'I don't know anything about them,' replied my father.

'You do,' said the man.

'You had better leave the room,' suggested my father. 'You better go outside.'

'I will not go out and you cannot put me out,' expostulated the man.

What happened next was subject to a sizeable amount of interpretation—my father said one thing, the man who wanted the horse clippers said another, and a third man, who was at that time working for Dad and happened to come into the room as events unfolded, said something else. Police court dismissed it as a trifling affair, which it was if you ask my father or the third man who entered the room.

I don't know how trifling it would have been for the man who got shot in the leg. Because when I say 'shot in the leg', I admit I'm sugar coating it. A less sugary description is the man got shot in the knee. Right through his kneecap. My dad kept a twelve gauge shotgun leaning against the kitchen cupboard, and one of those through your kneecap at close range would not be pretty. It would mess up your day.

I was only a small boy at the time and I don't recall what happened to the man afterwards. Ma never talked about it but then again Ma never talked about anything much at all, except to rouse me for getting grass stains on my good Sunday pants. I do recall there was a man who got about town with a limp, though, so maybe that was him.

I can't see the boats now because there's a mist come in and it's swallowed up my view of the breakwater. Out the window I can see the cheesewood bushes and a goose, but that's about it.

Whatever happened to that man Dad shot? I ask the woman.

She's dragging a big box across the floor. She stops and looks at me.

Sorry, hon, she says, *What did you say?*

That man Dad shot, over the horse clippers. What happened to him?

She's looking around the room now, as if she's trying to find someone. She looks alarmed. Does she think the man who got shot is here and can answer for himself?

I'm not sure, Richard, she says. *Would you like a cup of tea?*

What I'd like is to know what happened to that man my father shot, and if any bastard's stolen my mooring, and where the hell they've hidden the ladder, but it seems to me that a man can't get answers today, all he can get is a cup of bloody tea.

But I'm a gentleman and Luce would have my guts so I say, Yes, thank you, and the woman goes into the kitchen, leaving the big box right there in the middle of the floor.

ABIGAIL

'Abigail, come down here.'

Early afternoon. Abigail lay on the bed in her childhood room that wasn't hers anymore, dozily watching sunlight inch across the floor until it was beaming through the window. The room had grown stuffy. At the sound of her mother's summons, a tug-of-war played out in Abigail's mind. The instant resentment that she didn't have a choice but to comply hauled against the realisation that she did. The obedient child against the rebellious child, the bound crim against the autonomous woman. It tangled up in the space of a few seconds but by the time she rolled off the bed and came to the top of the stairs, she felt tousled and angry.

Her mother was standing at the bottom of the stairs. At her feet was a large cardboard box.

'She speaks,' Abigail said.

Her mother ignored that.

'What's in the box?'

'Come here.'

Abigail didn't move. 'Do you have another animal in there that's going to attack me?'

'You're still mad about the goose? That's just Kitten. He's harmless.'

'You called your goose Kitten?'

'What else would I call him?'

'Puffer jacket?'

'I want my jeans back. You can't wear them undone like that. Don't make me come up there.'

Abigail was wearing her mother's jeans and a T-shirt of her father's that read *Holden Repair Kit* with a picture of a hand grenade. Slowly, the stairs squeaked in reverse: ninth, seventh, fourth. She ensured she found every squeak, stepping on it with her full weight. The closer she got to her mother the more the air between them seemed to compress. Time slowed and strung out. Her mother wouldn't meet her eye as she descended, but Abigail saw Nell observing each footstep, eyes darting between Abigail's feet and body and hand gripping the rail, until she stood on the floor in front of her, the box between them.

Finally Nell looked her in the eye. Neither of them spoke. This went on for quite some time, this looking and not speaking; it went on for so long Abigail began to wonder if Nell had forgotten that it was *she* who had summoned *her* in the first place and was instead waiting for Abigail to explain herself. Outside the waves crashed and the sun crawled across the sky and trees pumped sap and meanwhile, Abigail and her mother stood at the foot of the stairs, looking at each other, not speaking.

Abigail moved first. Hooking her thumbs in the waistband of Nell's jeans, she shoved them down. Wriggled her hips, inching the denim down her legs. Once she had the jeans off, she handed them across the box.

'Thank you,' said Nell, folding the jeans and setting them on the sideboard.

Once again silence fell, only now Abigail had no pants on. She dug her nails into her thigh and gave it a delicious hard scratch.

Nell clucked her tongue. 'Is that a bite? Don't scratch it.'

Abigail eyeballed her mother, scratching harder.

Nell pointed at the box. 'All these clothes were donated last year for bushfire relief,' she said. 'Then the pandemic hit and we weren't allowed to give anything out. Since then the box has been sitting in the shed and I haven't had a chance to look at it. I want you to go through it. Anything old or stained, toss it. Anything in good condition, wash it, fold it and bag it up. Then you can take it down to the gift shop, where they'll sell it for charity. As payment for your time you can keep whatever you can wear.'

Abigail glanced into the box and laughed. 'I'm not wearing any of that.'

'What else are you going to wear?'

'I didn't come here nude. I have some clothes.'

All her mother did was rub her eyes. Nell rubbed her eyes and twenty-three years evaporated, as if they had never passed at all. As if the old press-dial phone was still there, the photos still on the walls, as if Hamish and Dylan were climbing out their window and Abigail was leaning out above them, hissing down in the dark *Where are you going?* and they were hissing back *Be quiet.* Her mother rubbed her eyes with that same stifled exhaustion, resignation and frustration that had always communicated to Abigail she'd done something wrong, but she couldn't know exactly what that wrong thing was because her mother wouldn't tell her. Instead, Nell would simply hold it against her for hours or days. Palms pressed by her mouth, middle fingers against her eyes, thumbs cupping the curve of her jaw: this was a secret handshake, martyr style. Christ was crucified in the same way Nell Fancy rubbed her eyes.

'There goes another saint,' Abigail said. But her brothers weren't there to snigger. Rather than fortified, she felt like an arse. Now she saw the deep grooves around her mother's eyes, and those momentarily vanished twenty-three years came roaring back. It wasn't only Abigail who'd been through the wringer. Her mother had, too.

What would a good person do?

As hard as prison was for her, she knew it wasn't easy for those outside, either. Nothing to do from afar but witness and worry. She thought of the thankless work of a fisherman's wife: the three am starts; the stink of fish and diesel filling every pore; the quiet fear always present no matter how gentle the weather or adept the men. And of course, there was the weight of Port Kingerton: parochial; foolish; full of hot air. Abigail felt churlish. Her defences began to crumble.

Taking a step closer, she looked inside the box. The first thing she pulled out was a hot pink miniskirt, slippery and elastic with a metallic sheen.

'Nothing says bushfire relief like an eighties hooker.' Abigail stretched the skirt at her waist. 'It wouldn't even cover my pubes. Although maybe that's the point?' She waggled her fingers at her crotch. 'Advertising. Like those blow-up figures at car yards that flap about in the wind. Come on in, folks. There's bargains inside.' She gave the waistband a few tugs; the fabric went see-through. 'I mean I'm sex positive, but this is something else.'

'Enough.' Nell grabbed the skirt and tossed it aside.

'You're keeping that one for yourself?'

'I saw a pair of pants that would fit you,' her mother said, rummaging.

Abigail retrieved the pink skirt and pulled it over her neck like a snood. When Nell looked up, she struck a pose and pouted.

'Take that off; it's not yours.'

'I thought you said it was payment for my time.'

'You haven't done a thing yet.'

'Call it an advance.'

'Take it off.'

She tugged the skirt off her neck, hooked it over her finger and shot it down the hall where it landed on the modem. Green lights blinked beneath the pink fabric.

'Abigail, I'm serious. This is something helpful you can do.'

Abigail nodded seriously. 'Bushfire relief. Got it.' She went to retrieve the skirt, and when she turned back her mother was wearing over her jumper a large beige bra with impressively pointed cups.

'I don't think they're flame retardant,' Abigail said.

Nell looked down. 'I don't know, I reckon these would be pretty dousing.'

'Depends what lights your fire. Let's find out. Hey, Dad?'

Nell gave a reluctant laugh. 'All right, stop it.'

'You're right. Wrong demographic. Hey,' she yelled, 'Grandpa?'

'Abigail,' her mother said irritably, wrenching off the bra and dumping it back into the box. 'You always go too far.'

Always.

Personal improvement group—or bullshit group, as the inmates called it—discouraged the use of superlatives. *I'm* always *fucking up; I'll* never *get my shit together; I'm* always *wrong.* 'Is it true?' the social worker would ask. 'Think about it. Always? Never? Is it *really* true?' Loath as she was to admit any kind of lightbulbs in the nick, it made sense. *You always* came with the message that this horrible thing you're being accused of—in this case, *always going too far*— is a discomfort that has run through the other person, at all times, for as long as you've known them. And if it's your mother saying it? That's forever. What a horrible, gutting thing to think.

The urge to throw something was overwhelming. To take every piece of crap from the box and hurl it into the sea. To drive over it with a car, to drop a match in it and set it aflame.

But Abigail could not go back.

The anger was protective, ego's bodyguard coming swift to cover up a wound, to shield her from the shame of a scolded child. She could thank bullshit group for that gleaming rabbit turd of wisdom, too. Oh, what forces it took to muster that anger! Abigail set her hands on the edge of the box, closed her eyes and breathed in. Breathed as if she were perched in a hut in Tibet, sucking up the Himalayas themselves.

She realised that the thing about coming home is it makes you a child again. It makes you forget you've grown your arse up. All the work you've done sloughing the labels you grew up believing about yourself—that you're lazy, bad-tempered, don't listen—it all goes out the window and the adult you thought you were—self-realised, independent, capable of lighting the stove—regresses.

People who stay in their childhood towns, she wondered, how did they do it? They up-grow under witness, perhaps; they are able to shuck their shitty kid labels because the same people who gave them those labels witnessed the growing up happen. Or maybe they don't grow up. Maybe they never stop being what other people say they are, and it goes on and on, generation after generation, until it's just a town where everyone thinks they know who everyone else is, but no one knows who they really are themselves.

Abigail opened her eyes and saw red.

THEM

Down at the breakwater boat ramp a minor melee was developing.

Young Dick arrived to see Twitch on the road with the tractor, waiting for the ramp, which was presently occupied by Fish Fisher and his tractor, long beard waving in the wind. Four cray boats were queued in the water, ready to come out. A crowd of locals were gathered by the ramp, pointing and staring.

'What's going on?' Young Dick said, striding up to Col Morton, who suddenly seemed to be everywhere.

'Well,' said Col, in an uncertain, drawn-out way. 'Fish is here for Lofty's boat.'

'And?' said Young Dick. Fish Fisher always collected Lofty's boat for dry dock. Every year for the past fifty-odd years. What was the big deal about that?

'Well,' Col repeated. 'Do you see Lofty's boat?'

Young Dick looked to where Lofty's *Queenie II* was usually moored and saw empty water. He searched the harbour, past the breakwater to open sea.

'But then Twitch arrived for your boat,' Col said, 'and Fish sort of ... barged onto the ramp before him, like in protest or something, and now he's not moving.'

Young Dick turned back to Col with a frown. 'In protest? Of what?'

Fish Fisher—white haired, flannel shirted, wizened as a scrap of boot leather—was sitting on his antique Massey Ferguson in the middle of the ramp. The trailer was backed to the waterline. In the water, Young Dick's boat was first in the queue and he could see his deckie, Spike, leaning against the gunwales, watching. This congestion would be easily rectified if Fish would just cede the ramp for a few minutes, Young Dick knew, but given that the old fisherman had turned the tractor off, folded his arms and was glaring down at the crowd yelling, 'I'm not moving, so you lot may as well bugger off!' it seemed that was not about to happen.

The crowd parted willingly as Young Dick made his way to the tractor.

'G'day, Fish,' Young Dick said, propping a congenial foot on the Massey's wheel rim.

'Dicky,' replied Fish.

'Quota came a bit late this year, eh?'

Fish nodded. 'Crays not crawling much this year.'

'Maybe global warming, you reckon?'

'Maybe.'

Both men scratched their chins thoughtfully.

'Reckon you could move aside, mate?' said Young Dick, after a respectful pause.

Fish sniffed. 'Not till some bastard tells me where the boat is.'

'What d'ya mean?'

'Someone took her. *Queenie II.*'

Young Dick felt a stab of impatience. 'I don't reckon,' he said. 'Probably Lofty's taken her out for some salmon, and maybe you got your wires crossed on when to pick her up?'

'Nothing wrong with my wires, Dick,' said Fish.

Fish Fisher and Old Man Loft went a long way back, Young Dick knew. He also knew that Fish was acting oddly because, a few months back, Lofty's wife had left him for another man. To a white heterosexual man of his father's generation this was an insult of almost indescribable proportions: being a cuckold was akin to losing one's penis. Probably worse. At least a lost penis can be covered up with trousers—a lost wife is obvious. Especially in a small town, where the success rate in hiding private affairs is inversely proportionate to how hard one tries to hide them. In other words, the more someone in Port Kingerton tried to hide their dirty laundry, the more public—and dirty—it became.

So, Young Dick figured now, Fish was scrambling, trying to retain his best mate's decency in a situation that Fish perceived, incorrectly, was somehow making Lofty appear indecent: a miscommunication. An unintended public stand-up. An *I'll meet you there then* that hadn't happened and now everyone could see it, and thought they were a pair of silly old fools.

'Some bastard's stolen *Queenie II*, Dick,' said Fish, glaring down at him. 'And I'm not moving till I find out who.'

Young Dick waited.

Waited some more.

'All right,' he said finally, pulling out his phone. 'How about I call Lofty?'

The sky continued to darken and wind began to gust. The Southern Ocean smashed against the breakwater. The crowd shifted and murmured. Twitch climbed down from the tractor cab to smoke against the back wheel, wind pulling the smoke sideways.

'Fish? I'll call him. We'll get this sorted out.'

Young Dick waited again, but this time he let it grow uncomfortable. The wait became tense enough to make Fish's jaw clench. Anyone will rush to fill a silence if left long enough, so Young Dick let that silence prove like rising bread until Fish finally opened his mouth. The crowd inclined forward.

'He hasn't been the same since … You know how …' Unable to finish, the old man lowered his head in shame.

'Barbara left? Yeah, I know.'

'"Left" is putting it nicely. His wife ran off with a bikie. Leaving the poor bloke without even a clean shirt to his name. Then that bone washed up yesterday, and now his boat's gone …' The old man leaned down, putting his face closer to Young Dick. 'If you ask me, someone here knows something.'

'About what?'

'That bone. And the bikies. And Lofty's boat.'

'That's three separate issues,' Young Dick said, as respectfully as he could, 'that don't have anything to do with each other.'

'I reckon they do.'

'The bone's nothing,' Young Dick said. Although he wasn't quite ready to share everything he knew about the femur, he was ready to say that much at least, because he really was keen to get this minor spectacle cleaned up. 'And what would a bikie want with a fifty-three-foot cray boat?'

'Why you asking me? Maybe Barbara isn't enough.'

There was a collective intake of breath from the crowd who, while pretending not to, had been eagerly following every word.

Young Dick rubbed his head. The obvious response here would have been to ask *Why?*, but he was not about to tug that thread in such a public setting. Rapidly this conversation was turning into something that should have happened behind closed doors, not out on the boat ramp with half the town listening in. Spike was still waiting on the boat, along with three more behind him, and although every deckie knows patience is a virtue, very few of them actually have any. When crays go for over a hundred dollars a kilo, a sense of haste is also a virtue.

Once again Young Dick considered the harbour. Lofty's *Queenie II* was nowhere in sight. It was perfectly reasonable that the two old fishermen had gotten their times mixed up. But Young Dick couldn't shake a feeling of unease. Because fifty-odd years *was* a long time to have been doing this routine task together. If a communication mix-up was possible, it was also possible the men would have it down to a fine-polished ritual, almost without the need for communication at all.

Stepping closer to the tractor, Young Dick said, 'All right, mate. I'll have a word around the place, see if I can find out what happened. Soon as I've got my boat out.' He pointed to the water, where Spike was standing at the bow, gesticulating aggressively, as the sky darkened even further.

Fish eyed him warily.

'We'll get this straightened up. I'm sure it's nothing. Coppers aren't worried about that bone at all. And if someone's nicked *Queenie II*—bikie or not—they'll have me to answer to.' Now Young Dick gestured to Twitch, the big man stacked like a pile of bricks beside the tractor wheel. 'All right?' Young Dick said. 'But I need you to move, cos Spike's about to blow a gasket.'

The two men exchanged a long stare. Seagulls bickered; waves gnashed.

'All right, Dick,' said Fish at length. 'But you find that boat, okay? A man without a wife needs a boat.'

Goddamn, Young Dick thought, as he saw tears in the other man's eyes.

'I'll find it,' he promised.

Thunder rolled in the distance.

OLD DICK

Here's the truth about Port Kingerton: it's not a shithole.

You ask any prick from the city and they'll tell you Port Kingerton, way down there in the south, is a skidmark on the state's underpants. But I'm here to tell you differently. Skidmarks don't provide millions in lobster export to the state's economy, do they? Nor do they provide work and meaning and refuge for folk who don't like the chatter and bustle and bright lights of big towns.

Because that's the thing about the city—it never gets dark. I've been up to the big smoke a few times and I didn't care for it at all. Luce did. Luce loved the cakes in the tea shops and the cardigans, apparently, were much prettier. But I don't have much need for cakes and cardigans myself, and in the city it's always light, even in the middle of the night. The city light smudges out the stars and makes for strange cold shadows.

I like how in Port Kingerton, it gets proper dark. That's when the stars come out. When the night is so black you can't even see your own hand in front of your face. So dark you couldn't see someone *else's* hand in front of your face. You can't hide from that kind of dark.

But in that kind of dark, you can hide anything.

ABIGAIL

The red track pants were thick fleece, with deep pockets and the price tag still dangling. She also found an oversized cable knit jumper, unworn, a pale buttery colour with sleeves that ballooned over her fingertips. Red track pants and a warm baggy jumper. After two days shivering in her floaty dress, Abigail didn't want to admit how much she loved them.

It took most of the afternoon to sort, wash and fold the box of donated clothes. Another thing she wouldn't admit: with each fold, her resentment eased. Carrying the box up the stairs to her room was not an option, so she dragged it into the lounge room, sat on the couch and went through the contents piece by piece.

As she worked, sunlight flooded the room and tiny wrens fluttered at their reflections in the large window. She could hear the pound of the ocean. Her grandfather chatted, telling her about 'that blow-in who bought the second fish-and-chip shop' and she said, 'Didn't Patty Smith own that shop?' and her grandfather replied, 'Yeah, now her kid owns it.' Patty Smith had moved to town before Abigail was born and her kid was born here—she went to school with Abigail's brothers. Abigail felt an unexpected fondness for a town that never changed. Her grandfather moved on, telling her how slack men were these days and she had to concede he wasn't entirely wrong—'a man's got to be able to lift stuff,' she agreed—and her grandfather said, 'Bloody oath. Something heavier than their phone.' The floorboards were warm under her bare feet as she padded back and forth from the dryer with armloads of clean laundry that smelled like fabric softener instead of industrial detergent. At one point her father brought her a cup of tea.

It wasn't unpleasant.

Until it was time to take the clothes to the gift shop.

Abigail stood inside the garage, garbage bag of clothes at her feet, eyeing her father's gleaming Chevy Silverado. Its fob was on the kitchen counter, sitting next to a bowl of pears.

She opened the driver's door. The cab smelled like leather oil, faintly of diesel. The gift shop was a few minutes away, that's all it would take. Drive to the shop, dump the clothes, drive back. Return the Chevy safely to the garage, engine barely even warm.

'Fuck,' she said.

She closed the door. Hauling up the sack of clothes, she hit the button for the roller door with her elbow and headed out the garage on foot.

Halfway down the drive, her arms were wobbling and her lower back screamed. Dropping the bag onto the drive, she put her hands on her hips, blew out a breath.

She left the bag and returned to the house.

Out in the backyard, she stood on the lawn and narrowed her eyes against the glare of the afternoon sun. A couple of horses grazed in the far paddocks, the odd gull wheeled in the sky and chrysanthemum buds waved in the wind but otherwise she couldn't see movement. She studied the stables and the yards, tracked the fences, looked left and right as if she was crossing the street.

Slowly, she made her way across the grass, alert for any sounds of hissing or honking, primed for the flap of a feather.

No goose. She relaxed, muttering obscenities under her breath.

In the stables, she waited for her eyes to adjust to the gloom. There was the familiar close smell of fresh sawdust, hay and horse piss. She peered into each stall as she passed. All were empty apart from the final one on the left. As she approached, she heard the muffled heavy sound of hooves on straw, the clank of an empty feed bucket.

Abigail stopped at the half-door and looked in.

Staring back at her was a handsome bay riding pony. Snowy white blaze down her face, big brown eyes. At the sight of Abigail, the horse lifted her head and nickered, nostrils flapping. Abigail's gaze travelled past the pony's head, along her sleek neck, past muscled shoulders to see enormous, bulging flanks. The pony looked almost wider than she was tall.

'Well, well,' Abigail said. 'You're fat too.'

That's when she saw the second set of feet, behind the pony's rear hooves. Work boots, jeans, a pair of legs unfolding, then out from behind the mare stepped a man. Tall, solidly built, hair cropped short. Rolled shirt-sleeves, black zippered vest.

'Obviously,' she said, 'I don't mean you. You can lift.'

The man didn't say anything.

Holding his gaze, she tilted her head, setting her elbows on the stable door. 'Who are you,' she said, 'and what are you doing to my mother's horse's arse?'

The man patted the pony's rump and Abigail took note of his big hands. Still he said nothing, so she asked, 'You're the vet?'

He gave her a single nod.

'Okay, vet. Why is this mare pregnant in autumn?'

Abigail knew foaling season was typically in spring—the beginning of cray season. As a kid it wasn't unusual for Abigail and her brothers to have been alone at breakfast, getting ready for school, just the three of them rattling around the echoing house while her father was out on the boat, her mother out with a broodmare. But here they were in mid-autumn, cray season over, and this mare was ripe as a peach and ready to drop.

The vet's eyes trailed back to the pony. Finally he spoke. 'She broke out.'

'Broke out?'

'Got in with a stallion.'

'Aren't those guys usually, like, double-fenced?'

'She's determined.'

Abigail looked the mare in the eye. 'Hussy.'

'You're Abigail,' the vet said, and her name in his mouth gave her a low stab of desire.

'Have we met?'

'Nope.'

Smiling, she scooched up closer to the stable door, hiking herself onto her toes and bringing her breasts onto her forearms. 'How can that be? You're not *new* in town, right?'

'Yep.'

She stopped scooching. 'Yes, you're new? Or yes, you're not new?'

The vet looked at her for a beat before he said, 'New.'

'Did you have to break through a fence, too?'

Now he stared at her and did not answer at all.

Granted, it had been some months since Abigail had attempted to flirt with anyone (and suggesting handies to the screws didn't count), but this was going atrociously.

'Have you got a name then, new vet?'

'Nate Ruskin,' he said finally. He took a step towards her and held out his hand, and Abigail shook it and it was the most sex she'd had since last winter.

'Pleasure to meet you,' she said. 'How long have you been in this shithole?'

'Not glad to be back?'

'No.' She took one elbow off the stable door, rolling her body sideways to look somewhere else, because she was starting to feel annoyed at herself and therefore also at him.

'Six months,' he said. She heard him step closer and now she had the impression he was throwing her a lifeline.

Six months? If Patty Smith's kid was born here, owned a local business and was still considered a 'blow-in', what did that make the vet?

'So how'd you make it into town?' she asked.

'How did I gain acceptance, you mean?'

She laughed to hear it said so plainly, from someone who a few minutes earlier had barely disclosed his name. 'Of course that's what I mean.'

The vet bent to retrieve a bag from the stable floor. He came to the door and she stared up at him, all six-foot-plenty of him, before slowly stepping aside to let him out. As he left the stall, the mare came up to the door, pushing her face past Abigail's shoulder in a humid waft of horse.

'Who says I have been accepted?' he said.

'You're here.' She indicated the stables in which they were standing. Her mother's.

The pony nudged the vet's sleeve and he scratched between her eyes, returning to his brooding quiet.

Abigail straightened, but she still didn't reach much higher than the vet's breast pocket. 'Well,' she said. 'It's been nice, but I've got a wheelbarrow to find, and no doubt you've got other horses' arses to attend.'

'Tell your mum I'll be back to check on this one again tomorrow, if she lasts that long.'

Abigail nodded at the mare. 'How much longer?'

'Any day now,' he said. He gave the mare a final pat then stepped away. 'Did you say you're looking for a wheelbarrow?' He indicated the direction of the feed room with his chin. 'You'll find nothing in there. It's a mess.'

'Oh, Nate Ruskin,' she said, smiling again. 'If only you knew what kind of mess I am used to.'

Nate's eyebrows twitched.

Then, pinning her ears, the mare sunk her teeth into Abigail's upper arm.

THEM

Jessica Bram watched the spectacle at the boat ramp through the front window of the gift shop. She saw old Fish Fisher in his tractor staging an unexpected sit-in, she watched that beefsteak, Twitch Witchens, looking perplexed and Spike Flaherty, on the deck of Young Dick Fancy's boat, looking pissed off. Jessica watched Young Dick Fancy stride up and make it all better.

Hanging the *Back in 5 minutes* sign, Jessica slipped out and hurried across the street.

She sidled up to Col Morton. 'What's going on?'

Col glanced at her. There was something unreadable in Col's eyes, Jessica noticed. He lingered on her face a moment and then his head tilted, almost imperceptibly, as if something curious had happened.

'Lofty's boat's missing,' Col said.

'Missing?'

Col nodded. 'Fish thinks stolen.'

'*Stolen?*'

They blinked at each other, mystified, then out came the explanation: Fish wouldn't move the tractor because he claimed someone stole Lofty's *Queenie II* after the bone washed up—maybe someone knew something about where the bone came from and they needed to dispose evidence offshore, Col conjectured—but Young Dick Fancy talked Fish down. There was also something about Lofty's ex-wife and a gang of angry bikies, but Col didn't want to say much more about that.

'Weird,' Col finished.

'I'll say,' said Jessica.

Jessica wasn't looking at Col, she was looking towards the ramp, where Spike was lashing Young Dick's boat into the trailer, but she felt Col's eyes on her again. Very casually, without looking at Col, Jessica said, 'First a bone, then Abigail Fancy comes back, now this.'

Col said nothing, but he didn't look away.

Early yesterday morning, when Mrs Potts's dog had dragged the bone out from under a pile of kelp, Mrs Potts had shooed the dog away, returned home and mentioned it to her son, Damon. Damon promptly headed to the beach, saw the bone himself and called the police. And Damon Potts called the police because he was a massive suck-up. Somehow always relegated to peer in from outside the inner circles of Port Kingerton, Damon had decided, in this case, to plant his flag firmly into the fertile centre. One look at that chewed white bone sitting on the sand and Damon Potts had known: this was his moment. If it turned out to be a cow or a roo as some people would say, so be it. He would take the gamble. Because if it wasn't? If it was human, as his desperate, striving instinct had told him? Well. Damon Potts would forever be the person the cops spoke to first. He might even become a *suspect*. How awesome would that be? How *lucrative*, down at the pub!

This was the story Jessica Bram recounted to Col Morton now, verbatim, and Col said, 'I know, Pottsy's a tosser.'

'Yeah,' said Jessica, 'but look at it now—he was right, wasn't he?'

'Right about what?'

'There's something to be in the middle of. Something is *happening*.'

'Something what?'

Jessica pointed. 'Human remains. The Fancys. Stolen boats.'

Now Jessica looked at Col and saw he was chewing his lip. Brows furrowed, his attention was again focussed on Young Dick Fancy, who was standing on the ramp as Twitch eased the tractor forward and Young Dick's boat inched out of the water.

'You know what this means, don't you?' Jessica said, in a tone that suggested it was obvious, and while it wasn't obvious at all to Col, he didn't want to admit that, so he made a non-committal noise that he hoped covered all potential responses, because he knew Jessica would continue anyway. Which she did.

'The Fancys will be all over it.'

'And?'

'And I've had enough of those arrogant twats owning the place.'

It was a risk, Jessica knew, throwing such a bold line at Col Morton. Especially with Young Dick barely a hundred metres away. Everyone knew Col and Young Dick were tight. But everybody also knew that, even though Jessica's grandfather Ed and Old Dick Fancy's wife Lucy had both died years ago, finally putting to rest that long era of cock fighting, any respect between the Brams and the Fancys remained tentative and grudging.

So Jessica Bram wasn't about to waste this opportunity to express herself.

'You're just nervous cos Abigail's back,' Col said, but he didn't sound certain.

Jessica shook her head. She knew a pivotal moment had arrived. The cracks were already showing.

In Port Kingerton, it was time, once again, to choose who was right.

And who wasn't.

While his boat was coming out of the water, Young Dick had been paying attention. He saw Jessica Bram emerge from the gift shop and pull Col Morton aside, and he marvelled about how time could fold away in an instant. All those years Abigail had been gone now felt like a heartbeat to Young Dick as he saw Col and Jessica draw together.

Whenever teenage Abigail had come home from school stormy-faced and swearing, it was usually Nell who dealt with it. Later, Nell would fill him in: someone called someone a skank; a chunk of hair sliced and tossed in the axolotl tank; a not-insignificant brawl that resulted in eyebrows painted with white-out. All Young Dick could do was wonder about old grudges dying hard. It was as if the animosity of their grandfathers had been passed to the girls in their blood.

Young Dick had always wondered if, in the end, he could have done more. Abigail and Jessica, a Fancy and a Bram, periodically expressing their hatred for each other was hardly new. And after a generation of smashed windows, burnt-out cars and sunken boats, Abigail and Jessica throwing eggs at each other seemed quaint. Young Dick had worked hard to put the animosity of his father's generation to bed, to return the town to a state of pleasantry. But in doing so, he'd let himself become complacent. He'd dismissed the girls' hostility towards one another as petty, childish rivalry.

It was a grave mistake. And Abigail had ended up taking the fall.

Now that his daughter was back, he vowed, he *would* do more.

Inspecting the hull of his boat, cold seawater dripping onto his head, Young Dick fought a sudden weariness. All he'd ever wanted was to fish for half the year and to potter about the house the rest. To look after his family, help Nell with the horses, maybe grow a few carrots.

But no.

His father's disease, and bloody politics, and this town's ability to cling to umbrage with glee meant constant vigilance. It meant Young Dick was always placating, always talking down, always watching.

Unfortunately, Abigail's return had diverted his attention. It was only for a moment, but he had looked away long enough for the pot to begin to simmer. Before he had had a chance to sow the correct story about the bone, Lofty's boat going missing was enough to turn up the heat, for things to threaten to boil over.

And the way Col Morton and Jessica Bram were looking at each other, Young Dick worried he may have left it too late.

OLD DICK

I reckon that young woman's found the ladder. Either that or she's about to hide it again.

I'm sitting in my room, waiting for that cranky Pom to come on the tele, and I hear a knock. I don't want company. Can't a man die in peace? But I say, Come in, because I'm polite.

Nobody comes in, so I turn back to the TV.

The knock comes again.

Fuck off.

Grandpa, says a voice, laughing. *The window.*

There she is, waving at me from outside the glass. Christ Almighty, that black eye. Looks like someone flogged her with the Old Testament. Not that she'd ever snitch, but if I find out who's responsible I'll take their legs off with a butter knife.

When I get to the window I see she's standing there with the wheelbarrow. A person with access to a wheelbarrow probably also has access to other handy tools, like ladders, so that's when I get suspicious.

What are you up to?

Can you open the window?

Who's asking?

I need to walk to town and these boots are giving me blisters.

Blisters are good. Toughen up the soft spots.

She rattles the window. *Just pop the latch.*

Haven't you heard of a door?

I don't want to see Mum.

It seems to me a strange place to go to try and avoid someone—into their own house—but I do as she asks and open the window.

She climbs inside and honestly it hurts me to witness, the way she flails, so I can't imagine how much it hurts her. But she manages, and she's inside and hobbling to the doorway, checking up and down the hall.

While she's gone I inspect the wheelbarrow through the window. I see a garbage bag filled with I don't know what, and frankly, I don't want to know. Plausible deniability and all that. But where there's a wheelbarrow there could very well be a ladder, so I get as close to the wide-open window as I can and peer out.

Ahh, smell that salt. A man could die happy with that salt filling his nostrils, tasting his last breath.

There's a young woman standing beside me.

Thanks, Grandpa, she says. *See you later.*

Who is this woman and why is she going out my window?

I do not know this woman, Luce. I swear.

ABIGAIL

Swapping her boots for her mother's sneakers was a relief only in easing her blisters. Because now she looked proper small-town: track pants, oversized jumper, sneakers.

'You may have my pants,' Abigail said, leaning back against the pull of the wheelbarrow as it gathered speed down the drive, 'but you'll never have my soul.'

The pony's teeth had left crescent-shaped stains on her sleeve and her bicep would have an unholy bruise, but any pain from the pony's bite quickly became old news as she once again navigated her parents' steep-arse driveway. The fifth time in less than twenty-four hours. But *Can't go back* was a mantra in her head, blunting the pain, enabling her to wrestle the barrow down the drive, past the pines and onto the road.

Can't go back.

Down the hill, towards town.

Can't go back.

Wheelbarrow squeaking, salt wind lashing.

Can't fucking go back.

At the bottom of the hill a footpath appeared, flanked by lawn, dotted with the odd picnic table. She even passed a gas barbecue. Ignoring the footpath she continued on the road. There never used to be a footpath; there never used to be lawn or picnic tables or public barbecues. Those things are for tourists and there never used to be tourists. As a kid, Abigail zigzagged her bike up and down the road to town, and there was none of this *kerbing* bullshit either. New houses had sprung up facing the ocean, mansions of plaster and glass, predictably punned: *Sailor's Rest*; *Summer-by-the-Sea*; *Afar to Remember*. Most of them looked empty, and she laughed at the idea that anyone would want to holiday here, but who could deny gentrification?

She wheeled the barrow onto the white centre line, because that never used to be there either, and she'd walked a kilometre and not met a single car.

And then, a little way up the road, someone was walking towards her.

At school Abigail's class had been only a handful of students. Eight on any given day, maybe ten. That same handful of Kingo kids were thrust together whether they liked it or not for most of the years that formed them. So it was easy for Abigail to recognise that the woman coming towards her was Jessica Bram. Her walk gave it away, the chin-up way she carried herself, somewhere between a flounce and a hurry. She'd watched Jessica Bram walk like that across classrooms, across the quadrangle, across the beach when she was six, twelve, sixteen.

Lawyers and cops like to say how hard it is to get a prison sentence in Australia. Cops say the system is too soft on crims; lawyers say, unless you've done something very heinous like murder six backpackers or be poor, a prison sentence is usually a last resort. Funny though, Abigail always thought, how it certainly wasn't that way for the people in prison. The number of women in Australian prisons over the past few decades had quadrupled—did that seem like a difficult place to get into?

Taking a firmer grasp on the wheelbarrow handles, Abigail reminded herself how quickly assault would land her back inside. The barrow wheel had started to squeak, a *wheep* emitting with every second footstep. The distance between her and Jessica closed, and when Abigail was within earshot, Jessica called out, 'Heard you were back in town.'

Abigail kept walking.

Jessica reached her, then turned and fell in step alongside. 'Never a dull day in Kingo, eh?' she said. 'You won't believe what just happened. Old Man Loft—you remember him? Old dude with a gazillion kids? His boat is missing.'

Abigail made a point of travelling her eyes down and up Jessica's body. Leggings, ballet flats, curly hair in a high ponytail. It was the kind of glance she might have given the front page of the *Accountant's Monthly*: incurious, mostly bored.

'Some people are saying it was stolen,' Jessica said.

Abigail walked on. *Wheep.*

'Been a while,' Jessica observed. 'What've you been up to?'

Abigail almost laughed.

'I'm managing the gift shop at the moment. Mum's on her own in the deli till next week.'

Wheep.

'Got three little ones. Married Smithy's cousin—remember that hottie?'

Wheep.

'He's still hot.'

Jessica kept going and Abigail was unable to tune out. Jessica lived with said hot husband and children in the old cottage house a block from the foreshore, at the far end of the esplanade: 'You know the one, it used to have a piano on the porch?' Her husband drove courier vans across the Victorian border and, three days a week, the kids went to the local daycare while she worked in the deli or the gift shop or, if David Wimple was stuck—'which he often is, ha ha'—behind the counter at the hardware store and Abigail did not give a shit.

'So,' Jessica said, after a pause. 'As if Lofty's boat going missing isn't weird enough on its own, apparently he's also been threatened by bikies. I'm thinking blackmail.'

Wheep. Wheep.

'Because—did they tell you? A leg bone washed up yesterday. You know, an actual human leg. Pottsy's ma found it. Remember Damon Potts? He's still a wanker. So probably it's all connected. Anyway, hey—what's Dylan up to these days? Still in Far North Queensland? I heard he was working on a mine.'

Wind picked up. Abigail could feel it gusting against her back, urging her forwards. The church passed on her left, and, ahead on her right, it looked as if half the town was clustered at the boat ramp. Something lurched under her ribs. Now the sky purpled and the wind ominously dropped.

'So, you in town for long?' Jessica asked. 'Just visiting your folks?' Finally she left a gap, waiting for Abigail to speak.

The gift shop was only fifty metres away. Tunnelling her gaze, Abigail marched on.

'Wow, Abs, you could at least say *hello*. You're not still pissed about that stuff with the baby, are you?'

Whee—

Abigail stopped. Leaning into the barrow, she picked up the garbage bag of clothes and thrust it at Jessica. Startled, Jessica stumbled backwards, grabbing reflexively at the sack.

'That's for the gift shop,' Abigail said. 'You're welcome, bitch.'

Then she turned the wheelbarrow and headed home.

Two minutes later the first flash of lightning tore the clouds. Light faded, the air turned chill, the sky opened and rain hammered down. Abigail pushed the wheelbarrow into a wall of water.

Only once before in her life had she been this soaked. When she was eleven, Abigail had been a Girl Guide for two months. Once a week her mother had driven the two-hour return trip to the bigger town, hoping the outdoorish camaraderie might expand her world beyond the few other girls at Port Kingerton Primary. At first there was novelty: making damper; tying knots; singing songs. But it quickly turned out that the girls at Guides were, pretty much, the same as the girls in Kingo only with less fish in their day-to-day lives. Abigail wanted to quit. Nell wrung her hands.

Then a camp came up. A weekend in a pine forest, working towards their Survival Skills badges. For the prospect of one more weekend, Abigail grudgingly mustered her waning enthusiasm and went to camp. The girls giggled and shrieked, the campfire crackled. Night fell and they crawled into their sleeping bags and at some point it began to rain. Their shelters, shabbily constructed triangles of fallen pine, provided no shelter whatsoever. Abigail woke to find herself lying in a freezing puddle in the dark, sleeping bag sloshing around her. Those were the days before mobile phones, when enduring hardship was considered character building. Was it? Maybe. Doubtful, she always thought. Rather than strength or bravery, what she remembered feeling was wet and helpless, and the unquestioned yet maddening sense of being trained to wait for an adult to tell anyone what they were permitted to do. And the adult had climbed into her car to escape the rain, leaving the girls to fend for themselves and, you know, build their characters. Survive. The following week she'd refused to get in the car. That was the end of Girl Guides.

As she trudged uphill in the rain now, barrow filling with water, Abigail wondered at what point an experience stopped being exactly that and became a wound. For the other girls, that camp could be a memory of adventure, a hilarious story. But for her it had been yet another example of how little liberty she felt in life: school; peers; how she spent her time—rarely did any of it seem to be her choice. Everyone always talked about how *free* children were but she'd spent most of her childhood longing for adulthood, where you could eat whenever you were hungry, go to the toilet without asking permission, not be labelled a *slow learner*

if you found trigonometry tedious or *difficult* if your peers
were little punks. But growing up she'd endured that same
mind-dulling routine, those same kids, day after day, year
after year. And when she had a problem with it, it meant
something was wrong with *her*—she was inattentive; she
was distracting; she *just would not cooperate.* Those same few
people told her what and who she was whether it felt true to
her or not.

And now she'd returned to the place she swore she never
would because she had no other option. Abigail was desperate to maintain her freedom, but now she had to consider
whether she was more wounded by her time out of prison
than in it.

At least in prison, she thought, no one lied to you that
you were free.

THEM

Most Wednesday afternoons, the front bar of the Port Kingerton Hotel was occupied only by its two regular drinkers, one at each end of the bar, retired old fishermen bent over their beer foam. But by four pm on this particular Wednesday, the bar was crammed. Outside, rain poured. Thunder shook the pub windows. Inside was rowdy, stuffy with the smell of wet wool and booze.

Col Morton's day had been excellent. As he stood in the clamour of the pub, with his third pint going down sweetly, he had to wonder if, in fact, he had ever had a better day. Cray season was over, his boat was in dry dock and he'd pulled in almost two tonne. Not that anyone would ask, because a fisherman's money business is his own, but if they did, Col would tell them that was the reason for his cheer: a simple celebration of a good season.

That wasn't the reason, though. Not entirely.

It wasn't that exciting things didn't happen in Port Kingerton, it was that this particular excitement Col felt so *inside* of. The events of the past two days—human remains washing up; Abigail Fancy's shock return; boats going missing—he hadn't heard about from someone else, who'd heard it from someone else. He had been *right there* when it happened. He, Col, had been the one to ask Young Dick Fancy if the bone was *a problem*. He had witnessed Young Dick's surprise and delight at the sight of his only daughter finally returned home; he'd seen the four hot sausages Abigail swallowed down whole. Fish staging a weird sit-in at the boat ramp? Col saw it. Lofty's spookily empty mooring? Col saw it. He'd seen it all. He knew it all. He was the one people had been sidling up to, wanting to know, *Is it true?*

An almighty clap of thunder shook the pub. Glasses rattled and everyone cheered.

Col's deckie, Little Jase Turner, was working behind the bar, because that's what Jase did the other half of the year. Hustling through the press of bodies, Col found Jase's brother, Adrian, and together they shoved their way to the bar.

'One day hauling my pots,' Col said to Little Jase over the din, 'the next pulling my pints.'

'Funny,' said Little Jase without any mirth.

'Hey, douchebag,' said Adrian to his brother. 'You fixed that porch light yet?'

Jase replied that he had not, at which Adrian began ranting about his brother's mediocrity and ineptitude and Col tuned out. He didn't want to think about the Turner brothers and their mother's back porch light. No, what Col wanted to think about was that precious moment in time when someone went from not knowing something to knowing it. When Col got to see the surprise and intrigue dawn on their face, shiver down their body, and know that he, Col, had caused it.

Was it better than sex? Col wondered now, downing the last of his pint as thunder quaked the pub's foundations. Quite possibly, it was. And that particular thought startled him, then excited him further, because he decided that he would need to compare the two, and rather urgently.

Late that afternoon, Jessica Bram decided to take up running.

The fact that her running track would be the footpath that traversed the length of the esplanade, past the pub's windows, along the shopfronts, past the beach and boat ramp and up the hill towards the Fancys' house, was a coincidence. Seeing Abigail Fancy only an hour or so earlier looking like a bloated sow in red track pants while knowing that she, Jessica, looked like a nymph in her Running Bare tights was also a coincidence. Jessica Bram just wanted to run. That's what she'd tell anyone who asked. So she pulled on her tights and laced up her sneakers.

The rain and thunder carried on for a while, and Jessica waited in her lounge room, idly stretching her quads, snapping a few selfies and scrolling her feed. Finally the rain stopped and she set off.

As Jessica ran out her front gate and to the end of her street, her legs felt like springs and her ponytail bounced from side to side. The sound of her sneakers hitting the wet pavement was satisfying. Water lying on the concrete from the rain came up in little sprays on the back of her tights but she did not notice.

About sixty seconds in, Jessica's breath began to labour and her knees were hurting. But then she turned the corner and heard noise spilling from the pub—voices, laughter and a bass beat that perfectly matched the cadence of her footfalls—and she discovered a second wind. Imagining she was tucking her shoulder blades into her back pockets, Jessica happened to run past the pub's front windows.

The rain stopped and the storm disappeared out to sea, but behind the bar, Little Jase Turner hardly noticed. Port Kingerton had a population of about three hundred people and he was fairly sure every one of them was currently inside the pub.

His boss, the publican Larry Dinwiddle, had gone down to the cellar to change out an empty keg already and Jase was working the bar alone. The bar that was three deep, a phenomenon Jase had only ever seen on TV.

Halfway through a pint of sparkling ale the tap sputtered. Swearing, Little Jase pulled out his phone and messaged Larry to change the sparkling keg while he was down there, then told the sheep farmer at the bar in front of him he'd have to wait a few minutes. Someone booed. A glass broke.

Little Jase wrung a towel and frowned.

Col Morton stepped outside the pub to light a smoke. The wet footpath gleamed with bits of late-afternoon sky that had broken through the clouds. Col could hear the ocean raging out beyond the breakwater as the storm headed away, blowing itself off towards the continental shelf. Clamping his smoke between his lips, Col thought of how, on top of all the good things that had already happened, he wouldn't have to get up early tomorrow morning—the first time in six months he could sleep in. He was stretching his arms above his head happily when he heard footsteps coming around the corner.

Other than when they were kids darting around the schoolyard, Col had never seen Jessica Bram run before. So at first he thought someone was pursuing her and his automatic reaction was to brace himself to run as well.

'Hey,' he called. 'You right?'

Jessica stopped in front of Col, bright spots of colour on her cheeks.

'What?' she asked, breathing heavily.

'I said,' Col said, 'are you all right? Is someone chasing you?'

'No. Why?'

'You're running. Thought maybe you were in trouble.'

Jessica laughed, and Col could see the strap of her sports bra peeking out from under her shirt. The strap was pink, the same colour as her cheeks. His insides suddenly felt weightless.

'I'm just exercising,' Jessica said, tousling the blonde curls of her ponytail through her fingers. 'You should try it sometime.'

Col widened his stance, planting his feet. He folded his arms across his pecs and squinted into the middle distance through the cigarette smoke wafting in his face. 'You reckon I'm not fit?'

Jessica put her hands on her hips and, brazen as you like, looked Col Morton up and down. Col felt it physically, the way her eyes ran the length of him, as if she was stroking him with a firm, warm hand. Now his insides dropped heavily.

'Pretty crazy day, huh?' he said.

Jessica nodded. 'Crazy,' she agreed. Then she stepped closer, tucked herself up alongside him and he could smell something nice, something vaguely female, like shower gel or clean skin.

'So,' she said, 'what does Young Dick think happened to Lofty's boat?'

Col hesitated. He answered carefully, because Jessica was standing very close to him and his head was a bit fuzzy. 'That's not for me to say.'

'People reckon it's related to the bone.'

'How so?'

'Think about it. Lofty's wife ran off with a bikie.'

'And?'

Jessica turned to Col, and he could see her eyes alight with that very same intrigue he had been fantasising about all afternoon. 'I reckon Lofty's scared,' she said. 'I think *he* thinks the leg bone was a message from the bikies and now he's shitting his pants. So he's done a runner.'

Col swallowed. 'What message?' he managed to say.

She shrugged. 'How should I know what Lofty thinks? "Don't come looking for your wife?" "Don't try and get revenge"?'

'Okay,' Col said, slowly, 'let's say you're right. Let's say Lofty thinks the bone is a threat and he's skipped town.

Why, then, wouldn't he tell Fish not to collect *Queenie II* for dry dock?'

Again she shrugged. 'That I don't know. Maybe Fish is play-acting to keep the peace.'

'With the bikies?'

'Yeah. Or Lofty.'

Col was getting confused. He wanted to follow Jessica's logic though, because, as he saw the intrigue burning in her eyes, he suddenly found himself unable to deny that she might be making some salient points. But he didn't have a chance to mull it further, because Jessica changed tack.

'*I* don't think that's what the bone is, though,' she said. '*I* think it's got something to do with Abigail coming back.'

'Lofty's boat went missing because Abigail came back?'

'No.' She laughed. 'Keep up.'

'I'm trying,' he said honestly.

'I think Abigail is back *because the bone washed up.*'

Col paused. He reminded himself he was talking to Jessica Bram. Granddaughter of Ed Bram, nemesis of Old Dick Fancy ever since Lucy had left Ed for him. He paused some more. He wanted to believe Jessica was simply playing out that old rivalry—after all, it wasn't as if that rivalry had died with Ed. It wasn't as if Abigail and Jessica had not had their own stoushes. It wasn't as if Col Morton hadn't stood on the sidelines watching as the insults, eggs and rocks were thrown.

'Hang on,' Col said. 'You think the bone brought Abigail here?'

'Yes.'

'Why?'

She shrugged a third time. 'Damage control? Something's been uncovered that shouldn't have been?'

'But Young Dick says the bone isn't a problem—'

Jessica took a step back, annoyed. 'Honestly, Col, think for yourself.'

'He knows what he's talking about,' Col said, but his voice lacked the conviction of a few moments ago.

'And you don't? Come on.' She stepped closer again, nudged him with her elbow. 'You're a skipper. You're smart, Col. A hundred times smarter.'

'Probably not a hundred ...' Col trailed off, because Jessica's upper arm was now touching his. Heat from her hip and thigh radiated onto his own.

When unexpected things happen, it can be mind-altering. Interruptions to mundane routines can provide an opening to possibilities that had previously been considered impossible. One's beloved boat might spring a leak, for instance, which opens a skipper to the idea of buying a new boat, something he may have sworn he would never do. Or a woman a man had not seen since she was a girl and he a boy, a woman so long unseen that she'd become mythical, might show up tender-bare-legged and swallow four sausages right in front of that man's face, and then that man might start seeing all the women around him anew. Suddenly he might become acutely aware of the very *bodily* nature of these women, their physicality, the way all their *parts* came together to make them as a whole much greater, much more tangible, than anything he had noticed before.

Had he ever noticed Jessica Bram's legs before? Col wondered now. Had he ever noticed that her cheeks were plump and ruddy and that she actually had, you know, ankles? No, he had not.

'He's lying, isn't he?' Jessica said quietly, her breath hot on Col's throat. 'Young Dick. That bone isn't *nothing*. He's trying to bury something. He's covering his arse. Yeah?'

'Covering what?' Col asked weakly.

'Who knows?' she said, breathily. 'The Fancys are as dirty as you can get.' Another nudge closer and more parts of Jessica were dangerously close to touching more parts of Col.

Okay. Col was a straight man, he was divorced, he had eyes. Yes, he had looked at Jessica Bram's breasts. Possibly a lot. But looking at Jessica Bram's breasts—or any woman's, for that matter—was like looking at the sky: it was just … there. You noticed it because you couldn't not notice it and if you tried not to notice it you'd look like an idiot. He was polite about it though, surreptitious. He wasn't a sleaze. But in the same way the sky was always there, so had Jessica Bram always been there, and Col Morton had never really *seen* her before.

Now, he did see her.

He saw her very, very much.

And he thought of how impossible things had been happening and he thought that, now, anything was possible.

OLD DICK

I grew up with two brothers. Both younger than me.

I wasn't the first-born son. I did have one older brother but he died when I was only a little tacker. I don't remember him at all, and nobody talked about him except for the fact that he died, which isn't much of a legacy to leave, is it? So that's really all I could tell you about him. He's buried up at the cemetery, but I only know that because I found the grave when I was a teenager getting up to mischief.

Like I said, that's all I can tell you.

That's why it was me who ended up with Dad's cray licence, not my older brother, because I happened to be on the right side of the dirt. Alive. A strong, willing, healthy young man—that was me. When Dad decided he'd had enough of pulling pots, I took over. I sold Dad's old Huon pine boat and got myself a sleek forty-eight footer which cut through the chop like it was the cream on Ma's trifle. I remember how dark it was the first morning I took her out but the sea was settled, smooth as a blanket, like she was telling me it was all right with her that I was in charge now. A true lady, the sea was, my first day as captain. I never forgot it and I made sure I was grateful and said *please* and *thank you* to her every day after that. Every single day. Even when she was so rough she stripped the lining of your guts and you came off the boat quivering like a soldier in the trenches. And I made sure my deckies knew to say it too, and if they didn't, it was their turn to scrub out the live tanks with a toothbrush.

Luce says I should think about my younger brothers sometimes and how maybe they would've liked Dad's licence. But what would that do? I can't help the order we came out in, that was up to Ma. I can't help that there's only so many licences and catch quota handed out, that's up to the politicians. Bastards. Fisheries say they're trying to maintain cray stocks for future generations, but we all know it's not about that—it's about control and lining their own pockets. How many politicians give the slightest rat's arse about looking after nature, taking care of the sea and land? None, that's how many. Blackfellas have been telling everyone that for centuries but do we listen? Ha! If the average white bloke isn't listening you can bet politicians are as deaf to it as my left nut.

Sorry, Luce.

Anyway. I'm not saying it doesn't cause tension, the way licences and quotas are guarded as fiercely as the crown jewels. It does. It's hard work but there's money in crays. If he wants, a man can work less than half a year and spend the rest of it with his feet up, polishing his Mercedes. Not that you'd see many fishermen caught dead in a Mercedes, but you get my point. Pretty much the only way to get a rock lobster licence is to get it from someone who dies. So yeah, maybe my brothers would have liked it. They've fished with me, but ultimately it's not in their name. Their bank account. Their empire. They're the spares to the heir, a shadow to live in their whole lives.

So what do my brothers do, being Fancy of name but not of empire? Well, one runs the pub, which means no one wipes their backside in Port Kingerton that he doesn't know about. The other drives trucks, which is also fair money if you know the right people, and handy too, if stuff needs to be moved from one place to another.

I see you're thinking about your brothers, says the woman.

If you say so.

And the pub. Would you like to go and say hello to the Dinwiddles?

I don't know why she's talking to me about going to the pub when there's sixty-eight pots to pull.

Let's go into the lounge room, she says, and now I'm in the lounge room. She's blocking the window again. I'd like to check and make sure no bastard's stolen my mooring but I'll have to wait till she's out of the way.

Looks like rough weather coming, she says.

Winchman better hold on tight, I say.

I've seen drowned men. I wish I hadn't but unfortunately when you work with the sea, it's an occupational hazard.

So when the young woman comes in looking like a drowned man I'm confused, because she's not dead, she's very much alive, and I know she's alive because she's swearing like holy hell. That's another thing I'm familiar with: swearing. But she's carrying on in the kind of colourful language I reckon would make even a sailor blush.

Hair plastered to her skull, face white as a corpse, hands blue—but she's stomping and raving. What is she on about, effing this and effing that? What is a jessicabram? Is that like a Netflix?

Oh, good, here comes the young fella. This should be interesting.

ABIGAIL

The rain ceased immediately after Abigail made it up the driveway for the sixth time in twenty-four hours. Should the goose have appeared she would have snapped its neck. Luckily for them both it was nowhere to be seen.

Leaving the wheelbarrow in the garage, she wrung water from her clothes, making puddles on the garage floor, dripping onto her father's gleaming Chevy. Just as she stepped inside the house, the rain stopped. Quiet hummed. Not a drop on the roof. Birds chirped.

'You've got to be kidding,' she said.

Her arms felt like jelly, her legs trembled and she couldn't feel her fingers. Her bicep throbbed from the horse's bite, her thigh itched from the insect sting. She still had no money, no phone and once again she had no clothes. Her credit was shot, she owed thousands in arrears. She had come here because she needed to get away, to start over, to

be a self-governing private person, but she may as well have
mounted a camera on her head, livestreaming her every
move, for all the privacy she actually felt. Everyone knew
who she was—everyone had decided, long ago, who she
was—and there was no changing that.

Six months of repressed rage bubbled up, quick as the
snap of her fingers.

But it wasn't six months, it was two years since her first
stint inside. It was twenty-three years since she left this town.
It was six thousand years of motherfucking patriarchy.

She stood dripping on the chic woven beachside mat
and heard the rain stop as if timed on purpose, like the
way women inside are locked in at three pm but their kids
don't get out of school until three thirty so there's no way
for mothers to hear their children's voices on the phone—
even if they did manage, somehow, to get to the front of
a line two hundred women long. She heard the rain stop
as if on purpose and felt in her gut the sensation of going
from a person to a number, a no one, a scrap of property of
authorities who own you wholly yet abhor you, too. They
blame you as if you have incredible power for harm yet
they tell you, legally and with the backing of society, that
you are worthless and powerless. They hate you yet they
want you.

Her father appeared. He held up his hands, saying,
'Hey, hey.'

'No,' she said.

'Abs, it's okay.'

'No.' She backed into the side table. The modem toppled
and fell.

'All right.' He lowered his hands.

Heavy breaths into a sudden silence. Water shivered from her hair.

'I can't go back.'

'I know.'

'I have to start over.'

'I know that, too.'

'But this goddamn town.'

Her father shifted on his feet. 'After yesterday, I think everyone's a bit ... stirred up.' He eyed her carefully. 'I'm sure it's temporary.'

'No,' she repeated. 'It's always like this.'

'All right, I'm not arguing.'

Footsteps sounded in the hall and she looked up to see her mother holding a tumbler with a finger of amber liquid. Wordlessly, Nell handed her the glass. Abigail threw it back with a grimace. She hadn't liked her mother's brandy when she was sixteen and she didn't like it now although she had drunk it both times.

'Dry clothes,' her mother said. 'Then let's sit down.'

'Look, Mum—'

'We'll sit,' Nell repeated, catching first Abigail then Young Dick in a firm gaze.

'She can't sit down when she's drowning standing up.'

Abigail's grandfather wheeled towards her, a clean towel folded on his lap.

'Here, chicken,' he said, handing her the towel. 'Dry yourself off, then you can think straight. No one can think straight after a dunking.'

She took the towel, plush and smelling of sunlight.

'I can't say I've had too many mishaps myself,' her grandfather went on, 'but you've gotta learn to hold on, girl, if you can't keep yourself upright when the sea bucks. But don't beat yourself up. The lesson is: never lose respect for the sea. She always wins.'

'You're right, Grandpa.'

'No one is better than the ocean. No man, no woman— no one. People are arrogant. They think they can outsmart nature. I don't know why. When did we get so dumb as to think we're smarter than everything else? I don't know when that happened, but I certainly don't agree.'

'I don't know, Dad,' said her father.

'And I don't agree, either,' Abigail said.

'So you'll hold on next time, girl?'

'All right,' she said. 'I'll hold on.'

'We'll sit,' said Nell.

So there Abigail found herself a short while later, seated at the dining table. Her parents on one side, her on the other, her grandfather at the head of the table. Abigail had pushed back her chair, propped one foot on the chair beside her, knee up, wrist draped over her knee. It was a pose she would not have been permitted at sixteen, but at thirty-nine she would like to see them try. On the table was a bottle of brandy and three glasses.

The western wall of the dining room was floor-to-ceiling glass overlooking the scrubby rise up to the lighthouse. The sun was sinking, beaming yellow through the glass, and her mother had rolled a see-through screen down, throwing a hazy light through the room.

With a grunt, Abigail leaned forward and splashed brandy into a glass. Her mother chewed the inside of her cheek and glared at her but said nothing as she swallowed it down.

Other than the addition of the screen over the windows that had happened at some point in the intervening decades, very little had changed about this scene from Abigail's childhood. The dining table, the scrub outside, the lighthouse a point in the middle distance: the lines and orientation of things was the same. The sounds of the horses calling from the paddocks, the unceasing background noise of the ocean pushing against the shore. She experienced a feeling of succour she didn't recognise right away and told herself it was just the brandy.

Her mother said, 'What are your plans?'

Abigail laughed.

'What about your friends?'

'Come on. You know I don't have friends.'

It wasn't true, but neither was it untrue. Because what kind of a friend would it make her? If she asked to share their bathroom, to field their kids' questions, to be privy to the inside of their fridge and hear their noises at night and see their underwear, until she could find a half decent–paying job with an employer who did not mind that she had two prison stints to her name? She was just plain lucky the restaurant had turned a blind eye to her first stint inside. To most employers one sentence was off-putting enough. But two? She'd be lucky to get a job scrubbing toilets.

Not to mention, she was open game. The threat of going back hung over her head, waiting for someone to abuse if she didn't do or say or act how they want. That vulnerability? She hated it. It filled her with rage. But it was precisely that rage that had gotten her into this mess more than once. It was precisely that knee-jerk reflex to protect herself, to make herself feel better—to *run*—that she had to overcome.

'No mates?' said her grandfather. 'Their loss. Pass the brandy, will you? A man's arms aren't six foot long.' Nell poured out a small measure and slid it down the table. He held up the glass and squinted. 'Bloody hell, tide's out.'

'You shouldn't be drinking at all,' Nell said to Old Dick, then turned to Abigail and added, 'And neither should you.'

'Fuck off.'

It was fleeting and she saw Nell tried to stifle it, but Abigail caught it: her mother suppressed a smile.

'All right, we've gotten unproductive,' said her father. 'So you don't have plans and you don't have friends.'

Abigail saluted with her empty glass. 'You got it.'

'That's easy then. You'll stay here. Get work here. Stay the hell away from the city and get back on your feet.'

'I went to the city to get the hell away from here.'

'What about her husband?' said her grandfather. 'Is he a useless prick?'

'I'm not married, Grandpa. But if I was, he probably would be.'

'There's your problem. Too many pricks.'

'Amen to that.'

'What work?' her mother said to her father. 'What work is she going to get here? I thought you didn't want her in town.'

'Now the truth's coming out,' said Abigail.

'She's been here one day and you've already sent her into town on errands,' her father said. 'There's plenty she can do around here. The veggie garden needs a makeover. And that feed room could do with a clean-out—'

'I'd rather not,' Abigail said, thinking of how many times she'd already hauled herself up and down that driveway.

'How much do you actually need to clear up your debts?' her father said. Now both her parents looked at her directly and calmly. Because here was a place in which the Fancys shined: cleaning up debt.

She stared at them, saying nothing.

Her grandfather said, 'You need someone knocked off?'

'I'm good. Thanks anyway, Grandpa.'

'Because back in my day, if we had a problem—'

'No problem,' her father said quickly. 'Everything is okay.'

'It's sorted?'

'It's sorted.'

'If you say so.' Her grandfather sounded dubious but went quiet and she saw, for a moment, her father wrestling internally with something she had never seen before. He looked flustered. It was as fleeting as her mother's suppressed smile a few moments ago, but it was there. She watched her mother put a hand on her father's forearm and squeeze it, and she thought if there was ever a reason to get married it was that—the way a lifetime of stories could be shared in a single tender arm squeeze. She looked away.

'Okay,' Nell began. 'You're not on parole.'

'Correct.'

'So you don't have to report to anyone. And you can't drive.'

'Of course I can drive.' Abigail mimed holding a steering wheel.

'You probably shouldn't even joke about it.'

'Who's joking? That's how I drive. How do you drive?'

'Fine,' her mother said. 'You're not *allowed* to drive.'

'Until 2037.'

Her father set down his glass with a clunk. 'They took your licence for fifteen years? For driving unlicensed?'

'Disqualified,' she corrected him. 'Gotta keep criminals off the streets, Dad. Rapist politicians and paedo priests go free but it's we who don't pay our annual stipend to state revenue you *really* need to watch out for.'

'This is the problem with leaving justice to coppers,' said her grandfather. 'The state's a wet blanket. Justice is easy served, you just have to know when it's a new moon and the night will be dark enough.'

Abigail nodded. 'And where there's no CCTV.'

Her father poured himself more brandy.

'It wasn't only driving disqualified,' said her mother. 'That was just one of the charges.'

'That was the charge they got to stick,' Abigail said. 'You throw enough shit at the wall, something will stick. I've forgotten how many charges they actually gave me in the beginning.'

'Six,' her mother said, and began to count on her fingers. 'Driving while disqualified. Taking a conveyance without consent. Misuse of a motor vehicle—'

'*Driving with attitude*,' Abigail said.

'—driving in a manner dangerous to the public—'

'Again, the attitude thing.'

'Property damage. Intending to damage property.' Nell folded her hands on the table. 'And if you hadn't threatened to rearrange his teeth, you might have gotten bail and had time to get your affairs in order before you went inside.'

'It was an offer,' Abigail said. 'That guy needs an orthodontist.'

Her father poured again; brandy sloshed to the brim.

'That makes no sense,' her grandfather said crossly. 'How can you damage property *and* intend to damage it? What is this, a time warp?'

'Shit at a wall, Grandpa,' Abigail said. 'Shit at a wall.'

THEM

Schnitzels, Little Jase Turner decided. A load of chicken schnitzels could be piled onto trays and sent along the bar. People could eat them with their hands—no one would mind. Little Jase certainly wouldn't.

The crowd was getting peaky and Little Jase recognised that filling everyone's stomachs would dull the alcohol and quell the excitement sparking through the air. So when a dairy farmer from out of town decided to order a bourbon and three others elatedly concurred it was a marvellous idea to move from beer to spirits, Little Jase made a decision.

But Cook wouldn't be in for another hour and Jase was feeling as spiky as the crowd. His head ached. Every few seconds someone yelled, making the blood vessels in his ears constrict. It didn't help that Limp Bizkit's *Greatest Hitz* was playing on the jukebox.

Surely schnitzels couldn't be too difficult to cook, Jase thought, shooting post-mix cola onto four glasses of bourbon. Just drop them in the fryer, right? He reckoned he could probably dump some chips in too.

'Oi, give us four more, while you're there,' someone shouted.

'You can wait,' Jase shouted back.

'Oh, come on!'

Jase sidled up to Larry, who was busy with the Guinness tap.

'I'm gonna make some food,' Jase yelled into the publican's ear.

His boss either didn't hear him, or didn't care, because the publican simply shrugged and went on pouring.

So Little Jase Turner left the bar and headed into the kitchen.

It was official: Col Morton's day could not get better. Not that any kind of rational thought, such as the ability to make an objective assessment of one's day, was currently running through Col's mind. No, what was presently occupying Col's mind was how Jessica Bram's arm was sort of cutting off the circulation to his head and he didn't even care. She basically had him in a headlock. It was the first time he'd had sex with a woman who had semi-strangled him during the process. Not that he was about to complain, because to be honest he wasn't entirely sure he didn't enjoy it immensely.

Col tipped to the left and almost overbalanced. He put one arm out to steady himself and knocked something, and it hit the floor with a metallic *bong*.

'Ssh,' Jess hissed, or at least Col thought she hissed—he couldn't really hear anything, his ears were filled with a rushing sound.

The room was dark, only a little fading daylight came through a narrow window high on one wall. A dull bluish beam fell next to Col's hand, reflecting off the steel bench-top. Briefly Col had wondered, when Jessica dropped her pants and hoicked herself up, if her arse would be cold on the steel. But then she'd opened her legs and put him in a headlock, so his concern for the temperature of Jessica's arse had been very brief indeed.

Col had gotten married in his early thirties, much like any other bloke his age at the time who had been living with a woman for a while. It hadn't worked out—she wanted kids, Col didn't; she wanted to move away, somewhere bigger and more anonymous, Col didn't—and Col had been largely single ever since. Sure, there was Tinder, but the pool of suitable women in Port Kingerton being as limited as it was, it usually meant a long drive. And most of the time Col couldn't be bothered with a long drive, he really couldn't. Not after a three am start and ten hours on a cray boat. And not when it was off season and he'd rather be tinkering with the old F Truck or helping out his farmer mates with the calving or lambing.

The point is, when Jessica started issuing what sounded like instructions in Col's ear, he had to focus hard to hear them, because he had come to the understanding that although the past two days had been exciting, it was definitely *not* better than sex. How could he have even entertained the notion that anything could be better than this? He had just needed a reminder, that was all. And that's what

Jessica Bram had been kind enough to do, by shoving him through the doorway around the side of the pub, dropping her pants and hoisting herself onto the bench: remind him what sex was like.

'Are you listening?' Jessica said.

'What?'

'I said pull out.'

'Oh. Now?'

'Well, before you're done.'

'Righto.'

Jessica let go of Col's neck. She put her hands behind herself on the bench and her eyes trailed to the ceiling. Her tights were hanging from her left ankle, swinging from side to side. 'I still can't believe Abigail Fancy came back yesterday, same day as the bone,' she said.

Col stopped. He drew back and looked at Jessica. 'What?' he said.

'Keep going,' she said impatiently.

'Okay,' said Col, and he did.

'It's just … *too* coincidental. Don't you think?'

'Um,' said Col.

'I mean—'

'Uh—'

'That Abigail—'

'Uh-huh—'

'Abigail Fancy—'

'Oh god—'

'Abigail Fancy should come—'

'Oh god, ohmygod—'

Col flailed, knocking something else to the floor with a crash, grabbing at the nearest cloth he could find.

'Hey,' Jessica said. 'That's my tights.'

All the kitchen lights came on.

When Little Jase Turner entered the kitchen and hit the lights, he was thinking about chicken schnitzels and not expecting to see Col Morton's white buttocks and woolly thighs thrusting merrily against the stainless steel countertop where only yesterday Jase had helped Cook slice a bucket of tomatoes for the Greek salad. Nor was he expecting to see Jessica Bram's face over Col's shoulder, looking annoyed, complaining about jizz on her tights while a metal salad bowl spun to a stop on the floor.

'What the actual?' said Jase.

'Hey,' said Col, turning only his head to face Little Jase, 'can you fuck off?'

A command from Col—his boss, his skipper—and Little Jase responded without thinking. Mumbling under his breath, he turned his back on the partially clad pair and shuffled towards the fridge. He would pretend the kitchen was empty; he would pretend they weren't there. When necessary, a deckie is good at turning his back and getting on with his task while pretending he can't see things.

'Honestly,' said Jessica, sliding off the bench and wriggling her tights back up. 'There's a tea towel right there.'

'I couldn't see it,' said Col. 'It was dark.'

'Yet you could see my tights, like, behind you?'

Col shrugged and grinned, pulling up his jeans.

'Jesus, Col, that's a lot of jizz. My ankle is soaked.'

'I aim to please.'

'It's not a compliment. Don't you wank at all?'

Over by the fridge, Little Jase glowered and pulled his shoulders up to his ears. The crowd in the bar wasn't getting any quieter, his head hurt and tomorrow he was supposed to help Jessica Bram's husband replace the roofing iron on his carport and now he would have to do it with the image of Jessica's naked thighs imprinted in his mind.

After a minute, although it felt to Little Jase like a very long time, the side door to the kitchen opened and closed. Silence fell behind him. Exhaling in relief, Little Jase dropped his shoulders and turned around.

To see Col standing right behind him.

'Are you kidding?' said Jase.

'Nope,' said Col, a supreme smugness writ all over his face. He was a man on the other side of a border, a man who had crossed a boundary, and now there was a gap between the two of them filled with trumpeting angels and also razor wire. It seemed to Little Jase as if Col stood taller, admiring the view.

'I have to work with her husband tomorrow,' said Jase. 'What am I supposed to say?'

Col hitched his shoulders, nonchalant. 'What do I care?'

'Young Dick won't like it.'

Now Col's bravado slipped. Only a fraction, but they both noticed it. Col felt it like a pebble dropping in his belly and Little Jase saw it in the way Col abruptly shrank an inch. But Col rallied, because his balls were empty and he could think straight.

'He'll be all right,' Col asserted. 'Besides, he doesn't have to know.'

Little Jase couldn't help the laugh that came out. It echoed around the kitchen. 'Of course he'll know. This will be all over town by sunset.' Little Jase pointed to the narrow strip of window. 'And the sun's pretty much already set.'

'She's harmless,' Col said. 'It was just a bit of fun. And you don't have to worry about her husband—she told me that she and him have an "understanding",' Col made air quotes with his fingers, 'a kind of "don't ask, don't tell" situation. The dude drives a courier van across the border. I bet he's got a few extras on the side, over there.'

'Whatever, man,' said Jase, holding up his hands. 'Don't care, don't wanna know. But I don't think Jess Bram's harmless. And I reckon Young Dick's gonna have words.'

Col's high started to deflate. He suspected his deckie was right.

OLD DICK

Something fishy is going on. I can't put my finger on it yet, but I will.

People have a certain way about them when they're hiding something. Shifty faces, crabbed body language—you can see the secrets in people if you know how to properly look. These days though, no one looks properly at anyone else. Too busy making up their own version of events. Too busy staring at their phones to notice if their own bum crack was smoking, let alone if anyone was acting shifty.

Anyway, what I'm saying is, they're acting queer. The whole lot of them: the young fella, the woman and that new one, the girl with the black eye. She makes a good cup of tea, though, that new one—strong and hot and just enough milk to scare it. No one makes tea like that anymore; seems to me people drink everything except tea, what with their pumpkin and dandelion lattes. Since when did dandelion become a drink? In my day dandelion was a weed you had to hit with a good squirt of Round-Up. Although they say now that weed killer gives you cancer and I can't say I'm surprised. Nasty shit if you got it on your hands, up your nose or in your eyes. I know a few people that happened to but I'm not saying anything more about that.

Dad, we don't need to talk about that right now.

I'm just saying, dandelion isn't a drink.

It's good for you, Grandpa. Cleans your liver.

Clean your own damn liver. Pass the brandy.

We're all sitting at the table and we've been sitting a while. I know it's been a while because earlier the sun was coming through the window and hitting me right in the eyes, so the woman closed the blinds, but now the sun is gone and it's dark out. I can see the beam flicking from the lighthouse. Calling the boats home.

They've been talking about a lot of things, those three. I must admit some of what they're talking about is going over my head but I'm getting the gist. The girl with the black eye stole a car and drove it like the clappers and the woman and the young fella don't want her to do that again, ever. I'm with them—stealing's a low blow. Unless, of course, the bloke whose stuff you nicked deserved it, and I'm not saying people *don't* deserve to have their stuff nicked from time to time, especially if they're a lousy prick, but a man's got to have some integrity and respect other people's property.

Or woman. Sorry, Luce.

Believe me, Grandpa, he is a lousy prick.

Oh, well, in that case—no harm, no foul, I say.

Cops say otherwise.

Clearly you're getting the wrong copper. You haven't greased the right palms. Boy, have I taught you nothing? What are you doing, not greasing the right palms? This isn't how I raised you. A man's in charge of his environment but you're letting your environment be in charge of you. The only thing you can't be in charge of is the sea. No man controls you—what are you thinking? If you've lost control of the men around you you've lost it completely. Do you need your head read or what?

And what fresh hell is in this cup? Hot cow shit? Pass the brandy.

Oh, Grandpa. I've missed you.

I've seen a woman laugh before—I'm a good bloke, I know how to keep the gentler sex happy—but I've never seen a woman laugh so hard she started crying.

Jesus. I think she's gonna lay an egg.

ABIGAIL

That night, Abigail couldn't sleep. She tried to get comfortable and failed. She tried not to think of her and failed—she was all Abigail could think about. Hours crawled, tipping into despair, pushing sleep even further away. Against the grief and guilt she tried to find her shield of anger but the tears she'd cried at the table earlier seemed to have eroded the anger somehow, even though she convinced herself they were only tears of laughter.

In her late twenties, around the time she had been living in the wine region south of the city, bartending at a pub, she'd dated a guy who, whenever he could not sleep, swore by making himself yawn. He claimed it would trick his brain into believing it was sleepy. She would wake to the sounds of jaw cracking, sighing, stifled howling as he attempted to make himself yawn and neither of them would be asleep. It wasn't the thing that had sent them on their separate ways but it certainly contributed.

Lying awake, she thought about him—he was in web development, or coding, or something like that—and then she thought about some of the others, the sweeter ones like him, and they began to blob together, like adding dough to more dough, until she felt the weight of them, all those come and gone, perfectly nice men, and she started to feel panicked.

Twenty-three years ago, arriving in Adelaide after seven hours in Zac Murphy's Corolla, she'd been blitzed with adrenaline and possibility. The city all slanted-light and glinting, the shunt of peak-hour traffic pulling her in. She'd felt brazen with anonymity—she could go anywhere, do anything, and not a single soul knew who she was. Now, in her childhood bedroom in the dark, she felt as if she were experiencing the reverse of that day. Exhausted and wrung out, her sense of self in tatters, on public display. She had tried it all, tried everything for escape, and none of it had worked.

Long after midnight, sleep came in short plunges from which she bolted out, disoriented and reeling. The quiet and the dark filled her head with impossible noise. It was as if she could sense the loom of something thunderous, a tidal wave of emotion drawing up behind her.

At some point before dawn she muttered, 'Hell, no,' and heaved herself out of bed.

In the kitchen she made coffee, but the unbearable quiet continued to scream. How quickly being the only body in a room had become unnerving, in spite of how, inside, the one thing they all longed for was solitude.

Clinging to her coffee cup, Abigail looked out the kitchen window and saw the stable lights on. Relief flooded through her.

The backyard was chilly in the pre-dawn dark. Listening to the distant roar of the sea, she didn't notice the goose until it was on her. A white streak barrelled out of the dark, hitting her mid-thigh.

Scalding coffee slopped onto her fingers. Aware that it was barely gone five am she stifled her curses, throwing her now empty cup at the goose but missing by a lot. She tried to defend herself, grabbing at a wing, a beak, a slimy webbed foot, until her flight instincts kicked in and she ran the rest of the way to the stables, goose honking at her ankles.

Panting, she doubled over in the stable breezeway. After her soaking in the rain yesterday she had washed the red track pants and now they were splattered with rapidly cooling coffee.

'Son of a bitch,' she said.

'He only attacks strangers.'

She straightened up to see the silhouette of Nate Ruskin standing in the breezeway. 'Nell didn't believe me,' he said, coming into the light. 'I had to go out there, offer myself like a sacrifice, so she could see it for herself.'

'Can't you just—' She made two fists and jerked them apart.

The vet narrowed his eyes, as if considering it. 'No. I've got to keep your mum on my side.'

'I'll vouch for you,' she said. 'I approve of a man who can get himself up early.'

He stepped closer, hands in his pockets. 'Comes with the job. I've got two hundred heifers to AI today. Had to check Bo early.'

'Bo?'

'The mare.'

'Ah,' she said. 'The fat hussy. So anyway, this goose? You dispatch it, I'll sweet talk Nell. Have you ever eaten roasted goose?'

A faint smile played at the corner of his lips. 'I don't reckon you've got that much authority with your mum, from what I've heard.'

'Has she been talking to you?' Abigail threw her hands in the air. 'She's ignoring me but, sure, talk to the vet.'

They walked towards the mare's stall, footsteps echoing out of time on the pavers. The pony stuck her head over the stable door and whinnied. Abigail stood back, out of reach of her teeth.

Nate let himself into the stall, running his hands over the mare's neck. 'Hey, lady,' he said quietly. 'How you doing today?' The pony pressed her nose to the vet's jacket, nudging insistently until he pulled a carrot from his pocket.

'Flirt,' Abigail said. 'Do you bribe the cows before you feel them up, too?'

'If I could fit two hundred carrots in my pocket, I would.' He disappeared behind the pony.

'You were only here yesterday,' she said, then hesitated. 'Is something wrong?'

'No,' he replied from behind the horse. 'Just dropping off a foaling alarm for your mum. Long day. Not sure when I'll be back.'

'Right. Two hundred heifers.'

He came towards her again, bringing with him the scent of soap and coffee, although she considered that maybe the latter was coming from her pants. Up close she could make out a dimple in his chin.

The last time a man had laid his hands on her in desire had been close enough to a year ago, and she now felt this keenly, this long almost-year, as her eyes settled on that dimple. A smooth cleft in his chin; she imagined she could see the pores there, the hair follicles shaved at the skin. She imagined him only a short while earlier, leaning into the mirror with the razor, one hand gently pulling the skin taut, foam sliding down his jaw. She wondered if he would be shirtless when he shaved. He struck her as the type to keep his shirt clean before it got very dirty.

'Damn,' Nate said.

She blinked out of her daydream to see him frowning at his phone.

'My second farmhand just cancelled on me. Shit. The first one pulled out last night and I thought I could manage with one, but with both of them out …' He swore again.

'How many other AI techs will be there?'

His eyes flicked to her.

'You can do, what—thirty? Fifty?—yourself in a day. Not two hundred.'

Nate lowered his phone. 'There's four of us.'

'Can't one of them spare you a hand?'

'Maybe.' He tapped his phone against his thigh, looking at the mare. 'I don't want to cancel. It's a big dairy. Lucrative. But maybe I should. Otherwise I'm not sure when I'll be able to get back here again.'

'Because it's lucrative here, too?'

He didn't answer but his eyes widened briefly.

She pointed to the pony. 'Has she waxed up yet?'

Now he considered her a long moment before answering. Those eyes. She could dive into the pools of them, swim in them and never touch the bottom.

'No.'

'She'll be fine a while longer. And even if she foals without you,' Abigail added, 'she'll cope. Like horses have forever, before dudes and their foaling alarms.'

'All right,' Nate said. 'Are you a vet?'

'God, no. You think I *like* getting up at five am, Nate Ruskin? I much prefer it in bed.' She let her eyes trail down his torso, his legs. She felt him watching her. She lifted her gaze back to his and said, 'I spent two years working at a thoroughbred stud. I can help you.'

He looked surprised, faintly amused. 'Racehorses?'

'Yes.'

He rubbed his chin. 'Horses aren't cows.'

'No. But if you've seen one quadruped vagina, you've seen them all.'

He gave a short, unwitting burst of laughter. 'Don't you have better things to do? You've just got home.'

'Better than getting out of this town for a few hours?'

He drummed his fingers on his thighs. 'It's a long day on your feet.'

'I have feet.'

'The pay isn't great.'

'We'll discuss it.'

He drew a long breath, holding it in. Abigail watched his chest expand, imagined she could see his heart beating. She wanted to unzip his vest and press her ear to his chest to hear the drum of it. 'Your two hundred cows are synched in oestrus. They need you today. And you need a hand.' She spread her arms. 'I'm your woman.'

Five minutes later, Abigail flung open her parents' bedroom door. A groggy mumbled 'What?' came from the dark.

'Mum,' she said. 'I need to borrow your jeans again.'

Nate had a late model four-wheel drive, an expensive one, but the interior was like an old paddock beater. Dried grass and mud caked the footwells, manured boots and flannel shirts littered the back with coils of rope, an axe, skeins of baling twine and, oddly enough for a vet, a fence strainer. He drove it like a paddock beater too—fast—and when she pointed it out, he shrugged and said, 'It's a vet thing. We all do.' But she noticed their speed drop a little and after a moment he added, 'But I do only have a few points left. Coppers aren't as forgiving as they used to be of country vets.'

'Of anyone,' Abigail said.

When she'd climbed into the car, Nate had moved a cache of food off the passenger seat: thermos of coffee; bread rolls; six bananas and an apple-walnut pull-apart as big as a dinner plate and she'd asked brightly, 'Wife pack your breakfast?'

'No,' Nate said.

'No wife, huh?'

His eyes slid to hers. 'No.'

'Girlfriend?'

'Occasionally.'

She grinned at him.

As they flew down the esplanade she watched the sleeping town flash past: beach; lawn; playground. Shops tightly shut, windows dark, though there was a light on out back of the first fish-and-chip shop. Nate turned left at the T-junction and, as town disappeared behind them, the tightness in her chest began to loosen.

The heater blew warm air, making her sleepy. She poured coffee and handed the cup to Nate; he drank in a few mouthfuls. He told her to help herself, so she did. The coffee was strong and bitter, waking her up. Sunrise was an apricot smudge in the east, the sky scribbled with cloud. Flat fields of dairy pasture stretched out, dotted with the dark humps of cattle.

After they had been driving a while, Nate said, 'So you worked at a racehorse stud. Have you always worked with animals?'

'Just sometimes,' she answered.

'What about the other times?'

She allowed her eyes to shift back to the side window, to the pastures green-grey in the dawn. She came from a long line of fishermen who had not only always been fishermen but had aspired to be nothing else. Her mother was her own woman, no doubt about that, but Nell was also a fisherman's wife and a riding pony breeder and had also aspired to be nothing else. Abigail hadn't wanted to fish or breed ponies—and that meant she'd had no idea what she actually wanted to do. So when she'd stepped out of Zac Murphy's Corolla and the city glinted and a never-known freedom stretched in front of her, she had resolved, in order to fully shuck the Kingo backwater, to do everything.

'Probably easier to tell you what I haven't done,' she said.

'All right. Go.'

Caught off guard by his sudden interest, she laughed. 'I've had a lot of jobs, that's all. Although my latest one I stayed at a few years. It feels like a place I could work a long time.'

'Where do you work now?'

Worked, she thought, with a fresh pang of shame. *Past tense.* Although she hadn't expected to, she'd loved working at the restaurant. Especially after the kitchen manager went on maternity leave and she'd stepped into the role. La Paperella was a tiny, bustling Italian fusion joint tucked between a 24-hour ice-cream shop and an upscale tattoo parlour at the good end of Hindley Street. The lunch crowd were Adelaide's up-and-coming corporate types schmoozing clients; the dinner crowd drew locals for Chef Mia's famous linguine allo scoglio (it wasn't on the menu; diners who knew had to ask for it). But it was the breakfast shift Abigail had loved the most, when in came the writers to moan over their laptops and huge lattes, when revellers who still hadn't slept rolled from the last club to wolf bruschetta, eggs and coffee. Vibrant, creative, pulsing with life. It was work that felt anonymous but connected, plugged in. That she'd stayed there long enough to become management—almost five years—was testament to how much she loved it. Prior to the restaurant, her longest tenure at any job had been thirty-two months. (Forklift operator at Port Adelaide. Excellent pay but the hours were crap.)

Abigail took a breath. 'Back of house at a restaurant. A really nice one. But,' she coughed lightly, masking the regret in her voice, 'I've had to move on. In the past I've done nanny work, retail, admin. I've driven forklifts at wineries, loaders at quarries and once, for a very short time, a pink stretch Humvee for hire around the Barossa Valley.' She looked over at Nate. 'Three weeks of shrieking, drunken hens was three weeks too many.'

She went on: the swanky underground bars; the creaking old country pubs; the wineries oozing tourists. The organic veggie farm in the Hills, destroyed by bushfire. The years at elite racehorse studs, working for svelte women and their bland but astonishingly wealthy husbands doing stable-hand work, groundskeeping, maintenance. Finally she shrugged. 'So I'm not entirely unfamiliar with a semen gun.'

Hearing it laid out like that, each job one after the other, she sounded like a spoiled kid who couldn't choose what toy to play with, growing bored and moving on. She wanted to reiterate how much she loved the restaurant, how dearly she wanted—needed—to stop running, but to her horror she felt a lump forming in her throat. The restaurant had forgiven her two weeks inside, but still she'd returned chastened, wary, only to find nothing changed: the same lunch crowd; the same dinner crowd. Same Chef Mia making jokes bawdy enough to burn the filets. The relief of forgiveness had been so unexpected she'd cried into Mia's apron. But five months? It was too long. Too much to overlook. It meant replacing her.

Enough. Abigail shook it off, shedding the rising gulp of emotion like a coat. She turned to Nate, the vet sliding his sunglasses on as the morning sun tore through the windscreen.

'Tell me about those girlfriends.'

Abigail knew that working with a herd of penned cattle was loud and dirty. She knew that the stink of cow shit became all you could smell; she knew the lowing of the beasts and the metallic clang of the crush, the heavy-wet scrape of hooves, would ring in your head until it was all you could hear.

In that way, it wasn't unlike prison.

After a two-hour drive to the thousand-acre dairy farm, Abigail took a pair of overalls from the back of Nate's four-wheel drive and got to work. She prodded up reluctant cows, swept away fresh dung dropped in piles about Nate's boots, helped him peel off any particularly sticky shoulder-length gloves. She fetched, ferried, shovelled, wiped, hosed. She called, cajoled, petted and, sometimes, sympathised with the wide-eyed maidens. At lunch time, the farmer's wife lugged out a huge pot of spaghetti bolognese and she tucked in with the rest of the farmhands, and the pasta was so warming and tasty and everyone was talking and joking and free to walk away whenever they wanted, if they really wanted. When someone barked an instruction, Abigail obliged and didn't mind that there wasn't time for pleasantries when an ovulating cow was breaking for the gate. When an especially chunky heifer stomped a muddy cloven hoof right onto Abigail's boot she let loose a string of invectives that set the other farmhands howling with laughter. No one asked her where she was from or why she was here because no one cared—the work was all that mattered. They were united. Two hundred cows is a lot of cows.

In that way, it was nothing like prison.

By late afternoon most of the cows had completed their date with the vet, tottering out of the shed carrying the seeds for their new progeny, the germs of the farmer's next millions.

Abigail wasn't unfamiliar with days on her feet. At the restaurant it was not unusual for her to spend eight or more hours largely upright—fetching, ferrying, cajoling—but she hadn't worked at the restaurant for half a year. She was also far from being in the best shape even without the bruises, blisters and bites.

As the sun started to fall towards the western horizon, sending flares of yellow through the shed, Abigail felt herself flagging. Trying to isolate the part of her body that was hurting the most to try and surreptitiously relieve it, she realised there wasn't a beginning or end to her discomfort. From head to toe, she was hurting.

Only a handful of heifers to go. She swept another pile of dung away from Nate's boots, counting down the minutes. There was still a two-hour drive home, but after nine hours of this, the drive would be nothing. A heated cab, some more coffee, the rest of that apple-walnut pull-apart—she could do it.

It was the second-last heifer who decided to make a break for it. Almost two hundred other cows had not managed to kick between the rails, but this one did, striking squarely on Nate's shin and opening his skin like a peeled banana.

Bleeding into his boot, Nate staggered backwards, dropping and breaking the semen gun. While the station manager clucked over the wasted bull junk and another farmhand rushed to examine the vet's wound, Abigail sidled over to the crush by the cow's flank and leaned on the rail to ease the pain in her lower back.

The heifer was agitated, pushing her massive body back and forth against the tiny cell, blowing hot grassy breath.

A small group had formed around the vet, passing iodine, towel and duct tape. Abigail could see Nate laughing and wincing.

'Being locked up sucks,' Abigail murmured to the cow. 'But you'll be out soon.'

She looked into the paddock. Most of the freed cows had wandered towards the horizon and only a few stragglers remained, lowing confusedly. The cow next to Abigail bellowed, pushing against the railings.

'Knocked up without even saying hey to a bull,' she continued in a quiet voice. 'Bit of a raw deal.'

It had been one of the first things she'd heard Jen say: *Do you know there was a time when humans didn't know that sex caused pregnancy?* Early one morning at the restaurant, Jen had come in with two other dancers, all aviators and big hair, smelling of that indescribable chemical perfume combination that came to be as familiar to Abigail as her own apartment. The three women ordered everything on the breakfast menu then feasted like Vikings. They laughed a lot. They paid in cash hundreds. Abigail could not focus on her other customers, her attention captured by the glittering women spilling over the corner table as she overheard Jen on her soapbox, thanking the discovered link between semen and pregnancy for the origins of patriarchy, the loss of female mystery and power. 'Egalitarianism fell to the male orgasm,' Jen liked to say. Abigail had felt all the hairs on her arms stand up.

The cow bellowed again. Abigail put a hand on the animal's flank, steamy against her palm. She glanced over at the station manager bothering over his bull semen and said quietly to the cow, 'I spoof, therefore I am. Not much has changed, huh?'

She patted the cow. Like her herd mates outside, this cow's body would become pregnant and her hormones and instincts would drive her accordingly. One day, nine months or so from now, this cow would feel the urge to wander away from her herd, to lie down; her body would heave and heave and then she'd find this little thing that she wanted to protect with her life. Would she know what was happening?

It came before Abigail could understand what it was. A stinging sensation like ants biting all over her skin. Memories that she had managed to push down for so many years rushed to the surface. The taste of metal on her tongue, icy cold fingers, breath steaming in front of her. And now she could smell it: the seaweed; the blood; the disgusting reek of a public toilet block.

Perhaps the cow picked up her sudden distress, or perhaps the animal startled when Abigail gasped and grabbed the rail to hold herself upright, but whatever it was, somehow, the cogs on the crush lever crunched and the gate screeched and sprang open. The cow leapt free.

Shouts rang out. The cow's hooves skidded on the concrete as she fled, flattening yard panels and gates like cardboard, galloping headlong out the open door towards the field and the rosy horizon beyond.

When Abigail was a teenager she had been banned from riding the quad bike. So banned, in fact, that her mother had sold the quad and bought a clapped-out Mighty Boy ute for Abigail and her brothers to use in the paddock instead.

She'd bunted Hamish against a fencepost and cracked his rib. It was an accident. The jerk shouldn't have been standing there, she protested. Nell had been more pissed about the five-hour wait in Emergency on top of the two-hour round trip to hospital than the actual injury. A greenstick fracture, painful breathing for a week or so; Hamish bounced right back and threw Abigail's Walkman off a cliff. Abigail and her brothers had maintained that the selling of the quad in place of a tiny stupid-looking ute was a grave injustice but they discovered soon enough that if the grass was wet down the bottom of the far paddock they could get the Mighty Boy sideways, so they stopped complaining.

So it was many years since she'd been on a four-wheeler, but it came right back to her.

The quad was parked just inside the shed door; the cow ran right past it on her dash for freedom. Abigail got to the quad, mounted it, thumbed the ignition and was away.

Eyes on the cow's rump, she blasted out of the shed and into the paddock. Cold air whipped into her eyes and her fingers around the handlebars went frigid. Divots in the ground clacked her teeth together. The cow, hearing the engine behind her, threw a random left, then a right, then another left, but Abigail kept at the heifer's flank, switching with her in a wide circle until they were headed back in the direction of the yard. The rest of the crew had opened the yard gates and stood nearby, helpfully waving their arms.

At the last moment the cow banked a hard left, avoiding the yard gates.

The quad was fitted with an anti-crush cage and the smallest reassurance flashed through Abigail as she hauled around in time with the cow and felt the floating sensation of all four wheels not quite being on the ground. Time stretched enough for her to consider her own stupidity. She had acted without thinking and was that not the exact thing she had been trying to change about herself? Was that not the reason she had come back to this place, this town that had tried to tell her what she was, to prove that they were all wrong, that she could be something else? *Stupid, stupid.* There was nothing to be gained from this. There was only what could be lost. If she could go back in time, she would. Back a few minutes in time and the cow wouldn't escape and Abigail's two feet would stay firmly planted on the shed floor. Freedom heifers were not her problem.

Clods of mud flew, runnels carved into the earth. The quad touched down and she sat back on the seat as the cow baulked, pivoted, then trotted resignedly back into the yard.

Abigail puttered in behind the cow and killed the engine.

'Nice work, Evil Knievel,' said one farmhand, clapping her shoulder. She clenched her jaw and said nothing. A short while later, the cow was pregnant.

THEM

To Sheila Rocket's vexation, Adrian and Jason Turner's mother had been unforthcoming with her lemon slice recipe.

Yesterday, when Fish Fisher had been protesting his inability to take Lofty's boat out of the harbour because the boat wasn't there, Sheila Rocket, after her nice chat with Adrian out the front of the hardware store, had popped over to visit Eleanor Turner under the guise of enquiring after that lemon slice, only to discover that: one, Eleanor Turner no longer had the recipe ('From the Scouts' fete?' Eleanor had said with a frown. 'Gosh. That was back when all my bits still pointed up.') and two, she had not actually spoken to her son Jason since the barbecue at Young Dick's the night before. ('He's too busy with work, out all hours. I've been at him to replace the back porch light for months.')

Now, a day later, Sheila Rocket was in Penny Bram's kitchen. Also in Penny Bram's kitchen was Beverly Din-widdle, the postmistress, wife of Larry the publican. The three women had not even made it to the table—three cups of tea cooled on the bench between them, while the two visiting women perched on stools and Penny Bram just stood there, not even leaning against the counter, because although Penny was partially kept upright by her long years standing behind the deli counter, she was also vertical with indignation.

'I'm not going to answer that, Bev,' said Penny. 'How would I even know?'

Mrs Dinwiddle looked perplexed. 'Jessica is your daughter.'

Sheila Rocket, who had initially come to Penny's because she was still on the hunt for information about Young Dick's barbecue from two nights ago, sat motionless on her stool. She had just learned from the postmistress that last night at the pub, events had transpired that were arguably as event-ful as the night prior. Possibly more so.

'Jess is a grown woman,' Penny said. 'I don't know anything—and frankly I don't *want* to know anything—about ... *that.*'

Sheila wasn't convinced. Twice a year, Penny Bram and her daughter Jessica travelled to the city and spent a weekend at a luxury hotel, lounging in robes and getting room service and pedicures. Everyone knew they did this because Jessica always put it all over Instagram. Everyone concealed their envy over the Brams' ability to indulge in such hedonism by saying outwardly that they considered it peculiar and a waste of money, while deep down inside they wished they could do it, too. The point is, everyone knew Jessica Bram and her mother were close, in much the same way that everyone knew Young Dick Fancy and Col Morton were close. Only rather than painting his toenails to prove it, Col Morton had offered his foot for a bullet.

'You have a special relationship with your daughter,' Mrs Dinwiddle said. 'It's something I've always admired.'

Sheila nodded vigorously. 'Yes. You're a very good mother. We should all aspire.'

Penny rolled her eyes.

The postmistress tried another angle. 'Look, Larry said he didn't know *for sure*. He just said that Jason Turner came out of the kitchen with schnitzels and his eyes looked like train windscreens, and Larry had to give the kid a nip of whiskey.'

'"Train windscreens"?' Sheila wanted to clarify.

'That's a direct quote,' Mrs Dinwiddle confirmed.

The image delighted Sheila. She made a mental note for when she would need to recall it later.

'I thought you should know,' Mrs Dinwiddle said. 'In case there's talk. I thought you should hear it from me first. I was, you know, concerned.' She reached out to pat Penny's hand but realised too late that both of Penny's hands were tucked in her back pockets, so, after an awkward hesitation with her hand extended and hovering, she patted the counter by Penny's tea cup.

'Gee, thanks, Bev,' said Penny.

'I'm only trying to be a friend.' A note of defensiveness crept into Mrs Dinwiddle's voice.

'We both are,' said Sheila.

'Well,' said Penny, finally picking up her tea. 'I don't know what to tell you. Jess hasn't said a thing. Hey,' she interrupted herself, setting the tea down without taking a sip. 'Did you hear Abigail Fancy is out with the new vet today?'

'No. Really?'

'Really,' Penny said, pleased to take the spotlight off her daughter. 'At Twelve Mile Dairy. You know, the big one.'

'The new vet, from here in town?'

'What other vet would I be talking about?' said Penny, irritated. 'It's hardly the old one. He's dead.'

'I'm just making sure,' said Mrs Dinwiddle, equally irked. 'I like to have my facts correct.'

'Nathaniel Ruskin,' offered Sheila. 'Nice fellow, if a bit quiet. He helped my Sissy when she got sick. Turned out she had gallstones. Did you know a Maltese can get gallstones?'

'He's a blow-in. He won't last.'

'Maybe,' said Penny. 'Although we don't have any other vets in town.'

'I hope he stays,' said Sheila. 'My Sissy liked him.'

'Patty Smith says he's shifty,' said the postmistress, frowning. 'She said her daughter said he's been in to get chips a few times, but he doesn't speak much. I've met him a few times myself and I have to say, I can't disagree with Patty. I suspect he thinks he's better than everyone.'

'Patty Smith is a blow-in herself,' pointed out Sheila, before reiterating, '*I* like him.'

'He's Nell Fancy's pet,' Penny couldn't help but say.

Mrs Dinwiddle couldn't disagree with that either, but she wasn't about to say that out loud.

'I didn't know Abigail Fancy was a vet, though,' said Sheila. 'When did that happen?'

'She isn't,' said Penny. 'She's waitressing, last I heard. Well—' Penny gave a short laugh, '—before she went to prison for vandalism, that is.'

'Vandalism?' said Sheila. 'I thought it was joyriding.'

'Hoon driving,' the postmistress said in a knowledgeable tone.

'She went to prison,' Penny repeated, putting down her cup. 'For the *second* time. Does it really matter what for?'

The other women murmured in agreement and went quiet. Sheila picked up her tea but found it had gone cold. The silence dragged. Penny Bram's house was a block back from the esplanade; the sound of the ocean was dulled. The only noise to break the silence was a half-hearted drizzle that started to patter against the kitchen window but gave up just as quickly. Sheila forced in a sip of cold tea.

Finally Penny said the thing they were all thinking: 'Why is she back?'

Each woman exchanged a glance with the other.

'Bev?'

The postmistress blinked, finding herself in the spotlight.

'You said Nell came back a second time yesterday for her parcel. What did she say?'

Clearing her throat, Mrs Dinwiddle shifted on her stool. She wondered how she could put it in a way that didn't suggest the *exact* truth: that Nell had disclosed nothing. That when she, Beverly Dinwiddle, had asked the question burning on the whole town's lips—*why on earth has that girl come back after everything she went through?*—Nell had not even seen fit to give the postmistress of forty-seven years and wife of Larry Dinwiddle, publican for seventeen, a simple piece of information.

Well, Mrs Dinwiddle thought to herself. Maybe she hadn't asked Nell those words *precisely*. She'd been tactful about it. Asked in a roundabout way. The point is, when she had enquired about Abigail's return, Nell Fancy had snubbed her. Twice. Never before had the postmistress felt the bewilderment of being outside the circle. Nell had left the post office the first time, and Sheila and the two fishermen's wives who had witnessed the snubbing turned to the postmistress in mute disbelieving joy, and Mrs Dinwiddle had had to shoo them outside and hang the *Back in 5 minutes* sign on the door to recover. Later, Nell returned with the ID the postmistress had cleverly thought of, and once again Mrs Dinwiddle had asked but once again Nell revealed nothing. So, when her husband had come home from the pub late last night with a story hot as a dropped coal, the postmistress had found a way to put herself back into the circle where she belonged. But it was important that she did it right. It was imperative that Mrs Dinwiddle put herself back in the circle *with* the Fancys, not *against* them. And because Col Morton was undoubtedly *in* and Jessica Bram arguably *out*, their frolic in the pub kitchen— no matter how alleged—blurred the lines of certain circles to the point where they were almost indistinguishable.

Carefully, Mrs Dinwiddle said, 'That's between me and Nell. I'm really not at liberty to say.'

And in doing so, Beverly Dinwiddle hoped she carved a line of her own.

What Penny Bram wouldn't disclose, of course, was that she had spoken to her daughter Jessica and knew about Jessica's dalliance with Col Morton in the pub kitchen, because earlier that day, Jessica had taken a bottle of cranberry juice from the deli fridge for a UTI.

Also, Eleanor Turner still had that lemon slice recipe and continued to make it for her sons—she just wasn't about to share it with Sheila Rocket.

OLD DICK

The young fella is doing that thing again. That thing where he plasters himself to the window like some kind of glass barnacle.

I've seen him do it often enough. He puts both hands above his head, palms flat on the window, then he leans his whole body against the glass, forehead to knees, then stays like that. He looks like he's been thrown against the glass. It makes him a silhouette; his body makes a shadow like those chalk outlines on the concrete where dead bodies were. Sometimes he stays like it for a few minutes but I swear I've seen him stay there longer than a man should. What's he even looking at? It's not like you can see the boats through that particular window. Through that window all you can see is scrub and more scrub. And the lighthouse.

I'm not looking at boats, Dad.

Maybe he's watching something suspicious. After all, it's not like suspicious activity only happens around boats—the scrub can hide that kind of stuff, too. It's pretty dense, that ti-tree scrub, the way it's knitted together, hunkered down on the slopes against the salt wind. You get yourself in that scrub, it's hard to get out. Everything looks the same. Anything could get lost in there, except rabbits and foxes. We used to go shooting but you're not allowed to do that anymore. Instead they've let the vermin take over, and now a man isn't allowed to shoot things, even if they're feral and you'd be doing the world a favour by knocking them off.

Where did that young woman go? I ask. She makes a nice cuppa tea.

The young fella blows a patch of fog on the glass. *Abigail's working today. Out of town. Thank Christ.*

Does he mean she's out at sea—is that why he sounds so relieved? That young woman doesn't look like much of a fisherman, I have to say. And to be honest I never did like the idea of women on boats. There's certain language that needs to be used on deck, or messages that need to be passed along, that shouldn't be for the ears of the gentler sex.

Sorry, Luce.

She's not out at sea. She's at a dairy with the vet.

What vet? What dairy?

Do you want a cup of tea, Richard?

Now the woman has appeared and she goes to the window, too, although she stands side-on to it, not like a glass barnacle. The young fella doesn't move. He's starting to piss me off. Acting like a drongo. There's no point sticking yourself to a window when there's work to be done. No one's going to give you money for sticking yourself to a window like a swatted blow fly.

Now a phone's ringing, but no one moves to answer it. Do they want me to? It seems to ring for a long time then it goes quiet. Shortly there's another ringing sound, a different one, and it's enough to drive a man bonkers. Someone answer the damn phone.

Hey, Twitch.

The woman has a phone to her ear and she's looking straight at the young fella.

You're looking for Dick?

Plastered to the window, the young fella shakes his head.

If he's not answering, he's busy … I don't know. But he did say he was going to … You're kidding … No, don't do that. I'll have a word to Dick. Okay, mate. Bye.

I'd like a cuppa, but the mood in the room has taken a nose dive. What is wrong with these two? Do they need me to off someone?

Incredibly, the young fella gets even closer to the glass. It's like there's no skeleton in him at all anymore, he's just a skin sack stuck to a window.

Still no sign of Lofty's boat. And Lofty himself is AWOL.

The glass barnacle does not move.

Also, apparently Col Morton's slept with Jessica Bram.

There's a loud, drawn-out squeaking sound. It's the young fella's palms dragging down the glass. Finally he comes away from the window.

Twitch is threatening to take Col to the lighthouse.

I've never found the lighthouse particularly funny, but apparently both of them do.

I'd like to know more about this fellow who needs a lesson. Stop laughing. A trip to the lighthouse is serious business. I'll get the jemmy bar.

No, thanks, Dad.

The woman says, *I'm only going to ask this once. Did Lofty have anything to do with the bone?*

The young fella takes a big breath, like he's standing at the foot of a mountain, and he's only just looked up and realised how massive the climb's going to be and he's having second thoughts.

I think it's got him spooked. About some other things, from twenty-four years ago.

What things? What are they talking about?

And where's my cuppa tea?

ABIGAIL

Ten hours after driving to the dairy in the half-light, they were driving home in the half-dark. Abigail had stopped noticing individual discomforts in her body and instead felt like an all-consuming existence of hurt, pain from scalp to toenails. Grimed and sweaty, she was sure they both ponged to high heaven but given they stunk equally they cancelled each other out. It was the first time in months she'd felt *alive*. Some spark within her had been blown on and begun to glow.

The farmer's wife had given Nate a plastic tub of sandwiches, which was sitting between Abigail's feet. She was incredibly hungry. To distract herself from the sandwiches, she asked Nate if he had plans for the weekend.

'I've got another dairy tomorrow,' he said. 'A smaller one, but I'll be beat. Probably call it an early night.'

'That sounds amazing.' She sighed, wondering if she'd become a drag.

'I'll have my son with me next week. I'll need the rest.'

She glanced at him. He'd washed his face but a smear of dirt remained by his ear. 'You have a son?'

'I do.'

'How old is he?'

'Fourteen. Leon.'

'Does he live here?'

'Melbourne. With his mum.'

'His mum?'

Nate exhaled through his nose but didn't offer anything else. She imagined reaching over, thumbing away the dirt from his skin.

'How often do you see Leon?' she asked.

'One week a month.'

She wanted to know more, but she was beginning to feel as though she was battering him with questions. And she knew how that felt, so she let him be. They drove for a while, neither of them speaking, Abigail continuing to try and ignore the sandwiches.

Finally, Nate said, 'What about you?'

'What about me, doll?'

She caught a fleeting smile on his lips. 'Any plans with your folks?'

'They didn't know I was coming, so probably not.'

'They didn't?'

Maybe the vet already knew she was just out of prison; it was likely some Port Kingerton mouth had already blabbed it. But something in his manner suggested he didn't. Nate might be a silent type but he didn't seem uncomfortable in her presence. It was a discovery most people backed away from, retreating into themselves with a mixture of embarrassment and fear, as if she were carrying a virus. But if she wanted someone to trust her, she had to be honest about it: *just so you know, I've been to prison.* Disclosure was a gamble—admit it and run the risk of abandonment, hide it and ratify your own disgrace. Damned if you do and damned if you don't. *What would a good person do?*

Abigail rested her elbow on the door, chewed a sliver of fingernail. A craving for a cigarette hit and she looked longingly at the sandwiches.

'No,' she said at length. 'They didn't know I was coming. I haven't been home for over twenty years. But I was kind of over a barrel.' She glanced sideways. His expression was impassive, his eyes watching the road. 'I've been in prison,' she said, trying to keep her voice even. 'Five months. And if I don't want to go back, I've got to start again. So it's hello, Kingo, and fuck you very much.'

Nate said nothing.

'Screw it,' she said. 'I'm having a sandwich.' She leaned forward to try and lift the plastic tub out of the footwell, grunted, adjusted the seatbelt and tried again.

Taking a hand off the wheel, Nate leaned over and pulled the tub into her lap. Immediately she wanted to push it back down so he would lean over her again.

She took a sandwich and peeled up a corner of bread. 'Roast beef,' she said. 'Well, I guess she had some lying around.' She tried not to think of the heifer from earlier, railing against the crush. But the sandwiches were good: fresh bread, tender beef, cheese and caramelised onion.

'Your mum told me. About prison.'

Mouth full of sandwich, her head snapped towards him. The car went through a rut in the bitumen, something in the back gave a sharp rattle.

She struggled to swallow. 'You knew?'

'Yeah. It's not my business, but—' he shrugged, '—small town.'

'You didn't say anything.'

'I wanted to when you jumped on that quad.'

'And yet you refrained. Aren't you a gentleman.'

'Except for the cattle pimp thing.'

She waited, taking another bite of her sandwich, but it didn't come.

'Oh, come on,' she said, after a while. 'Don't you want to know?'

'Know what?'

'Why I went inside.'

Nate took a breath, as if truly considering it. Then he lifted one shoulder in a shrug. 'Yep. But I assume you didn't murder someone, so again, maybe it's none of my business?'

'How do you figure that?'

'Figure what?'

'That I didn't off someone.'

'Five months doesn't sound like a murder sentence.'

'Plenty of people would disagree,' she said. 'They think sentencing in Australia is too weak. And it's usually men like you who are the most opinionated about these things.'

'Like me?'

'Moneyed; rural.'

He laughed; her mocking was a gentle arrow. For a second he took both of his hands off the wheel, turning his palms up. 'I'm too busy to get online and tell everyone how wrong they are.'

'Again, the cattle pimp thing.'

'Someone's gotta do it. People like cheese.'

Abigail suppressed a smile and turned back to the window.

Nate offered her twenty bucks an hour, but she refused and got him up to twenty-five.

'A little steep for a rookie,' he said, counting out cash under the glow of the cab light. They were parked at the top of the Fancys' driveway. Night had fallen in earnest.

'Who are you calling a rookie?' Abigail said, taking the money and folding it into her back pocket. 'So I'll see you tomorrow?'

'Maybe I can't afford you the whole day.'

She shook her head. 'I can't work the whole day. I've got stuff I need to do.'

'How did we end up here?' Nate said. 'You're setting the terms and I'm not even convinced you're good at this.'

'Mate, seriously? I'm not going to dignify that with a response.' She climbed out of the four-wheel drive, turning to face him through the open door. 'Did you not see me on that quad?'

Nate's features were picked out by the light overhead, his face partially in shadow. She could see the line of day-old stubble along his jaw. The smear of dirt was still there. 'I'll pick you up at eleven,' he said. 'Whatever you need to do, do it before then.'

Abigail licked her thumb. 'You've got a little something,' she said, motioning to her own jaw. He frowned, looked in the rear-vision mirror. Tried to rub the dirt away but it didn't come off.

'So do you.' His finger drew a line in the air from her face, to her neck, down her chest.

She blew him a kiss. 'See you tomorrow.'

The house was lit up, voices chattering, TV blaring and her grandfather yelling about a ladder. The inside of her jolted and withdrew, curled like a poked sea urchin. A longing for her tiny apartment, for the dull anonymous drone of the city, joined the rest of her physical aches.

She came into the kitchen to find her father at the counter, her grandfather at the table and her mother standing between them, hands on hips. Nell's mouth was open, as if to speak, but when Abigail entered she closed it.

Abigail considered staying quiet. She could grab something to eat, say good night and disappear. She yearned for sleep. But the tension in the room hummed like a plucked wire. It was clear she had walked into the centre of something, and ignoring it or pretending she didn't notice would only make it more awkward and obvious. Her mind flashed back to the weightless feeling of the quad with its wheels off the ground. *What would a good person do?*

'Everything okay?' she asked, warily.

'Never you mind,' her mother said. 'It doesn't concern you.'

'Great.' Taking a fifty from her back pocket, she handed it to her mother.

'Fifty won't go too far. Not with the amount you're eating.'

'I'm getting more tomorrow,' Abigail said. 'Oh, and Teflon tape.'

'What?'

'Never you mind. It doesn't concern you.'

'Thanks, Abs,' her father said, coming forward. 'But you should keep it, so you can, you know—' he gestured at her, as if indicating her entire body '—get back on your feet.'

'Speak for yourself,' her mother said, pocketing the cash. 'I'd like my jeans back, too.'

'Be careful whose money you take,' her grandfather said from the table. 'They might want to collect it later. With interest. Sometimes it's blood. Other times it's your balls.'

'And on that encouraging note,' Abigail said, 'I'll retire to my room for the rest of the evening. Good night.'

'Not so fast,' Nell said. 'There's something you should know.'

Abigail bit back another retort about things that did not concern her. 'As soon as I've been to the shops tomorrow, you can have your jeans back.'

'It's not about the jeans.'

She took in the three of them ranged across the kitchen, each staring at her with a certain expression. Her mother's barely veiled fury, her father's pity mixed with hope, her grandfather's concern and calculation. She felt weary to her bones.

'Can it wait till morning?'

Her parents exchanged a glance. 'Let's get it out of the way now,' her mother said.

Abigail sat at the table.

Her grandfather asked, 'What the hell happened to your eye?' and she replied, 'Wrong end of a cow,' and the old man nodded knowingly.

Her father's phone rang. Pulling it from his pocket, he glanced at the screen and shoved it away. 'There's been some developments,' he began without preamble.

This is what Abigail learned: the cops had a strong suspicion who the thighbone from yesterday might belong to. No one else in town knew that particular piece of information yet. In the meantime, the discovery of said thighbone had caused nerves throughout town to fray. Some of the more *lawfully questionable*, her father said, ('Dodgy buggers,' her grandfather said), were reconsidering the shady behaviour of their past and wondering just how shaded it might continue to be. Or if it was going to become exposed to the daylight, washed up like a femur on the beach.

'So what you're telling me,' Abigail said tiredly, 'is that Kingo is currently having a collective arse clench.'

Her mother rolled her eyes.

Her father said, 'Yes,' and went on: Old Man Loft's cray boat had gone missing. No one knew where it was. To compound matters, Lofty himself seemed to have disappeared, too. Presently Fish Fisher was laying siege to town with accusations that bikies were behind it and that the disappearance of both Lofty and his boat was *evasive action*, her father said, ('Pants shitting,' her grandfather said).

'And this concerns me how?' Abigail asked, fighting the droop of her eyelids.

'I'm getting to that.'

People were fabricating their own stories about the origin of the bone. There were also plenty of stories being made up about Lofty, Fish and the boat.

'Town is getting … uncomfortable,' her father said.

'Like genital warts,' her grandfather said.

'Look,' Abigail broke in, 'I get you're trying to keep me in the loop. But I've no idea what any of this means, and honestly? I don't care.'

Her parents exchanged another meaningful look. Her father went to speak but Nell cut him off. 'There's talk about what happened before you left,' Nell said. 'Renewed talk. About all of it.'

A cold prickle stole over Abigail's body. Suddenly she was wide awake.

'The timing is unfortunate,' her mother added. 'The bone washing up on the same day as you—'

'They think I had something to do with this thighbone?' Abigail felt her voice could cut glass.

Silence fell in the kitchen.

'Well?' she prompted, looking between them.

Her father opened his mouth, but it took so long for his words to come out she began to wonder if he was going to speak at all. 'People seem to be ... re-evaluating,' he said finally.

'Re-evaluating what?'

Her parents sighed like one united organism of sufferance. She wanted to punch something.

'Alliances,' her father said. 'Who's on whose side and who's keeping whose confidence. Navel-gazing about the past. Rehashing old grievances. All of it really. You name it, they're talking about it.'

Abigail muttered 'Fuck's sake' under her breath. It was beginning to seem like a cosmic joke, all of it.

The first time Abigail went skydiving, she convinced Mark to go with her. As the single-engine aircraft made its rattling climb into the sky, they strapped themselves to strangers then plummeted down over Semaphore Beach. The initial freefall had felt so physically inconceivable she didn't have words to describe it. A few years later she talked Jen into it and once again she was dropping from the sky, weightless, obliterated, the roar in her ears and the breath ripped from her lungs.

As another wave of disorienting homesickness crashed over her now, Abigail was reminded of that sensation of freefall: a bodily scream that there is no earth beneath your feet. And she thought that feeling homesick when you were at home, when there was nowhere else to go, was possibly the most unnerving thing she had ever felt.

'Listen,' her mother said, and Abigail heard an attempt at conciliation in her tone, 'we're just saying you should keep your wits about you. If people talk to you—which they will—just keep it together.'

'Why wouldn't I?'

'You threatened to tear Adrian Turner's balls off.'

Abigail gave an incredulous laugh. 'How do you even know that?'

'I'm just saying. Keep a hold on your temper.'

'Your concern is noted.'

Nell threw up her hands. Young Dick's phone rang. Again he ignored it.

'You're going about this the wrong way,' her grandfather said. 'You want the girl to behave herself? Stop terrorising young blokes? Keep her mouth shut? Just say so. Stop farnarkling about.'

'I think that's the gist, Grandpa,' Abigail said. 'Although I'm not sure why it's my responsibility to keep the fuckwits in this town calm when I've been away twenty-odd years and back all of five minutes. Seems to me any "re-evaluating of alliances" is none of my business.'

Her grandfather turned to her parents and said, 'She makes a fair point.'

Her father's phone chimed, and Nell said, 'Just turn it off.'

'It's Twitch.' Her father read the message then swivelled in his chair, looking towards the doorway. He stabbed the screen in reply. 'He's here,' he said. 'He's coming in.'

Abigail heard the sound of the back door opening and closing. Heavy footsteps, then a bald head appeared in the kitchen doorway, followed by a very large man. Black T-shirt straining at the seams, black jeans, tattoo snaking up one side of his neck.

Abigail couldn't help it: her face stretched into a grin. Somehow she was out of her chair and across the kitchen and Twitch wrapped her in an embrace, lifting her off the ground.

'You smell like crabs,' she said, when he set her down.

'You smell like cow shit.'

'You got old.'

'You got fat.'

She laughed and punched him in one enormous arm. Her fist bounced harmlessly.

'Your mum's telling everyone you look amazing,' Twitch said. 'She's not lying, eh?'

Abigail turned to her mother in surprise. Nell's face remained impassive.

'Although.' Twitch frowned, gently taking hold of her chin, his eyes roving over the bruised side of her face. 'Tell me they look worse, yeah?'

She withdrew from his grip, saying nothing.

'Am I interrupting something?' Twitch asked, glancing around the table. 'Good.' He clapped a hand on her father's shoulder. 'All right, Dicky?'

'Who's this meathead?' said her grandfather.

'This is Twitch, Dad,' said her father. 'Fisherman. You've met plenty of times.'

'Good to see you again, sir,' Twitch said to Old Dick, smiling.

'Sod off.'

Abigail put her arm around her grandfather's shoulder and squeezed. 'God,' she said. 'You're excellent.' Straightening up with difficulty, she announced, 'This has been fun, but I'm knackered. And I've promised that lovely vet my services again tomorrow, so—'

'You're working with Nate Ruskin again?' her mother asked.

'Yep.'

Nell looked at Young Dick. 'She's going to snap that man in half,' she said, wistfully. 'And we only just got him.'

Abigail opened her mouth to respond and was interrupted by a rapid knocking on the back door. Her mother, father and Twitch exchanged a loaded glance, before her father closed his eyes and said, 'That'll be Col.'

Nell turned to Abigail. 'Now, his balls,' she said, 'you *can* tear off.'

THEM

When Col Morton drove up to Young Dick's house and saw Twitch's ute parked there, he felt a sudden urge to piss.

Col took his time putting the ute in park and shutting off the engine. He reflected, not for the first time that day, on how screwing Jessica Bram in the pub kitchen may not have been one of his wisest ideas. One of his more exhilarating ideas, true, but possibly not the wisest.

Let it not be said that Col Morton was an unwise man. For this was something that he, Col, prided himself upon: his ability to *think* about the consequences of things. By his mid-thirties, Col had been captain of his own boat; he had avoided the bond of a missus and kids that make a fisherman's life both easier and harder; he'd never had crabs (the pubic variety).

But to see Twitch's ute parked there, black paint gleaming under the Fancys' back porch light—that squeezed Col's bladder all right. Squeezed the wisdom that seemed to have fled last night at the sight of Jessica Bram in her running tights right back into him.

Col ascended the steps to the back porch. Raised his fist to knock, then hesitated.

Perhaps he'd been a bit stupid, but spineless Col was not. It takes a certain fortitude to get where Col Morton had got in this town and he reminded himself that a moment of weakness shouldn't take that away. So right there, where his fist was raised to knock at Young Dick's back door because Col and Young Dick had that kind of relationship, Col checked himself, and instead of knocking like a person timid with contrition, he rapped the door like he always had: assured of his own importance.

They left him standing there longer than Col liked before Young Dick called, 'Come in.'

When Col went in his limp returned.

Around the table in the kitchen were Young Dick, Nell, Twitch, Old Dick and—there she was—Abigail. Thinking of the sausages, Col felt the blood leave his face then flush it with heat. He was a few years younger than her so he'd never experienced it himself, but he knew Abigail was an easy sort. Giving and generous with her affection, the boys used to say. He'd once seen Brian Wimple kissing her behind the bus shelter and been unable to look away. Now Col felt himself struck by the same desire. All he wanted to do was look at Abigail, so instead he looked at everyone else.

'G'day, Fancys,' he said, clearing his throat. 'Twitch.'

Twitch made no acknowledgement of Col's greeting. The big bald man just held Col's gaze, unblinking, in a way that was neither cold nor angry. Actually, Col found that he could not make sense of Twitch's expression at all.

No one told Col to have a seat, so Col continued standing in the doorway. It looked to everyone as if Col were trying to affect a casual pose, momentarily resting one elbow against the door frame, then crossing one foot over his ankle, but in the end he gave up. He stood up straight, putting his hands behind his back.

'Is there a problem?' Young Dick asked.

Col didn't reply but his Adam's apple bobbed as he swallowed.

'Well?'

Again Col swallowed. Again he cleared his throat. Finally he said, 'Just having a little fun, is all, Dick. No harm meant.' His eyes darted to Abigail and the expression on her face made him feel dizzy. Was that ... *arousal* he could see in her eyes? Did she know about him and Jessica, and was she picturing it, the way he had been picturing her, in the pub kitchen last night? *Oh god*, thought Col, *Abigail Fancy is thinking about sex. In the same room as me.*

Nell started to laugh. 'No harm meant? The woman is married, Col. She has three kids.'

'Apparently Jess and her husband have an under—'

'I don't want to hear it,' said Young Dick.

Col went quiet.

'Wait,' Abigail said, and the sound of her voice turned Col's insides to warm liquid. 'What's this "fun" you had, and who's this married Jess?'

Oh, thought Col. Abigail *didn't* know. Now his bowels sunk into his shoes.

Young Dick stood up. He went to the counter and flicked on the kettle. Taking down two cups, he dropped in tea bags, leaned against the bench and waited for the kettle to boil. Col thought Young Dick completed these actions with the calculated deliberateness of an executioner.

What Col did not understand was this: Young Dick was not thinking about Col and Jessica Bram in the pub kitchen. When Nell had told him about it, Young Dick had found the piece of news about as interesting as weather: it played a part in the landscape of one's day, but it wasn't especially remarkable. Because between the surprise of his daughter's return, his father's increasing verbal outpourings, a washed-up femur and a missing boat and its skipper, Young Dick's interest in Col Morton's sexual activity bordered on non-existent.

But, like most people, Col was prone to solipsism. He thought his own internal worldview was fact; he believed that *his* reality was the *only* reality. Col assumed that everyone else was thinking about the same things as he, and that what he believed to be true irrefutably was.

So Col entered the Fancys' kitchen and thought he felt tension, and decided that tension was a result of what he now judged to be his betrayal of Young Dick—from his knocking boots behind enemy lines. In a perverse way, this misconception only heightened Col's sense of self-importance. But the fact was, Young Dick was tired, and merely wanted to know what Col Morton was doing unannounced in his kitchen on a Thursday evening. Nell didn't care about Col, either: she was worried about Abigail. Twitch, while enjoying the look of discomfort on Col Morton's face, was wondering what to buy his youngest granddaughter for her upcoming birthday. Old Dick was wondering when he would get his cup of tea.

And Abigail?

'Tell me what's happened,' said Abigail.

Col chewed his lip and considered the ceiling. He continued to avoid Abigail's eye. 'I'd rather not talk about it with ladies present.'

Abigail leaned back and screeched with laughter. 'Tosser.'

'I don't get it,' said Old Dick.

'Sounds like this guy's dipped his wick in someone he regrets,' said Abigail, pointing at Col, 'and thinks he shouldn't explain himself around Mum and me because we're not cock-carrying members of society.'

'That makes sense,' Old Dick said. 'Sorry, Luce.'

Abigail took her grandfather's hand and squeezed it. Nell leaned over and patted his arm. Young Dick set tea in front of Old Dick and Abigail.

'So who'd you bone, Col?' Abigail asked.

Col kept his eyes somewhere around the light fixture.

Then Abigail said, 'Hold on. Mum said "married". And you said "Jess". Col—did you fuck Jessica Bram?'

Silence fell in the kitchen. Everyone heard a different tone in Abigail's voice; each witness filtered her question through the lens of what they themselves thought about Col Morton right at that moment.

To Col, Abigail sounded incredulous, like they were fifteen again and sex was an awesome, slightly alien concept.

To Young Dick, his daughter sounded somewhere between bored and mildly disgusted.

Twitch thought Abigail was pissed off as hell, because it was Jessica Bram who'd started the accusations about her twenty-four years ago.

Old Dick thought deckies had gotten too fresh these days and needed a good kick up the backside.

But it was Abigail's mother who heard the truth in Abigail's voice—and that truth was, simply, that Abigail thought the idea of Col Morton and Jessica Bram was hilarious. Because, goddamn, what a juicy can of worms that opened.

How far back did the grudge between the Fancys and the Brams go?

It would depend who was asked (it would also depend who was doing the asking) but in Port Kingerton it was generally accepted the grudge began when Lucy—back then she was Lucy Neal—ran off with the young fisherman named Richard Fancy when she was betrothed to another young fisherman named Edward Bram.

Now, 'ran off' would also be a description that varied, dependent upon who was doing the telling. Lucy Neal was a catch. In a remote fishing outpost where the young ladies tended towards unpolished and swarthy, Lucy was pretty and refined. But not in a way that would put a man off his work. She might be sweet but she had backbone. She liked tea cakes but she also sucked the meat from lobster legs, and she once waded into a freezing soak up to her waist to rescue a stuck calf.

Some said Ed Bram might have stood a chance had Richard Fancy not stood to gain so much. Lucy, the only child of a local beef farmer whose great-grandparents had slapped ashore on one of South Australia's first colonist ships, came with a substantial land inheritance, and the marriage of Richard's father's rock lobster licence with Lucy's father's land was a merging of assets too beneficial to overlook.

So, whether Lucy ran, or was pushed, also varied from one story to another.

But if those closer to the situation were asked—Lucy herself, say—the story contains nothing about assets at all. Simply: Dick Fancy was a cat. To Lucy he was handsome and playful, quick-witted and honey-mouthed. Lucy had *liked* Ed Bram, but she had not *loved* him. This she realised when she began spending more time with Dick Fancy after her father employed Dick to undertake odd jobs around the house: fix a sagging gutter; sweep the chimney; remove a dead possum from the rainwater tank. These were jobs Lucy could have done herself but when she came of age and Edward Bram began calling, her father decided someone else was better suited to those tasks and that someone else could only be Richard Fancy.

That it's likely the grudge appeared earlier than Old Dick and Ed was rarely commented upon.

Because by the time Abigail Fancy and Jessica Bram began scrapping over who got to hand out the orange slices on Miss Partridge's story-time mat, new grudges began to be far more interesting than old ones.

Especially when the intervening generation had laboured for peace. And frankly, peace is boring.

OLD DICK

I don't recall asking for a cuppa tea, but it appears I've got one. Look at it there, steaming away in front of me. I'd rather be making sure no bastard's stolen my mooring before I die than drinking tea with this lot, but you can't always have everything you want.

The way I see it, this deckie needs a good kick up the backside. Standing there wringing his hands, not looking his captain in the eye? In my day he'd be icing his arse for a week.

Okay, so he's been messing with a skirt he shouldn't have messed with. Blah blah blah. Have these people never met a deckie before? They'll chase after anything that moves and even a few things that don't. It's not worth fighting. It's better to just let them get it out of their system. A man with skirts in his head is a man daydreaming, likely to get himself knocked into the reef. I'd rather they flog it out themselves somewhere I don't have to know about than me flogging it out of them with a piece of hose.

Now the deckie looks like he's seen a tiger snake and he's backpedalling himself into the doorway. Gives his head a hard, loud clunk on the architrave.

The young woman with the black eye is laughing. She makes me nervous when she laughs because I really do worry that something is going to come out of her, she laughs that hard.

The young fella says, *No one's flogging anyone, Dad.*

The meat-headed bloke with the tattoo up his neck says, *Speak for yourself, Dicky.*

That's enough, the woman says. She sounds stern but she takes my hand and squeezes it. I like it when she does that. Reminds me of Luce. Now the young woman's hugging me again. Jeepers, they're handsy, this mob.

All right, I say. I'm dying, but no need to make a song and dance of it.

Look, I say. You want to make a deckie behave himself? I'll tell you what I know. Listen up.

ABIGAIL

A bustle of activity went around the table.

Chairs scraped as her father and Twitch stood up, Twitch issuing a suggestion to Col that he wait outside and gird himself for the lighthouse, her father countering with an instruction that there was no need for that kind of talk. Her mother proclaimed Old Dick needed milk in his tea and that *Doc Martin* was about to start, and wasn't it cold enough to light the wood stove?

Over the top of them, Abigail called out to Col, 'Was it worth it?'

Backing rapidly from the kitchen, Col met her eyes over Twitch's broad shoulder.

She grinned.

Then Col vanished as Twitch cuffed him on the side of the head.

Abigail left the kitchen and made her way upstairs. In the shower she closed her eyes and leaned her head against the tiles, letting the hot water rinse away the stench of cow. Her ears rung; she could feel her pulse in her feet. Moving as if she were asleep standing up, she brushed her teeth, pulled on the *Holden Repair Kit* T-shirt, clicked off the bathroom light.

She found Nell sitting on her bed.

'I told you,' Abigail said, 'you can have your jeans back tomorrow.'

'You didn't finish your tea.' Her mother pointed to the bedside where Abigail's cold, half-drunk cup of tea was sitting.

Abigail climbed into bed. She tried to pull the blankets up but Nell's weight pinned them in place. Waiting for whatever it was her mother had to say, the heaviness of her mother's body at her feet, Abigail felt time collapse and once again she was fifteen. Anticipating a lecture.

From downstairs came the low drone of men's voices. Neither Abigail nor her mother spoke for some time.

She'd almost drifted off when Nell said, 'I wanted …' She cleared her throat, shifted her weight, and started again. 'I wanted to see if you were okay.'

'I'm fine.'

'After what was brought up, in the kitchen.'

'I said I'm fine.'

Her mother's jaw clenched.

Abigail changed the subject. 'Why'd everyone hustle out?'

Nell sighed. 'Noise can upset your grandfather. Your father prefers it if people don't overhear everything he says.'

She struggled to sit up. 'Why?' Abigail thought that even if her grandfather didn't seem lucid, he wasn't unaware.

Surely he knew when he was being silenced. He'd said *I'll tell you what I know* and the room emptied.

Her mother looked uncomfortable. 'Because once he gets started, it's hard for him to remember where to stop. His memories come out mixed together. What really happened gets confused with story, or town legend. His concept of what's confidential has gone.' Nell paused, staring into the middle distance. 'We've worked hard to make sure the past stays there. To keep things peaceful.'

'Peaceful,' Abigail repeated, deadpan. 'Does that mean something different to you than it does to me?'

Her mother didn't reply.

'That seems cruel,' Abigail added. 'To close Grandpa down like that.'

'We care about him,' Nell said crossly. 'We're looking after him. Living with dementia is not easy. Living with your father-in-law who is living with dementia is not easy, either. It's been six years. You haven't been here and I don't need your opinion.' Pressing her hands to her face, Nell rubbed her eyes in that long-suffering way.

Eight years ago, when her grandmother died, Abigail thought of coming back. Just for a couple of days. But she'd made excuses—pathetic ones, she can't even remember what they were—and stayed away. Six years was a long time, she conceded to her mother now.

'After Lucy died he was never the same. When he started forgetting to eat, he moved in.'

Abigail could say it. *I'm sorry I wasn't here.* But she didn't. Her grandmother died, her grandfather declined, her brothers left and her parents became caregivers again and she wasn't here. She felt like a lowlife.

'He keeps saying he's dying,' Abigail said.

'He is. But I suppose we all are.'

Abigail was quiet.

'Time passes differently for him. He talks about dying when he remembers Lucy died.' Nell gave a short smile. 'Usually when he's said something rude. He's waiting for her to tell him off. And his memory might be declining but his emotional responses aren't. Especially the strong ones.'

'His personality hasn't changed.'

'No. He's always been a gruff bugger. It's an important part of his identity, disease or not.'

Abigail laughed softly.

Another quiet settled between them. Muffled voices continued to float up from the lounge room. Abigail took a sip of her cold tea. 'Hell,' she said. 'I am tired.'

Her mother's expression was guarded. 'And yet, you're going out again tomorrow.'

Abigail pushed her fingertip around the rim of her cup. 'I need the money.'

'We can give you money.'

'No.'

'Don't be stubborn.'

'Don't be *you*.'

'Are you really that broke?' her mother asked. 'You were managing a high-end restaurant.'

'It was still just a fortnightly salary. It's not like I had investments. Throw in all those fees and fines and it's—' she snapped her fingers '—gone.'

'I wish you'd let us help you.'

'I'm here, aren't I?'

'Why don't you tell me—'

'Jesus Christ, I'm tired of telling. I'm tired of explaining. For what? Who's actually listening? Because what I will *tell you* is after a while, all the explaining? Starts to feel like it's not actually for *me*, but for *you*, for everyone demanding their goddamn pound of flesh. And I give it, and give it, and give it, and it's *still not enough*.'

The men's voices had gone silent. Nell's eyes were hard. Abigail's heart galloped against her ribs.

'So,' her mother said. 'You're not fine.'

'I never was,' she replied. 'Not for any of you.'

The next morning, Abigail walked to town in a cold drizzle. Shabby clouds dashed across a pale sky, light rain coming in bursts that made her squint, mist clinging to her eyelashes. After yesterday's storm, fresh mounds of seaweed piled the shore and stunk the place up.

All she wanted to do was buy a cheap phone and some clothes while speaking to no one. But speak to no one in Port Kingerton? Fat chance.

'Miss Fancy,' said Mrs Dinwiddle from behind the counter as Abigail stepped into the post office. 'By my very own eyes.'

Abigail considered the postmistress and found that Mrs Dinwiddle looked exactly the same as she had twenty-three years ago, as if she had reached an approximate physical age somewhere between fifty and eighty and stayed there, preserved, unaffected by the passage of time. Same tight-curled white hair, small chin sunk into drooping jowls. Abigail recalled those jowls swinging when the postmistress

marched out the back door of the post office to shoo
Abigail and her friends off the stone wall under an over-
hanging peppermint gum where they would sit smoking
Escort Blues or sucking Chupa Chups.

A shuffle of movement to Abigail's left. Glancing over,
she saw three ladies begin intently studying a rack of greeting cards.

Mrs Dinwiddle side-stepped into her line of sight. 'How
are you, dear?'

On display were three phones: eight hundred dollars,
three hundred dollars, ninety-nine. All too expensive. *Fuck!*
She chomped on a fingernail. Then something caught her
eye, the flash of a red sticker. Stepping closer to the counter,
she pointed and said, 'I'll take that one.'

'I'm sorry?'

'That phone. Forty-nine bucks.'

'It's damaged, love.'

'Does it work?'

'Of course.' Mrs Dinwiddle looked flustered. 'I wouldn't
sell it otherwise. A small crack on the screen is all. But don't
you want something a bit … fancier?'

Abigail looked over at the rack of greeting cards and the
ladies' eyes bolted down again.

'It's locked to a network.'

'You get more than one network here?'

'Surely you want something better,' Mrs Dinwiddle said,
her face pinking. 'For Instagram and so forth. This one is
only two megapixels.'

'What's a megapixel, Bev?'

The postmistress looked lost.

Abigail put three fifties on the counter: one singly, two next to it. 'That's for the phone; that's a bank deposit,' she said, pointing to each pile.

The postmistress picked up the cash but made no move towards the register. 'I saw your mum yesterday. She told me all about how you were back.' She left a long pause and Abigail began to wonder if she would ever walk out of here with this crappy broken phone. 'Must be nice being home after all this time?'

Shifting her weight to the side, Abigail jutted one knee, leaned forward and dug her fingers into her itchy thigh. She kept scratching until Mrs Dinwiddle finally bent under the counter, retrieved the box and handed it to her.

Another long pause. Mrs Dinwiddle's eyes darted across her face, left and right, like tiny search lights.

'Is ... is there something else, dear?'

'Change, Bev.'

'Sorry?'

'You owe me a dollar.' Holding up the box, Abigail tapped the price sticker.

The postmistress went puce. Abigail took her dollar in change, finalised the cash deposit, and left the post office.

The rain stopped and the sun was out. Abigail crossed the street and walked onto the lawn in front of the beach. She stood in that scrap of sun, breathing the seaweed-heady air. Only a few cray boats remained in the harbour. The ocean foamed against the breakwater.

Wet grass stuck to her red boots as she walked. She passed the playground. The splintery old lighter on tractor springs was gone, replaced by a plastic tunnel slide. She remembered carving *Jess Bram is a ho* into the side of that lighter with a compass, lead paint flaking onto her fingers. The phone booth in which they'd prank freecall numbers—*Hi, Anita Sickadick? No? How about a Welladick?*—had been replaced with a wifi hotspot. Public art, rusted steel tubing contorted into geometric shapes, painted in seagull crap. The old toilet block was gone. They had bulldozed it not long after she left. A new one stood under the trees a little further west.

She had to stop and swallow. Press her fingernails into her palms.

A weird sense struck her. Town seemed hushed for a Friday morning. Although she was used to the relentless clamour of prison, and before that the city, so maybe Kingo was always this quiet. She couldn't remember. She had a feeling like she was being watched but when she looked around there was no one in sight.

Far ahead, beyond the rise towards the scrub, she saw the point of the lighthouse. Last night Twitch had joked about taking Col Morton up there. Col Morton had rooted Jessica Bram in the pub kitchen, apparently, while Little Jase Turner made schnitzels. Had Twitch's joke about beating the crap out of Col been for her benefit? Did people still think she gave a toss about Jessica Bram? *We've worked hard to keep things peaceful*, her mother had said.

'Peace my arse,' Abigail said, and a seagull strutting nearby stopped and aimed one beady eyeball at her.

Tearing open the box, she fished out the phone, hairline crack trailing across the screen from top to bottom. She put in the SIM and turned it on. She went through the start-up menu and, after what felt like an age standing by the wifi hotspot, began to type.

Hey.

Three dots appeared, then, *Thank god. Thought you died or something.*

Lol no.

How is it?

Still a hole. IOU $90. Send deets.

WTF for?

Bus ticket and Maccas.

Nope.

Yes fkn.

Fine.

Three dots wiggled, then Jen's account details appeared.

Thanks. Kiss the babies for me. And thanks, u know?

I do. Take care babe. Give em hell.

Abigail thought maybe she might cry, but she didn't. After making the transfer to Jen she checked the time; less than two hours before Nate would pick her up. The sun disappeared and the misty rain returned. Shoving the phone in her pocket, she tossed the box in the bin. Then she crossed the street and went into the hardware-cum-surf store.

THEM

Penny Bram was refilling the pie warmer when she heard the squeak of the deli's back door. Rather than actively placing frozen pies into the warmer, however, Penny had been holding the tongs and looking out the window.

A few minutes earlier, town had been busy and Penny had had a run of customers. There had been coffees to brew, hot pasties to place in brown paper bags and all the morning papers had gone. Then, as abruptly as if someone had thrown a switch, the street fell silent. At first Penny didn't notice, moving into the lull by retrieving the tray of frozen pies, but when the quiet continued she happened to glance out the shop's front window, and there *she* was.

Abigail Fancy, strolling casually along the beachfront.

Firing off a quick text to her daughter, Penny stood in front of the pie warmer, a still-life in the act of filling it, watching Abigail out the window until she heard the back door opening and turned to see Beverly Dinwiddle's frame appear through the plastic strips.

'Bev,' Penny said. 'If it's a toastie you're after, I'm all out.' It would only take Penny a few minutes to make a sandwich, if that's indeed why Mrs Dinwiddle was here, but Penny was still piqued with the postmistress after yesterday morning, when she had bailed Penny up in her own kitchen and practically called her daughter Jessica a slut.

But the postmistress did not want a sandwich.

'I've just had Abigail Fancy in the post office,' said Mrs Dinwiddle.

'Oh?'

'Yes. And I'm afraid to say, she's up to something.'

'How so?'

'She purchased a phone.' The postmistress came behind the counter and stepped right in close to Penny Bram, so close that Penny could smell the rose-scented talc the postmistress sprinkled on herself after her morning wash.

'A phone?' said Penny, pushing aside pies to make room for pasties.

'Yes.' Mrs Dinwiddle leaned in and stage whispered, 'A burner phone.'

Penny set down the tongs. 'A what?'

Mrs Dinwiddle gestured to the front windows, out of which both women could see Abigail standing by the wifi spot, ripping open a box.

'A burner phone,' the postmistress repeated. 'Something that can be used to make illicit calls and dumped. Untraceably.'

'You been watching *Breaking Bad* again, Bev?'

Mrs Dinwiddle sniffed. 'I'm not interested in gossip. I'm just passing along something that may be important, for the future. Because of, you know—' She pursed her lips and lifted her chin, indicating the sordid business between Col Morton and Penny Bram's daughter Jessica in the pub kitchen that she did not want to spell out explicitly.

'I see,' said Penny. 'And how exactly does this—' now Penny waved a hand at the window, Abigail Fancy '—concern me and my "future"?'

'She also deposited cash.'

'How much cash?'

'I'm not at liberty to say.'

Penny reconsidered Abigail Fancy out the window. Now Abigail had discarded the box and was staring intently at the phone in her hand. A few seagulls had landed near her feet. Penny told herself that the reason Nell's daughter appeared so transfixing through the window was not because of who she was, but merely because her red pants were so bright against the green of the grass and the blue of the harbour, circled by the snowy dots of the gulls. It was an arresting display of colours, that's all. Penny would tell everyone that's why Abigail had caught her eye: the colours.

Two doors up, at the gift shop, Jessica Bram was also staring out the window.

Jessica happened to be looking at her phone when the text from her mother came in—*Abigail Fancy out front*—so Jessica had looked out front and indeed, there was Abigail, limping painfully along the grass.

A few minutes earlier Jessica had also been busy with a sudden rush of customers: a fisherman's wife bought six miniature potted succulents; a pair of tourists bought a handful of postcards; a hippy from just across the border had wanted the display of crystals unwrapped so she could hold them in her hand and decide which one was calling to her.

Jessica liked working in the gift shop. She liked its unpredictable, eclectic flow of customers, so different from the deli, whose mind-dulling patterns she could set her watch by. When the hippy had picked a smoky quartz and left, the store was empty, so Jessica sat down and took out her phone. But she had not gotten far in deciding what angle of her breasts to send to Col Morton when her mother's text appeared and she had been obliged to leap to her feet and go to the front window.

So, yes, there was Abigail Fancy, alone on the grass in the middle of town, opening a box and taking something out of it. What was it? Jess wondered briefly, then recognised the item as a phone.

Jessica watched Abigail for a while, waiting for her to do something, but nothing happened. Abigail continued to stare at the phone. Jessica had to wonder what Abigail was doing. As far as she was aware, Abigail Fancy was not on Instagram, Twitter, Snapchat, TikTok, Pinterest, YouTube or LinkedIn; once, Abigail had been on Facebook, but a while back Jessica noticed her account had disappeared, or Abigail had changed her name to something untraceable and unfriended any mutual friends through which Jessica may have been able to find her, or those mutual friends had changed their names, too. So, given how long Abigail was staring at that phone, Jessica had to assume Abigail was messaging someone. Jessica watched and waited, but Abigail appeared to take no photos or videos of herself, nor anything else. Not even a seagull.

Then Jessica's phone buzzed with a message from her mother.

Dinwiddle says Abigail Fancy bought a burner phone

Jessica pressed her nose against the glass. In the time it had taken her to glance down at the message, Abigail had moved. Now she was putting something in the bin.

Jessica sucked in a short breath.

omg she just put it in the bin! she typed to her mother.

She deposited cash too, her mother wrote.

how much

Dinwiddle says 'literally too much for her to say'

Jessica jerked back from the window as Abigail stepped onto the street.

Adrian Turner was in the hardware-cum-surf store when Abigail came in. He was standing by the light globes, right by the entrance, looking for a ninety watt bulb to replace his mother's blown back porch light which his useless little brother still had not fixed. The door opened and there she was.

Abigail Fancy, gliding into the store: a vision in red pants and boots, hair in glorious disarray from the salt mist. Strands of it, blonde as cut wheat, clung to her flushed cheeks and moist lips and Adrian had the image of peeling those strands of hair from her mouth with the crooked tip of his finger; he imagined feeling her humid breath on his knuckle, how his own lips might part in mirror of hers. He remembered the sensation of her hot breath in his face in the car on Wednesday morning.

Instantly Adrian's head snapped back to the light globes, searching with a renewed sense of urgency, now feeling intense gratitude for his brother having not already done it.

Abigail's footsteps moved behind Adrian, slowly away from him, clop-clopping down the aisle. He ached to turn around, to see where Abigail's attention was directed, to find out what need or interest had called her into the store.

'Abigail, love!' called David Wimple from behind the counter. 'Long time. How's things going, eh?'

Adrian waited for the sound of Abigail's reply but when it did not come he swivelled his head, peering over his shoulder into the dim depths of the store. He couldn't see her; the shadows of cheap surfboards had swallowed her up. He caught the store owner's eye. David Wimple shrugged.

Turning away from the light globes, Adrian stepped into the aisle. He made his way along it, pulse rushing in his ears. Reaching the surfboards at the end of the aisle, he turned and found Abigail at the back wall. Her head was bent forward, her hair falling loose across her face. In her hands was a blue work shirt wrapped in plastic. As Adrian watched, she set the shirt back on the shelf and picked up another; the plastic made a dull rustle.

A gift for her father, maybe? Adrian wondered. Or her brothers? Hamish and Dylan worked up north, FIFO workers on a gold mine. He dismissed that idea. Her brothers would buy their own shirts. People were saying Abigail had spent yesterday with that new vet, the blow-in who had replaced dead old Carlisle—maybe the shirt was for him? At that thought, Adrian felt sour.

'Are you going to watch me the entire time?'

His mouth went dry. Abigail lifted her head to look at him and he saw the bruise around her eye had lightened at the edges to a greenish hue. She was wearing a baggy jumper and the neckline had slipped, revealing the milky ridge of one collarbone. He wanted to press his tongue to it.

Adrian cleared his throat. 'Sorry,' he said. 'Just wondering if you want some help?'

'You work here?'

'Oh,' Adrian said with a diffident laugh, shaking his head. 'No.'

'You just like to offer assistance to customers in any store?'

'Uh, no.'

Abigail returned to looking at the shirt. She dropped it back on the shelf and picked up another. When she moved, all of her moved, all hips and breasts and belly, and Adrian felt a desperate sense of not knowing what to do. Three times in his life he had kissed Abigail Fancy—once under the old lighter at the playground; the second time at a party at Ricky Leake's house; and the third time she had turned her head away at the last minute but his mouth had still connected with the edge of hers—and he could feel every one of those kisses tingling on his lips now. He watched as she moved away from the shirts and towards the rack of pants, a single rail with a few pairs in shades of blue and brown. Her fingers played across the hangers as if checking for a particular size, and watching her fingers flick and listening to the barely audible click and scrape of the hangers sent a frisson of hypnotic pleasure across Adrian's scalp. She took a hanger off the rack and Adrian blinked rapidly to wake himself up.

'What do you think?' Abigail said, turning her body square on to Adrian and holding the pants at her waist.

A few years back, when Adrian and his kids' mum were still living together, he had once worn a denim shirt with denim jeans and his ex had called him a dickhead. In terms of fashion sense, Adrian knew that pants went on legs and a T-shirt on a torso, maybe a jumper if it was cold, and that was it. His two daughters didn't seem to care much about clothes either, as long as the item was not yellow (the five-year-old) and didn't have annoying seams (the three-year-old), so Adrian could not even claim to have absorbed some fashion insights from them. And his ex? Adrian tried to remember, but come to think of it, he couldn't picture Sal from the neck down at all, even though he saw her every day. *Huh*, he thought now, *maybe Sal was right*. He *didn't* pay attention to her.

'You having a stroke?'

Adrian started as if a gun had gone off. He realised he had not answered Abigail's first question about the pants, and now she had asked him another and still he was standing there, slack-jawed as a dog in the sun.

'I'm not looking for your actual opinion,' Abigail said. 'Relax.'

'They look nice,' Adrian said at last. 'They suit you.' The pants were a kind of dark green with reinforced patches at the knees and pockets all over the place.

Abigail snorted softly, and the sound unclogged something in Adrian. She went to put the pants back on the rack but for some inexplicable reason, Adrian found himself continuing.

'Very flattering,' he said. 'I like the colour.'

Abigail glanced back down at the pants. 'Khaki does it for you?'

He was trying to stop but the words seemed to keep coming. 'The pockets would be really handy. You could keep your purse and phone and ...' he flailed, '... lip gloss in there.'

Abigail's eyebrows twitched.

'And I like how the bottom of the leg is, like—' he found his finger pointing, waggling, '—cut out, that way, in a curve. It's trendy—'

'I think it's just cut for work boots but okay.'

'—and figure-hugging—'

'Good to know, Giorgio.'

'—and slimming—'

Abigail returned the hanger to the rack. 'Dude,' she said, and he thought she was trying not to laugh but he couldn't be sure, 'stand down. I think you're about to say something you might regret.'

Adrian felt his eyeballs darting about, between the pants and shirts and Abigail. He could not find an explanation for what had just occurred, the things that had spouted out of his mouth about pants. Adrian Turner did not care about pants; he did not care what anyone wore unless they were wearing nothing and he'd rather they weren't (his little brother) or were wearing something and he'd rather they took it off (pretty much any woman over the legal age). But he found himself with such a desire to hold Abigail's attention, to insert himself into her day. Is this what feminists were going on about, he thought, when they talked about male entitlement? Was he mansplaining, he wondered, to his horror.

Abigail crossed her arms and considered him, and Adrian felt undressed. 'Look,' he said. 'The other day, when I saw you. I'm sorry I brought up … the past.'

Abigail said nothing.

'I wasn't thinking straight, I guess. That was uncool.' He could see her nostrils flare slightly, her chest expanding as if she were taking a deep breath. 'It just took me straight back to when we were kids,' Adrian explained, 'seeing you on the side of the hill like that. All these fun memories came up.'

'Are you serious?'

'Well, no. What I brought up … that memory wasn't fun. Sorry.' But he'd said it now, he'd cracked the ice, so he ventured, 'Did you keep in touch with her?'

'With who?' she asked, but he heard in her voice that she knew.

'Honnie.'

A beat. Then, 'No.'

'Ever? Not even after—'

'I said no.'

He gulped. But he'd asked. And he had the sensation of being stronger for it. Had anyone else in Port Kingerton been brave enough, Adrian wondered, to voice that *thing* they had all been thinking? Had anyone else—all those folk stalking about, talking big, reckoning they knew it all— had the balls to actually walk up to Abigail Fancy and put it there, at her feet, like a steak in front of a tiger? They had not, Adrian told himself. Overinflated chicken shits, the lot of them.

'Listen.' He took a step towards her. 'If you need anything, I'm always around.'

'Oh, yeah?' said Abigail. 'What might I need?'

Adrian felt a grin spread slowly across his face. 'Ah, you know,' he said with a shrug. 'To, like, talk, maybe? Or just hang. Whatever.'

Abigail tapped her lips with a finger, a thoughtful expression on her face. 'Hmm,' she said. 'Talk or hang. What a choice.'

A long pause ensued and Adrian began to wither inside, but then Abigail smiled. 'So what's your take on all this?' she asked.

'The ... pants?'

'The leg bone,' she said. 'And Lofty's boat.' Then she stepped closer to him, lowered her voice and added, 'And Col Morton shagging Jessica Bram in the pub kitchen.'

Adrian felt he was soaring.

OLD DICK

Ask me how long I've lived here and I'd tell you this: I can't say.

Maybe I got here yesterday, or maybe I've always been here. A man can't always keep track of these sorts of residential things, he has better things to do. Luce would know, though.

By 'here' I mean this house—not Port Kingerton. Don't even dare ask me how long I've lived in Port Kingerton because I'll knock your block off. I was born here, just like my father and my grandfather and my great—no, wait, I think that one floated here from England. My point is, I've been here forever. So the house doesn't matter. I can't see the house right now, anyway. I'm in the middle of a paddock.

This is the back lawn, Dad. Thought you might like some sun while it's out.

What are you calling a lawn? This is a paddock, boy. Look at that clover and ryegrass. And look there—a goose. Who wants goose turd all over their lawn? No one, that's who. So it's a paddock.

The mare's gonna foal soon. You want to take a look at her? Make a bet when it'll be born?

All right, I'll look at your mare. But I'm better with heifers, it must be said.

I know, Dad. You're good with cattle. Mum was, too—remember? She could always pick which cow would calve next. Every time. He gives a laugh and I don't know why he's amused because he's right. Luce never got it wrong.

Speaking of Mum, look at that—your chrysanthemums are coming into bloom. That's special. Luce loved the 'mums, didn't she, boy? You remember? I feel so happy, seeing those yellow and pink petals. Bunches of them on the kitchen table in autumn, brightening up the dreary days when cray season's finished and the weather cools and the skies turn grey—

Wait, I say. Wait. Why've you got a mare foaling in autumn?

The young fella sighs. *She got out.*

What kind of a farmer lets his mares run loose, getting themselves into trouble? A drongo, that's who. No wonder you don't know when she's gonna foal. Give me a look at her. I'll do my best, but you're really better off asking Luce. She'll know. She always knows. She knew when that girl was in trouble and she was right.

Dad—

No, listen to me. Because I didn't listen to her. Your mum told me there was trouble. She said that man was a bad egg, but I said there's no proof. I thought she was just being a gossip—your mum was queen of the grapevine, after all— and a man can't go accusing another man of that kind of unpleasant business without proof. But she was right. Because they found the child, poor little mite, and then what happened? All hell broke loose. Because I didn't listen to your mother. So listen to me, boy, because it's when people start ignoring each other and making up their own stories and believing those made-up stories as if they're real, that the truth gets lost and no one can tell their elbow from their arse anymore. That's how lynch mobs happen. I know because I've seen it. The minute you stop listening? People lose their heads.

ABIGAIL

Dubiously, Abigail considered the work shirt on the bed. Dusty plastic wrapper, orange 'clearance' sticker faded and peeling. After buying the phone and shirt, she had just two dollars left.

A vague low-level anxiety gnawed. Her fingers fluttered with the craving for a smoke.

So, there it was: a return of that old urge to run. When she'd settled at the restaurant, into her tiny apartment in the city, she'd thought that perhaps, finally, she'd outgrown it. That she might be experiencing what everyone else seemed to at a certain point in life: the desire to *settle down*. But now she could feel that familiar pressure, an inner voice goading her forwards. Just like that cow breaking for the gate, the promise of liberation was within reach, if only she'd hustle.

She took the shirt from the wrapper. Although she'd not been at all interested, David Wimple at the hardware store had told her this particular size had been discontinued. 'That's why it's on clearance, you see?' he'd said, while Adrian Turner, hovering behind her, kept talking about how handy pockets were. The shirt reached her knees but at least it buttoned up.

In her parents' bedroom, she took a pair of her father's work pants. She attempted to roll the hems but gave up. She'd tuck them into her boots.

Descending the stairs, she wondered how she was going to manage another day with the vet, then remembered the two dollars in her pocket, dredged up a reserve of determination and headed out.

Less than an hour away, today's dairy was closer than yesterday's, and this time only thirty cows required Nate's services.

'A walk in the park,' Abigail said, mostly to reassure herself.

Nate glanced across at her. He was freshly shaven and smelled minty clean. 'Head-to-toe Hard Yakka?' he observed.

'You have a trained eye for workwear.'

'Not usually,' he said.

'You're flirting? Be still my beating heart.'

He didn't answer, but since he had raised the topic of clothing, she felt unashamed to give him a thorough once-over. In the daylight she was able to take in the way his jeans were snug around his thighs. She wanted to run her hands over his quads. Had her stomach not rumbled at that moment, she very well may have.

It was an amiable ride to the dairy. Not an unpleasant afternoon. A repeat of the day before—sweeping, fetching, cajoling—but there was a sense of being less time-pressed, more relaxed. This farmer was not worth the millions of yesterday's; the underwritten sense of commercial urgency and authority was gone. She'd swear the cows felt it too, as they held their great swaying rumps politely for the vet to thrust his arm inside and not a single one of them shat on his boot or kicked him in the shin.

'How is it?' she asked Nate of the wound on his leg.

'It stings a bit,' he admitted, and Abigail found she adored him for the way he didn't try to bloke his way out of it, ridiculously playing it up or down.

The hours passed and she ate, kept herself hydrated and did everything she could to stay on her feet, knowing each hour was worth twenty-five more dollars, a rate so generous it would be an insult to every farmhand if she didn't earn it. Especially in her tenuous position. So she made sure that she did.

Which was how her guard went down. The pleasantness, the industriousness, the measured husbandry of her aches and fatigue—this was how, when the farmer's wife came out to the shed late in the afternoon, Abigail didn't think to keep herself aside, to maintain a certain aloofness, and instead came forward to take a cup of coffee, smiling.

The farmer's wife was a rugged woman in her sixties, check-shirted and hard-bitten, jeans cinched high over wide hips. Abigail could imagine her smacking a rolling pin against her palm one minute, roping calves the next.

'I know you,' the woman said, after a moment's critical appraisal. 'You're Nell Fancy's girl.' She held her hand out flat, halfway down her thigh. 'Last time I saw you, you were this big.' She turned to the farmer, a grizzled man with grey hair sprouting in clods from his ears. 'What're you doing hiring a Fancy kid?'

The farmer appeared confused. 'I dunno.'

'You should've checked with me first. Before you went off getting girls.'

His reply was inaudible.

'Especially a Fancy.'

Abigail's blood went hot.

'She's with me,' said Nate.

The farmer's wife sized up Nate. 'You hired her?'

'Sure,' Nate said mildly.

'You know she went to jail?'

The words ricocheted around the shed. One of the cows in the yard outside let out an indignant bellow. The farmer's eyebrows twitched, cracking open his craggy face in surprise.

An unsettling sensation came over Abigail. Later she would recognise it as time slowing, a pause of the clock. Words lifted in her throat and her tongue prepared to release the barbs of an instinctive reply—*Mention this shit again and I'll rip your fucking balls off. You're welcome, bitch. I'm never fucking coming back*—but what unspooled in front of her was a vision of the immediate future, a future that all of a sudden she did not want. If she defended herself, if she stood up to the farmer's wife, she could see the situation inflaming, the woman's indignation justified, her scorn validated. Possibly a bloody punch-up. But if Abigail said nothing, if she bit her tongue and swallowed her defence, she would simmer in a stew of resentment, sick with anger and regret and self-betrayal, and later she would erupt with

it, lashing out at someone or something else. Either way—
defend or submit—Abigail would lose. The two-way choice
in front of her was maddening and intolerable.

But it was also, she realised now, utterly false. Because
that old two-way street—react or simmer, lose or lose—was
no longer the only path. And that path only existed if she
believed it was all she had.

Now it dawned on her. There was another route.

What did she really want? Realising that she did not want
either of the first two options cracked open the understanding that there could be another. In this provoking place she
found herself, and would always find herself because life was
a mercurial freaking dance, she could carve a new, never
before taken, path out. *So, what do I really want?*

The problem was, she couldn't answer that. Not in the
split second the answer was required. All she could do was
stare, coffee cup halfway to her mouth, her speechless gaze
drilling holes into the farmer's wife as she continued to be
peeled open. Throw the coffee cup into the shed wall? Offer
a humble yet assertive explanation for her presence? Drop
to her knees in exhaustion and fall asleep on the concrete?

After what felt like an eternity, she drew breath to reply
but Nate cut in. 'That's true, Jackie,' he said, 'but I can't
afford not to. I've never seen anyone so good on an ATV.'

So it would be door number three, Abigail realised. Laugh
till you wet yourself.

Night had fallen by the time they left the dairy. They drove
in silence, the only sound the wheels churning on the road
and insects hitting the windscreen. Headlights made a

narrow tunnel in the dark, the white line flashing beneath the car.

Abigail fought the urge to lay her head against the window, imagining the cool glass against her temple. Instead she sat up straight, held erect by the last dogged shreds of her pride.

'All right?' Nate asked, after a time.

'Yep,' she replied, more curtly than she'd intended, because she was wearing his pants and not for a good reason.

No one else would have noticed, but that was no consolation. *She* knew. And Nate knew, because it was his spare pants she'd had to ask after, surreptitiously and red-faced, and was now sitting in, and goddamn if they did not do up. The past few days had been marked by an inordinate amount of borrowing other people's too-small clothes and she had reached the end of her rope. Listening to the farmer's wife, feeling as though she was standing in front of the magistrate again, experiencing the horrifying spread of warm liquid between her thighs had done it. She was dangling, facing a drop of god only knows how far before she would hit the ground.

Can't go back. Cannot, will not, go back.

'Okay,' Nate said, after another silence. 'I want to know.'

'I don't want to talk about it.'

'Not that,' he said, and had the mettle to put a hand out and gently squeeze her leg, just above her knee. If she hadn't recently pissed herself she might have been turned on. 'I want to know why you went inside.'

It wasn't a secret, her criminal record, but she needed a quid pro quo first. Before she laid it all bare, she needed from him the sharing of something more intimate, a little more endearing, than a total of two hundred and thirty cows' arses and one emergency pair of pants.

The cab was dim, lit by the bluish glow of the instruments on the dash. Nate was picked out by this glow and she slid her eyes up from his shoulders: his Adam's apple; the soft skin of his throat; the line of his jaw; the cleft in his chin. He caught her looking and held her eyes a beat longer than familiar. There were stars of light on his pupils.

'Okay, vet,' she said. 'I'm going to need something from you first.'

'Such as?'

'What've you got?'

He quirked his eyebrows.

'Come on. You spend your days handling the back ends of animals. Haven't you ever been embarrassed? I'm sure you've got dirt as long as your arm.' She leaned in. 'Even with those shoulder-length gloves.'

He flexed his hand on the wheel, making the muscles in his forearm shift beneath the skin. She resisted the urge to put her teeth on his bicep.

'I'm shite at texting,' he said.

'Weak,' she said.

'No.' He seemed adamant. 'It's how everyone communicates and I can't do it. It's like I'm cursed.'

'Really?'

'I once told a client she needed a good beefing.'

'"Beefing"?'

'Yes. Like a rogering, only with beef.'

'What did you mean to say?'

'That she needed good bloodstock. For her breeding cattle.'

'How'd you mess that up?'

'I don't know.' He sounded genuinely puzzled and frustrated, and she tried not to laugh. 'I told another client he needed to be put down.'

'Harsh.'

'And I once sent a photo to my ex with the words "next you'll want to knock these off".'

'I don't know what to ask first,' she said. 'The photo was of ...?'

'A Rottweiler's scrotum.'

'And it was meant for ...?'

'My first-year apprentice.'

Abigail dissolved into a fit of laughter.

'That's not all,' he said. 'I told an elderly alpaca farmer he was full of manure. I told a worried cat owner she categorically did have rabies. I sent a close-up of a Barber's pole worm to my son's religious ed teacher. And,' he finished, 'I don't know how many times I've sent "I love you" to clients instead of my son.'

'I get it,' she said, trying to recover, aware they had no more spare pants. 'But who hasn't had autocorrect make them look bad? I need something else. Your son's mum?'

His face was unreadable. 'What about her?'

'You're a long way from your son. What happened?'

He took a moment to answer. 'She's been far away from me for a long time.'

She waited, but her question went unanswered.

'So?' Nate said, after a while.

She watched night-dark paddocks flash past the window. She wondered where to begin. What it might mean to tell him.

When she had first moved to the city, it had not taken her long to discover the novelty in being able to say anything she wanted about her past. She could fabricate a backstory as colourful or as plain as she desired. For the first few months she slept on the couch of Zac Murphy's cousin, a self-employed part-time fridge repairman who cared only for his bong, but then she got a job as a live-in nanny for a wealthy young couple in Rose Park. So while for Zac Murphy's cousin she had simply been stir-crazy to get out of a small town, for the wealthy young couple she became an undergrad on her gap year ('Humanities,' she'd said vaguely) whose parents were in primary production ('Aquaculture') and found she was able to breathe. Her name conjured only blank stares or polite smiles; 'Fancy' meant nothing. She even liked herself better. Nanny work cheered her; it was hard to dwell on fear and anger when twin two-year-olds were refusing to nap and demanding cheese. For a few years she moved from one wealthy family to the next, chasing small children until she grew almost as exhausted as their mothers. She moved, found something else to do. Again and again.

But blood runs deep; shadows cannot be avoided forever. As the years passed and so did her twenties, her thirties, blood came up and spotlights swung into dark corners, illuminating the shadows huddled there.

So, she would run. From one job to the next, one place to the next. Booze or men or drugs could block it only for a while, until the next thing—the next town, job, bloke—offered hope. Liberty. Rest and restoration. If only she could run fast enough, she could be free.

Until she couldn't. Running will do that. Abigail had run hard and fast enough that each stumble and fall started to pile up: possession, hoon driving, driving under the influence. They didn't go away.

Her heart began to trip. 'Do you want the short version or the long version?'

'We've got time,' Nate said.

Abigail remembered the expression on the face of the farmer's wife—surprise, deflation and awkwardness—and how, when Nate had said, *She's with me*, Abigail had felt the unexpected shock of solidarity, the relief of it.

So she took a breath and began.

THEM

'Ade, can I ask you something?'

'You can pass me the screwdriver.'

Little Jase Turner picked up the screwdriver and handed it to his brother. They were on their mother's back porch and Adrian was balanced on a plastic patio chair, arms above his head, attempting to remove the cover over the porch light. Behind him the sunset was pink as the inside of a mouth, casting everything in a washed-blood hue.

'Why would Abigail need a burner phone?'

'What?' Adrian said, looking down at his brother from under his armpit. 'What are you talking about?'

'People are saying she bought a burner phone from the post office. And she deposited a bag of cash.'

'Don't believe everything you hear.'

'Well,' said Little Jase, scuffing his toe on the porch, 'that's what I wanted to ask you about.'

Adrian grunted. The screw was threaded. *Son of a bitch*, he thought. He did not want this right now. It was Friday night, the kids were with his ex, the footy was about to start and there was an unopened bottle of Jack Daniels on the passenger seat of his ute. An hour earlier, Adrian had popped open the pad of his thumb in the pipe bender. Split it like a ripe plum. He hadn't been paying attention, his head stuck back in the hardware store, full of the low murmur of Abigail Fancy's voice as she'd stepped close to him, close enough that he could still smell the scent of her hair, and asked him to imagine Col and Jessica in the pub kitchen. And Adrian had imagined it, and he hadn't stopped imagining it since. Only it wasn't Jessica Bram in his mental image, it was Abigail. And it wasn't that knobsack Col Morton, it was himself.

'Just whack it,' Little Jase offered, recognising the light cover was stuck.

'Whack your face,' Adrian answered, but he flipped the screwdriver and hit the butt of it against the cover.

'So what happened?' Little Jase asked. 'Was it like people are saying?'

'When?'

'When she left. Abigail Fancy.'

'She skipped town,' said Adrian, hitting the stuck light cover again and feeling his patience dwindling. 'And that was it.'

'Okay. *Before* she left, then. Was it, like, *really* bad?'

Adrian dropped his arms. The light cover remained glued to the eave. He reminded himself that his little brother was exactly that: little. Jase was twenty-seven—fifteen years younger than Adrian, a result of some later-in-life frolicking by his mother that he avoided contemplating. Jase had barely been in kindergarten when Abigail left, but that didn't mean he hadn't grown up with the stories. Adrian considered his brother now and saw the boyish innocence in his dipshit face.

'It must've been bad enough for her,' said Adrian. 'Because she took off when she was only sixteen.' He considered the light cover again, giving it another sharp rap. 'People were pretty mean to her. By the time she left it had been going on for a year or so. If I'd been putting up with that kind of crap for that long, I probably wouldn't stick around either.'

'Putting up with what?'

Casting his mind back, Adrian felt a surge of guilt. Earlier at the hardware store, Abigail had popped her hip and smiled up at him from under her eyelashes, and he'd felt giddy at the sound of her voice. Now he was overcome by the realisation that all those years ago, he had not helped her. At the time he'd thought that if not even her father or brothers could help, what use could he, Adrian, have been? He recalled the moment he had driven past Abigail, pedalling her bike furiously up the esplanade, and he could see something vivid and glossy down the back of her T-shirt, and as he got closer he saw that it was red paint. Some of it was in her hair. Someone had thrown red paint on her and he didn't stop. Why? he asked himself now. To hell with her family—why didn't *he* help?

'I was a chickenshit,' Adrian said, driving the screwdriver against the stuck light cover, but it remained fast.

'Tell me something I don't know,' Little Jase said. 'But that doesn't answer my question.'

'Fuck your question.' Adrian hammered the screwdriver against the light cover until the plastic shattered. A shower of dead beetles rained onto his head. 'I was too scared to go against the crowd. I did what everyone else did without even thinking about it because *that's just what we do*. There, you happy now?'

The two brothers glared at each other. Adrian was holding Jase responsible for everything: his darkening mood; the pain in his thumb; that unopened bottle of whiskey. He was even holding him responsible for his sudden churn of guilt and self-castigation.

'Do you think it's true, what people say she did?'

'Here's what is true,' Adrian told Jase. 'If I have to get down off this chair, I'll wring your neck, you freeloading douchebag scrote. You live here. Why am I always the one fixing the broken shit?' He shook clots of matted dust and spider webs from his hair. His phone buzzed in his back pocket but he ignored it.

'I just think, if it *is* true, why the hell would she come back? So maybe that bone—'

Adrian climbed down from the chair and his brother went silent. Adrian took his time dusting himself off. When he finally looked up, Little Jase was at the other end of the porch, eyeing him warily.

'Come here,' Adrian said. 'I'm gonna—'

Little Jase held up his phone. 'It's Twitch,' he said. 'He wants us at Young Dick's. Now.'

OLD DICK

My dad always said that if you want something done right you have to do it yourself. Then Ma would say that was a load of horse droppings.

As a kid I found this contradiction confusing, but it turned out they were both right. It's just a matter of balance.

For instance, one year my dad bought his own Christmas present. He wanted a pair of those fringed leather chaps (nobody knew why; it was the same year his brother died so we all reckon the grief just temporarily messed with Dad's head) and he knew Ma wouldn't be seen dead buying a pair, so he bought the chaps himself. Drove all the way to the big town, to one of those fancy saddlery outfitters. Wrapped them up, fringe and all, and set them under the tree. After Ma put them in the fireplace with a squirt of kerosene she didn't speak to him for a couple of days and then Dad snapped out of it and all was right again. My point: sometimes doing things for yourself isn't recommended; it's best to let others do it.

But then, when Billy Loft's cup-winning thoroughbred stallion was found poisoned stiff in his stall, Dad knew the only way to deal with the man responsible was to put him in craypots and dump him out on the reef. Neat and tidy, not troubling anyone who doesn't need to be troubled.

So, you see? It's all about balance. You have to think: Whose shoulders am I putting this burden on and do they need it, or should I just do it myself and do it right? And for that matter, who's putting a weight on *my* shoulders and do *I* need it, or should I tell them to get stuffed?

I can see the young fella thinking, mulling that over. He's chewing his lip and giving me a long hard look. A thinking look. The kind of look that heralds the arrival of an epiphany.

That's right, boy, I say. Listen to your dad.

That's the problem, he says, *I've been listening to you too much.*

Codswallop. If that were true you wouldn't be in this mess.

ABIGAIL

For a long time Abigail might have called her childhood lousy, but prison set her straight.

Sitting in Nate's four-wheel drive in the dark, she told him that. She explained that being surrounded by women whose lives were underscored by abuse, addiction, neglect, hounding by men, cops, DOCS or Centrelink, she realised that a childhood of feeling gently neglected, deeply frustrated or her identity railroaded by her name did not constitute lousy. Getting in trouble for stacking her roller skates down the hill? Not lousy. Chewed out for breaking Dylan's rib, for wagging school, for smoking? Nope. Getting into a fight with Jessica Bram at the playground while the other kids stood around throwing bark chips at them? Still not lousy.

'Sure,' she said, 'being run out of town at sixteen wasn't easy, but eventually, I learned not to complain.'

'*Sixteen?*'

'Yeah. Spent my seventeenth birthday on the couch of a bong-smoking fridge repairman.'

'I'd think that's something to complain about.'

Abigail looked straight ahead. 'There was a woman inside with me who couldn't laugh. Prison sucks—it's designed to break people and it does that very well, so don't get me wrong, it's certainly not a party, but often enough, there's laughter. Sometimes it's sarcastic, or cruel or whatever, but it happens. But one woman didn't laugh at all. Ever. No one knew what had happened to her, to take that ability away, but it wasn't hard to guess. She was there when I arrived and still there when I left.'

Nate was silent.

'I'd had a bit of petty theft in the past.' She picked at a thumbnail. 'My brothers and I just being dicks. Shoplifting, nicking bikes and leaving them somewhere else, breaking into sheds. Gateway stuff, I suppose you could call it.'

Nate glanced over at her. 'Your brothers are the twins, right?'

'Yeah.'

'Where are they now?'

She tore off a shred of thumbnail with her teeth. 'North,' she said, spitting out the nail. 'Queensland, sometimes the Territory—pretty much as far away from here as they can get.'

'They don't like Port Kingerton either?'

'No, they were happy here. They probably would have stayed, if not for Dad. When Grandpa got worse after Grandma died, Dad told them to get as far away as they could.'

Nate went quiet.

'It chafes, you know? This town. They've all decided what you are. They believe their own bullshit into reality, and then you can't argue with it.' She watched the darkness pass by for a few more moments. 'We had a new regular at the restaurant,' she said quietly. 'Smooth fucker. Convinced the sun shone out of himself. Most people have a bit of, I don't know, *niceness* in them, even when they're having a bad day, but this guy never did. He was convinced he was better than everyone and wanted everyone to know it.'

'Ah,' said Nate. 'One of those.'

'Never took his sunglasses off. Even inside. Eight hundred dollar shirts. Never said anything other than what he wanted to order—"macchiato" or "eggs Florentine"—no pleasantries, no "have a nice damn day". The only other time he'd speak was when he had a problem with something, which was often. His macchiato wasn't hot enough, his eggs too runny, table water too room temperature. Or he didn't like the music, or the way the table was set, or he thought the wait staff were too rushed or sloppy or—this one's fresh—not friendly enough.'

'Sounds nice.'

'We had a new waitress,' Abigail said, then paused. Heat rushed to the back of her throat. 'Melinda. Really nice chick. Single mum with two little kids. She'd been up all night with a sick toddler and she made a mistake. Forgot to put gluten free on his order and his eggs came out on rye sourdough.'

'Was he allergic?'

'No. Just a fuckwit.'

'I see.'

'He'd always ordered rye sourdough. Every day. Until that one day he changed his mind. He lost it. Got right in her face, called her "inept", told her he wouldn't even feed this food to his dog. Then,' she shifted on the seat, trying to ease any one of her aches, 'he called her fat.' She looked over at Nate. 'She was five months pregnant.'

He said nothing, catching her eyes in the dark.

Abigail felt her heart starting to pound, her eyes beginning to prickle. 'When I came to talk to him, to try and smooth things over, he asked to "see my papers".'

'Your what?'

'My vaccine pass. He asked to see mine, and then all the staff. Started demanding to see all our certificates. It just ...' She flexed her hands, trying to stay present, to stay in her body. 'It wasn't okay with me. The way he demanded ... to see ...' She trailed off, frustrated, unable to find the words. She recalled his face, the pretentious manscaped triangle of beard, the butt-hurt, overweening expression. 'His entitlement was a trigger,' she managed at length. 'Why should I show *him* my private medical shit? What right does *he* have to know about my body?' Now his image was replaced by a memory of Melinda, her cute tired smile, tiny diamante stud in the side of her nose; Melinda leaning over the counter, holding her phone for Abigail to see a photo of two small kids asleep on the carpet, crashed out after playing, arms flung above their heads.

'Mel didn't come into work the next day.' Abigail cleared her throat. 'Took a bunch of pills. She lived, but, yeah.'

'Shit,' Nate said. 'Sorry.'

'Yeah.'

'So. You killed him—rye sourdough?'

'No. I took his Maserati.'

'Oh.'

'It's possible he, uh, "dropped" the fob in the bathroom. It's possible I picked it up. It's possible I took it up the M1 to see if it really did have a top speed of three hundred and two. It's possible, when I was done, I left it in the carpark of a gay strip club with a message keyed into the bonnet.' She picked an invisible piece of lint from her pants. 'It's also possible my licence was still disqualified. And that wasn't the first time.'

'You stole his Maserati before?'

'It wasn't the first time I'd been caught driving disqualified.'

'Second?'

She sighed. 'Fifth.'

She remembered the feeling of the Levante beneath her, supple leather and slick gleaming instruments, the effortless power of the car's muscles eating up the bitumen like cream. She'd buzzed the window down and the wind that tore in was all warm spring grass, rolling country. She'd put her hand out the window to feel the blast of air. Like skydiving, the wind pressed into her open mouth and she could not breathe, her laugh ripped from her so she could not hear it.

She never saw the traffic cop with the radar hiding behind a bush at the bottom of a long, revenue-raising hill. The cop knew Abigail, they all did, and with her face and hand out the window he saw her coming. So did the camera; her grin was unmistakable. The cop hadn't bothered to go after her, simply called it in. Someone said there was a photo online, another photo the cop had taken of the radar gun with her speed registered on the screen—228—but she hadn't looked for the photo herself. She'd seen the speedometer on the Levante, that was enough. She'd felt the wind in her hair like a lover's fingers raking her scalp. She had felt, for a little while, the freedom. Rinsed clean. The freedom that she craved with every cell of her being.

'What was the message?'

Abigail glanced up.

'The message keyed into the bonnet,' Nate said. 'What was it?'

She paused for a long time before answering. '"I heart dick".'

'Does he?'

'Who cares? I shouldn't have done it.'

'Steal his car?'

'No, he deserved that.'

'The speeding?'

'Are you kidding?' She laughed. 'Come on—a rich arse-hole, a luxury SUV out of the realms of most people's dreams let alone touch. You can't tell me there's not a law-yer, an upstanding copper, even a judge who wouldn't, deep down, if they were *really* honest, want to give it a go.'

'Then which part shouldn't you have done?'

'That message.' She shrugged. 'I've got no beef with gay dudes.' There had also existed a photo of the SUV with *I* ♥ *DICK* carved into its glossy azure multicoat, but that one was only on Abigail's old phone.

At least, she had pointed out to her weary lawyer, since her first stint inside for driving while under the influence, she hadn't touched the drugs again.

Nate was slowing for a corner, the kind of remote country intersection where only three cars passed a day yet inevitably, because no one bothered to give way, someone died. They had come to a complete standstill, Nate looking left and right into the dark, and she wondered if he was taking such care because she'd just described driving at two hundred and twenty-eight kilometres an hour.

'And for that you got prison time?' he said, accelerating again.

'Once you have a few things on your record, it's ...' She spread her hands. 'A snowball. Especially if it's all similar offending.' Then she checked herself, hearing the voice of her lawyer in her head. 'I've made mistakes. I've driven home from parties knowing I shouldn't have. I've been loud and a nuisance on the road. I have an aversion to authority so I hate renewing my licence, even if my disqualifications are up. But once you're in the system, it's hard to get out. It's designed that way. And, as much as I know it's important to "take responsibility"—' she quirked her fingers in air quotes '—there isn't a single person alive who hasn't made mistakes. Done stupid shit. The only difference is I got caught. If I've been imprisoned for not sticking to the rules, for being reckless with other people's safety, I reckon plenty of politicians should be in prison, because they keep cutting welfare and healthcare and stealing Aboriginal kids. And millionaires who can afford to contribute to that welfare and healthcare, but pay eighty whole bucks in tax. But they're the ones making and enforcing the rules. You can't stay at the top unless there's people below you.'

Nate was quiet.

'None of those women I was locked up with deserve to be there. They're not a danger to society. Most of them have just been dealt a shitty hand in life. But me? I don't have an excuse. I've just been an arsehole.'

'Have you, though?' Nate said, and Abigail thought she could hear frustration in his voice. 'And who hasn't been, at one point or another?'

'Jesus.'

'I'm serious.'

'I know you are. I'm saying Jesus was never an arsehole.'

'How would we know? Maybe he was. Maybe he got annoyed if his bread wasn't right, too.'

Something in the consideration of that struck Abigail as funny. She pictured the frustrated Christ, experiencing a moment as fallibly human as any other—the failed expectations of desire—and she wanted to laugh. But she stifled it, because Nate didn't have any more spare pants.

Twenty-five minutes later they turned into the Fancys' driveway.

Abigail said, 'What the—'

'Looks like a party,' Nate observed.

'Yeah,' she said. 'But it doesn't look like fun.'

THEM

It may have been true that Jessica Bram and her husband had an understanding, but it was also true that Jessica Bram's husband had no such understanding for Col Morton.

This was unfortunate for Jessica. It meant her liaison with Col did not evaporate from discourse with her husband quite as swiftly as she would have preferred. In fact, her husband was going on and on about it, rather than executing his usual hand chop through the air, wink and feigned *I don't want to know*, which he tended to renege on later, in bed, when he did want to know, very much, and in florid detail.

'Col sodding Morton?' Jessica's husband hissed when the kids were finally asleep. 'Are you kidding me?'

'Since when,' Jessica hissed back, 'have you cared?'

'When it's one of the sodding Fancys' henchmen, that's when.'

'Col's not a *henchman*. Calm down.'

'Don't tell me to calm down. Col took an actual literal sodding bullet for Young Dick. Have you forgotten?'

'Stop saying "sodding". You sound like a twat.'

This had gone on a while, wife and husband circling the island bench in the kitchen while the kids slept, Jessica texting her mother in the intervals her husband took between being outraged to gather his thoughts. *Huz doing his nut,* she wrote. *Pissed about Col.*

I don't blame him, Jessica's mother replied. *You didn't think about that one, did you?*

Nope, Jessica responded, annoyed. *Why should I?*

Did you forget who Col is?

Jessica pocketed her phone in disgust. Her husband was still pacing. Thirteen years separated Jessica and her husband, and although she seldom registered the gap in their age, right now she felt it keenly: his hair turning silver; the weathered skin on his face and hands; the look of jittery exhaustion in his eyes.

'Col's no one important,' Jessica said. 'And neither are they, despite what everyone thinks.'

Her husband rested his hands on the bench and considered her at length. 'Don't you remember what that was like?' Then it was as if all the outrage left him. He came forward and took Jessica in his arms, resting his chin on her head. 'I don't want any trouble.'

'There isn't going to be any,' Jessica mumbled into his shirt.

'They're mates, Col and Dick. Col made sure of it.'

'Just because Col's a brown-noser doesn't mean Dick Fancy bothers who he sleeps with.'

'He might when it's a Bram.'

Gently, she thumped a fist against his pecs. 'I'm not an "it".'

His arms squeezed. 'Babe, maybe you're too young to remember.'

'I wasn't born yesterday. I know what it was like.'

'You didn't live it. It wasn't pleasant, Jess, living in a war zone.'

Jessica drew back. She pushed the hair away from her forehead, revealing the jagged cord of scar tissue in her hairline. 'I lived it,' she said, waiting until his eyes found the scar and he nodded. She let her hair drop.

Having Abigail Fancy throw a rock at her head was not the same as living in a daily state of malcontent and division, Jessica knew. A bit of bitchy mouthing off, handfuls of bark chips flung and kids chanting, *Wham bam, thank you, Bram*, was a mere scratch on Port Kingerton's greater record of unrest. There was a time when locals scurried about avoiding eye contact, when shopfronts were boarded up, a new car was liable to go missing, a new boat likely to sink. Old grudges—hard feelings so long-held and unquestioned the horizons of them had disappeared altogether—seemed to hold together the concrete and iron of the place as much as the damp and salt rust. Once, tourists had never visited. Even the seagulls barely touched down for long. The relative peace that existed in Port Kingerton now had not been gained quickly or without effort. These things, Jessica knew. But even so, she had to admit to feeling a thrill of excitement. Stirring in her was a sense of being the instigator, a scintillating knowledge of being the driving wheel. A shift was happening and Jessica, at the forefront of it, felt the lure of power.

Her arms tightened around her husband. 'Speaking of trouble,' she began, but was interrupted by her phone buzzing. Her mum again.

Something happening at Fancys'.

What? Jessica wrote.

Mum—what?

What's going on?

Mum???

But Jessica's phone remained maddeningly silent.

Nell was in the stables. Filling the mare's hay bag, she watched Bobo tear into it with gusto.

'Still not off your food,' Nell said. 'No foal yet then, eh?' She patted the mare's neck and straightened her rug where it had slipped, exposing a jutting flank.

That's when Nell heard the sound of a car arriving at the house. At first she didn't think much of it—cars were always coming and going—but when it was shortly followed by the sound of another, then more, Nell pulled out her phone and shot a string of question marks to her husband. Irritation ran through her at the thought of another impromptu town meeting. The noise was upsetting for her father-in-law. And the freezer was running low on sausages. Actually, the entire house was low on food. Between Abigail's arrival, foal watch, Old Dick's increasing agitation, the bone washing up and the hectic buzz of town, neither Nell nor her husband had had the chance to visit the bigger town for groceries.

Oh, who am I kidding, Nell thought. *It's Abigail.* Of course it was. Nell could tell herself she was distracted and busied by other things but it was Abigail consuming every scrap of her mental energy. In coming back here, her daughter had proceeded to take up any space Nell had left, including her jeans and all the food, too.

Not that Nell hadn't wanted that. Not that Nell, for years now, had not wished fervently that her daughter would come back. The boys had each other but Abigail had always been alone. Even surrounded by girlfriends as a teenager, Nell had witnessed her daughter keep the other girls at a distance, letting them circle her but with a kind of impossible push, a never-connection, the way magnets repel one another.

Nell listened to the cars arriving and wondered why, even before that poor girl, Abigail had seemed intent on pushing everyone away. And then Nell thought of her own mother, an alcoholic for as long as Nell had known her, and her mother's mother, also an alcoholic, and thought, *Maybe that's why.* Maybe aversion—to other people, to connections, to *feeling things*—can run in the genes, thread little stitches of repulsion into one's DNA. Or maybe sometimes there simply isn't an explanation.

No response came from her husband. No messages from Abigail either. Not that Nell was expecting any, but the knowledge that her daughter had a phone again and was at least in messaging range had filled Nell with such a staggering relief she had not been able to hide it and Abigail had rolled her eyes and said, 'You're making me want to give you a fake number.'

A yelp came from the backyard, followed by the angry honks of a goose. Breaking out of her reverie, Nell gave

Bobo one last pat, let herself out of the stall and strode from the stables to find out what on earth was happening.

Col had a splitting headache. He had taken two Panadeine Forte but they had barely made a dent in the pain. When Young Dick summoned him, Col had been tempted to take a couple more pills and stay home on the couch with half-a-dozen beers, screw the lot of them, but he didn't. Col might have made some errors of judgement the past couple of days, but he couldn't deny he'd now had some sense knocked into him.

If only it hadn't taken a broken nose to do it.

So Young Dick called and Col responded. Now he was driving up the Fancys' driveway with his head pounding and his guts feeling like a sack of snakes. Headlights flared in his rear-vision mirror, causing him to squint, which hurt more than Col would have thought it was possible for eyelids to hurt. When he reached the house he saw the taillights of two more utes pulling in before him: Twitch, who disappeared straight into the house, and Adrian Turner, who lingered outside, appearing to wait for Col. Col cursed under his breath.

'Oof,' said Adrian upon clocking Col's face. 'Ran into a door, did ya?'

'Fuck off,' Col replied, but his nose was plugged with blood and it came out *Fug*.

'Now, now,' said Adrian with a laugh. 'It was worth it, right?' He elbowed Col and Col stared at him blankly.

'Right?' Adrian repeated, nudging Col again, eyebrows waggling, and then Col understood. Adrian thought the current state of Col's face—eye sockets turning purple, nose swollen, beard crusted with dried blood—was the result of him screwing Jessica Bram. And Col, who only moments ago had thought for the first time in his life that he did not want to be at the Fancys', now sensed a glimmer of opportunity. He began to feel fortified. He began to feel glad he came.

Lifting his chin, Col replied evasively, 'I'm not answering that.'

'Why not?' said Adrian. 'Doesn't seem like you're shy about it. What did you think the pub kitchen was—a private suite?' He chortled. 'Oi, Jase,' he bellowed suddenly, as his little brother's wagon pulled up. 'Come check out Col's face.'

Adrian was acting nonchalant, his talk full of swagger, but the truth was, the sight of Col Morton's mashed face had sent a bolt of horror into his groin. Until this point, Adrian had not even been sure he believed that Col *had* slept with Jessica Bram. As far as Adrian was concerned, his little brother Jase had always been a twerp who was not indisposed to flex the facts to get what he wanted and, in this case, Adrian had assumed all Little Jase wanted was attention, to get in on the action that had fizzed around town the past couple of days.

But it must be true, Adrian realised now. All day people had been saying Twitch was threatening to take Col to the lighthouse for pissing off Young Dick by shagging the enemy. And look, here was Col, face like a dropped pie. Only a fist could have caused that havoc. A big, meaty fist on the end of a big, powerful arm.

Okay, sure, admittedly Adrian had leapt to the assumption his little brother was lying about Col and Jess because his brother had been there at the Fancys' the night Abigail had arrived and eaten a dozen sausages straight off the grille, and Adrian had not been, and Adrian had been blinded by furious envy. But Adrian reminded himself now it was *he* who had felt the warm press of Abigail Fancy's breasts on his hands on the steering wheel. It was *he* who had stood in the hardware store today, giving Abigail advice on pants, flirting outrageously. The score was even and his brother could bite it.

'What, man?' said Col.

Adrian blinked. 'What?'

'You're staring at me,' said Col. 'You wanna kiss me or something?' Col tried to form his lips into a pucker but it hurt too much.

'You wish,' replied Adrian with a laugh, but they both heard the nervousness in it.

'Far out, that's nasty.' Little Jase appeared beside Adrian, looking awed and disgusted by Col's face.

There came the low burble of a V8 and Trisha Loft's HSV appeared. The men waited for Trisha to spot them and leave but she didn't. Instead, Trisha parked and walked over. Col's gladness that he came soared to even greater levels, because Trisha's choice to endure a group situation meant Young Dick must have insisted. Whatever it was Young Dick had to say, it must be important.

Then the front door flung open and Twitch yelled, 'What's this, a cake and arse party?' and they all filed inside.

Less than forty minutes later, the front door opened again. First out was Little Jase Turner, stumbling on the top step, followed closely by his brother Adrian, face like a clap of thunder, then the rest of them. Last out was Col Morton, who hobbled over to the edge of the drive and vomited neatly into the cheesewoods.

That's when Abigail and the vet pulled up.

OLD DICK

I hear engines.

Revving, idling, the crunch of tyres over gravel. Sounds like a fleet coming, one by one. There's doors slamming—*thud, thud, thud*—and there's boots stomping and the walls shake. I am below deck while the footfalls above go back and forth, back and forth, and the waves pitch us about like a walnut shell in a storm drain.

Shut up, would you? I'm trying to watch my show. A man can't watch his show while the boat's pitching and the deckies are yawping like seagulls around the burley.

The woman comes in and hands me the remote control. I like her, she's nice. She puts a hand on my shoulder and asks me if I need anything. Cuppa, bikkie, sandwich?

Drop anchor, I tell her. Pots ahoy.

She smiles and the hand on my shoulder gives a squeeze. She tells me to turn the volume up on the TV if I want and I tell her the only volume that needs adjusting is coming from the pie-holes of those deckies.

Right, that's it. A man can't watch his show in these conditions. I can't even hear what the cranky Pom's saying.

Look, I know you're all excited, but it's time to pipe down. Fretting like a bunch of yarded heifers is going to achieve jackshit.

No.

No. Get away.

Here's the truth. You want it? Maybe if you know it, then you'll know why I'm telling you to shut your yappers.

No, I said. Are your ears painted on? Come near me and I'll knock your block off.

We knew that girl was in trouble. We knew it before the rest of you. Well, Luce knew, and she begged me to do something, but I said I wouldn't interfere until I was certain of the truth, because interfering in another man's business isn't my nature. All right, it is in my nature, but it depends on the type of business.

And then I was certain, so I did interfere. I took care of it.

Where are we going?

The truth comes out. Eventually it all comes out. Like an infection, it won't go away unless you cut it open, until you put it in the salt water, and it burns, and burns, and burns.

ABIGAIL

'An ice dealer?' Abigail said.

'That's the story,' her father answered.

Once again she found herself seated at the long table in the dining room, surrounded by her mother, her father and her grandfather at the head of the table. Only this time her grandfather had in front of him a cup of regular black tea— nothing made from dandelions, no brandy. The brandy was on the floor alongside Nell, out of the elderly man's line of sight. Abigail had already watched her mother surreptitiously lean down with her cup more than once.

Abigail was so tired she thought she might die. 'In that case, who gives a shit?' she said, yawning so widely her jaw cracked. 'You won't see me crying about a dead ice dealer.'

'A human bone was found,' Nell said, and Abigail thought her mother sounded almost as tired as she felt. 'That bone very likely belongs to a person known to police who's been missing for a couple of months. Case closed.'

'We hope it's closed,' her father said, with a glance at Nell. 'Just now, I've told a few people what Dettwyler's told me. Or at least I've told them the gist of it.'

Abigail didn't want to ask, but she recalled her parents' insistence that she know at least enough not to threaten anyone bodily harm. So she said, 'The gist being?'

'What your mother just said. Cops have been aware of a missing person who'd been known to visit the area from time to time.'

'Not a local?'

'No. From interstate. When the borders were closed during the pandemic he got around the checkpoints by coming through the pine plantations.'

'Needs must,' she said, draining her tea.

'I won't have ice here, Abs,' her father said, his voice quiet and steely. 'You know that.'

'So you topped him?'

Her mother laughed.

'Say what you like,' her grandfather spoke up, 'I never touched those sheep.'

'I know you didn't, Dad. They got out on their own. The gate was open.'

'Useless mutton.'

'So you've told everyone the thighbone belongs to a missing ice dealer from interstate,' Abigail said. 'You've told everyone that's the story according to the cops. And now everyone's happy, and going to get on with their lives, yeah? Back to fishing and judging the shit out of everyone. Super. I'm off to bed.'

'That's what I've told a few people,' her father said, 'in the hope it will get back to Lofty. I'm not sure why he's panicking, but I need him to stop. When people panic they start gabbing. And I don't want old Lofty gabbing.' Her parents exchanged another glance before Young Dick looked nervously at his own father, muttering into his tea about stolen sheep and dead stallions.

'Gee,' Abigail said, unable to stop the sarcasm creeping into her voice, 'really? People talk shit when they're scared?'

'Abs—'

'Tell me more about the crap people spin when they're afraid. Explain to me how a group of people, all believing their own terrified bullshit, can make a reality out of nothing. Better yet, explain that to all the witches they burned.'

Her grandfather's fist came down on the table, making the salt and pepper shakers clunk together. 'I thought I told you,' he said, turning to her father. 'You've got to keep a crowd calm.'

Her father rubbed his face. 'That's what I'm trying to do, Dad.'

Abigail's head was starting to pound. The stink of cow manure lifted from her clothes, she was ravenous and her eyes stung with fatigue. She wanted to go to bed; she did not want to be sitting here at her parents' table, yet again discussing the stupid, insular politics of this pipsqueak, self-absorbed town filled with obsessive braggarts who thought they were the centre of the universe.

Her grandfather laughed. 'Pipsqueak town,' he said. 'Good one. But you know who isn't a pipsqueak? That Bram fellow. He might look harmless but he's slimy as a snake.

Don't ever turn your back on him. He'll knife you soon as he'd give you the time.'

Abigail saw her father's jaw clench.

'Dad, I'd rather we didn't start talking about Ed Bram again. What I'm saying has nothing to do with him. Ed Bram is dead.'

'Ha,' said her grandfather. 'Serves him right. When's the funeral?'

'Twenty-four years ago.'

Old Dick furrowed his brow. 'I think I'm busy that day.'

'So that's the story,' Nell said, leaning across the table to regain Abigail's attention. 'Okay? The cops believe the bone belongs to a wanted crim with plenty of enemies who's been missing a while. He went missing nowhere near here. The bone has been in the water a few months, probably washed in from the deep current. There are no suspects here. There won't be any investigations locally. If anyone asks, that's what you know.'

'Yippee,' Abigail said.

'And if anyone asks about Lofty or tries to tell you something about his missing boat, you cut them off. The bone has nothing to do with that. Change the subject. Distract them, point out something shiny if you have to.'

'Aye, captain.'

'I'm serious, Abigail.'

'For fuck's sake, I get it. *Don't mention the baby.*'

Silence dropped. She stared at them, looking from one face to the next. The three of them stared back at her. The silence was so complete the growl of her stomach echoed into it.

'Well,' she said, after an excruciating, drawn-out minute. 'That's what you're trying to say, right? May as well point out that elephant in the room.'

'How come,' her grandfather said, 'she gets to talk about that and I don't?'

'We are *not* talking about that,' Nell said, her voice icy.

'We were,' Old Dick countered. 'We were talking about it just a few minutes ago, when all those deckies were here making bedlam. We were talking about it then and all of a sudden you told me not to, and then everyone buggered off and now I'm sitting here drinking tea like a useless prick, wondering what the hell happened.'

Abigail looked at her father, who was gazing down at the tabletop, blinking rapidly. Abruptly he stood and walked to the darkened floor-to-ceiling window, put his hands on the glass and gazed towards the lighthouse sending its blue-white pulse across the scrub and ocean. She watched her father press his body against the window as if he could push through it, walk out into the scrub and the night.

Quiet fell again, and in it the ocean heaved. Abigail's stomach continued to gurgle. Her mother disappeared and came back, placing in front of her a steaming bowl of potato and leek soup. Studded with chunks of bacon, garlic and parmesan scents wafting up; Abigail took to the bowl as if she had never eaten. For a while all that could be heard was the clink and scrape of her spoon against the bowl, the susurrus of the sea, the mumbles from her grandfather. As she ate, Abigail felt the silence turn from grim anticipation, to an uncomplicated quiet, into something that felt almost pleasant. When she was done she dropped the spoon into the empty bowl, pushing it away with a satisfied sigh.

Her mother broke the quiet. 'You went to Hansens' dairy today, didn't you?'

The sense of pleasantness faded.

'Did you see Jackie? Did she recognise you?'

'She did,' Abigail said carefully, aware that she was still wearing Nate's pants.

'And?'

'And what?'

'And what did *you* say,' Nell said impatiently, 'when Jackie recognised you?'

It took Abigail a beat to realise her mother wasn't concerned for how Jackie Hansen had treated Abigail, but the other way around: Nell was worried about what Abigail's reaction had been to the other woman. Maybe she could tell her mother about her odd revelation, the way time slowed, the way the future unfolded and she understood that there were options beyond blind, unthinking reaction. But that could lead to explaining why she was wearing Nate's pants.

Abigail belched. Nell pursed her lips. Her grandfather said, 'Who stepped on a frog?' And, from over by the window, her father's phone chimed.

'I didn't say anything—' she began, but was cut off by her father growling, '*Bloody* hell.' He was frowning at his phone, thumbs stabbing.

'What's going on?' Nell asked.

'Twitch says something's happening at the drive-in.'

'What something?'

Her father handed his phone to Nell. Abigail watched her mother skim the screen, then calmly hand the phone back.

Nell turned to her. 'You were saying?'

'I've no idea,' she replied truthfully. Now that she'd eaten, her fatigue returned tenfold. Eyelids struggling to stay open, vision fuzzing at the edges. The lure of sleep, so longed for, was all she could feel. The stairs were an Everest, insurmountable. There was a couch in the lounge room. A few steps. She could make it.

Nell came around the table, took her elbow and helped her into the lounge room.

Expansive, soft, corner couch. Deep cushions giving under her knees and hands, sinking for an exquisite eternity. Her mother's face looking down at her, ponytail hanging over her chin, disappearing as she covered her with a blanket. Then there was nothing.

THEM

The drive-in at Port Kingerton did not have a projector room. Nor did it have a screen, any kind of audio outlets, or a snack bar wafting popcorn and hot dogs. There were no gates or fences, no tickets or admission fees.

Nobody ever watched a movie.

Instead, what Port Kingerton had was a vacant lot, a few utes and an old forty-four gallon drum.

As far as anyone could tell, the vacant lot had always been vacant. Tucked on the esplanade between the gift shop and the second fish-and-chip shop, the vacant block was a wide square of land topped with too much gravel to be called weedy and too many weeds to be called gravel. Its location was convenient: hot chips right there; the pub only a short stumble. Its adoption of the moniker 'drive-in' happened back in the early noughts, when Brian Wimple, whose lounge room fronted the street at the other end of the vacant lot, bought a new big screen TV and someone walking along the esplanade realised they could make out Sigourney Weaver onscreen flame-throwing an alien. In early years they gathered on warm summer nights, sitting at the end of the lot with Brian Wimple's lounge curtains and front door wide open, but that soon progressed into a gathering of utes, a crackling fire and the realisation that no one cared about watching a movie, anyway. It was just an excuse to sit around drinking in public. Celebrating the end of cray season, or the beginning of cray season, or mid-season. Or someone's birthday, or new ute, or, you know, it was Friday and not pouring too hard with rain.

After the events that had transpired and seemed to keep on transpiring, what else were they going to do but gather together to rehash it, blow wind into it, nut it out—set it on fire?

So just after sunset they began to gather.

Even though some of them knew they weren't supposed to.

Adrian Turner hadn't intended to come. Still replaying the scent of Abigail Fancy's hair, Adrian had promised himself a solitary evening to nurse his tenderised heart and popped-open thumb with that bottle of Jack Daniels on his passenger seat. But then his little brother had pissed him off about his mum's porch light, and Young Dick had called, and Col Morton was sporting a smashed-up nose after banging someone he shouldn't have, and Old Dick Fancy had started ranting about the baby, setting Young Dick's gathering into a tailspin, and Adrian's Friday night had taken an unexpected tangent.

Adrian left the Fancys' house, drove down the steep driveway and into town, with his thumb throbbing and his mind reeling. He didn't like either of those sensations, so he reached for the bottle of whiskey, clamped it between his thighs and removed the cap. He took a long slug, screwing his eyes against the burn in his throat. Then he took another.

As he came into town proper, a knot of brake lights shone red on the road ahead and he slowed, frowning. A few utes were turning into the vacant lot. Pulling up on the street, Adrian buzzed down the passenger-side window.

'Oi,' he shouted, leaning across the centre console. He palmed the horn, two short blasts.

Col Morton, standing beside his ute, turned his head.

'I thought we'd canned it tonight?' Adrian called.

Col opened his mouth to answer, but closed it again. Gingerly, he put a hand to his busted face. Then Adrian's little brother drove over the kerb, bumping into the lot. Jase nosed his wagon into the growing crowd and got out of the car.

'Hey,' Adrian called, hitting the horn again. 'Come here, dickhead.'

His brother either couldn't hear him, or ignored him long enough that Adrian muttered under his breath, drove into the lot and pulled up, idling, next to his brother. For a moment Jase looked as if he might continue to ignore Adrian, acting as though he could not see him, but then Jase's shoulders slumped and he opened the door and slid into the passenger seat. Adrian rolled the window back up.

'Did you not hear Young Dick?'

'It'll be right,' said Jase.

'Go home.'

'It's my first night off in weeks,' Jase said. 'You all got to party the other night for the end of season and I didn't. Trisha said she's coming. I haven't hung out with her properly in ages.'

At that moment, they both heard the rumble of a V8 and looked up to see Trisha Loft cruise past without stopping. The horn gave one long blast, a middle finger held high from the driver's window.

'Oh,' said Jase. 'I guess she was kidding.'

Adrian pinched the bridge of his nose.

'Dicky doesn't care if we hang out,' Jase went on.

'He said we should stay home tonight. Not even ten minutes ago. You were standing right next to me when he said it.'

Little Jase laughed. 'Come on. He's not Hitler.'

Outside the car, yellow flames began to lick up from the oil drum. A burst of laughter; the ocean roared in the dark. A few more cars had arrived.

'You all got to party,' Jase repeated. 'I'm staying.'

'If you'll remember,' said Adrian, 'that party was when you caught Col bare-arsed where he shouldn't've been and now Col's face is busted up.'

Jase looked longingly towards the group of parked cars. Six of them now. He looked back at Adrian. 'Do you know something I don't?'

'There's nothing else to know. You heard everything Young Dick said.'

'Yeah—and what about what Old Dick said, hey?' Jase laughed. 'Talk about a cat among the pigeons. Ed Bram, eh? Do you think he did it?'

Adrian said nothing. He wanted to smack the kid. His brother was letting his imagination run wild, getting caught up in all the rumours. It was overwhelming his common sense.

'So you believe Young Dick?' asked Jase. 'The bone's a missing ice dealer?'

'Of course I do,' replied Adrian. 'And it's not Young Dick who says so, it's the cops.'

'Some people are saying it's a bikie.'

'The bone belongs to a bikie?'

Jase's shoulders hitched. 'Or it's a message *from* a bikie. A threat. Some people reckon that's why Lofty's boat's missing—cos he's skipped town. Just like Abigail did.'

'You're an idiot.'

'It explains the burner phone,' Jase continued as if Adrian hadn't spoken. 'She's in on it, with the bikies. Probably met one in prison.'

'In on what?'

'That's what I was trying to ask you about, but you were too obsessed with Mum's precious porch light.'

'All right,' said Adrian, nostrils flaring. 'What exactly do you want to know?'

'Do you think it was hers?'

There was that surge of guilt again, curling through Adrian's gut. 'What I think is irrelevant,' he said, realising that much was true at least. 'Whoever needs to know, does. Also what I think is that you should go home.'

'Do you think she's hiding something now?'

The last of Adrian's patience evaporated. 'Listen up,' he said. 'At the pub the other night you cooked up all that food to keep everyone chill, yeah? That was smart. So why are you acting like a dumbarse now? Can't you see that the same thing needs to happen tonight? Dick just told us where the bone came from. And then he said to leave it.' Adrian lowered his voice. 'That means *leave*.'

The brothers stared at each other, each equally bemused by the argument, though neither for the same reason. Little Jase was stumped why his older brother was so insistent he go home—why care so much about a few blokes standing around idly at the drive-in? Adrian was baffled why his younger brother was not bloody well listening to him—why was he ignoring a directive straight out of Young Dick Fancy's mouth?

Little Jase's frown eased first. Understanding dawned on his face. 'I get it,' he said. 'You're jealous.'

Adrian blinked. 'What?'

'You're jealous,' Little Jase repeated. 'Because I was there on Tuesday night, when she came back. I was at the barbecue and you weren't.'

'What?'

'Ha ha,' Little Jase sang, pointing at Adrian. 'I saw her first. You wish you were me!'

Adrian slapped his brother's hand away. Little Jase dropped his hand but didn't wipe the mocking smile from his face.

Screw this, Adrian thought. The footy had already started, he wanted to FaceTime the kids before they went to bed and his injured thumb hurt like a bitch; he had forgotten it and acted without thinking in slapping Jase's hand away. Adrian took in the group standing around the lot—Col, a Wimple, Ricky Leake, a few other not-importants—and decided he no longer cared. On their heads be it.

'Your funeral,' Adrian said. 'Get out of my car.'

'Ade,' said Little Jase, now placating. 'It'll be all right. I just want to hang out for a bit.'

'Get out.'

'Why don't you stay for one beer?'

'Get the fuck out of my car.'

Little Jase complied and Adrian drove off, catching in the rear-vision mirror a glimpse of his little brother, arms hanging at his sides, watching him go.

Next door to Brian Wimple's, Penny Bram had an excellent view of the back half of the vacant block from her kitchen window. All she had to do was lean over the sink, lift up onto her toes and press her cheek against the glass.

Along with her cheek, Penny was pressing her phone against the glass. Trying to hold herself steady, she angled the lens, taking photos and video. For a short while she watched the proceedings at the drive-in, until she heard the sound of the back door open and close then hurried footsteps up the hall.

Penny tried to straighten up but her lower back seized. She winced, thrust a hand out to steady herself and knocked a glass into the sink. 'Damn it,' she muttered, taking in the broken glass littering the unwashed plates and cups.

Jessica came alongside her mother to peer out the window. 'I thought you said Adrian Turner was there?'

'He is,' Penny said, stepping away from the sink, rubbing her back. 'Check the photo I just sent. He's right there.'

'He's not there now.'

'He must have moved.'

'That's Little Jase Turner,' Jessica said, 'standing next to Col.' She pressed closer to the glass. 'And Ricky Leake, Tom Craft, Brian Wimple—'

'Watch out, there's broken glass there.' Penny clucked her tongue, taking Jessica by the arm and moving her sideways. 'You didn't have to come over.'

'Good excuse to get out of the house.'

'Himself still pissed off?'

'Yes,' Jessica said. 'I've never seen him go on and on like this. He says he's annoyed about Col, but I think it could be something else.'

'It's nothing else,' said Penny, taking out the bin and dragging it towards the sink. 'He's annoyed about Col. And I don't blame him. You two and your ridiculous "understanding". Call it what you like, but if you ask me, it's cheating, plain and simple. But okay, *okay*.' Penny held up her hands as Jessica rounded on her. 'I won't start on that.' She began picking pieces of glass from the sink.

Jessica centred herself at the window. 'Did you hear she went to the hardware store?'

Penny paused, a shard of glass between her fingers.

'She bought dark clothes,' Jessica said. 'And someone else told me a whole heap of duct tape and rope.'

Penny's fingers slipped and glass sliced into the pad of her thumb. Blood rose and a sharp sting went into her hand. Penny experienced a rush of such sudden and intense maternal grievance that it caught her off guard. Old fury and sorrow combined with a new outrage, and she dropped the piece of glass into the bin before kicking the bin away. It slid across the lino, butting against the cupboard on the other side of the kitchen.

Jessica's eyebrows lifted in surprise.

Penny stepped closer to her daughter. By the time Jessica was fourteen she was already taller than her mother—height came from Jessica's father's side, the only decent thing he had left them besides Jessica herself—so Penny had to thrust up her chin to look her daughter in the eye.

'Listen to me,' Penny said. 'All that business is long over. We've made sure of it. Forget Abigail. If she's up to something, so what? Let her commit her own crimes. You need to wash your hands of it.'

Feeling her own indignation rise, Jessica glared down at her mother. 'Easy for you to say. You weren't the one whose childhood was made a living hell. She turned everyone against me. Remember that time she wrote "scrag" on my locker and *I* had to stay back after school and wash it off? Or when she told her brother to ask me out and then not show up, and I stood at the phone box for like two hours while they all hid across the street and watched?'

'I remember,' said Penny quietly.

'She called me a bastard.'

'I know.'

'Because I have no dad.'

'I know, honey.'

'What do you think she's up to?' Jessica cried.

And Penny cried back, 'I don't care.'

They blinked at each other, shocked. Penny thought of looking through the deli window that morning, her eyes caught by the red pop of Abigail's pants against the green grass, and realised it was true: she no longer cared what Abigail Fancy was up to. Yes, at first she had been curious.

At first she had been swept up by gossip but now what Penny cared about was her daughter, and her son-in-law's tested patience, and her grandchildren who had only known Port Kingerton as a sleepy fishing hamlet, a place of peace. What Penny cared about was not watching Jessica spiral into the same melancholy and obsession that had marked her late teens and early twenties, even after Abigail Fancy left and the town moved on from that whole horrendous mess, turning its face to other quibbles, other targets. Abigail left and Jessica had clawed herself into respectability, onto a platform of, if not high esteem, at least something like tacit approval, and they, the Brams, had got on with life.

But now it seemed to Penny her daughter was willing to smash that platform down, all because Abigail was back with a burner phone and duct tape.

So Penny said as clearly as she could: 'Don't squander the truce, Jess.'

Jessica stepped away from the sink. 'What truce?'

'You know what I'm talking about. Young Dick and Nell and me, we've worked hard for it.'

Jessica snorted.

'It's true,' Penny went on. 'Your grandfather and Abigail's grandfather ... it wasn't nice. People went missing, property went missing—even animals died. And you had to be on one side or the other, and neither side was peaceful, or right. Maybe you don't remember—'

'I do remember,' Jessica interrupted. 'Why does everyone think I don't? She threw a rock at my head. I was unconscious.'

Penny pressed her lips together.

'Everyone talks about this "truce" like it's a real thing,' Jessica said, 'but where is it? When I went up to her and said "hello", Abigail ignored me completely. She wouldn't say a single word. Oh, except for calling me a bitch. Does that sound like a truce to you?'

'Jess—' Penny began, but was interrupted by a knock on the door.

'Yoo-hoo, hello?'

At the sound of Sheila Rocket's voice, Penny and Jessica stared at each other, mother and daughter wordlessly communicating their options. Let Sheila in? Make an excuse and usher Sheila out? Pretend no one was home?

Too late. Sheila was inside, bustling into the kitchen with her Maltese terrier skulking at the end of its lead. The dog was wearing a tartan coat and its collar had a series of jingling bells.

'I just happened to be out walking Sissy when I saw your lights were on,' Sheila said. 'So I thought I'd stop in. Oh, hello, Jessica.'

Penny's house was hardly on Sheila's way anywhere; Sheila Rocket's house was at the other end of the esplanade. Also, it was nine pm—what seventy-year-old woman walks her dog at nine on a Friday night? But no one had time to acknowledge that because there was another knock, another voice calling out, 'Hello? Penny?' and setting the dog off into a fit of furious barking as Beverly Dinwiddle came in.

'Sissy, sit,' Sheila cried fruitlessly.

'I was just passing by,' the postmistress said, raising her voice over the yapping. 'Nothing urgent, but there's something I thought you should know. Oh, hello, Jessica.'

'I'll put the kettle on,' said Penny. 'And if you want, we'll sit on the front porch, where we can see the whole drive-in.'

Col Morton had not wanted to come to the drive-in. His face was a font of pain and he still felt like throwing up, even after losing his guts into Young Dick's cheesewoods while that goose attacked him from behind.

As far as Col was concerned, Young Dick had told them all in no uncertain terms that the issue with the thigh bone was over, and they should go home and stay there. Col had not needed a lot of convincing. After leaving Young Dick's, home was where he'd intended to go. Really, he had.

But then, driving down the esplanade, Col had seen the vacant block and the oil drum, a few cars parked. Those cars didn't belong to anyone important, and Col pictured sitting at home alone with his face throbbing like murder, then he pictured sitting out in the cold fresh air, breathing wood smoke and salt and listening to a few no ones talk about nothing, and that sounded more appealing. Also, and perhaps most persuasively, in surrounding himself with a few not-importants, Col saw another opportunity to feel like a hero. And between the pain in his nose and his perception of Young Dick's displeasure with him, feeling like a hero was better.

So Col pulled into the vacant lot.

'Hey, man,' said Brian Wimple, strolling up to Col, then he stopped dead. 'Shiiit,' he drawled, whistling. 'That looks nasty.'

'So's your sister,' said Col.

'Is that really Twitch's handiwork?'

Col shrugged. 'I'm no snitch.'

Brian handed Col a joint. Col smoked until his face stopped hurting. Little Jase Turner showed up, followed by his brother Adrian, and for a while Col worried he might be pushed from the top of the food chain—especially when Trisha Loft cruised past—but in the end, after the Turner brothers conducted a conference inside Adrian's ute, Adrian drove off having not even set foot on the weedy gravel, so Col's position was safe.

It did not take long for Jessica to grow bored. On her mother's front porch, she listened to her mother, Sheila Rocket and Mrs Dinwiddle dissect the town from one side to the other while she scrolled Instagram and kept an eye on the developments in the vacant lot—of which, even after some time had elapsed, there were none. Other than Col Morton and Little Jase Turner, Jessica saw no one of any import. Brian Wimple was handing out pot, but what else was new?

A few times, Jessica was sure Col had seen her, his face turned in what appeared to be the direction of her mother's house, but when she stared back at him, he turned quickly away.

Jessica's wine glass was empty. Her phone read 9.18pm; she'd been watching the vacant lot for almost twenty minutes. She tuned into the conversation around her ('No, no,' Sheila Rocket was saying, 'It was his great-uncle, not his grandfather ...') then tuned out, flicking to the photos her mother had sent, zooming in and out. That was definitely

Adrian Turner's ute. So where was Adrian now? He wasn't on Instagram so Jessica couldn't check, and there were no new posts from Little Jase Turner, nor Col. As she was flicking over to check Facebook, a text came in from her husband, which wasn't unusual, but in it he asked after her whereabouts, which was. Was he really that nervous about Col? she wondered. @ *mum's*, she wrote. *Back soon.* She hesitated, then added *xxx* before sending.

Over at the vacant lot, the men continued sitting around the fire. Other than the occasional arm lifting to drink, no one moved. The ocean rumbled and soughed, leaves rustled, a boobook hooted.

'... ten cents,' Mrs Dinwiddle said, 'and back then that was expensive, for a stamp ...'

Idly tapping her phone against her thigh, Jessica had the idea that she could go over to the drive-in, inject some fizz into the situation. She could see what they were talking about, and find out how Col was doing. Because although she had not seen Col today, Jessica had heard that Twitch had taken Col to the lighthouse and people were saying that Col was nursing a black eye. Jessica was experiencing conflicting feelings about this knowledge. In part she found it thrilling, almost titillating—the idea of an old-school manly punch-up over a woman's honour. But also, more annoyingly, Jessica suspected any bruising on Col would only serve to remind people that Abigail Fancy was back, because Abigail was *also* currently sporting a black eye. And that particular bruise Jessica *had* seen for herself.

'... seventy-eight hectares, or is it seventy-nine?'

Jessica yawned and glanced at her mother, who shot Jessica a look that she could not interpret.

'What's that?' said the postmistress suddenly, sitting forward.

All four heads swivelled to the vacant lot.

'Where?' said Sheila.

At the drive-in, the fire flickered. Col took a drink. Crickets chirped. Nothing else happened.

'Never mind,' said Mrs Dinwiddle, deflating.

Pushing back her chair, Jessica stood. Her mother's eyes went wide in a silent plea. Jessica left the porch, went into the house and made her way to the bathroom.

Her mother's bathroom was small and spotless, everything in its place: clean cake of soap on a tray, hand towel hung just so, tiny pot-plant trailing leaves down one side of the vanity. Jessica locked the door. The older women's voices continued to murmur. Jessica checked her reflection, fixed her ponytail, swiped mascara from beneath her eyes. Rummaging in a drawer, she found lip gloss and slicked some on. She lifted her shirt, rearranged her breasts. Then she changed her mind and pulled down her pants. She arched her back, snapped a photo. Hit send.

Jessica returned to the kitchen. Filling another glass of wine, she went out to the front porch, put her feet up and waited.

OLD DICK

Everything has gone quiet. No voices, no footsteps. Even the TV is silent.

You might wonder where they all went, but I couldn't care less. A man doesn't have the energy or inclination to care about where all the noisy bastards went when it's time to kick the bucket.

Richard, honey, you're not dying today.

I want to ask the woman what she knows about dying. Has she ever died before? No. She hasn't. The way I see it, until you can call yourself an expert on any matter, it's best to keep your mouth shut. But I'm a gentleman and Luce would have my guts if I back-talked a lady, so I don't say anything.

Oh, now *the cat's got your tongue, has it?*

The woman is standing there with her hands on her hips. If I had to guess, I'd say she looks mad, but sometimes I can't tell how women are feeling just by what's on their faces. I swear, a woman's face was designed that way on purpose—looking like one thing, but thinking or feeling another thing altogether—just to make men say something stupid and get themselves into trouble.

Now her face changes again and she sighs, and if I had to guess, I'd say she looks wistful.

Could have used a little of this silence earlier, she says.

What in the blazes is she talking about?

It's late, are you tired?

I'm not tired, I'm dying. There's a difference.

Now she's sighing again, looking out the door and talking about Abigail being asleep finally and she doesn't know what she's going to do. *There isn't any time*, she's saying. *We need time, but there isn't any.* I look at the clock and tell her it's about half past nine. For a few seconds she looks at me, puzzled, and then she smiles but it's a sad smile, so maybe it's not a smile after all. Now she's sitting on the bed and putting her hands over her face and I still don't know what to say, so I don't say anything.

The young fella knocks on the door frame. Why's he knocking? The door's wide open. This isn't a dunny and I'm not sitting here taking a dump.

Sorry, Luce.

Now *his* face? His face, I understand. That's an expression I'm familiar with. If I've seen that face on one man I've seen it on a hundred. I've seen it on boats, in paddocks, at the pub. I've seen it when the night was so dark you couldn't see anything at all. That right there? That's a man as angry as a cat with its tail on fire.

ABIGAIL

At first, when Abigail awoke, she did not know where she was. Emerging into consciousness felt like being yanked from the bottom of a well. Dim, shadowed room; lying on a lumpy surface, mouth tasting faintly of garlic. Then she remembered: the couch. Home.

She was cradled on her side, hip disappearing into the rift between two cushions. So bizarrely comfortable, all her aches vanished, as if this couch had been engineered just for her at this exact point in her life. How long had she been asleep? From another room she could hear the murmur of her parents' voices, the clink of a spoon against a cup, the tick of a clock.

Yawning, she stretched her arms and the muscles along her spine and down her legs shuddered back to life. Digging awkwardly in her pocket, she retrieved her crappy new phone and checked the time. Almost ten. Barely an hour she'd been asleep yet she felt as rested as if she'd slept all night.

'What the hell was in that soup?' she muttered to the empty lounge room.

Blue light from the tiny screen illuminating her face, she keyed in a text: *Missing the cows?*

The reply came after a few minutes. *Pining.*

This is the problem with pimps, she wrote. *They can't get enough. How's your leg?*

Nate began to reply then stopped, then started again. This went on for several minutes, and she was close to setting the phone aside when the message finally dropped in:

Leg fine. Hows your enema?

She let out a burst of laughter. She could picture Nate staring at his phone, disbelief mounting, wondering how he could take it back.

*everything
**all your body
You know what? Forget it.

Abigail wrote, *Sadly I know you didn't mean that in a sex way. Right now I'm comfy but tomorrow could be hell*

But then Nate's response pinged in, and had she not been wedged into the cushions, she might have fallen off the couch:

How do u know I didnt mean it in a sex way?

'Oh, it's like that, is it?' she said, smiling and settling into the cushions.

Then her mother came into the room.

'You're awake,' Nell said.

Momentarily blinded by the phone screen, Abigail blinked into the dark. 'What did you put in my soup?'

'Nothing. But there might have been hops in your tea.'

'Might have been?'

'Was.'

There was a click and Abigail's vision flooded white. 'Jesus,' she cried, screwing her eyes shut. 'Do you mind? And I was already tired—you didn't have to roofie me.'

'Oh, please,' said Nell. Abigail heard the huff of a cushion as her mother sat down. 'It was just a few flowers. Less than what's in a beer.'

Abigail cracked open one eye. Her mother was sitting on an armchair opposite, lit by the glow from a small lamp. 'I'd rather have had a beer.' Abigail picked up her phone. 'Now can you leave? I've got a vet to sext.'

'Leave him alone. He's a good vet.'

'I've no intention of compromising his veterinary skills.'

'No, but you'll compromise my relationship with him. Then I'll have to go back to calling someone from the bigger town, and the travel fees are ridiculous. Ruskin coming here was a godsend.'

'Even if he's a blow-in?'

'Even then.'

Sleepiness was tugging at Abigail again. She fluffed her hair and pouted her lips, angling the phone a little further, pulling down the neck of her jumper to expose some bare skin, the dip of her collarbone. The shutter clicked; the message whooshed off.

'Abigail, can you listen to me?'

Something in her mother's tone made her look up. Among the mild impatience and exasperation, a sharp edge crept in.

'What are you going to do?'

'I'm sending Nate a ph—'

'Forget the bloody vet,' Nell said. 'You know damn well what I mean. And I'm tired of arguing, so please answer me. If you're going to stay here, we're going to have to talk.' Her mother leaned forward, elbows on knees, and repeated, 'What are you going to do?'

It was an excellent question.

Currently she was tucked on a couch, belly full of potato and leek soup, flirting badly by text with a hot vet. Less than a week ago, she had been lying in her narrow bunk on a thin mattress after an unsatisfying dinner of slop-in-a-box, staring at the blue slice of floodlight cutting across the ceiling from the skinny window, claustrophobic and lonely. A year ago, she might have been sitting on an orange bar stool drinking half-price shots of tequila at a bar that had old number plates and horse bridles hanging from the walls, surrounded by drunk stable-hands.

She thought back further. Five years, ten years, twenty. Certain details stuck—shivering, stamping her feet against the cold in line outside a club, breath and cigarette smoke fogging up into the night; the heavy roll of a horse in a straw-filled stall; headlights strobing on tree trunks through switchbacks in the Hills. But other memories were spongy, harder to pin down. That time she had slipped on a mossy trail and sprained her ankle, hobbling three kilometres back to the car with her arm over a friend's shoulder, the air sharp with eucalyptus and campfire smoke—when was that? That time she caught the flu and couldn't get out of bed for three days and Mark had actually shouldered open the door, lock splintering through the architrave, to check if she was okay—when was that? Her life had become a series of murky eras, defined by jobs, by people who'd come in and out, most of them already ghosts. There was her childhood in Port Kingerton, there was the leaving, and then there was two decades of whirlwind: years spent chasing a desperation to forget, hoping the next thing—town, job, lover—would wash her clean, make her safe. Would convince her that she wasn't the contemptible person she believes she is.

But now: returning home. An ending and a beginning as clear-cut as yelling out the window of Zac Murphy's Corolla, *I'm never fucking coming back.*

What was she going to do now?

Her mother waited.

Abigail realised she was too tired to argue anymore. Too tired to try and hide. Her mother was right: they could not keep sniping at one another.

'Abigail?'

'I can't go back.'

'To the city?'

'To prison.'

'I know that,' Nell said, as if it was obvious. Then she added, more gently, 'But you can't work with Nate Ruskin much longer.'

With difficulty, Abigail sat up. She let the blood in her body redistribute itself. 'You know what's crazy? The night before I got out, I was shitting myself. I hated every minute in that hole, and yet there I was, about to get out, and I was terrified.'

Her mother narrowed her eyes. 'Of coming back here?'

'Believe it or not,' Abigail replied with a mirthless laugh, 'no. I was scared to get out because I was scared of having to go back *in*. Being in prison sucks, but being *sent* to prison is horrendous. Unless you've been through it, you can't imagine the humiliation. And your entire sentence is in front of you. Once you're inside, it blows but at least every day is a day closer to getting out. But outside ...' She trailed off. What was she trying to say? What was more terrifying than a torture you were currently enduring?

The threat of something worse: that it could happen again, and again.

'Outside, it's the devil you don't know.'

Nell considered her for so long, Abigail wondered if she would speak at all. 'There are devils from your past here, too,' Nell said finally. 'Are you ready to face them?'

Abigail repeated what she had said to her mother last night: 'I'm here, aren't I?'

The phone chirped.

A photo: pale yellow botfly eggs speckling the underside of a horse's belly.

Oh god. Sorry.

Hey, she wrote, *as far as dick pics go, I've seen worse.*

THEM

Almost ten pm. No moon; the stars scattered chips of ice in the sky. A dense mist slunk off the ocean, leaving beads of moisture on hoodies, slicking the duco of the utes. Someone threw another stick in the fire and sparks flared up. A car stereo was tuned to Triple M playing hits from the 90s, making them all nostalgic for their teens.

Col's phone beeped. He drew it out and saw a flesh-coloured blur. He blinked a few times, pressed his fingertips carefully into his eyelids and tried again, but the photo remained opaque, a fuzzy, pinkish square.

Col looked up. He was seated on the tailgate of his ute, parked with a few others in a rough circle, all reversed around the fire. Tailgates down, blokes lounged, legs swinging, tins lifting to mouths.

When Col first arrived his vision had been fine. Sure his head hurt, but his eyes were working. Now, Col realised as he glanced around the group, he could not see very well at all. If he squinted he could make out Little Jase Turner, a few feet away, but across the circle, past the fire in the drum, he could see only indistinct shapes.

Col wasn't drunk, but he was stoned. Plus he was cold. And the others were being far too loud. The men's laughter was strident, their voices drilling into his head then pushing out from the inside of his skull.

Col frowned at his phone, holding it at arm's length, then bringing it close to his face, right under his throbbing nose. Nothing worked. He couldn't see the photo. He couldn't even read the text to see who it was from.

'What you got there?'

Col lifted his face and found someone standing alongside him. A tall, skinny silhouette smudging out the stars.

'Pottsy,' Col said. 'When'd you get here?'

'I been here a while,' Damon Potts replied in his reedy, nasal voice. 'You been asleep?'

Col ignored Pottsy and got back to trying to interpret the blur on his phone. Was that an elbow? he wondered.

'Who's that?' Pottsy said, coming in closer. Then he whistled, long and low. 'Da-a-amn, I'd hit that.'

'You couldn't hit a bitch on heat, Pottsy, you wanker,' someone yelled. Raucous laughter rang out and Col thought his forehead might pop open with the intensity of the sound. He imagined the front of his skull shooting off, the pillow of his brain bursting out like an airbag.

'Fuck off, Pottsy,' Col muttered and went to pocket his phone, but before he could it was snatched from his hand.

'Hey! Give that back.'

'Hel*lo*,' said another voice, with an appreciative whistle, 'who's that?'

'Niiice.'

Col clambered to his feet but found himself plonking right back down again, tailgate smacking into his rear. The edges of his vision flashed white with pain.

'Wait, is that … Abigail Fancy?'

'What?'

'Lemme see!'

Once again Col tried to stand but the ground beneath him had begun to list. He spread his feet, bent his knees, braced his thighs like any good sailor, but the earth continued to pitch from side to side. A sour taste rose in his mouth. Col did not want to chunder again. Not in front of these blokes. Suddenly all he wanted was to go home. Dimly it occurred to him that he should have listened to Young Dick earlier when, after Old Dick had started ranting about Ed Bram and the baby, Dicky's face had paled and he'd hastily suggested they all call it a night, quiet like, just for a few days. To let things settle back to normal. Col felt the pain of a bullet entering the instep of his foot, shattering the tiny bones there, and began to feel incredibly sad.

'That's not Abigail.'

'It is. That's her arse for sure.'

Col mumbled, 'Gimme back my phone,' but no one was listening.

'As if you'd know Abigail's arse.'

'That's not her. Look, see the bathroom? It's too neat.'

'Why are you looking at the surroundings?'

'I'm telling you, that's Abigail.'

'It's not. The Fancys aren't that neat. Have you ever seen their stables? I had to get a shovel from the feed room once, took me an hour to find it.'

There was a brief silence, then, in a resigned but authoritative tone, a voice said, 'That's Jessica Bram.'

Col blinked in the direction of the voice. Jessica had sent him a photo of herself? Now he experienced a spark of hope. He tried to place the voice but he was having trouble thinking straight. Everything was starting to sound muddy, under water.

'How do you know that?'

A long pause, then, 'Because I've been there, man. See that cluster of freckles, next to her hip? I've—'

Whatever else was said was drowned out as laughs and whoops pealed up into the night, and then Col passed out.

When Jessica saw Col crumple to the gravel, her feet dropped from the table. Straight away she glanced at her phone as if it would tell her what to do and when it didn't, she stared at it for some time until she heard her mother say, 'What's going on over there?'

'Col's fainted,' Jessica said.

Growing up, it could have been said that Jessica Bram was the underdog. But one of the people who would never say that was Jessica herself. Not because it wasn't strictly true, but because it was a notion she simply refused to entertain. Jessica Bram may not have been popular, a part of the 'in crowd' (as limited a crowd as that could be in a town with a teenage population that barely filled one classroom), but she was no shrinking violet. Where others may have accepted their diminishment in a kind of doomed surrender, Jessica Bram did not. When the other kids tried to put Jessica down, she ignored them. If they insulted her curly hair, or scoffed at her city-bought clothing, or queried her lack of father, Jessica straightened her spine and imagined their words as radio static. Because, as her mother always told her, *You have just as much right. Your grandfather was born here. They are no better than you.* And when Abigail Fancy threw a rock at Jessica, hitting her on the forehead and knocking her out, when she got to her feet Jessica picked up that rock and threw it right back.

And look where that dogged self-belief had got her, Jessica thought to herself now. To a place where she could send Col Morton a selfie—a boy who, at school, would hardly deign to look at her; the man who had thrust his foot out when a rifle had been aimed at Young Dick Fancy—and, by the power of her bare flesh, cause him to swoon away.

'Col's fainted?' Penny said, rising from her chair.

'Looks like it.'

For a good long minute they both craned their necks, then Jessica stood up. 'I'm going over there.'

'What? Why?'

'I can't sit here watching. Col might need help.'

'He has help,' Penny pointed out, indicating the men now gathered in a tight circle, although none of them appeared to be helping the lifeless form of Col. Mostly it seemed they were staring down dumbly, scratching their heads.

Before her mother could say anything more, Jessica jumped from the porch and headed across the street. She jogged a few steps, checked herself to a walk, then jogged again. Something was swarming within her, sending her insides into a flurry of anticipation, and she felt hurried and impatient, yet also like she needed to be chill. Casual.

Jessica arrived at the scene to find Little Jase Turner on his knees, putting Col Morton into the recovery position. Little Jase patted Col's cheek, shook his shoulder.

'Col, mate,' Little Jase was saying, but Col wasn't really answering. What Col was doing instead was making a wet, indecipherable groaning sound.

The pitiful sight of Col's face, slit-eyed and turgid, sent a wave of nausea through Jessica. She did not know quite how to feel. All her earlier bravado vanished. She watched as Little Jase cursed Col for not letting him take the time off a while back to update his First Aid certificate, because now he couldn't remember jackshit.

'Foooshhh,' said Col in a low bellow.

'He's all right, isn't he,' said Brian Wimple, 'if he can talk?'

'I wouldn't call this talking,' said Little Jase.

'Should we, like, call an ambulance?'

'Yeah, right. People bleed out before they can get an ambo. Quicker to drive him to hospital ourselves in reverse.'

'Okay then, should we drive him to hospital front-ways?'

'Who's the most sober?'

'Nooo,' said Col, his voice barely audible among the ensuing analysis of each man's state of inebriation. 'Hoshtal.'

'What's that, Col, mate?' shouted Brian Wimple, as if his own volume would help him comprehend Col's lack of it.

'Noo. Shittal.'

'Bloody hell, Col, I can't understand you.'

'He doesn't want to go to hospital,' Jessica spoke up from the circle's edge, and the men startled and turned to her in surprise because no one had seen her arrive. Jessica saw Col's eyes, embedded as they were in dark swollen flesh, swivel towards the sound of her voice.

The men froze as they came to the collective realisation that only moments ago they had been studying a close-up of what was allegedly Jessica Bram's arse. Now that very same arse was alongside them, in real life, attached to a real woman. Feet shifted, throats were cleared. The dank sea mist continued to roll in; stars winked in the sky. No one said anything or looked at anyone else.

Finally someone mumbled, 'Oh, hey, Jess.'

'How've you been?' said someone else.

'Good, thanks,' Jessica replied.

At their feet, Col groaned again.

Little Jase pulled out his phone and announced, 'Twitch is on his way.'

It was the verbal equivalent of a cattle prod. The men burst into a flurry of activity. Or at least, they burst into what *felt* like a flurry of activity when largely stoned and drunk. Empty cans were picked up and tossed clanging into the backs of utes, blunts were stubbed out and stowed in pockets and those pockets were then patted fretfully, as if conducting a self-frisk. Shoulders were un-slumped, chests inflated, fingers raked hastily through hair.

Would they have behaved so guiltily had Jessica Bram and the cluster of freckles on her hip not wandered in? Possibly not. But as it was, the collapsing of Col, the arrival of Jessica and, most troublingly, the knowledge that there had been an edict issued earlier by Young Dick Fancy that there probably shouldn't be a drive-in tonight—an edict they had blatantly flaunted—threw into stark relief for each of them that they had reason to feel guilty.

And, it must be said, a few of them still weren't convinced the arse on Col's phone hadn't been Abigail Fancy's. And those few continued to harbour the image of the lace-edged underwear and creamy skin in their minds, like the after-burn of glancing at the sun, and the arrival of Twitch bloody Witchens would make it a harder fantasy to continue har-bouring. After all, if anyone needed an illustration of what it meant to defy the Fancys, they needed to look no further than the mangled face of Col Morton.

By the time Twitch arrived, everyone was seated back in a casual circle. Col had been hauled to his feet and set wonkily on the tailgate of his ute. Alongside him sat Jessica, occasionally putting her hand up to right Col whenever he leaned dangerously in any direction.

Twitch parked on the road. Slowly, the big man got out of his ute, slammed the door, turned to face the group. Hitch-ing his pants, he strolled onto the vacant lot. Weeds flattened beneath his boots, gravel crunched.

'Hey, fellas,' said Twitch, congenially enough. 'What's going on?'

'Not much, man, just chewin' the fat.'

'Good season, eh?'

'Yep,' said Twitch, looking to Col Morton. Barely percep-tibly, his eyes flicked to Jessica Bram seated alongside.

'You right, mate?' said Twitch.

Col's eyelids fluttered, his mouth opened to reply, then shut again.

'I think he might have a concussion,' offered Little Jase. 'But he doesn't want to go to hospital. Or at least, we think he doesn't.'

'Oh, yeah?' said Twitch, stepping closer to Col. Crouching, Twitch put his face into Col's line of vision. 'How many fingers am I holding up?' he asked, giving Col a peace sign.

Col's teeth began to chatter. He knew he needed to answer Twitch's question correctly, otherwise Twitch probably would take him to hospital. And Col did not want to go to hospital. He wanted to go home to bed. Plus, he knew Jessica Bram was sitting beside him; he could feel her occasional nudge on his shoulder or elbow, encouraging him into a position that resembled upright, and he wanted to believe that *she* believed his broken nose was a result of his bravery and virility.

So Col concentrated, and found that if he blinked rapidly enough his vision cleared, just for a second.

'Two,' Col said.

Twitch gave him the bird. 'How about now?'

'Three.' Col's voice was triumphant.

Twitch dropped his hand. Turning to the group, he asked, 'Did he lose consciousness for long?'

The men exchanged a glance. No one wanted to lie to Twitch, but no one had actually paid that much attention when Col collapsed to know the correct answer.

'I don't think so,' said Little Jase. 'He dropped, and then was speaking, almost straight away.'

'Not that we could understand what he said,' offered Brian Wimple. 'But he was making noise at least.'

Twitch ignored the pesky stoner Wimple kid and directed his focus on Little Jase Turner, who, although he had ignored Young Dick's suggestion to go straight home tonight, at least had a head on his shoulders that Twitch could respect.

'He spewed at all?'

Little Jase cut a glance at Col before answering, almost remorsefully, 'Yeah. Earlier, up at Young Dick's.'

Swearing under his breath, Twitch glowered at Col, as if Col had purposely gotten himself a concussion in order to ruin Twitch's Friday evening.

'All right,' said Twitch. 'You lot clear off home. I'm not going to repeat myself. Col, get your arse in the ute. I'll take you to hospital.'

Twitch turned to Jessica, pinning her with his gaze. Jessica felt it, the danger of it, shoot straight up her spine. Raising her chin, she held Twitch's eye coolly.

And there, in that locking of eyes, they all felt the presence of a twenty-four-year-old ceasefire. When Ed Bram died and the sniping stopped, and it had been like the sun came out. They felt the presence of that ceasefire manifest itself in the vacant lot before them, running like swell, gathering speed and then hitting a reef—smashing to foam.

Jessica opened her mouth to say something, and then they all heard it, faintly:

Whomp.

Every head turned towards the sound. Towards the sea.

Far out on the ink-black water, a fireball exploded in the dark, golden flames in the sky.

A boat was on fire.

OLD DICK

Come closer.

Closer, boy. A man can't shout his final dying words.

Now listen to me. That fellow Dad shot? You know the one I'm talking about?

Which one?

What?

Grandfather shot several men, Dad. I'm asking— which one?

Several men? I admit my memory can deceive me—I am eighty-two or -five or -nine, after all—but I would swear on the good book there was only one man who ever got a bullet from my father. All right, my father was given to bouts of flightiness, a bit of a spooky horse was my old man, but never did he shoot more than one—

The horse clippers. The poisoned stallion. That guy who tried bringing smack in. The missing pots—

Oh, those ones. I wasn't counting *those* ones. Who cares about those particular dipshits? Good riddance, I say.

Well, which one then?

I'm talking about the man Dad shot in the foot.

The young fella looks perplexed. *Shot in the foot?*

That's what I said.

Grandfather didn't … I can't remember him … in the foot. He tended to, uh, you know—and he pats his chest, as if checking for his keys in his breast pocket—*quick, like.*

Don't cast your eyes down like that when you talk about your grandfather, boy. What are you—ashamed? Your grandfather was a great man, a formidable man, a respected man who didn't go letting his environment be the boss of him. From what I've been hearing around here lately, you could stand to learn a few things from your poppy. Deckies running wild, unmarried women flogging cars, nags foaling in autumn. Maybe it's you who needs a bullet in the foot.

The young fella gives a great walloping sigh. I can see him looking towards the windows, those big ones that look out over the scrub and the lighthouse, and I'm worried he might plaster himself to the glass again so I say something to keep him here in front of me.

Well, who *did* get shot in the foot?

He rubs his chin, keeps looking at the windows. I come closer to him, close enough that my knees bump into his. I remember someone getting shot in the foot. I remember it like I remember the sound of your mother's laugh, boy, so don't go trying to tell me I'm not remembering right.

No, you're right, Dad. Someone did get shot in the foot.

Who?

Col Morton.

Who?

Fisherman. Now he laughs a little. *The one Twitch teased about taking to the lighthouse.*

That scared-looking fellow who chased a skirt he shouldn't have? He got shot in the foot?

Yeah.

Why? What'd he do? He doesn't look like he could do much trouble, to be honest.

He's no trouble. Just tries too hard to be liked by everyone.

And then he liked a sheila he shouldn't have?

The young fella thinks that's funny. *Yeah*, he says. *Although, honestly? I don't care. I know I'm supposed to care, so I've acted like I do, but I don't.*

Why should you care?

Because the sheila was a Bram, Dad.

Let me tell you something about that Bram fellow.

You've said enough about Ed Bram for tonight, he says, and there's that pissed off cat face again.

Now the woman comes in and she's saying something about an Abigail harassing a poor vet, and am I tired and do I want to go to bed?

A chiming sound. The young fella puts his phone to his ear.

ABIGAIL

Abigail woke again to the sound of rapid footsteps. After five months in prison her body responded automatically. Bolting upright, she launched herself off the couch, perfectly awake, heart hammering, adrenaline coursing through her veins.

As her surroundings came back into focus—the couch, the armchair, the dim lounge room—relief flooded through her. A lump formed in her throat and she had to swallow repeatedly to make it go away.

In the hall, she found her mother running towards the garage door calling, 'Richard, it's not your problem.'

'What isn't Dad's problem?' Abigail asked, as everything in her body began to hurt again.

Nell turned to her. 'There's a boat on fire.'

As her parents piled into the front of the Chevy, Abigail opened the door and climbed into the back.

'What do you think you're doing?' her mother said.

'Getting into the car,' she replied. 'I'd have thought that was obvious.'

'You can't come.'

'Like hell. I'm not missing this.'

'You need to stay here and look after your grandfather.'

Abigail paused. Then, 'Wait,' she said. 'Do not go without me.' Fixing first her father then her mother with what she hoped was her most earnest and piercing gaze, she alighted the Silverado, returned inside, retrieved her grandfather and wheeled him into the garage. She helped him into the back, buckled his seatbelt, and said, 'All right. Let's do this.'

The car did not move.

'Giddy up,' said Old Dick. 'No one's boat's getting any less torched just sitting here like a limp dick at an orgy.'

'Oh, for heaven's sake,' said Nell.

'A family outing,' said Abigail. 'Isn't this nice?'

Her father put the car in reverse and backed out of the garage.

As they cleared the scrubby bushes lining the road, Abigail could see, out in the harbour, a bright golden speck. A ball of flames.

'That's a boat on fire, all right,' said her grandfather, sounding happy. 'That takes a man right back.' Her father was repeating, over and over, 'What the hell have they done, bloody hell, what have they done?' Her mother was eerily silent. There was something awe-striking, almost unbelievable, about the sight of those flames; candlelight against the water and the star-pricked sky. Closeted inside the car, her parents seething and her grandfather waxing reminiscent, Abigail felt as if she were not quite awake, possibly still asleep on the couch after drinking her mother's hops-laced tea.

They sailed down the hill, rocketed along the esplanade. As they came into town she saw people and cars spilling out of the vacant lot alongside the second fish-and-chip shop and laughed under her breath.

'So much for them going straight home,' her mother said.

'No one's listening. They've gone crazy,' her father replied.

Pulling up in the middle of the street, her father was out of the car and heading up the jetty before Abigail had managed to unbuckle her seatbelt.

Two streetlights, one at each end of the beachfront, bracketed the dark street with wan glowing pools. A little light fell onto the kerb from the windows of the second fish-and-chip shop. A third lamp dangled above the boat ramp but as far as Abigail was aware it had never worked—as kids they'd used it as a slingshot target. But she knew the dark would deter no one. People seemed to be arriving as if out of the night air itself, drawn from houses by the spectacle out to sea. Footfalls ran past, a shoulder knocked into her.

'Watch it,' she snarled.

No reply.

Nell came alongside her.

'Whose boat is it?' Abigail asked.

'I don't know,' her mother said, but she sounded so cross Abigail knew she did.

Another figure made to dash past, but Nell reached out and grabbed them. There was the sound of feet skidding to an abrupt halt.

'Oh hey, Nell,' said a man's voice, sheepish. Abigail did not recognise the face. Black hoodie, grizzled beard, stout build—he could be anyone.

'Tom—were you at the drive-in?'

He took a moment to answer. 'Um, yeah. Sorry, look, I wasn't going to—'

Her mother cut him off. 'Did you see anything?'

'With Col?'

Now Abigail heard a frown in her mother's voice. 'What? No, I mean the boat, quite obviously. What happened with Col?'

'Concussion, I think.'

'Col Morton has a concussion?'

'Um ...'

'Forget it.' Nell released the man and he ran off.

'Maintaining your excellent rapport with the locals, I see,' Abigail said.

Her mother made an indecipherable noise in her throat. 'Stay here.' Without waiting for a reply she struck off towards the jetty.

Abigail returned to the ute. 'You okay, Grandpa?'

'Good enough,' he replied, sounding content. 'Haven't seen fireworks in a long time.'

'I'll be right back, okay? Don't go anywhere.'

'Where would I go? I've got a nice view from here.'

Abigail headed for the jetty. She could see people spilling onto the beach, raised arms pointing out to sea, and now there came the sound of an outboard motor firing up and a tinnie went speeding over the black water.

Her boots clomped on the weathered boards. Water burbled beneath her and she was struck by a memory of the harbour floor below, clogged thick with weed, the jetty timber salt-bleached, glinting with fish scales and stained with guts. More memories flashed thick and fast: clutching hot chips on a freezing day; a handline dangled in the water;

smoky campfires on the beach. The playground. Rocks thrown. The toilet block, bulldozed to dust.

Turning sideways, she barged through the crowd. Faces flashed in her direction, voices muttered angrily, but then those voices died away. Feet shuffled sideways, bodies retreated as the crowd parted in front of her. A hush fell. And then, behind her, whispers started up, moving after her like a small dog on a lead.

'That's her.'

'That's Abigail.'

'That's Abigail Fancy.'

At the end of the jetty, she found her mother framed by a small group of men. Between them and the main crowd there was a gap, like the barrier between the stars on the red carpet and the riffraff. Her father had disappeared.

'I thought I told you to wait by the car,' her mother said.

Abigail ignored her. Searching the faces of the men standing with her mother, she recognised Twitch, Adrian Turner and his brother Little Jase, while the fourth looked vaguely familiar but she did not care enough to try and place him.

'Where's Dad?'

Her mother gestured in the direction of the tinnie speeding across the harbour, towards the burning boat.

'He's not going to try and put it out, is he? That thing's gone.'

No one answered.

'Whose boat is it?'

Again no one answered.

Glancing from one man to the other, she said, 'Where's Col? Off for a sneaky shag with Jessica Bram again?'

Adrian Turner stifled something that sounded like a cough. Little Jase shuffled his feet. The fourth man, the one she couldn't quite place, was standing close to Twitch and murmuring at him.

And then, they stood there: Abigail, her mother, and four men of her parents' inner circle. They stood and they all stared, rather impotently she felt, at the boat on fire in the water. The flames billowed, flickering a palette of bright yellow to dark chemical orange.

What did they think they could do? There was nothing to be done for it, the boat was on fire and would continue to be on fire, until the flames exhausted their fuel reserves, or until the damage to the hull became such that the seawater streaming in pulled the boat beneath the waves. Either way, the boat would be gone. There was no saving it. Some things are inevitable and this was one of them. Inevitability, Abigail realised as she watched the drifting inferno, was a self-perpetuating thing. What had to happen would happen. Time, growth, decay—any attempts to delay or halt the inevitable was pointless. Arrogant. She may not always have a choice about what would happen, but she always had a choice about her reaction to it.

Standing at the end of the jetty, she looked out over the dark ocean and knew there was nothing between her and Antarctica. Twenty-three years of running and she had come full circle.

She placed a hand over her belly. 'There's a chance we'll be okay,' she murmured. 'If we want to be.'

The boat exploded. A sudden commotion erupted on the jetty behind her. And then there was a splash.

THEM

Col Morton was sitting in the back of Twitch's ute, trying not to throw up for the third time.

Col felt lousy. He felt lousy for several reasons: his perceived betrayal of Young Dick; his broken nose, which hurt tremendously; his collapse in front of the other—most of them less important—men at the drive-in. Nobody thought him a hero, they thought he was a swooning loser. But the lousiest thing of all was being slumped in the back of Twitch's ute while everyone else was getting in on the action, watching the drama of the burning boat.

Meanwhile, all Col could see was the window of the second fish-and-chip shop, because that's where Twitch had parked in order to use the light from the shop window to more closely examine him. And then Twitch left to follow the flames.

Alone in the back of the ute, Col heard the shouts and gasps of the crowd. He heard more cars arriving, more footsteps running. He heard the high whine of a tinnie racing across the harbour and imagined the roar of the flames. He had the bright idea to message Little Jase Turner and ask what was happening, but when Col examined his pockets he found them empty, and realised someone else still had his phone. Probably Pottsy, that tosser, who'd snatched it from him on account of a certain photograph before he'd fainted.

That thought made Col remember Jessica Bram. She had been there at the drive-in only a short while ago. Col was lying on the gravel and Jessica's voice had swum into his ears.

Where was Jessica now? Col wondered. He tried to sit up straighter. He turned his head but a wave of nausea made him grit his teeth. He still hadn't seen the photo—the selfie that may or may not have been of Jessica—and he felt a renewed sense of desire to get out of Twitch's ute, to go find his phone.

Gingerly, Col crawled to the edge of the tray and climbed out.

Adrian Turner had received the phone call from his brother when he was not quite halfway through the bottle of Jack Daniels. He'd said goodnight to his kids, and his popped-open thumb had stopped hurting. The footy was down to the last five minutes and the Magpies were up by one point. Adrian did not want to talk to his brother. He let the call go unanswered, but then a text came in saying *SOS* and the phone rang again immediately.

'What?' said Adrian.

'Col Morton's flaked it and a boat's on fire.'

'You're shitting me.'

'No. Check your messages.'

Two photos pinged in: a blurry yellow speck on black and a blurry Col Morton prone on the gravel. So Adrian had rolled off the couch and headed for his keys.

Now Adrian was standing at the end of the jetty with Nell, Twitch, Spike and Jase, and they were watching the boat burn. Adrian realised he was more drunk than he had thought. This was serious, this torching of a boat, and Adrian knew it would be necessary for him to be sharp of mind. He took a few lungfuls of cold sea air, hoping it might sober him up.

The crowd on the jetty suddenly fell silent. People edged apart and then the figure of Abigail Fancy stood before him.

Adrian thought he heard Nell say to Abigail, 'I thought I told you not to drive the car?'

Adrian could feel the slap of the water against the jetty pylons beneath his feet. In the back of his mind he knew it was the whiskey pushing him off-kilter, so he focussed hard on being sober. Abigail was asking questions about the burning boat and Adrian was brimful of the desire to answer, but he recalled earlier that day at the hardware store, the way he had gone on and on about pants, and he feared that if he opened his mouth he would have no control over what came out.

But then he heard Abigail say, 'Col's shagging Jessica Bram again.'

Instantly Adrian felt his tongue become too big for his mouth and his pants too small for his crotch. He cursed the flow of his own blood. Abigail took him right back to being eighteen again, all dick and no brains. All scandal and secrets, forbidden liaisons and rumour. Adrian could not help it—in spite of himself, in spite of how he had promised himself he would never mention it again in respect of not having his balls torn off—what happened twenty-four years ago came roaring back to him. The discovery by the beach. The inflamed town. The fractures, the tattled-to journos, the angry mobs.

Sharp of mind my arse, Adrian thought. He was useless like this. The only thing that was going to put the brains back in his head was a dunking, and he considered taking a quick leap off the jetty. He imagined plunging into the water and feeling jolted back into control of his body, but then the boat exploded, someone started yelling and someone else jumped into the water.

From their particular vantage point, Sheila Rocket and Mrs Dinwiddle could see it all.

News of the unfolding situation had come to the women as they were sitting on Penny Bram's porch watching the drive-in devolve after Twitch Witchens arrived, scattering the men like a dog through chickens. The postmistress received a phone call from her husband Larry, the publican, who had become aware of the situation himself after popping his head out the front door of the pub when someone exclaimed, 'Strewth! She's ablaze!'

Sheila, Mrs Dinwiddle and Penny had arrived promptly.
The two older women were pleased to find the bench by
the beach available, and took their position without delay.
Penny seemed to have disappeared.

So Sheila and Mrs Dinwiddle watched the Fancys
arrive and stride through the crowd. They watched Young
Dick disappear into a tinnie off the end of the jetty. They
watched the boat, engulfed in flames, continue to burn
out at sea.

'I can't see whose boat it is, can you?' asked Sheila.

'They're all in dry dock,' replied Mrs Dinwiddle. 'Except
Old Man Loft's.'

'Yes,' said Sheila, delighted. 'And who's that, on the jetty
with Nell Fancy?'

The postmistress craned forward. 'Tim Witchens, of
course, and Spike Flaherty. And the two Turner boys—'

'Yes, yes,' Sheila broke in impatiently. 'I mean the
short one.'

'Well, that's Abigail, isn't it?'

Sheila knew it was Abigail. She just wanted to hear someone else say it aloud. Because Sheila had spotted, skulking
by the beach, a flash of white-blonde hair, the unmistake-
able bouncing gait of Jessica Bram.

'I don't know about you, Sheila,' Mrs Dinwiddle began,
'but I'm getting the oddest sense of déjà vu.'

'It does take one back,' Sheila agreed, her voice thick with
reminiscence.

But Beverly Dinwiddle was not feeling reminiscent. It
was creeping up on her, too swiftly for her liking, the feelings of twenty-four years ago. It was the same crowd, the
same people milling about, voices raised in collective shock.

It was the same time of night, the same cold sea mist, the same breaking-point air of disbelief.

And there was Abigail Fancy, right at the heart of it. One girl raging against an entire town.

Mrs Dinwiddle thought of her desperation to keep Nell in the post office yesterday morning, her preposterous quip about ID and the confused dismay on Nell Fancy's face. She felt like a foolish old gossip. She felt ashamed.

She stood up. 'I don't think I ...' But the postmistress could not finish her sentence. It was too much, all this. Hurrying away from the bench, Mrs Dinwiddle pushed against the crowd, moving in a different direction to everyone else. Head down, she hurried on until she came to an abrupt halt. Someone had stepped in her way.

'Bev?'

The postmistress looked into the face of Penny Bram.

'Have you seen Jess?'

Mrs Dinwiddle nodded. 'She's over by the jetty.'

She was about to ask Penny what was wrong when she heard a commotion on the jetty, a *boom*, and saw the explosion reflected in Penny Bram's wide open eyes.

By the time the boat exploded, Young Dick and Trisha Loft had circled it several times in the tinnie.

It was Lofty's *Queenie II*, of course. Young Dick had known that even before he'd left home, before he'd seen the flaming vessel for himself.

Out in the open water waves pitched the tinnie about. Each pass downwind of *Queenie II* sent them through the path of thick, choking smoke. Coughing, Young Dick finally gestured to Trisha and she motored into the shelter of the breakwater, a safe distance from the burning boat.

They lifted and fell on the waves. They stared. Stars glinted behind the dying flames. Young Dick bucketed out seawater that slopped over the gunwales. It wasn't in his goddaughter's nature to say a lot, and even when the heat finally got too much for the gas bottle in *Queenie II*'s cabin and it went *kaboom*, Trisha merely shielded her eyes and flinched.

The boat sank swiftly. The sea went black.

'No one stole her, did they,' said Young Dick.

Trisha didn't reply. A black-hooded figure at the tiller; all Young Dick could see of her in the starlight was the pale skin of her hands and chin. She sniffed and swiped a sleeve at her face, so quickly he may have imagined it.

Finally she spoke, a husky voice from under the black hoodie: 'He's just getting old, Dicky.'

Young Dick wanted to know what that had to do with anything, but Trisha didn't answer. 'Well,' he said, 'you're gonna have to come up with an explanation. They're all going to want it—' he gestured to shore, the crowd '—or they'll keep making up stories.'

'I don't care what anyone thinks.'

'Your granddad might,' Young Dick said kindly.

Trisha cut her eyes to him. 'Why?'

'At the boat ramp, Fish told me—and everyone overheard—that your granddad became nervous when the bone washed up.'

'And?'

Young Dick felt a twinge of discomfort. 'They're saying...' He stopped. The boat rocked. He tried again: 'People think the bikies are after him. Because of your nan.'

Trisha said nothing, but she did not look away.

'Someone's started a rumour that when your nan left, your granddad tried to go after her and, in the process, pissed off the man she left him for. And that man happens to be part of a bikie gang, so ...'

Trisha dropped her face and made a small noise, and at first Young Dick thought she was crying, but then she snorted and he realised she was laughing.

'That's got to be the biggest load of shit I've heard in my life.'

And Young Dick, who was not unfamiliar with big loads of shit, had to agree.

Now Trisha looked at him. 'And what about you then, huh? Do *you* care what everyone's saying?'

'I wish I didn't,' he replied. 'But I feel like I have to. At least until Dad ...' He paused. 'You heard him tonight. The way all those stories came out—it sounded like he was implying Ed had something to do with the baby.' He gave a single bark of laughter, rubbed his face. 'He wants to stay involved. He needs it. Meddling, sticking his nose in—it's who he is. But it's getting harder to keep a lid on things that need to be kept ... lidded.'

'I know some of the things your dad says aren't ... *necessarily* true.'

'Unfortunately, others might choose to believe otherwise.'

Trisha shrugged. 'Like I said, it's best not to care what anyone else thinks.'

'Not caring what they think is easier when you don't have to deal with the consequences of what they think.' Again he pointed to the crowd.

'Why do you have to deal with it?'

'They ran my kid out of town.'

'Did they, though? Wasn't it her choice at all?'

Young Dick looked at Trisha in surprise. Where had that wisdom come from? Trisha was barely out of her twenties. Her statement was like a blast of fresh air. For all this time, it had been easy for Young Dick to blame himself, because wasn't that his job? To protect his child? But back then he didn't even know what he was protecting Abigail *from*. The cops' questions? He'd handled them. The town? He'd certainly tried—as much as he hated to do it, the lighthouse had been visited, more than once. Although he'd tried to discourage them the boys had done their part—quietly though, in sheds and back alleys. And he knew his father had been relentless in his enquiries, at least until he became distracted by Ed Bram going missing.

But maybe what Young Dick hadn't seen was that in the end there was nothing he could have done to protect Abigail from *herself*. From her own wilful stubbornness. Her own hurt and terror. No matter what he'd done—and he'd done a lot—Young Dick's power ended where Abigail's began.

'The sense of responsibility comes from somewhere,' he said. 'Maybe it's just in my blood.'

'Or maybe,' Trisha said, 'you should get over yourself.' There was a smile in her voice.

Young Dick chuckled softly. They were quiet a while, listening to the slap of the water against the hull.

'Trisha,' he said. 'Why'd he do it?'

'I told you. He's getting old.'

'And?'

'Do you need it spelled out?'

She waited, but he continued to stare at her.

'Dicky,' she said, and she leaned so far towards him that a lock of purple hair swung free from her hood. 'It's worth more as an insurance claim.'

Young Dick sat back. He waited until Trisha fired up the motor, then he began to laugh.

Unfortunately for Col Morton, he could not swim.

Almost no one knew this about Col—not even Little Jase Turner, who had worked on Col's boat for several years. This was poor human resource management, as it could put Col's deckhand and winchman in a precarious and potentially traumatising situation should Col ever fall into the ocean, but good HR practices tended to be something that the fishermen of Port Kingerton associated with hoity-toity office blocks in the city, not out on a boat with the swell and the gulls and the crays.

This was the reason for the widespread reluctance on the jetty to go after Col, when he was seen falling into the water. Everyone assumed Col could swim.

Except for Nell Fancy, who knew he could not.

'Col, get out of there,' Nell demanded into the dark water below the jetty, hoping Col could stay calm enough to put his feet on the bottom and stand up. Col had confided in Nell many years ago, not long after the foot-shooting, in what Nell had assumed was a way to inveigle himself into her good graces, but whether or not he was also *afraid* of water, and would panic and flail about, making things worse, she did not know.

'Col, answer me right this minute.'

Nell did not want to enter the water herself. It was cold. She did not want to leave Abigail alone with this crowd. And she did not want to turn this into more of an incident than it already was. If Col could simply stand up and climb out they would all forget about it and, now that Lofty's boat was gone, soon would all go home.

'Col!'

Damn it, Nell thought. Bracing herself, she took off one shoe, but before she could reach for the other, Twitch, Adrian and Little Jase Turner appeared, kicked off their boots and slid into the water.

Something was happening in the crowd behind Nell, but she was too focussed on finding Col to notice. The smell of old fish guts oozed from the warped timber and the strong stench of weed lifted from the water. The bottom was a thick disgusting mess—would Col even be able to put his feet on it?

Twitch surfaced nearby, spitting water. Adrian and Little Jase were wading away, gazes darting about.

'Where is he?' said Nell.

Twitch shrugged, but the big man was beginning to radiate unease. They were both racking their minds: How long since Col went in? A minute? Two? More?

Twitch may not have known that Col could not swim, but he was far more aware of Col's current state than Nell. Nell did not know that Col Morton was stoned off his nut— Twitch did. Nell knew that Col had a broken nose, but she did not know that he had, only minutes ago, fainted onto the gravel. Twitch did. So while Nell hoped Col could simply stand up in the waist-deep water, Twitch knew the depth was irrelevant—the man should not be in the water at all.

Then, barely audible over the noise of the crowd, Nell and Twitch heard it at the same time: a groan.

Col was clinging to the jetty pylon.

'What the hell are you doing?' said Twitch, sloshing towards him.

'Were you right underneath me the whole time?' said Nell. 'Why didn't you answer me?'

Col's teeth were chattering, hair slicked to his head. He mumbled something incomprehensible. Twitch got to Col but Col would not release the pylon. The pylon was sharp with barnacles and slimy with weed. Tomorrow Col would notice his hands and face covered in tiny cuts but for now, he did not feel the barnacles jabbing into his flesh. He was just grateful to have his head out of the water and the ability to draw air into his lungs. The plunge into cold water had been terrifying and unexpected but Col noticed that at least now he felt sober. His sinuses burned from the salt but he knew it would be good for him. Seawater, as much as Col did not like to enter it, was healing. Everyone knew that.

When it became evident that Col would not let go of the pylon, Twitch took one of Col's wrists, peeling back his arm, but Col just clamped more firmly with the other.

'It's healing,' Col mumbled.

'He doesn't want to come,' Twitch said to Nell. 'I'm not going to stand here persuading him.'

'Maybe he's scared of you,' said Adrian, appearing alongside Twitch.

Twitch looked between Col and Adrian. 'Why?'

'Because, you know—' Adrian made a fist and brought it to his own nose.

'Huh?'

The three men stared at each other. Then Adrian said, 'You took him to the lighthouse this arvo?'

'Yeah,' said Twitch. 'To help me pick up an engine block from Sparky. Not to beat the shit out of him.'

'You didn't?'

'Of course I didn't. Why would I?'

Little Jase waded up. 'Col's told everyone you clocked him. For, you know—' He made a pumping motion with his pelvis. Seawater sloshed about.

'I lied,' moaned Col. 'I tripped over. My shoelace was untied ... I thought it sounded better ...' The rest of his sentence was inaudible.

A ripple of alarm went through the crowd. Everyone, even Col, looked up.

Over the top of the crowd they heard a shout: 'Nobody misses that Bram fellow, do they?'

Col let go of the pylon, slipping beneath the water.

Col Morton was shot in the foot on the last day of summer in 2010.

The end of February in Port Kingerton could be unpredictable: hot, dry and windy or cold, wet and windy, or anywhere between the two. On this particular day it was hot. And windy. A severe fire danger warning was in place for the entire south east but Young Dick had a wether who needed to go in the fridge sooner rather than later. Maybe the summer grass had stayed unusually rich, or maybe it was a genetic quirk, or possibly the lamb had only got one testicle in the castrator band and had managed to keep one hidden up in its belly, pumping out testosterone, but whatever the reason, the lamb was growing rapidly, approaching the size of a small horse. For weeks he had been watching the lamb, clocking its massive growth, and he did not want to wait any longer. Young Dick did not like mutton. Something about the greasy smell of it boiling all day reminded him of the meaty-lanolin smell in his grandfather's out-buildings and it always made him feel queasy.

But Young Dick's butcher was also a CFS volunteer, so on that hot day the butcher was on standby to head to the fire station, unavailable to take the monster lamb himself. But no matter, the butcher said, if Young Dick could drop the carcass in the butcher's cool room he would get to dressing it tomorrow.

It just meant it would be Young Dick who would need to turn the wether into a carcass.

Young Dick wasn't squeamish. A fisherman couldn't afford to be. Bait, roe, guts—if one wanted to pull in several tonnes of crays a year, one had to be okay with gore. But it wasn't until he had the wether yarded, its bright eyes and fuzzy head looking up at him, hoping for a bucket of oats, that Young Dick faltered. He considered waiting until tomorrow, when the butcher would be available again, but he'd already troubled to yard the thing. Its fat flanks were heaving in the heat. He thought again of the smell of mutton, called himself a fool and shouldered the rifle.

The barrel quivered. The lamb blinked at him. Its nostrils flared with its breath.

Young Dick lowered the rifle.

Then Col Morton appeared. Young Dick had known Col since he was an infant. Col's father, although recently moved away, had been a good friend to Dick and Col himself had gone to school with Dick's kids. Col had been one of the few who had attempted to stick by Abigail, and although it had made not a scrap of difference, Young Dick had not forgotten the display of loyalty. Also, Col had recently purchased his own boat and that was no small thing.

'Morning,' said Col, reaching the yard.

'Yeah,' said Young Dick, surveying the wether. He swore he could see the animal growing before his eyes.

'Jeez, that's a whopper,' said Col.

'Yeah,' repeated Young Dick.

'Sorry to interrupt. Just got a question about my catch quota. I'll wait.' And Col waited politely for Young Dick to shoot the animal but the animal did not get shot. It kept breathing. It kept growing. Young Dick imagined its muscle fibres turning from melting tender to jerky tough as it stood in front of him.

Although he had never been one for machismo, Young Dick did not want Col to witness his hesitation. Mostly because that would give the sense of it dragging out longer. But somehow, without either of them uttering a word, Col seemed to understand. Nonchalantly, without spooking the wether, the younger man slipped into the yard. He stood alongside Dick and then an invisible question seemed to be asked: *May I?* And answered, *Be my guest*. Young Dick handed Col the rifle. Col raised the gun.

The hot wind gave a ferocious gust, lifting dust and grass seeds. Col inhaled lightly, held his breath, fingered the trigger.

And sneezed.

Aside from the fact that Young Dick was supposed to have surrendered that particular rifle in the amnesty in 1996, and also that Col held no valid firearms licence, none of them—not Young Dick, not Nell and certainly not Col—were willing to face the wait times at the hospital in the bigger town, which had blown out to stupendous proportions. There was blood, but it slowed swiftly. There was pain, but there was also the Fancys' brandy and codeine. There could have been infection but a twice-daily hobble through the seawater at high tide, Col's arm tucked firmly about Nell's shoulders, took care of that.

Besides, mere minutes after the gun went off, Col had felt his foot was quite fine. As soon as Young Dick Fancy had picked Col up and made a joke about Col having 'taken a bullet for him', Col found himself radically healed.

'Just promise me you won't tell anyone,' Col found the courage to say, reclining on Young Dick Fancy's couch with his foot elevated on a stack of pillows while Nell doused him with antiseptic and wrapped a clean bandage firmly over his entire lower leg. 'I'd never hear the end of the teasing.'

'Our secret,' promised Young Dick, fetching Col more brandy.

The wether lived for ten more years, eventually dying peacefully of old age beneath a pine tree.

But Col Morton had forever taken a bullet for Young Dick.

OLD DICK

There's something strangely beautiful about a boat on fire. Especially at night. At night you can't see the thick black smoke. You can't see anyone beating a hasty getaway. Black sea glinting orange, the glow like a sun out on the water.

All right, it's unlikely you'd find it splendid to look at if you *own* the boat, your livelihood blazing away like that, but what I'm saying is, sitting here in this car watching that boat burn—I like it. I can't say I haven't seen the odd boat torched but it's been a long time since I could take a back seat, watch the flames and say, *I had nothing to do with that.*

At least, I don't reckon I had anything to do with this one.

The young fella is carrying on a bit, though. Acting unsettled. He could stand to be a bit more stoic in the face of a torching. Stuffing us all into this car, racing down the hill into town, and now I'm sat here and there's a throng of people wandering past and peering in the windows. I'm starting to feel like the Pope. I wonder if this glass is bullet proof.

Boom. There she blows! What a sight, fire raining down.

They say, now, that nothing ever really goes away. I've heard kids talk about there being no such thing as erased. *Nothing can be truly deleted from the internet*, they say. But I think folks these days are just too out of touch with the earth. Too busy worrying what's on their phone to make use of what's real, what's right in front of them. No one takes the trouble anymore to learn about the earth's elements, to study those things in nature that have been around long before the first humans stood up on two legs and started thinking we were better than everything else. Earth, fire, water: you respect those things, you harness them right? You're set for life.

Nothing disappears things like fire.

Nothing swallows things like deep water.

Nothing holds a quieter dignity than giving a man's mistake back to the earth. Or, for that matter, a mistake of a man.

I'm trying to take a short stroll along the jetty to watch the boat burn.

Clear off, you bastards. A man can't watch the boats when you're gathered around bleating.

Oh, but it's all *Mr Fancy* this, *Mr Fancy* that. It's *How're you doing, sir?* and *Old Dicky, old boy, old buddy, old pal, howthebloodyhellareya.*

I'm dying, thanks for asking. Now go away so I can watch the fireworks in peace.

I see a flash of pale yellow hair. It's moving through the crowd, bobbing up here then disappearing, reappearing over there only to blink away again. The yellow hair looks like a bright light waxing and waning. A lighthouse, calling the boats home. The yellow hair flashes closer, closer, until it's standing right in front of me, attached to a young woman.

Hello, Mr Fancy.

Well now, there's a face a man could never forget. Haven't seen you for a very long time. Call me crazy, Ed, but are you wearing a blonde wig?

It's me, Mr Fancy. Jessica.

You're not Ed?

She laughs. *Are you talking about my grandfather?*

Could be, I say. Is your grandfather Ed Bram?

He is. He died a long time ago.

How long is a long time ago?

Twenty-four years.

You call that a long time?

It is when you're forty. That's over half my life.

I suppose you're right. What did you say your name was again?

Jessica.

Whose boat is that, Jessica? I ask, pointing out to sea. But there isn't much left of the boat anymore, just a fizzing red spot on the water. As we look towards it, it blinks a few times and disappears.

That's Lofty's boat.

Was Lofty's boat, I say, and we both laugh at that.

Tell me, Jessica, why are these dickheads still carrying on? The boat's gone. What are they het up about?

The sea mist has gathered on her hair, glinting under the streetlamp. She's a nice girl. I appreciate that she has helped me across the grass towards the jetty. She has a gentle but steady grip on my elbow and now a man can walk onto the jetty like he used to do every day of his life. I can smell the salt and weed and fish. I can hear the ocean crashing against the breakwater like she's trying to get through it. Maybe one day she will.

Well, I think everyone's excited to see you.

Nonsense. I've been here every day for a hundred years. Nothing special about me.

Oh, Mr Fancy, says the girl. *That's not true at all. Don't you think everyone would be excited to see the man who killed Ed Bram?*

Why? I say. Nobody misses that Bram fellow, do they?

ABIGAIL

Crouched on the jetty beside her mother, Abigail was watching the men in the water trying to talk Col Morton off the pylon when someone behind her said, 'Um, Abigail?'

'Not now,' she said.

'Is your grandpa okay?'

'He's fine.'

'I don't think he is. That's him standing there—'

Abigail turned her head and saw the vaguely familiar man from the end of the jetty pointing a finger. She followed his finger to see her grandfather standing at the foot of the jetty, surrounded by a horde of townsfolk.

'Last time he walked was 2020,' the man was saying, but Abigail wasn't listening. Rushing through her was a dizzying sensation of having been flung back in time. Streetlamp picking out the tops of heads, faces cast in shadow: a leering, tittering swarm. All of a sudden she was fifteen again.

It hit her with such ferocity she grabbed the man to steady herself.

Grappling to her feet. Shoving her way along the jetty. How was it possible that she'd ended up back here again? Surrounded by a cold night, a clustered town, feeling alien, an outlier among a species she did not understand?

'Back off,' Abigail barked, her voice as hoarse as it had been twenty-four years ago. Silence descended and she felt the weight of their faces trained on her. 'Are you just going to stand there ogling?'

Her grandfather wobbled on his feet. She saw him lift his chin, open his mouth and shout, 'Nobody misses that Bram fellow, do they?'

That's when she saw the blonde woman standing in front of her grandfather.

The last time Abigail found herself face to face with Jessica Bram on this lawn, they were fifteen. Abigail with bark chips in her hair, Jessica a trail of blood down her face. Jessica crying angry tears, Abigail stony faced, wiping rock grit from her palms. There'd been a crowd watching then, too. *Slut*, Jessica had bawled. *Just admit it.* It wasn't the first time she and Jessica had clashed, but it was the first time no one had jumped to Abigail's side. The way her gut had dropped, to look around and find herself alone. The surge of utter disbelief and panic. She'd been the tall poppy they couldn't wait to cut down. It went on for a long year. For a whole year she put up with it, endured the blacklisting and jeering and lies, until she couldn't take it anymore and she was never coming back.

As she approached Jessica now, Abigail could hear the pulse of blood in her ears. Every cell in her body wanted to launch at Jessica and start tearing.

'Oh, hey, Abigail,' Jessica said. 'If I haven't said it already, welcome back.'

Abigail ignored her. She took her grandfather's elbow in a gentle grip and made to steer him towards the car, but he planted his feet and would not move.

'I said hello,' Jessica said.

Finally Abigail looked at her. She allowed her ribs to lift and fall once, twice. A host of responses ran through her mind before she decided on: 'Fuck off.'

'Do you have to be such a bitch?'

'No. It's a choice.'

A murmur went through the crowd. Someone sniggered.

'Come on, Grandpa,' she said. 'It's cold.'

'No, thanks,' he said. 'I'm having a nice chat here with …' He frowned at Jessica. 'What did you say your name was again?'

'Jessica. Ed Bram's granddaughter.'

'Oh,' said Old Dick, visibly disappointed. 'One of them.'

'That's right,' Jessica said in a rush. 'I am one of them, and proud of it. My mum and I are all that's left. We've had to do it tough in this town on our own.'

'Congratulations on your achievements,' Abigail said to Jessica. She took her grandfather's arm again, but he remained unmovable. It also seemed that Jessica wasn't done.

'How do you think it feels,' Jessica said, raising her voice, 'living here every day with the people who murdered my grandfather?'

Abigail felt a mounting dismay. Alarm and bewilderment crossed her grandfather's face.

'Murdered?' he said. 'Girl, what are you talking about—'

'Enough,' Abigail said to Jessica.

'No.'

The crowd stilled. An eerie silence dropped over the foreshore. Even the waves went quiet, as if the ocean itself held its breath.

Jessica marched forward and addressed the crowd. 'Doesn't anyone think it's convenient that she came back on the same day the bone was found?' She appeared to wait, but when no response came she went on. 'We all know the Fancys are covering something. That bone is obviously evidence, and she's back for damage control—'

'What?' Abigail broke in, stunned.

'She also bought a burner phone and deposited a mountain of cash, and bought dark clothes, rope and duct tape—'

'A hundred bucks is not a mountain,' Abigail said, uncertain why she was defending herself or for what. 'And it was Teflon tape. And *really?*'

'—to cover up her crimes. She's been to prison a dozen times—'

'Twice.'

'—and frankly she deserves to be in there forever, for what she did to that baby.'

And there it is. Time crunched to a standstill. Twenty-four years vanished, and it was 1999 and she was standing on this lawn, crushed beneath this mass of leering faces and she did not matter. There was nothing she could say or do because their own primal wounds were in control and their minds were made up.

The rock had been heavier than she'd anticipated. Where had it come from? Jessica yelled it—*slut*—and then the rock was in her hands and it was pelting through the frigid night air to hit Jessica just where her blonde hair met her forehead: *thwack*. The sound would never leave her, like other things would never leave her: stench of seaweed; metal stink of blood; reek of a public toilet block. Jessica had folded as though she was boneless and Abigail didn't hear her body hit the ground because she could still hear the dull smack of the rock on skin, she could still hear the ring of *slut* and the roar-whine in her ears. There'd been nervous laughter from the crowd then, as there was now, and she had spun on her heels, felt herself screaming, but could anyone hear it?

Why wouldn't anyone help her?

Her limbs turned to ice. *It's happening again. It's happening again, it's happening again, it's happening again.* Abigail was a statue—she *made* herself a statue. Because she could not go back and if she were to throttle Jessica Bram's skinny white neck, if she were to paint a crown of bruises about Jessica Bram's fluffy blonde head, she would go back undoubtedly.

'Lock them *all* up,' Jessica was saying. 'They killed my grandfather.'

Abigail could hear the sound of someone panting. Was it herself?

It felt like an eternity that she had stared down at Jessica's lifeless form. Later someone told her it had been only seconds, but at the time she'd watched Jessica slumped on the grass and thought, truly, that she had killed her. But Jessica got to her feet—someone put their arm around Jessica, Abigail remembered being surprised by that display of humanity—and Jessica wiped her face, dusted off her jeans and resumed as though nothing had happened, blood trailing down her face. *Admit it*, Jessica said. *You're a slut just like your grandmother.* Many years later, when Abigail recounted those words to Jen, Jen had daintily exhaled a stream of smoke and offered, 'Not every day you hear the words "slut" and "grandmother" in the same sentence. But mmkay.' To which Abigail replied, 'Especially when my grandmother crocheted doilies and thought risqué was a woman in trousers.'

But there it was, laid out for all to see—the man behind the curtain of Jessica's outrage: the legend of a woman. A woman running; a woman stolen like property; a woman making a choice, the sin of sexual agency. Did it matter what was true when your identity, your very genetic heritage, was rooted in it, born from the slight of it?

Now a murmur went through the crowd. Bodies jostled, the crowd parted, and Abigail saw her mother emerge, trailed by her posse of men. Col Morton appeared, soaked from head to toe and with what looked like the beginnings of two black eyes. Adrian Turner, his little brother and Twitch were wet from the waist down; a piece of seaweed clung to Twitch's leg. As Abigail stared, uncomprehending, Col moved his hands and cupped them in front of his genitals.

'Richard,' her mother cried, hurrying to Old Dick's side. 'Are you okay? Where is your chair? Adrian, get it, would you?'

Abigail watched as Adrian Turner retrieved her grandfather's wheelchair but the old man refused to sit, batting Adrian's hands away.

'What's going on?' Nell demanded.

No one answered.

'Abigail?'

'Well,' she began, slowly, 'apparently I'm a crime lord.'

She saw her mother's eyes widen, roving over her face. Then Nell glanced at the crowd and Abigail wondered what it was she could see in her mother's expression. It wasn't fear, Nell Fancy was far too on top of things in this town to feel afraid of it, but was it something like it? Trepidation?

No. It was disgust.

'Pathetic,' Nell said. 'Don't you all have better things to do?'

And Abigail wanted to laugh now because, as if on cue, heads dropped to consider their own feet. Throats cleared; bodies shrunk. No one could inspire the scolded inner child quite like Nell Fancy, but this was the first time Abigail had felt grateful for it. Only Twitch lifted his chin, crossing his arms and digging his knuckles beneath his biceps, bringing the muscles out like melons in his sleeves.

A voice came from the crowd: 'Jess?'

Abigail blinked. Penny Bram was stretching a hand towards Jessica.

'Let's go home,' Penny said.

'No,' said Jessica. 'Let's sort this out, once and for all.'

'There's nothing to sort out,' Penny said, and Abigail could hear the nervous plea in her voice.

Another murmur started up in the crowd, more shuffling and jostling, and now the postmistress appeared. Abigail saw Mrs Dinwiddle hesitate before opening her mouth and announcing, 'Jessica, maybe you should listen to your mother.'

Suddenly Old Dick spoke again. 'Listening to a mother is good advice,' he said. 'I didn't listen to Luce—get your hands off me, boy,' he said, as Adrian tried once again to usher him into his chair, '—and I should have. She's a mother. She knew when that girl was in trouble—I said get *off*—and I didn't listen.'

'You knew Honnie Zabowski was pregnant?' Jessica said.

Abigail turned to Jessica so fast her ears rang. 'You knew it was Honnie?'

And when Jessica looked at her, she couldn't make out whether Jessica's expression was one of incredible guilt or incredible triumph.

Honnie had been Abigail's friend for only eighteen months, yet Abigail thought of her every night. When she closed her eyes Honnie was there, materialising behind her eyelids, no matter how often, how resolutely, or however chemically she tried to push the image away. While Abigail herself lived and aged, Honnie remained a portrait suspended in Abigail's mind, always fifteen, a fixture in her internal landscape.

Honnie had come to town as a teenager with her mother. A distant cousin of the Lofts, they slid in without a ruckus and, not two years later, slid back out again in spite of one. Hardly anyone saw them go.

Everyone was too busy pointing at Abigail.

One of those kids at school so skilled at blending in no one's exactly sure how, one day Abigail discovered Honnie was in her orbit and liked her too much to wonder when she came to be there. Honnie was to Abigail what everyone else wasn't. She wasn't simpering. She wasn't pandering. She wasn't sulky, needy, phony. Honnie was thoughtful and funny, wickedly deadpan; she could make Abigail laugh to the point of breathlessness just by an offhand gesture, a tone of voice, a quirk of facial expression. More than once Abigail got sent out of chemistry for being disruptive when she was cry-laughing over Honnie's imitation of Mr Hall's lazy eye. Honnie kept red frogs in her pocket and when she shared them with Abigail they were gooey from the warmth of her body. In return Abigail gave her smokes and sanction. Honnie wore her thick hair in a sleek ponytail; she wore round glasses and huge jumpers over her big, soft frame. To Abigail, Honnie was a person-sized cushion: comfort and warmth and nothing not to like. She didn't know at the time that Honnie was so good at being *likeable* because she had striven to make herself that way, had made herself malleable, had erased herself so meticulously, shaved away any sharp or protruding edges in order to survive.

Abigail wished she had known.

She never stopped thinking about her.

No matter how much she ran.

Pure silence. As if Abigail's surroundings had evaporated and she stood in a vacuum. Then a whisper, a low hiss in the crowd that boiled swiftly to a hubbub, then a clamour. Questions hurled, shouts and insults began to fly.

Abigail's head was reeling. A kind of bewildered fury was coursing through her and she couldn't fully comprehend what was taking place. Was Jessica Bram really standing here on the foreshore in the cold night air, yelling at the entire town? Was Abigail really listening to this implausible melodrama? Again?

The urge to lie down, to close her eyes, to be tucked away in her cosy apartment in the anonymous drone of the city buckled her knees. That was the moment Abigail realised three things.

Firstly, she was tired of running and simply would not anymore. So be it. She would stop and face it, the tidal wave of emotion, and she would deal with whatever that meant, whatever that came with. She was not sixteen anymore. She was a grown-arse woman with a rich life and a biting conscience and a giant, flawed heart.

Secondly, she realised that just like this senseless crowd, just like herself blasting up the freeway in a stolen Maserati, Jessica Bram was acting out her own pain. She was doing whatever she could to gain relief. And while Abigail couldn't exactly love her—hell, she didn't even like her—in this place, this acting from a wound, she could *understand* her. Both of their childhoods had been spent cementing the stories about themselves, true or not, that were told to them by others. There was no difference between Abigail trying to prove who she wasn't—not just a Fancy, not just the daughter of a small town big gun, and Jessica trying to prove who she was—not just a Bram, not just the only child of a single mother. They were both searching for the exact same thing: freedom. The liberty to be whoever they really are.

That discovery caused everything she had thought about the past two-and-a-half decades to grind to a halt then shunt into reverse.

And thirdly, she realised Nate Ruskin was standing beside her, murmuring into her ear. Her mother's horse was in labour.

THEM

Trisha slid the tinnie against the jetty and Young Dick climbed out.

'Listen,' he began to say, 'about the insurance—'

Trisha raised a hand to cut him off. She held his eyes and nodded once, then the engine revved and Trisha cut a tight circle and motored away. Young Dick didn't know where she would go, but he knew wherever it was would be as far from the crowd as possible. He could see them clustered on the street in front of the drive-in. A seething, yeasty mass.

Standing at the end of the jetty, Young Dick took a moment to collect himself. He was furious. They had not listened to him. Less than an hour ago he had told them to go home and now look—there they all were, sucked to a whiff of ado like mosquitoes to a bared ankle.

Young Dick was struck by the thought that if he hadn't spent the past six years wishing deep down that no one felt the need to seek and heed his every instruction, they probably would have heeded him tonight. Since his mother died and his father's disease began to take hold, Young Dick had resentfully, unconsciously, rejected the responsibility he'd inherited from his father, his grandfathers. Young Dick didn't want to be a leader; he simply wanted to live his life, quiet with his family. Sure, he guarded some unfortunate truths he'd have to take to his grave, but regardless, for six years he had tried to wean the town from the Fancy reign and tonight it appeared they'd finally chosen to let go of the damn nipple. They had decided to ignore him and think for themselves.

And now he wished they hadn't.

Young Dick hurried along the jetty. Murmurs of consternation came from the crowd, punctuated by sharp jabs of a female voice raised in anger. He tried to place the voice. It wasn't his wife, and it didn't sound like his daughter.

Then Young Dick heard his father say, 'She knew when that girl was in trouble—and I didn't listen.'

And he thought, *Oh, shit.*

Adrian Turner was trying in vain to get Old Dick Fancy back into his chair. The old man's spine was bending and his knees were trembling, but he refused to sit. Every time Adrian offered his hands he was swatted away and Adrian was beginning to feel like an annoying insect. Plus his popped-open thumb was hurting. Old Dick had smacked it a few times and Adrian was reluctant to keep putting it in the line of fire.

The problem was, Adrian held so much respect for this retired patriarch, this hard-weathered, law-making, justice-dealing old cray fisherman, that his clumsiness felt like trying to put undies on the King. It just seemed wrong.

It also did not help that Abigail was watching his every move, his every fumble, and he felt as though he was failing a test he didn't know he was taking but that he lusted desperately to pass.

Let him speak, Adrian wanted to say. But at the same time he thought, *Dear god, someone make him stop.* Because now Jessica Bram was gaping at Old Dick Fancy incredulously. At the precise moment that Adrian copped a particularly forceful smack on his injured thumb he heard Jessica say, 'Honnie Zabowski is pregnant?' and, momentarily deranged by the flare of pain, Adrian blurted, 'She can't be. She's dead.'

When Mrs Dinwiddle heard Jessica speak the girl's name, tears came into her eyes. For the unwitting swoop of emotion the postmistress might have wanted to blame menopause but she was long past that; she was long past the point of even being able to *blame* that—not that she had ever actively mentioned it to anybody. In fact, all those years ago, when she had been weathering the change of life, Beverly Dinwiddle had told nobody, not even her dear husband Larry, and so, when she decided to come forward with the other women and have herself eliminated, no one had batted an eyelid. True, she'd received a few funny looks, heard a snigger or two, but the postmistress had done her duty for the town. At the time she'd been convinced, like everyone else, that it was the right thing to do.

Mrs Dinwiddle heard the girl's name now and thought bitterly, *I shouldn't have done it.* She wanted to correct

Jessica Bram. It wasn't a 'mountain' of cash that Abigail had deposited, merely two fifty-dollar notes. But that would be infringing upon Abigail Fancy's privacy.

And the postmistress had already, once before in her life, infringed upon Abigail Fancy's privacy.

Shame coiled tightly inside Mrs Dinwiddle. It is said that one's past mistakes come back to haunt one and, heck, the postmistress was feeling haunted indeed.

Twenty-four years ago, Beverly Dinwiddle had wanted to correct the town—*this isn't the crime you think it is*—but in order to do so, she would have been admitting to a crime. A violation. A month after the baby was found, the letter had come in, addressed to *Miss Abigail Fancy* in a teenage girl's handwriting (who else dots a lowercase 'i' with a loveheart?). The postmistress took the letter to the kitchen and held it over the boiling kettle. Then she opened the letter and read it. She'd watched herself as if she were witnessing someone else, a character in a spy novel perhaps, undertake this grievously immoral, not to mention thumpingly illegal, act of treachery. Tampering! Opening a mail receptacle that was not hers! For this act the postmistress knew she could be criminally liable. She could go to prison.

Just like Abigail did.

So Beverly Dinwiddle knew the truth, but she could never say *how* she knew. Over the years she had swung between trying to pepper the town with hints, to steer the narrative in the right direction, and wanting to stay silent, to put the whole awful mess to bed. When people eventually stopped talking about it, the postmistress had consoled herself that it was over, and resolved that one should begin each day with chin up and eye to the future.

Now she was riven with shame.

The postmistress knew the letter by heart. *Dear Abigail,* it began, in Honnie's loopy girlish script (dear god, she was but a baby herself!) *Perth is nice. I don't know anyone. Thank you for being there for me. I'm still sorry about your jeans. If you write to me I'll try and write back, but Mum says I shouldn't talk to anyone in Kingo ever again because of what happened with the baby. Sorry they think it's yours. Love, Honnie.*

Mrs Dinwiddle stepped forward. 'There's nothing to cover up,' she said. 'Ms Fancy here—' she gestured to Abigail, hoping it was a strong, forceful display of solidarity '—had nothing to do with baby Joan.'

And that's when David Wimple, owner of the hardware-cum-surf store, spoke up from the crowd: 'And she never bought rope, either.'

Col Morton was trying to follow what was happening, but his teeth were clattering together so loudly he could not hear everything that was being said. They'd all heard Honnie Zabowski had died of an overdose, somewhere in remote Western Australia, many years ago—why were they talking about her now? And why was Jessica Bram acting surprised at something Old Dick Fancy had just said?

And what was this about duct tape?

What is going on? Sheila Rocket thought. When Jessica had spoken Honnie's name, Sheila's heart had gone *ka-thump* in unbridled excitement. Sheila expected, like last time, a flare-up was about to begin. Anticipation swelled. But then something unexpected happened: things began to calm down.

Twenty-four years ago, when the town had mustered like this, it was supposed to have been a town meeting but devolved swiftly into a kind of ... what would be the word? Sheila wondered now. *Riot* wasn't quite right—there were no baseball bats or looting. *Commotion* would be closer, but it felt a bit dull.

Sheila strained forward, trying to catch what Abigail Fancy and Old Dick were saying to Jessica, and the word *uproar* came to her and she decided that would have to do. Twenty-four years ago the town had gathered like this in order to talk about the baby and instead became an uproar. Sheila had not seen the rock thrown herself but she'd heard it—a low, thick *thwack*. Did Abigail start it or Jessica? It didn't matter. Everyone knew the Fancys and the Brams had blamed each other for Port Kingerton's ills since time immemorial. That particular thrown rock had simply been the final crank in the opening of a steam vent, and there'd been no stopping what burst out.

It had been no small thing, having detectives from the city come to town. Interrogating the locals, canvassing the beachfront and shops and public toilet block; they even staged a recreation, with a mannequin in a wig and everything. For days Port Kingerton had crawled with police, news vans, reporters thrusting microphones in faces and photographers running sideways, snapping like paparazzi around royalty. At first everyone had been excited by the novelty of it, the sense of righteous importance. But it didn't take long before tolerance stretched thin. Tempers boiled over and everyone was very, very emotional, broken-hearted for that poor baby.

At least the nurses had given her a good name. Strong, after Joan of Arc. Because she had been a little fighter. It was because of that name that the women were galvanised when some menfolk suggested the females volunteer themselves for inspection. Gallantly. Self-sacrificingly.

Except, of course, for Abigail Fancy, who at the suggestion had stuck up her middle fingers and, eventually, fled town. If that was not an admission of guilt, Sheila, and so many others, did not know what was.

So now Sheila was waiting for the rocks to start flying. She was waiting for the wrestling and the hoarse-throated shouts. But instead, it just kind of ... fizzled out. Because last time, Sheila recalled, hadn't it been the twins, the Fancy boys, Hamish and Dylan, who'd started throwing punches? And they were gone. Banished, some said, at Young Dick's bidding. Here came Nell Fancy and her men—Twitch, Col, the Turner brothers, Spike—and then came Young Dick, and the next thing Sheila knew, in spite of Jessica Bram hailing them with questions, the Fancys were piling into their vehicle and driving away.

Sheila's interest sparked to note that Abigail did not leave with her parents, climbing instead into that new vet's four-wheel drive, but even that proved nothing of intrigue, because the vet followed the Fancys. Nothing happened that could indicate a family attempting to *disguise nefarious activity* or possibly being *rent asunder*—no driving in opposite directions, no piqued peal of tyres on bitumen. No middle fingers thrust out windows. Nothing. Just a quiet convoy driving, together, in the direction of home.

OLD DICK

The death of Ed Bram was an accident.

I'll admit it might depend on your definition of the word 'accident', but I maintain that's what it was.

People fall in the water all the time. Take a look at any headline from the local rag over the last hundred years and you'll see: MAN DROWNED OFF JETTY; BOY DROWNED OFF ROCKS; AN UNFORTUNATE ACCIDENT—WOMAN FALLS IN WELL.

It happens.

But the nice yellow-haired girl seemed to think I had something to do with Ed Bram carking it, and I told her, how could I push a man off the perch when I'm about to drop off it myself?

You hated him.

He hated me. Fair's fair.

She shook her head like she didn't believe me. *You started it*, she said.

Pfft. That grudge went a long way back, girl. Like bloody England and France. One bruised pride begets another. One stolen craypot makes missing bloodstock makes a girl shotgun-wedded makes three hundred acres extorted makes blackmail makes ransom makes a licence swindled from a deathbed—next thing you know, a hundred years has passed and we're still tatting for some other bastard's tit.

Richard, let's go home.

No. I want to watch the boat burn.

The boat sank.

Dad, here, take my arm—those hips aren't made to be stood on.

You worry about your own hips, I'll worry about mine.

Mr Fancy?

Jessica, not now.

You knew, Mr Fancy? You knew about Honnie?

Jess, for fuck's sake, mind the fucking door?

If you knew—Mr Fancy!—Hey!—Why didn't you—

The door slams and there she is in the window, yellow-haired, open-mouthed, but I can't hear what she's saying because we're driving away.

ABIGAIL

The house appeared, lit up in the dark, windows gold against a backdrop of stars. The sweeping driveway, salt-bleached stone, those cheesewoods oozing oversweet—whatever way you looked at it, Abigail thought, it was just a house. This castle of Kingo, this house of parliament—it was still just bricks and trusses mortared together by generations of hubris and baggage. Ordained only by belief; stop believing, and did any of its power exist at all? Did anyone's?

Abigail pressed her hot forehead to the cool glass of the car window, and as they passed the house to drive around back to the stables, she followed the bright house lights with her eyes, not moving her head, until her eyes hurt. Nate parked by the stables. When she climbed from the four-wheel drive she couldn't help a groan. Nate asked if she was okay.

'Just waiting for a goose up my arse.'

The vet laughed but she saw him glance nervously about in the dark.

Inside the stables, soft light spilled from the end stall. Nate's footfalls along the cobblestones were controlled and noiseless. Abigail sweated with the same effort to tread lightly.

They stopped some distance from the stall. The pregnant mare was pacing, churning up straw, biting at her flanks. Her tail was wrapped up in a red bandage and it swung like a baton. Next door, the mare's stablemate stood motionless, nose through the rails and ears pricked, and there was a long moment of stillness as Abigail watched the companion horse and Nate observed the pregnant mare, all of them quiet together.

Then her mother appeared.

'Nate,' Nell whispered. 'Thanks.'

Abigail felt there was an element in that single word from her mother—*thanks*—that went deeper than simply acknowledging the vet's presence in the stables at this particular moment in time.

Nell clicked her tongue. 'She waited till we were all gone.'

'Of course she did,' Abigail said. 'People around here have a tendency to feel entitled to peer up vaginas.'

Nell made a choking noise in her throat. Slowly, her head swivelled to Abigail, and Abigail could see all the whites of her mother's eyes.

Leaving the mare in privacy, Abigail and Nate tucked themselves into the cramped feed room. Nell declined to stay, and Abigail thought her mother walking away from a prized mare in labour showed how blisteringly uncomfortable she was in her presence.

And so she found herself alone in the dark with the vet. It had just gone midnight. Between moments of activity the mare dozed. Abigail felt the tug of sleep herself.

She was very close to Nate. Sitting on a stack of hay bales, pressed together shoulder to thigh; she could hear the breath going in and out of him. Beneath the earth and straw scents of the feed room there was something she imagined was his skin: warm and spicy.

'Why are you staying?' she asked groggily. 'Are you worried about her?'

Nate exhaled slowly. 'Which "her"?'

'Ah,' she said, understanding. 'You're worried about pleasing Nell.'

'I have to.' His head turned to her. 'This fucking town.' He said it so gently, with such an almost endearing humour, that Abigail felt herself smile.

'Precisely,' she said.

Everything she'd feared about returning to Port Kingerton had come true. Her mother's martyred silence, her father's lead-weight burden. Gossip, slander, grotesque made-up stories. But—by some miracle—she was still here. She had not fled.

'Duct tape,' she said. 'And a burner phone? Even for Kingo that's a next level fantasy.'

'What happened?'

She was so exhausted she answered without thinking. 'I opened their mother wound.'

He looked at her. 'Their what?'

'It took me twenty years to work that out,' she murmured. 'Before that I always assumed they just thought I was a slut.'

Nate continued to gaze at her without speaking. The mare was quiet in her stall.

'You'd think I'd be untouchable. Dad could tell practically anyone here to jump off a cliff and they'd happily ask which one. But you know what dies harder than anything? Misogyny. Not even their respect for my father could trump their hatred of me.'

She searched his face. It was too dark to make out his expression, but she could see the line of his jaw, the rough side of his cheek. She recalled the shocked relief that came when he spoke up for her in front of the farmer's wife, his casual confidence, downplaying the moment into something manageable, unremarkable. She remembered crouching bare-legged beside the four-wheel drive as he'd quietly handed a clean pair of pants across the bonnet, his eyes politely averted as he broke from his usual reserve to keep up a gentle but steady patter of conversation about nothing in particular, distracting her. Making her human.

'Surely,' she said, 'you've heard about the baby?'

She felt the tidal wave rushing behind her. The urge to run was so compelling she clamped her hands together. Fear and trepidation roiled through her. This had to come out. This had to come out of her.

Nate said, 'You want to talk about it?'

She said, 'Yeah.'

They were fifteen. *Fifteen.* Not girls, not women. They had bodies that could do everything a woman's body could do but Abigail wore a Tweety Bird nightie to bed and couldn't go to sleep until her mum kissed her goodnight.

Fifteen.

They knew the power of their bodies, the allure of their bodies, was dangerous. To exist inside these beings felt illicit, something that was both shameful and also, somehow, potent and vital. They were witches' potions, they were the strong dark liquor at the back of the cabinet, they were cigarettes smoked crouched behind brick walls. Forbidden, stolen, intoxicating.

Honnie had not wanted to go home. They'd been skulking around town, skidding their feet on the swings, folding long limbs into the tunnel slide together against the cold. Night fell and the two wan streetlights came on, but Honnie would not be drawn inside. Pooling their coins they bought a parcel of hot chips, tearing an opening in the paper and picking out chips that burned their tongues. Abigail kept suggesting they go home—to hers, to Honnie's—but Honnie was unsettled and refused. She didn't feel well, she said, and her mum would make her go to bed. And Honnie didn't want to go to bed.

'What do you wanna do?' Abigail asked, but Honnie just looked away, shaking her head.

So they kept walking. They peered into darkened shop windows, they hung around the back door of the second fish-and-chip shop, stealing a ciggie with Ricky Leake until Patty Smith ordered them to clear off on threat of Ricky losing his job.

For a while they sat at the playground. Shivering in the old timber lighter, breath fogging in damp clouds, ocean churning in the dark. Abigail's parents knew she was with

Honnie, and if she didn't come home with the dark, they would assume she was at the Zabowskis'.

Honnie needed to pee. Hurrying to the public toilet block, scurrying inside, arm in arm beneath the ugly glare of fluorescent light. Pine needles crunching like dead insects on the concrete underfoot. It felt even colder inside, the stone walls radiating the chill night. Abigail turned the hand dryer on, giggling at the roar of hot air as Honnie went into the stall.

The dryer clicked off. Abigail turned it back on. Off, on again.

'Honnie?'

No answer.

'You still peeing?' Abigail laughed.

No answer.

Shrugging, Abigail set the dryer going again. She must have set it a hundred times. The whir of hot air grew deafening. No one came in—why would they? It was Port Kingerton, a tiny fishing town at the butt-end of South Australia, in the bleak depth of winter.

After a while, Abigail wandered to the stall door. 'Honnie?' She put a hand on the timber, pressed it lightly.

The door swung open.

Abigail has spent her entire life trying to make sense of that moment. Flinging herself from planes, drinking until the world spun, plunging down freeways—all of it an attempt to parse the moment in life where nothing makes sense, when that split second feels like you're living something unreal: a fiction; a nightmare; a tale told by other people. But it wasn't happening to other people, it was happening to them. To Honnie, to her.

And Abigail could only watch in horror, she could only witness, and Honnie looked at Abigail with a face that she could never forget, the naked terror, the face of a child abandoned. And what could Abigail do, when Honnie said, *Please don't tell? Please don't ever tell, oh my god, Abigail, you have to promise me. Never tell.* There was blood on Abigail's jeans where Honnie clung to her, on Abigail's shoes where she had stood in it. Other things too, unmentionable things, substances they did not know could come out of themselves and at one point, Honnie, who had been sick, said, 'Looks like I didn't chew my chips enough,' and why did they laugh? Because it was absurd, beyond belief.

'Is it …?' Abigail said.

'I don't know,' Honnie said.

They looked down and tried to see, tried to understand, but they could not. How could they?

They were fifteen.

Cold, metallic taste in Abigail's mouth. The stench of urine and rotting seaweed and something different, musty and earthy and unknown but also—impossible!—familiar. Somehow known. How was that possible?

The world lies to women and to girls. It tells them they are petty, catty, each other's worst enemies. Cat fight, bitch fight, mummy wars. But when that stall door creaked open and Abigail saw Honnie cradling her arms, curtain of sweat-soaked hair and thighs streaked with red, Abigail knew one certainty: she was here. There was no cleaving from this. She was here for this girl, this abandoned, hurting, barely-woman, and she would not break. Whatever Honnie asked her to do, Abigail would do it. She knew this with the same certainty she knew the sun would rise tomorrow.

So Abigail asked, 'What do you want to do?'

And then she did what Honnie wanted.

That's where Abigail stopped. It felt crude to have said it all aloud, but being divested of it she was empty, all of it sucked out like water down a plughole.

She got to her feet and went to the feed room door, where she watched the mare pacing in her stall. The pony would fold herself to her knees, roll to her side, only to stand back up again. It looked like colic, but she knew the horse was simply repositioning her foal. It was instinctive behaviour, engrained in the mare's biological wiring. Just like that escaped heifer would nine months or so from now, this female animal was responding to the messages of her body. Both passenger and driver, both helpless and entirely her own, and only, source of power.

'Honnie didn't know she was pregnant,' Abigail said. 'She thought she had a stomach ache.'

She felt something, a slight ticking sensation on her hands, folded on top of her belly. Surprised, she looked down and saw she was crying.

Shouldn't it be easier for her, she often berated herself, that what happened had not happened to her directly? It was not her inside that toilet stall. It had not been her bedroom snuck into night after night, year after year. But vicarious trauma is still trauma—she'd learned that at bullshit group, too. A cousin of survivor guilt; the unmarked boy soldier holding his gun in trembling hands while his brothers' insides are heaped on the dirt around him.

Abigail returned to sit alongside Nate and put her face in her hands. For one beat of time it was as if there was nothing but awareness, a sense only of her *beingness*, and she was spellbound by it. And then, finally, the wave crashed. She cried for a long time.

When eventually she looked up, she saw her parents were in the room. Nate had taken hold of her hand. The space felt airless and heavy.

'She didn't know,' Abigail repeated. 'I didn't know. But she told me not to tell anyone, so I promised. I was shit-scared. I thought they'd put us in jail, Honnie *and* me.' She gave a short, ironic laugh that faded to bitterness. 'They always throw the women in jail.'

'The baby was alive,' her mother said quietly. 'We tried to tell you. This could've been different.'

In the beginning her parents had begged her to allow them to tell the truth, in order to take the heat off Abigail. *Just quietly*, her father said. *We won't make a fuss of it*. But Abigail's terror had been so overbearing, so absolute, that she had not wanted anyone talking about Honnie at all. The idea was unthinkable. Talking about it felt to Abigail like standing in that grotty, stinking bathroom all over again. And bizarrely, her grandmother agreed. *There's no getting through when men have their blood up*, Lucy said. *Better to keep it hush-hush*. Her brothers came home with bloodied knuckles, but it made no difference. Women's business, her grandfather had called it. Not our business.

'We made mistakes,' her father said. 'We wanted to keep you safe but we didn't do right by you, or by Honnie. Even though we did try,' he added.

And although Abigail knew he was referring to the money they had given Honnie and her mother, the swift and furtive squirrelling away interstate, she said, 'Like when Mum went to the doctor with the rest of them?'

She felt Nate give a jolt alongside her as the understanding clicked home. Abigail wondered if the mare out in her stall was picking up on the tension. How it might be affecting her.

Nell took a deep breath. 'I wasn't ...' She picked a piece of straw from her jeans, dropped it carefully on the floor. 'I never had the exam.'

Abigail stared at her mother. She never had the exam? She recalled Nell coming home from the clinic saying, *What's done is done*, and she'd felt the betrayal of it cut her in half. Not even her mother was on her side.

'You didn't?'

'No. I paid him off.'

'Wait,' her father said. '*You* paid Gregory?'

Nell nodded benignly.

Her father looked mystified. 'But I paid him, too.'

Abigail looked back and forth between them. 'What for?'

'To say that he'd ...' Her father cleared his throat and Abigail saw the discomfort in him. 'That he'd seen all of you. And nothing else. We wanted him to leave it ambiguous. We thought that way you'd *all* be safe—all you girls.'

'Well, that's what he did say,' Nell said. 'He refused to indict anyone. Do you really think I would have gone through with that?'

'I've lived the last twenty-four years thinking you did!' Abigail hissed. She had a feeling like she was coming apart at the seams.

'I can't believe he took money from both of us.' Her father shook his head. 'Sneaky bastard.'

Abigail let out another quick laugh. 'And as you'll remember, that achieved fuck all.'

Her parents exchanged a glance.

'A special kind of public hell is reserved for the woman seen to not want her child,' Abigail said. 'It hurts people's most fundamental wound: the need for their mother's approval. Doesn't matter that in this case it was a terrified fifteen-year-old girl abused by her mother's forty-five-year-old boyfriend. They can't even see it. Being told forever that women are inferior clashes with their deep need for their mother's love and confuses the shit out of them. All they see is themselves in that unwanted baby, a woman they can blame to feel righteous, and *bam*. Out comes the mob. Out come the torches and pitchforks.'

Again her parents caught each other's eye. Abigail was too furious and exhausted to try and interpret their wordless conversation. Nate was motionless and silent, but she could feel the heat from his body next to hers. She could hear him breathing. From the mare's stall came a snort, the sound of straw churned up.

'And that,' she said, 'I learned from my friend Jen, the stripper. Someone extra familiar with being both desired and loathed.'

THEM

When the Fancys drove away, all the bluster went out of the crowd. No one knew what to do. The town became a puppet with its strings cut, impotent and pointless, their animating force disappeared up the road in Young Dick Fancy's Silverado. Now they found themselves standing around frigid and soggy—and in Col Morton's case, soaking wet—and there was the collective feeling of being at the pub past closing time, when the lights are thrown on and all one can see is the mortifying, un-sexy mess. What had moments ago appeared alluring could now be seen for the pale ale slopped down its front and up-chuck on its shoes.

So they slunk away. Eyes downcast, mumbling about seeing each other tomorrow, maybe. Or next weekend. They headed home, each filled with their own measure of disbelief, confusion or rapture, each already conceiving the ways they would recount this night to themselves and to each other in the days and months and years to come—this night in which it seemed as though something had happened, but they could never quite put their finger on what that something had actually been.

Beverly Dinwiddle went home to her husband Larry, who was snoring on the recliner in front of the TV. The postmistress outlined the evening's events to the publican, who was one of very few town locals who had chosen not to attend the evening's public discourse, because, frankly, in order to maintain one's sanity running a pub in a small town, one had to have cultivated a significant measure of genuine disinterest in a public shitshow. But she told Larry all about it anyway—about Col Morton going for a swim, about Jessica Bram accusing Old Dick Fancy of murder (murder, for heaven's sake!), about Abigail once again facing a slavering crowd and how she, Beverly Dinwiddle, was feeling sadness and regret upon looking back at how the town had treated those poor girls.

Larry considered this, then said, 'Times were different back then. We didn't listen to girls like we do now.'

And although Mrs Dinwiddle patted her husband's hand and said, 'Perhaps you're right,' she went to bed feeling like that was not necessarily true. She had seen the protests on TV in front of Parliament House; she had seen the women marching with ferocious, fed-up faces. And the postmistress resolved, in the morning, to find a leaflet she could sticky-tape to the counter at the post office to signal her new-found women's liberalism.

Col Morton had sobered up enough to know he was not sober enough to drive, so Little Jase Turner gave him a lift home. It was a grudging kind of lift though, as Col's clothes were still dripping seawater and he didn't seem to be aware of the gross leak coming from his nose.

Pulling up in front of Col's house, Little Jase was relieved when Col got straight out of the wagon. No hanging about to debrief whatever the hell had just happened in town.

But then, as Col was about to slam the door, Little Jase said, 'Wait!'

Col bent down, peered inside.

'Is this your phone?'

Col looked. It was.

'It was being passed around,' Little Jase said, 'back at the drive-in. With the … you know. So I thought I'd better … you know.' He sniffed, cleared his throat. 'Privacy and that.'

Col went to pocket the phone, only to remember his pockets were a swamp. 'Thanks,' he said quietly.

A short while later, after Little Jase drove away and Col shuffled inside, stripped off his wet clothes and showered some heat back into his body, he climbed into bed. He pulled the blankets over his head. In a cocoon of darkness he lifted the phone to his face and blinked against the glow of the screen.

A curve of black underwear, a strip of lace around the top of one peach-fuzz leg. Three freckles like chocolate drops on a hip bone.

They'd said it was Jessica. Someone swore they knew. Col tried to remember, but the pub kitchen had been so dark and it was all such a blur. He looked at the photo for a long time and then, smiling and warm, he went to sleep.

Penny Bram walked Jessica home, loaded with things she wanted to say but unable to say any of it. She wanted to say, *What were you thinking?* She wanted to say, *Are you okay?* She wanted to say, *What on earth happened back there, did you have some kind of episode, has the UTI gone to your brain and affected your ability to think?*

Oh, but for a dollar every time Jessica and Abigail Fancy had fallen out! Penny had lost count. It began in kindergarten over who was going to hand out the orange wedges after story time—one got a braid yanked out, the other an eyeful of Clag Paste—and from then on it seemed their rivalry was set. Friends picked sides (Abigail's), boys picked sides (usually Abigail's, but Jessica was not without her assets). Teachers tried: separation; team projects; time outs; behaviour charts. Nell and Penny tried: phone calls; bribery; pleas; punishments. But the two girls just seemed to hate each other on a visceral level. Penny had once accidentally joked to Nell that it was as if Abigail had been born Trojan and Jessica Greek. To which Nell had replied archly, *Well, Helen made her choice, didn't she?*

'She didn't know,' Jessica said, finally breaking the silence. 'Abigail. She didn't know that we know the baby was Honnie's.'

'She's been gone a long time,' Penny said.

'I thought someone would have told her.'

No one knew exactly when the town figured out it was Honnie's baby. There probably wasn't a clear-cut moment. The baby was found wrapped in a thick wad of hand towel when an unknown person hammered frantically on the back door of the second fish-and-chip shop, and someone said the baby was Abigail's with enough conviction that no one questioned it. Even if she was a Fancy. Even if Young Dick tried his damnedest.

The first boy to claim he'd slept with Abigail had been followed by a string of others and at the time, in a town that prizes its boys, its next generation of fishermen, no one bothered to consider the boys were simply bragging or, more likely, lying. Especially when Abigail seemed to demonstrate her guilt by refusing to allow Doctor Gregory to examine her. For heaven's sake, even *Nell* went inside with the doctor. What possible other conclusion could they draw? That Honnie and her mother had left town before the examinations began skipped anyone's notice because the town was blinded by camera flash and, as a general rule, no one really noticed the Zabowskis anyway. Distant cousins of the Lofts, a single mother who slipped into town with her teenage daughter and made no waves, initiated no complaints or attempts to upgrade any public instalments, then slipped out when everyone was mightily distracted.

'Don't you think her parents would have said something?' Jessica was saying. 'Like, "Oh, by the way, no one thinks it was your baby anymore"?'

'Maybe they didn't like to talk about it,' said Penny.

'Like, "It's safe to come back"?'

'Maybe she wanted to stay away.'

Jessica went quiet again and Penny experienced a moment of reprieve, but then Jessica said: 'Grandpa knew there was a king tide that day. Why'd he go fishing?'

Penny sighed. If only she had a dollar for every time they'd been here, too, she thought. 'I don't know,' she said.

'He never got over her, did he? Lucy.'

'No,' Penny said. 'He didn't.' Now she eyed her daughter and allowed herself to say, in a rush of frustration, 'What the hell were you thinking, accusing Old Dick Fancy like that?'

Jessica took a long time to reply. 'God,' she said finally. 'Honestly? It just came out. I saw him standing there, holding court like a king, and next thing ... I don't know. I thought of everything I hate about them and ...' She drifted off, tucking her hands into her armpits. 'Weird,' she said softly. 'It's like I just wanted to tell him that I *know* him. I wanted him to see me.'

Their footsteps crunched softly. Icy night air drifted down the collar of Penny's jacket and she hunched her shoulders, trying to keep warm.

They reached Jessica's house and stopped at the gate. The front porch light was on, and both Penny and Jessica experienced a feeling of relief—a man nurturing a grievance doesn't leave a welcoming light. And although Penny's life had been marked by the bruises of her father's pride, she marvelled at this man who had managed to escape it, who seemed immune to insecurity, this man who had married her daughter.

'He truly doesn't mind, does he?' Penny said. 'He doesn't get jealous. With your ...' she waved a finger, 'whatever you call it. Open marriage.'

'It's a choice,' Jessica said. 'He chooses not to believe it matters.'

'It's not that simple. Not for everyone.'

'It is for him. Why not for anyone else?'

Penny laughed at the irony of her daughter's statement. Jessica shushed her; the kids were asleep.

'I want you to remember that,' Penny said, 'next time you choose to be offended by the Fancys.'

Lights clicked off across Port Kingerton. In garages, kitchen windows, Eleanor Turner's back porch. Homes fell silent, heads flopped onto pillows, eyelids fluttered closed. Dreams would be vivid, subjective or not there at all. Blackness fell over the town, except for the two dim streetlights, placed far apart, that continued to bathe the beachfront in a murky glow until a new day would begin.

OLD DICK

Maybe it wasn't an accident.

Look, all I can tell you is the way I see it. And the way I see it, Ed Bram went fishing on those rocks when he knew the tide was coming in and next thing anyone knew, Ed Bram wasn't on those rocks anymore. Nor was he anywhere else. He was gone a while. I couldn't say how long. All I know is he was gone long enough that a missing man became more important than the questions I should have been asking about that poor girl. The heads I should've been knocking. Luce never did let me forget it. Called me a windbag and a troglodyte and made pumpkin soup for tea for a week. I hate pumpkin soup.

Sorry, Luce.

But then Ed wasn't missing anymore. He was ... well, after the fish had their share he wasn't much of anything, anymore.

You think nature doesn't know how to take care of mess?

It took care of that other bad egg, too.

ABIGAIL

From the top of the cliff, Abigail could see all the way along the coast. The ocean was the colour of a glass bottle. Sand dunes unrolled and spray drifted, hazing the air. Insects clicked and buzzed in the saltbush around her. The narrow trail was deep pale sand, her boots sank and slid.

Breathing heavily, she emerged from the saltbush onto a square of lawn. In spite of the cold wind sweat trickled down her spine; her dress fluttered about her knees. Headstones stood in rows. Jam jars of flowers here, trinkets there. A clump of daisies nodded yellow heads and she plucked a handful on her way past. She kept walking until she reached the north side of the cemetery.

Dwarfing the surrounding graves was a solid cube of marble standing taller than her head. On top of the cube a spire soared another six feet and on top of the spire an angel crouched as if in grief, wings folded about itself. When she was a kid the gravestone had seemed normal. Now she thought it couldn't be more ostentatious and phallic if it tried.

FANCY, the engraving read. *In memoriam.*

'Hello, fam,' she said.

Buried beneath her feet were no less than eight of her relatives: her great-grandparents; two great-uncles and their wives; one small boy—her grandfather's brother who had lived only nine months; and her grandmother Lucy.

'Nothing's changed in Kingo,' she said. 'I'm blaming you guys.'

She lowered herself to her knees.

The foal had been born just after one am. A leggy bay filly with a white star between her eyes, sliding into the world with a little mess and no fuss. Nell was delighted: the filly was stunning and, after all, free—she had come without a stallion's service fee. 'That doesn't make it okay, though,' Nell had said sternly to Bo, feeding the mare a carrot as her new foal wobbled on damp legs. 'No more breaking out and getting into trouble.'

'Slut shaming,' Abigail said.

That's when her mother looked at her, hard, and said, 'How long *do* you have to go?'

And she replied, 'I'm thirty-eight weeks next week.'

Abigail lowered herself further onto the grass, stretching onto her side. Sunlight poured down and she closed her eyes, making her existence red-gold. In this position she imagined her silhouette like a seahorse, all bulging front. It tucked away when she was standing up, but maybe that was because, upright, there was so much more of her for her belly to be eclipsed by. All floating flesh, loose fabrics and mouth. All hard-pounding heart.

The grass radiated heat. Nearby she could hear the soporific hum of bees, the trilling of birds. She felt as if she could fall asleep forever. But she didn't have forever.

The judge had wanted to give her longer, but grudgingly cut her sentence short. Not even the criminal justice system wanted women giving birth inside. 'You pled the belly,' a friend inside said. 'It's how women in the olden days used to escape the noose.' Then she finished sadly, 'Not like it doesn't happen, though—the taking of our mamas. Not like some of us aren't raised by the state.' And Abigail knew how true that was, and there was nothing else that either of them could say about that. Because although they'd all seen the TV shows or heartwarming social media posts about children raised by loving foster carers, all gratitude and blessings and selflessness, in prison there were women raised in the foster system, too, and in those women there was a hole where the blessings should be.

As the years went on and the baby would have turned into a teen, then a young adult, Abigail found herself looking twice at the faces of some young women she passed in the street. Could it be her? Or her? Once, on the tram to Glenelg, she had stared at a young woman (same round cheeks; same small pouty mouth) for so long the woman had glared at her and moved seats. Abigail realised that in her mind Honnie's face was forever fifteen, and she simply could not imagine what Honnie would look like now. Or what her daughter might look like.

Eyes closed, Abigail draped an arm over her belly, spreading her fingers over the drum of her middle. She could feel a pulse of something through her, something tentative but brilliant, as though she had cracked open a door and let in hope.

'You're full term?' Nate said last night. 'You should have told me.'

'Why?' she replied. 'So you could stop me from working with you?'

And the gorgeous vet had nothing he could say about that, either. Before he left she pressed herself against him, and he returned the gesture, imprinting the length of his body against hers.

After a protracted, un-pretty minute, she was back on her feet. She spent a long time wandering among the gravestones. There was only the sound of the wind rustling the saltbush, the distant thunder of the ocean against the cliffs. Scrub wrens hopped about on the grass. Her hands lingered on the sun-warmed tops of the headstones, and she thought about what it could mean to be free of generations of judgement and fear, to not be held captive by frail, fickle ego.

Well, damn. She was getting all woo.

Abigail made her way back to the road. Her gait had become even more awkward and swinging, her pelvis feeling wide as a bus.

The sound of an engine, coming at a clip up the hill. She shielded her eyes as the ute pulled up alongside her.

'Hey, stranger.'

'Hey yourself.'

'Pretty crazy, huh? Last night?'

'Oh, Adrian,' she said. 'Just another Friday night in Kingo.'

He laughed. 'Hey,' he said. 'You still haven't told me how you got the shiner?'

'This?' She gestured to her eye. 'Walked into a door.'

His face darkened. 'You mean a bloke gave it to you?'

'No. I mean I walked into an actual door. Well, a door frame. I was leaving a room and someone called out to me, and I turned around but I was off balance because of this thing—' she pulled her dress tight and gestured, and she saw his eyes go wide '—and smack. Right into the frame.'

He winced. 'Did it hurt?'

'Yep.'

He gave her a sympathetic look.

'But feel free,' she said, 'to tell people whatever you want. That I got it in a pub brawl, or doing some sick parkour evading the cops, or falling off a stolen unicorn. You choose. Because it doesn't matter what happened. It only matters what anyone thinks happened.'

Her phone chimed and she pulled it out.

Hope you don't mind, wrote Jen in a group text, *but I've given your new number to a few peeps.*

Heyyy, Abs!

Yo! Girlfriend. Sooo glad you're out.

Love you, babes. Miss your face.

Abs! Welcome back sweetie.

You owe me a beer.

   Just cos you're the baby daddy? Wait your turn.

When you coming back?

Got a back-of-house job here waiting for you, just sayin.

Still carrying that kid around?

Abigail typed, *Couple weeks to go. And I miss your faces too. Now fuck off a minute, gotta kiss a boy and send a nude to a vet.*

Yasss

Kiss all the boys!

GET IT GIRL.

If you're sending nudes …

    Again, just cos you're the baby daddy? What is this entitlement?

Within her there was an unearthly tumbling, a stretching against the barriers of her and it tickled, making her laugh.

Taking hold of the window frame, Abigail leaned forward. At first Adrian retreated, but she kept going. She grabbed his shirt and pulled him towards her, and then Adrian understood. His face registered shock, then delight, then she couldn't see his next expression because she was kissing him.

ACKNOWLEDGEMENT OF COUNTRY

This story was written and is set on Boandik country. I recognise the traditional custodians of this country, the land on which I live and work, and pay respect to Elders past, present and emerging.

ACKNOWLEDGEMENTS

At many times during the writing of this novel I relied heavily on the assistance of others, without which I would have floundered indeed. I extend deep gratitude to:

Frances Loy, whose generous sharing of her experience was vital.

Katie Davies for kindly providing invaluable legal information; Bettina Engelhardt, who patiently answered police procedural questions and helpfully read an early draft; Leah Farrugia for teaching me about cattle AI (and for teaching Ben to eat tomatoes); Lorraine Murphy for cheerfully managing things so I don't have to; Isabelle Schubert, who read early chapters in record time, helping me understand they weren't incomprehensible; the inimitable Les Zig, always such a willing and sagacious source of counsel. I hope you'll all forgive where I have meandered from your considerable expertise and gone my own erroneous way.

Emily Maguire, with whom I was exceptionally fortunate to receive a mentorship through *Kill Your Darlings*, waded fearlessly into the first draft and in doing so provided the difference between productivity and despair. I am immeasurably grateful for her good will, wisdom and stratospheric talent.

Leisa Masters, for everything really, but also for never letting me forget what my actual job is, and for believing so wholeheartedly it makes it almost impossible for me not to believe as well (although god knows I do try). Kelly Morgan, for effusive cheering exactly when I needed it—how I miss our tea mornings.

Pippa Masson for her continued guidance and understanding, as well as the excellent Caitlan Cooper-Trent, and all the dear folk at Curtis Brown Australia.

The unparalleled team at HQ HarperCollins, most especially Rachael Donovan, for her confidence, enthusiasm and vision; Annabel Blay, for the most enlivening advice and care; Kylie Mason, who always inspires and makes tremendously better; the keen-eyed Annabel Adair, for fixing all my mistakes; Christa Moffitt for the spectacular cover design; Jo Munroe, Natika Palka and all the teams in sales, marketing and publicity who work hard getting books into this world.

To booksellers and librarians across Australia. Many cheers. You're marvellous.

My family: my mum, Julie, who is my very first and very best reader. Ben, who never baulks at the most random questions without preamble at any time of day (and now you're at the front *and* the back), and Addy and Leo. All unconditionally encouraging and patient. Thank you.

Those familiar with the south-east of South Australia may notice a resemblance, geographically at least, between this fictional town of Port Kingerton and the non-fictional town of Port MacDonnell / Ngaranga. In spite of the fact that these towns, fictional and non, share geographical locations and a primary industry of crayfishing, I wish to assert that, beyond those similarities, Port Kingerton and its inhabitants bear no resemblance to anyone (or anything) living or dead and are entirely the products of my imagination.

And finally, I wish to acknowledge the 3,011 women who are, at the time of writing, incarcerated in Australia. Of these, First Nations women represent a disproportionately high percentage. It is my personal belief that no woman should be in prison.

BOOK CLUB DISCUSSION QUESTIONS:

❖ From the opening lines of *The Fancies*, Abigail's reluctance to return to her home town is clear. However, Abigail's sense of desperation and lack of options is also apparent, although the reasons why take a little longer to reveal. What were your initial feelings about Abigail? Did your perspective of her change, as her past and criminal history is revealed? Do you think she is capable of staying out of prison?

❖ The novel is narrated from three perspectives: Abigail's, the townsfolk's (headed 'Them') and Old Dick Fancy's. How did this structure affect your reading experience? Did you have a perspective you found more preferable or compelling? Why do you think the author chose to present the story in this way?

❖ *The Fancies* takes place in a fictional small fishing town in South Australia. In what ways is this setting important to how the story unfolds? Why do you think the author chose to create a fictional town, rather than set the story in a real one?

❖ On the same day that Abigail returns home, a thighbone has washed up on the town beach. As the story unfolds, another event of significance from twenty-four years ago also begins to resurface. Why do you think the townsfolk so readily conflate these events? Do you believe the characters accepted the explanation given for the thigh bone? Did you?

❖ Abigail and her mother, Nell, have a tumultuous relationship. How does the author demonstrate the ambivalence of their mother–daughter connection? Why do you think Nell experiences feelings of frustration or even hostility towards Abigail, and can you relate or sympathise?

❖ Homecoming, for Abigail, results in a dramatic sensation of feeling like a child. Have you ever moved away from, or returned to, your home town? Can you imagine leaving a place as a relative child and returning many years later fully grown? How do you think that might affect how an adult views their sense of self?

❖ Old Dick Fancy is living with dementia, and as a result, one of his symptoms is described as a 'jumbling' of memories. His perspective often recounts the past, and there is sometimes a collapsing of the past with the present. What impact does this have on Old Dick's narration of events? Did you believe his voice to be reliable? How did you feel about the author's portrayal of living with dementia?

❖ The lifelong rivalry between Abigail and Jessica Bram has survived in spite of Abigail's two-decades long absence from Port Kingerton. Why do you think a rivalry developed between these two characters, and do you believe either of them would be capable of overcoming it? If humans are social animals, why do you think these animosities form and continue, sometimes for generations?

❖ A theme of this novel is judgement: the way people judge each other both individually and as a group; the assumptions we form and the stories we believe—whether they are true or not. What judgements did you form about Abigail? Did your feelings change as the ending is revealed? Has reading this story changed your perspective about forming or maintaining judgements of others?

talk about it

Let's talk about books.

Join the conversation:

facebook.com/harlequinaustralia

@harlequinaus

@harlequinaus

harpercollins.com.au/hq

If you love reading and want to know about our
authors and titles, then let's talk about it.

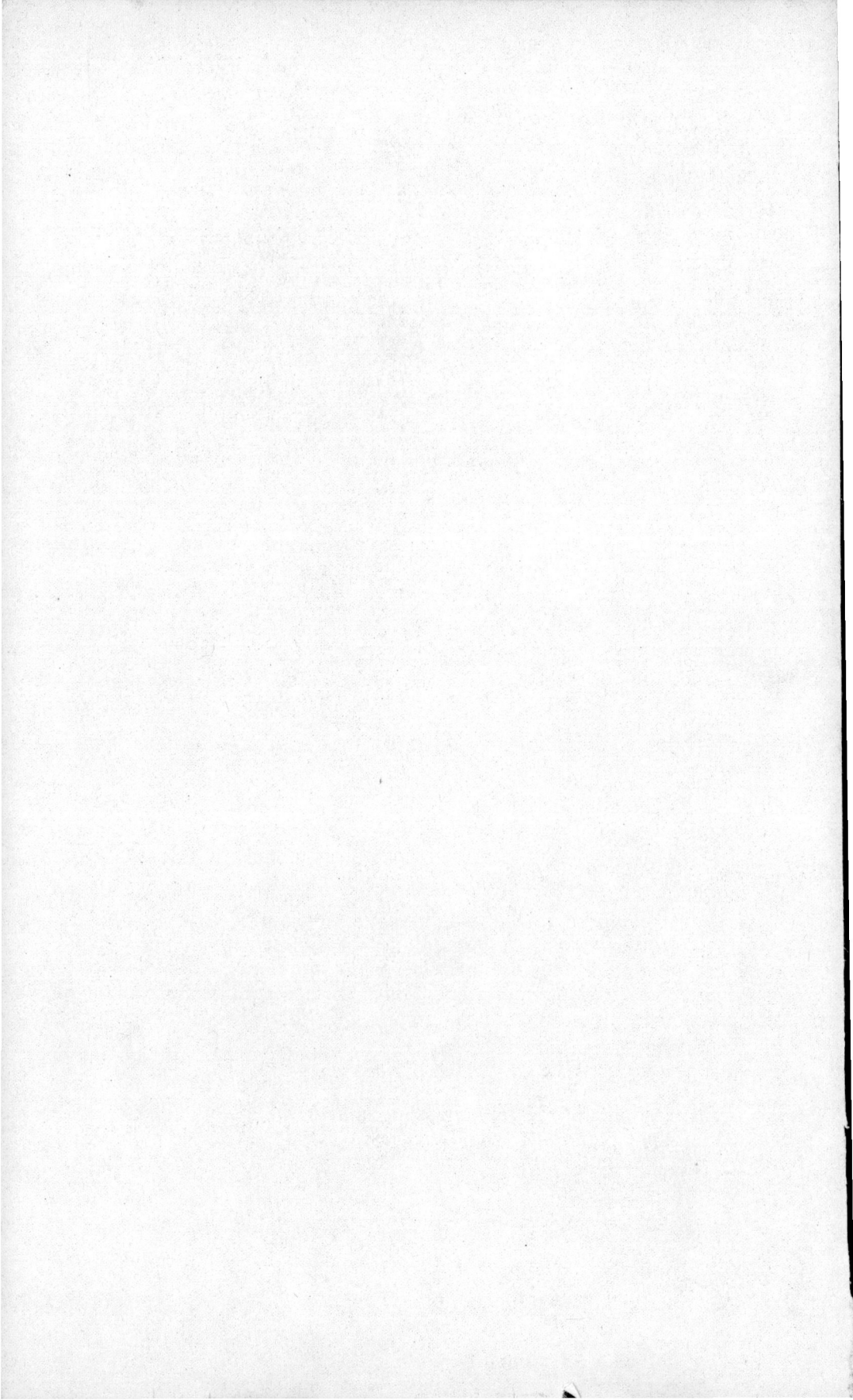